THE IMPOSSIBLE SEARCH FOR THE PERFECT MAN

DEBBIE HOWELLS

First published in 2013. This edition published in Great Britain in 2023 by Boldwood Books Ltd.

Copyright © Debbie Howells, 2013

Cover Design by Head Design Ltd.

Cover Illustration: Shutterstock

The moral right of Debbie Howells to be identified as the author of this work has been asserted in accordance with the Copyright, Designs and Patents Act 1988.

All rights reserved. No part of this book may be reproduced in any form or by any electronic or mechanical means, including information storage and retrieval systems, without written permission from the author, except for the use of brief quotations in a book review.

This book is a work of fiction and, except in the case of historical fact, any resemblance to actual persons, living or dead, is purely coincidental.

Every effort has been made to obtain the necessary permissions with reference to copyright material, both illustrative and quoted. We apologise for any omissions in this respect and will be pleased to make the appropriate acknowledgements in any future edition.

A CIP catalogue record for this book is available from the British Library.

Paperback ISBN 978-1-80549-251-1

Hardback ISBN 978-1-80549-249-8

Large Print ISBN 978-1-80549-250-4

Ebook ISBN 978-1-80549-252-8

Kindle ISBN 978-1-80549-253-5

Audio CD ISBN 978-1-80549-244-3

MP3 CD ISBN 978-1-80549-245-0

Digital audio download ISBN 978-1-80549-248-1

Boldwood Books Ltd
23 Bowerdean Street
London SW6 3TN
www.boldwoodbooks.com

In memory of Bernard

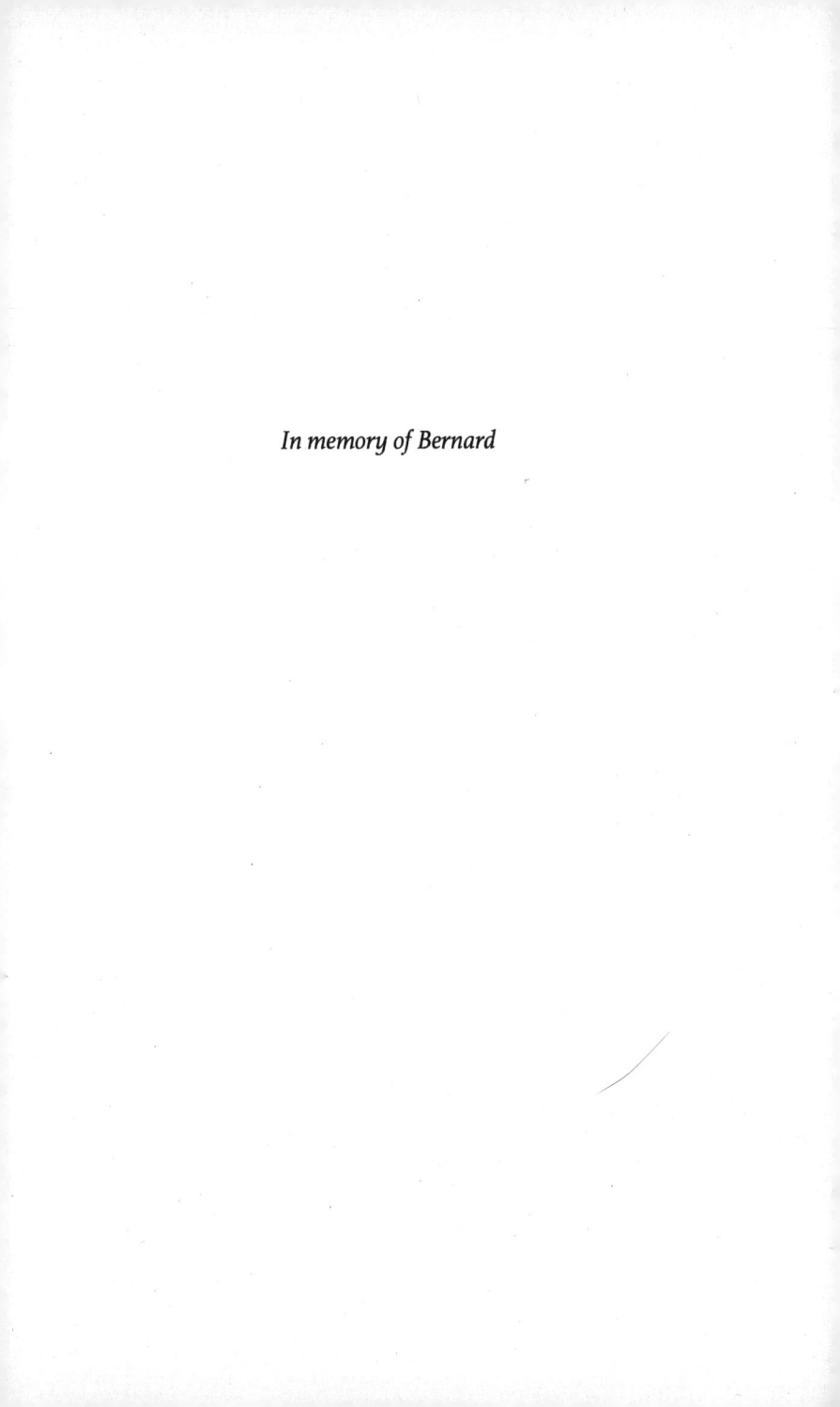

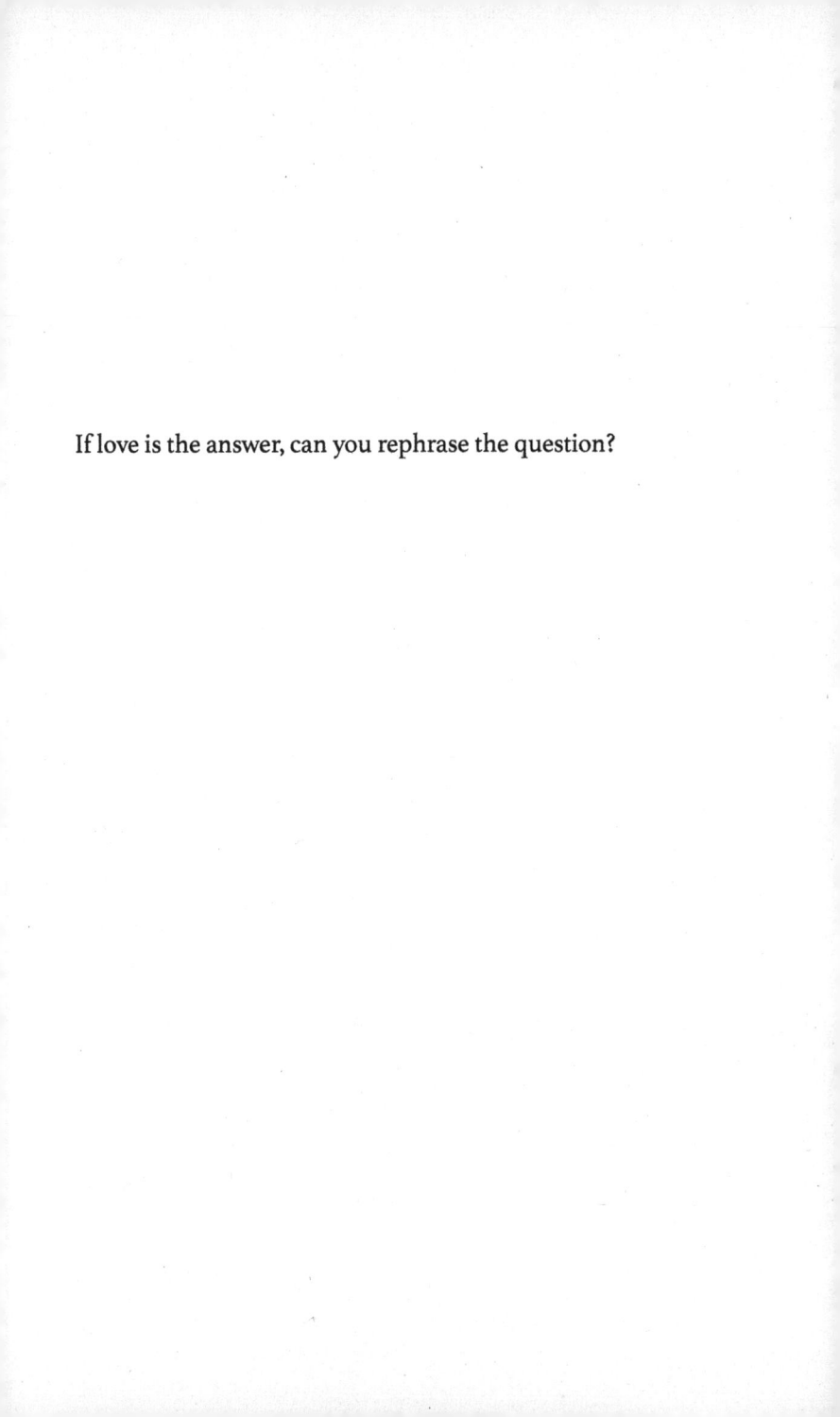

If love is the answer, can you rephrase the question?

1

I'm where every girl in the world wants to be. Wandering serenely through Tesco. In the middle of the night. And there's no one here, which is odd...

Actually, it's surprisingly peaceful, meandering up and down the wide empty aisles with only some vegetables for company. But hold on just a moment, I can hear something. Or rather someone... Holy moly. Not just any old someone either.

A positive vision appears around the corner, a knowing smile playing on his lips as I find myself gazing at Zac Efron and Ryan Reynolds all rolled into one beautiful, jaw-dropping specimen.

Clinging to his lean, sculpted frame is one of those tight T-shirts that leaves nothing to the imagination – I can make out every muscle, every curve of his tanned, glorious body. As he comes towards me, there's an intense look in his dark eyes and I'm getting a funny feeling, like goose-bumps all over.

I close my mouth, smooth my hands over my T-shirt, sucking in my tummy and attempting to look nonchalant, as though I bump into sex gods in Tesco every day. But. Oh crap. I don't know what to say now, because there is no T-shirt. In fact, I'm horrified to find I'm not wearing anything at all... Where the fuck are my clothes?

* * *

The luminous hands on my alarm clock read just before 3 a.m. when my eyes ping open to the sound of the heaviest of April showers hammering torrentially on our roof. I'm still blushing from the realisation that I'm completely starkers in the middle of a supermarket, with a gorgeous stranger giving me the once-over – except I'm not of course. I'm at home in my bed, fantasy and reality blurred for a few delicious moments longer as I contemplate the man of my dreams, still unmistakeably here in my head. What a time to wake up, just when things were about to get interesting... But by now, one thing I most definitely am is annoyingly wide awake.

Okay. So it's not the first time I've had a vivid, outrageous dream and as I lie in bed, I wait for the full-blown assault from my insecurities that always follows. General unease then escalates into complete and unreserved paranoia of mind-boggling proportions, while I explore the entire range of catastrophes waiting to befall me. Bankruptcy, life-threatening illness, divorce... because they're all there waiting to get me.

As I lie in my favourite pyjamas (I checked, just to make sure) I toss and turn restlessly, my imagination in full swing, at its absolute, spectacular worst. If I'm going to dream about flaunting myself at gorgeous men, why can't it be on a tropical island? Or is there hidden significance to dreams about lust among the veg aisle at Tesco's... More likely I just have a disturbed mind.

The warm, inert body next to me doesn't exactly help, emitting porcine snores at regular intervals, every so often interspersed with a particularly hoggish one – the kind that has about four syllables – putting an end to any hope of sleep. Arian is a world-class snorer, and not even a well-timed elbow in the ribs has any lasting effect on the din emanating from his nostrils.

My lovely husband is also a world class duvet-hogger. I tug the covers back over me – he doesn't even stir, but then Arian can sleep through anything. If the house fell down around us, he'd be oblivious to it, but he's oblivious to most things these days.

I know my fears and suspicions will shrink back to normal, only mildly paranoid proportions by daylight. And my imagination, I'm the first to admit, is inclined to get carried away. However, just lately, I'm beginning to wonder whether this is simply in my head, or if indeed something is going on.

Arian flies large aeroplanes for a big airline. We met six years ago when my best friend, Leonie, married his best friend, Pete. Leonie's cabin crew and we've been the best of friends since secondary school, where she stuck her oar in – *fuck off, you bitches* – and her finger up at the bullies who were making my life a misery.

Leo's beautiful, with smooth olive skin and long dark hair. After leaving school, with the same audacity that had endeared her to me in the first place, she lied about her age and pursued her dream to take to the skies. I, meanwhile, as was my due, accepted the rather less enthralling option of a secretarial job, in the dingy offices of Carpets-R-Us.

It might not have been so bad, if only Leo's life hadn't been full of excitement. A never-ending whirl of exotic destinations, fab shopping and hot men in uniform – I preferred to gloss over the 4 a.m. check-ins and the night Tenerifes – but it all served to make my lacklustre nine to five existence answering dreary Mr McKenzie's phone seem even more tedious than it was.

But when we were together we kicked our heels up, determined to misspend every second of our long-awaited freedom. We were far too young, we agreed, to tie ourselves down to just one man, so it was absolutely only fair, we told ourselves, to go on dates with lots of them.

So many men and so little time. That was us for years, until that fateful night stop in Tangiers when she met Pete, who was understandably smitten at first sight.

Tall and sandy haired (Leo's word, Pete's a ginger), he's besotted. And it was totally his fault I met Arian, then kept meeting Arian at theirs, again and again, because they're friends.

As I discovered, pilots can yap for hours – about holding procedures and rostering agreements, and other pilot-ish topics of conversation, such as dwindling pensions and the new junior with the big bazoomas. And then Arian asked me on a date.

It was easy to be infected by the magic between our friends. One date turned to many, culminating months later in a drunken proposal that surprised both of us. I detected a flicker of surprise on Leo's face when I told her. Or possibly it was a flicker of uncertainty, which, being Leo, she then hid forever behind a mask of enthusiasm and delight.

'Oh my God, oh my God!' Leo had jumped up and down excitedly. 'When's the wedding? How did he propose? Oh, Lou, this is the best news ever! Oh, I'm so excited!'

All without pausing for breath before she'd dashed off to tell Pete.

Looking back, her excitement was always greater than mine. Isn't a wedding, after all, just about the biggest day of your life? The biggest decision you ever make, and worthy of at least some peripheral soul searching before you tie the knot? Maybe for most people – but for me, it was the natural order of things.

The lead-up to our wedding simply flew by, filled with meetings with photographers, florists and of course food tastings, not to mention fittings of my elaborate and frightfully expensive Vera Wang wedding gown. Barely having a moment to think, I allowed myself to go with the flow, and just took completely for granted that this was how it was.

My mother – Lord bless her – as is her nature, complained about everything and secretly revelled in every stressful minute of it. A total mother-of-the-bride-zilla, she was in her element, organising everything to a degree that gave a whole new meaning to the word, positively terrifying everyone she came across.

But at last I was doing something she approved of. Oh yes, she was thrilled to bits that her previously slightly disappointing daughter had bagged herself such a good catch. Truth is, I think she was a teeny bit smitten herself, but there was absolutely no doubt that she wanted our wedding to be impressive, with no expense spared, with hundreds of guests, white doves after the ceremony, flowers simply everywhere and those hideous wedding favour things on the table that no one knows what to do with. She even managed to rustle up ten tiny bridesmaids I'd never even seen before and drafted in a professional speech writer, just in case my poor father let the side down.

I'm afraid to say that I was happy to take a back seat and let her. And it *was* an incredible day. But. After it was over, things between me and Arian just ticked along fairly uneventfully, much as they had before. Wasn't there supposed to be more?

With Arian away so frequently, it's like he has a double life – at home he does a bit of DIY and mows the lawn, but the moment he puts on his uniform, he steps into a parallel universe I have no part in.

And so, in between times, I am quite used to getting on with my own, somewhat less glamorous way of life. In a funny sort of way, it's worked, or so I thought. My biggest worry has been what to pull out of my extensive and mismatched wardrobe each morning. Until now.

This isn't a conclusion I've come to easily. And terrified though I am to confront it, there have been rather too many last-minute flight changes, more than ever before. He's extremely amiable these days, when he's here that is, which is less and less frequently. And he hums a lot in the bathroom. All this, despite the fact that we haven't had sex for two months, which probably goes a long way towards explaining my night-time fantasies about frolicking with Latino-type males in Tesco. But recently I'd go so far as to say that my husband has been avoiding all bodily contact suggestive of intimacy. I know in daylight hours, I'll convince myself that I'm just being paranoid, that nothing's changed and it's the gremlins of the night out to get me again. But... the fact remains. Arian has always liked a lot of sex.

In the beginning, just being in the same room as him would fill my head with carnal thoughts. Arian would walk through the door after being away for a night and barely say hello before we'd be tearing each other's clothes off like there was no tomorrow. Even his unpredictable working hours had their use.

I'm really sorry, Mum, we won't be able to make lunch tomorrow. No, Arian's just had a week of night flights again and needs to catch up... Yes, poor thing, he's exhausted...

Ha. Not much sleeping went on, I can tell you and it was easy enough to overlook any guilt at lying to a mother who'd long ago switched allegiance to her son-in-law.

Of course the frequency wore off a bit as the years went by, but nothing like this. Two whole months? Preposterous.

* * *

My alarm wakes me at 6 a.m. I long to close my eyes and drift back into oblivion, but I can't. The space next to me is empty and there are splashing sounds coming from the bathroom, against a background of energetic humming noises. Galvanising my weary body into action, I stagger bleary-eyed down the stairs to make a cup of tea, to be greeted by the mad, black creature that leaps up maniacally and wags her whole body at me.

Elmer is rather a scruffy flatcoat retriever. There aren't too many of them about and if you've ever lived with one, you'll know why. Reading my thoughts, she grins madly at me, one eye squinting, while grabbing at my pyjamas with grizzled jaws.

I let her outside; it's really far too early to be dealing with a demented dog. It's a beautiful spring morning, and I stand for a moment breathing it in, watching Elmer pogo madly across the grass. Rays of early morning sun are poking through the trees, catching the dew on the grass so it sparkles.

It's quiet and still and calms the madness in my head for a moment. I've always loved this garden, with its gently sloping grass and gnarled apple trees. There's an old garden bench among them, my favourite place on Sunday afternoons, curled up on a pile of cushions with a trashy book.

In the opposite corner, there's a bigger, very ancient oak, perfect for climbing and even more perfect for just sitting under in the height of the hottest summer, then at the far end is Elmer's stream, where she wallows for hours.

Arian appears and kisses me perfunctorily on the cheek. I feel a pang of I'm not sure what. Since when does my husband kiss me like he would his mother? Before, he'd have come and stood quietly behind me, his arms wrapped around me, his lips nuzzling my hair, hinting at far more than just a kiss.

Tall, with longish hair that's still damp from the shower, he's suspiciously bright-eyed and bushy-tailed this morning. It's good to know at least one of us slept well. And he's annoyingly affable. What *is* going on with him?

'Sleep well, Lou? You were out of it this morning,' he remarks happily.

Ironically because I was awake all night worrying about our marriage, buster, I almost say, but don't.

'Oh, my Lisbon's turned into a night-stop, so I won't be back until Saturday,' he adds oh-so-casually, not one iota of guilt on his face as he carefully avoids eye contact. 'Still, I'll cut the grass on Sunday and we could go out with Pete and Leonie then, if they're free?'

My stomach lurches and not about the bloody grass. And it's not that I mind him being away, because I don't. But today is Thursday. He was supposed to be coming home tonight. Two extra nights away. *Just like last week.*

What's equally annoying is his excessive need to socialise. I see people all day – I enjoy the little time we spend on our own, though of course I love seeing Pete and Leonie. And Arian's with people all day too, though for the most part, it's a smelly old co-pilot – or so he'd have me believe.

'Maybe we could have an evening in together, darling, just you and me?' I suggest as we go inside, knowing Leo's going to visit her mother.

'To make up for missing our anniversary?' I add wistfully, in my mind picturing a romantic candlelit dinner and chilled champagne, abandoned for all the right reasons as we rip each other's clothes off, unable to wait another second.

That does it. Now he *does* look shifty. My stomach ties itself in knots. And still I don't say anything.

'Um, let's see when I get back?' Arian literally grabs his flight bag and runs out of the house without saying goodbye, leaving me standing there, utterly perplexed. What about his case? He must have put it in the car earlier, I decide, more convinced than ever something's wrong.

But in spite of the apprehension growing inside me, all I can do now is wait. I don't have much choice. I know I can't go on like this, *not knowing...* So I decide. When he gets back from this trip, *somehow* I have to talk to him.

2

I still work in an office – and anywhere else, it would be as dull as the job as Carpets-R -Us, but as it happens, it's one of my favourite places in the world, because it's at the heart of a busy veterinary practice in Lower Shagford, a little village in the back of beyond, about eight miles from Winchester and connected to civilisation by miles of winding lane.

It's a blink-and-you'll-miss-it kind of village, with at its buzzing heart, a pub, a chippy, and an archaic village stores, surrounded by a scattering of posh country houses, tatty old cottages and, of course, the ubiquitous barn conversions. There are also the infamous allotments, the setting of many a village battle.

The drive to the practice twists and winds through chocolate-box fields full of pretty cows, until you come to what on first sight looks like a rather run-down old farm. On closer inspection, however, there's a jolly expensively tarmacked parking area in front of a stylishly converted cow shed, which has a big window and is my office. Then round in the yard, there are stables and barns deceptively full of impressively high tech vet stuff, like scanners and X-ray machines, and even a horse-sized operating theatre.

The drive continues on for another half a mile, ending in front of the rather imposing and grandly named Offleigh Manor, home to the awfully rich Mankly-Talbot family. Actually, they're the only reason we've got such a posh drive as they absolutely insisted on it for their fleet of expensive cars. Mr M-T works in the city, and has a very tiny wife called Amanda, who has perfect highlights and a tinkly laugh, and waves a hand weighted with gold at us whenever she drives past in one of her Mercedes. However, the only one of them we tend to see is Paris – known as PM-T. At sixteen, she's a sex maniac and rather prone to crushes.

Most of our patients are horses, though the odd other animal crops up from time to time. And there's never a dull moment because as well as the lovely horses, there are the owners, who are mostly a bit bonkers, because if you keep horses, you have to be. I mean, they cost a small fortune, half the year they're caked in mud and their designer wardrobes are more expensive than their owners'. But if you love your horse, such is your life.

The practice was started by Beamish, the senior partner, who's very old school and highly respected for his encyclopaedic knowledge of all things equine. I'd never imagined that a vet's life could ever be glamorous, but his client list is phenomenal, from sheikhs to racing yards and the most champion of show jumpers. Quite how such a fumbling, benign country gentleman has become such a legend is to my mind, astonishing, but that, perhaps, is why he is.

Then there's awfully nice Miles, who's very lanky and has worrying down to an art form. His encyclopaedic knowledge of legs and feet extends to equines only, because this is Miles and his entire brain is devoted to his job. He's also unaware that he's the current object of Paris's attentions – she rotates them. Every time his car pulls up, I glance at my watch, counting the seconds before she appears, lolling around decoratively in skin-tight jodhpurs and long leather boots, batting Cheryl Cole eyelashes provocatively at him, which is a waste of her time because Miles would only notice eyelashes on a horse.

Emma is the newest recruit, and everybody loves her. She's blonde, clever and gazelle-like. Maybe not in that order, but you get the picture and if she wasn't so unassuming I would most definitely have to hate her. Then there's Sam, the green-eyed vet nurse, with his soft, lilting voice which has a hypnotic effect on both horses and owners alike. I'm convinced he's secretly a horse-whisperer.

I share my office with Agnes, who has been there since the beginning and knows absolutely everything about everybody. Not that you'd ever know. She's fabulously discreet.

Which leaves Mrs Boggle, the cleaner. Poor Mrs Boggle is one of life's hard-done-bys. She wears dreary clothes, has whiskers on her chin and sighs a lot. Her favourite topics of conversation are death, funerals and Benidorm, so it's best not to get her started. She comes in three evenings a week on her ancient motorbike and she keeps the office nice and clean, in particular the men's loo, which personally I wouldn't touch with a bargepole. She's an absolute saint.

And what do I do? Well, I help Agnes in the office, answering phones, (*Good morning, Anstruther, Morgan and Willis, how can I help you?*) making coffee and am not averse to the odd bit of mucking out as long as there's a warm, velvety horse-nose breathing in my ear.

But I feel part of a strange little family when I'm here, and rumour has it, we're about to become extended. His name is Marcus. Marcus Fitzpatrick, actually, which sounds posh – and is far too long.

'Good morning, Anstruther, Morgan, Willis and Fitzpatrick, how can I help you', every time the phone rings?

I don't think so. Rumour has it that Marcus is a bit of a whizz kid. Posh and brilliant? Ego the size of a small planet? A few days here will bring him down to earth.

Elmer comes to work with me, and barks neurotically at the clients, so Agnes makes me shut her in a stable, which is fine because Eric's there too. He's Sam's awesome, elderly terrier with short legs and glinting eyes, who don't take no shit from no one. Elmer thinks he's God.

* * *

I agonise between my striped top or the plain black one before plumping for the black. Infinitely more flattering, but boring, so I add my trademark long patterned socks over my skinny jeans, and finish it all off with my Uggs. My latest funky wellies are safely in the back of my car.

Today when I get to work, however, there's already a kerfuffle going on.

'Good morning, Louisa,' says Beamish, his eyebrows bristling as he peers over his glasses at me. He's immaculately dressed in his old tweed jacket and polished shoes.

'Hi, Lou.' Lovely Emma's there too, looking stunning as usual with blonde wisps of hair already escaping from her messy ponytail. Even in her shapeless polo shirt and navy workwear trousers, she still manages to make me feel inadequate.

They're studying the diary together. Even in this computer age, Beamish still insists that all appointments are written down in the good old-fashioned way, and so we have this huge, hard-backed tome, without which he is convinced the practice would fall apart.

'Morning, all.' Then I hesitate, because there's clearly something amiss. 'Is everything okay?'

'Um. Fine.' Spoken slightly absently and Beamish's stock answer to more or less anything.

'Um, Beamish, could I possibly have the next two weeks off? Um, Beamish, can I order more champagne for our coffee breaks?' Chances are he'd probably still say, *'Um fine'*...

'Oh good,' I say instead. 'Excellent.'

Why, then, is he so agitated? Ah ha, I can guess. It's Sylvie.

It has to be – I've seen this happen before. Sylvie Williamson is a valued client with a grown-up Barbie-princess home and a collection of priceless horses who are her babies. As well as extremely wealthy, Sylvie's a widow, and for reasons none of us can fathom, has the hots for Beamish. Yes, even the middle-aged can get crushes, I've discovered. And they're just as embarrassing as teen ones, because completely out of his depth, there are no end to the lengths Beamish will go to in his efforts to avoid her. I earwig shamelessly on their conversation.

'Um, thing is, old girl,' Beamish is saying to Emma rather longingly, 'she has this, er, mighty fine stallion. Pure bred Arab. By Indiana's Dream... Simply extraordinary he is.'

Beamish looks wistful. He's rather partial to Arabs, especially when they're pure bred like this one. He must be off his nut. I knew one once and they're loonies.

'Point is, er, Sylvie says he's a little off colour. Seemed perfectly fine last week, but she wants us, er, me, um, to do some blood tests. 'I say...' he looks apologetically at Emma, 'would you mind awfully?'

Emma pats Beamish's arm. 'Of course not, it's no trouble. If you're quite sure you wouldn't rather go yourself?' She can't resist teasing him slightly.

'No. Um. Yes,' Beamish stutters gratefully.

'Louisa? Please get that phone?' Agnes's voice, sounding stern.

Once the vets are all out on their rounds, things quieten down, though not for long. We've a couple of horses coming in for lameness assessments, and they might be sleeping over, so I have two stables to prepare, just in case.

As there aren't any clients for her to terrorise, I let my lunatic dog out to help me. Then feel a rush of shame as it hits me. I've hardly given Arian a thought.

Agnes has the afternoon off, leaving me alone in the office which I am positively ecstatic about, but with a list of jobs as long as my arm to ensure I'm kept occupied. She obviously doesn't think I have any initiative. Mind you, she's exactly the same with the vets, giving them detailed itineraries, leaving absolutely nothing to chance.

Once she's left, I go and ogle at the clients' horses when they duly arrive, in their all-singing, all-dancing horsebox, which I wouldn't be surprised to find are kitted out with Jacuzzis and cocktail bars and disco lights. After all you know what that show-jumping lot are like. Not exactly early to bed with a hot water bottle and a mug of Horlicks. No. I'm sure these big horse shows are just one gigantic party, with all sorts of shenanigans going on once the horses are tucked up in bed.

The only other noteworthy event of the afternoon is a rather supercilious call from Marcus, the new vet-to-be, who, in a most imperious manner, leaves a message for Beamish to call him.

'I'd really rather talk to Beamish,' he says haughtily, sounding most put out when he discovers I'm the only person there – and completely up his own arse. 'Oh, I suppose I'll *have* to leave a message in that case...'

Well, very nice to talk to you too, I think to myself. Simply splendid first impressions all round. Presumably I sound so ditsy that I can't be entrusted with even a message.

And then, because I can't stand arrogance in any shape or form, I decide, most satisfyingly, exactly who his first client will be. Well, I contemplate to myself, he deserves it. There's a grumpy old sod called Henderson who never pays his bills, with a filthy-tempered horse with rather persistent warts. On its dick. Ha. Perfect.

Elmer and I get home by six, and it's not until I'm back in my kitchen that I think back to my suspicions of this morning, but almost instantly I reassure myself. *This is Arian, for goodness' sake. We're married... Of course he's not having an affair...*

I know I won't hear from him before Saturday. We don't text each other as a rule. It's never even occurred to me that's odd. Perhaps on this occasion, I should call him? He's my husband after all. But something stops me, because I'm not sure what I'd say. Then it occurs to me too, that these days we're spending more time apart than together.

As all these thoughts resonate in my head, it's as though I'm digging my head out of the sand. Uneasily, I go upstairs to have a shower. The house is stuffy and airless, and as I go into our bedroom to open the window, something catches my eye.

Now that *is* odd. Arian has left his night-stop case behind. Something makes me go and look inside it. I find very niffy socks and boxers, which have obviously been there much longer than just since his last night-stop, which okay, is still not exactly conclusive – but my bad feeling is getting worse.

Even more uneasy by bedtime, I've already resigned myself to another wakeful night. With Arian away, I switch on the TV at the end of the bed, pile his pillows on top of mine and watch *Titanic* for the umpteenth time. Elmer's lying beside me, which is strictly against house rules, but if my hunch is right, it's looking more and more likely that Arian's breaking a few house rules too. Elmer's suitably smug, then her eyes close and in no time, she's snoring noisily and letting out the occasional fart, which isn't that different to Arian.

* * *

An uneventful Friday comes and goes, and it's late when I eventually wake on Saturday morning, but at least I've managed to catch up on some sleep. Elmer doesn't care. She'd fester in bed all day if I let her. But as I contemplate Arian coming home, there are butterflies in my stomach and I'm filled with a sense of trepidation.

Maybe an intimate dinner to celebrate our anniversary isn't such a bad idea. Maybe sea bass or fillet steaks... Champagne, of course... And banoffee pie, Arian's favourite, with lashings of double cream All of which means a trip to Sainsbury's. But I have to try.

* * *

It's about half past nine when Arian eventually does get home and after all the trouble I've gone to, I'm annoyed. He's yawning and the atmosphere is instantly awkward as my plans collapse in front of me. I'd expected him an hour ago and the sea bass is brown and shrivelled in a surround of mushy tomatoes. But there's no trace of Thursday's air of joviality. He's pale and drawn, his eyes unable to meet mine.

He kisses me, with slightly more feeling than the morning he left. 'Pour me some wine?' he asks quietly. 'I'll just have a quick shower.'

And I'm left just sitting there, my stomach churning, a feeling of foreboding building inside me.

Another twenty minutes pass. He comes back in, his hair still damp and mussed up which I always find incredibly sexy. For a moment, I'm tempted to run my fingers through it, to see if I can't rekindle a bit of the chemistry that's been in such short supply lately. But he makes no move towards me, just stands drinking his wine.

The atmosphere is killing me but I'm still not sure what to say. Nor is he – in fact, neither of us speaks for ages, until at last, he turns to face me.

'Lou?' he says, before turning silent again, as though he's fighting an inner battle with himself. Then he puts down his wine and comes to sit next to me. He sighs, deeply, and takes both my hands in his. It's the most physical contact we've had in ages. Suddenly I'm very afraid of what is coming.

'There's something I have to tell you, Lou...'

His voice is low and serious. Then he sighs again and when he speaks, his voice is even quieter.

'I've met someone.'

And with those three innocuous little words, my life changes irrevocably forever. It's what I've suspected, but it's no less of a shock. As it sinks in, I snatch my hands away, suddenly dizzy, my heart fluttering out of control.

'I'm so sorry.' He sounds almost beseeching, as if he can't bear for me to think badly of him.

Sorry... Is that it? For destroying our marriage? For wrecking my life? Just 'sorry'? The wanky tosser bastard...

'At work?' I ask, sounding much calmer than I feel. I'm stricken, disbelieving, the breath completely knocked out of me, but I have to know the facts, so my cursed imagination doesn't go into overdrive.

He's silent again, then reluctantly, 'Yes.'

I should have guessed as much. 'So you've turned out to be one of those pilots after all, that plays away with the trolley dollies, just like you said you never would,' I spit viciously at him.

Trolley dollies... Leonie hates me using that phrase. But I'm determined not to cry in front of him.

'No. It's not like that. I wouldn't do that,' he argues back. How *dare* he argue.

'So who is it then?' I demand, feeling tears threatening.

'Another pilot,' he mumbles through his hands.

Oh God. Don't tell me he's gay. That really would be the insult beyond all insults. But he can't be. I would have known... *wouldn't I?*

'Her name's Karina. She's a first officer. We met about a year ago, and well, we just hit it off,' he finishes lamely, his eyes riveted to a spot on the carpet in front of him.

I bet they flaming did. Karina. You can just imagine it can't you? I certainly can. *Karina.* An image of a petite blonde in a pilot's uniform pops into my head, Scandinavian probably. I can see her now, long white-blonde hair, pouty lips and big boobs, like the girl in that stupid shampoo advert. Dead sexy, which explains Arian's apparent loss of libido around boring old mousy-haired me. I bet they snog on the flight deck when no one's looking and have intimate dinners in all the far-flung corners of the globe. And sex in all those enormous hotel beds. My imagination really can be a curse, and as I watch it play out slow-motion in my head, I feel sick.

'So all this time, all these nightstops... They've been a smokescreen for your infidelity, haven't they? Because you're too gutless to tell me, Arian. So why tell me now? You could have had your fling, got "Karina" out of your system without me being any the wiser, and we could have got on with the life we'd always planned together,' I rage, my voice getting louder and louder. But the damage is done, and I already know that it's far, far too late.

'I never planned this, you have to believe me. It just happened.' He sounds so *weak*. How have I ended up married to a weak man? There's nothing I detest more.

'Things don't *just happen*, Arian. You made a choice, you made it happen. You could have made the decision to walk away,' I rant, really incensed by now, losing all control as I feel tears pouring down my cheeks. 'And you've broken your marriage vows you lying, hypocritical arsehole. I hate you...'

Arian is staring at the floor. He hesitates for a moment. 'There's something else,' he adds falteringly, looking even guiltier than before.

I'm astounded. What else can he possibly throw in now? Hasn't he said enough? I stare at him bleakly, this stranger that I'm married to, wondering what's coming next.

He blurts it out. 'Karina's... pregnant.'

His words are like a physical blow. Actually, it might have been better if he'd said he was gay, because a homosexual husband would be easier than this. *A baby*. Oh, how I'd *love* one of those. More than one actually. Funny, but Arian's never been that keen. And then the penny drops. Heavily. That's why he's finally told me, isn't it? Karina's called his bluff. She's clearly not as stupid as he is. I give them about six months before she sees him for what he is.

But one thing is perfectly clear. If this has been going on for a year, my husband's been shagging two women at the same time. The thought leaves me numb. Incredulous at his betrayal. But out of nowhere comes a shred of self-preservation, because I already know I never want to see Arian or speak to him, ever, ever again.

'Get out.' I hurl what's left in my wine glass at him, which isn't enough to soak him, but sends him scarpering from the room. Elmer is looking guilty too, tail between her legs as she skulks neurotically at my side. I pick up the wine bottle and fill my glass to the top, then sit down, shaking from head to toe, still in a state of total shock as, seconds later, the front door slams.

For two hours I don't move. I'm completely immobilised, my mind blank. I don't even cry, just replay the last few hours over and over in my head, as I absorb the reality that my husband has left me. It's over.

3

It's only once the initial shock subsides that my emotions practically engulf me, as I find myself on a roller coaster like never before. My world, it seems at times, has completely fallen to pieces and the person who was supposed to be my staunchest lifelong ally, the one person I was meant to be able to count on, he's the one who's done this to me.

Thoughts skip through my head about what must doubtlessly lie ahead. Practicalities, such as splitting our money, joint accounts and other so-called necessities, but the single worst part is telling people, which for ages I can't bring myself to do.

Yes, I'm bitter, angry, hurt – I have every right to be. And no, I'm not in denial. I have no trouble whatsoever in grasping the reality of what's happened, and nor do I wish him to come back. It's just that I don't particularly relish broadcasting to the world that I obviously wasn't good enough.

Guess what folks, my husband's found himself another woman. Yes, she's young and pretty. Blonde actually, oh and guess what, she flies a big aeroplane. That's right, a jet... And she's pregnant too, did I mention that? A far cry from flaky Louisa with her mousy hair and weird dog.

By Monday however, when I should be going to work, I'm an emotional wreck, and for the first time ever I phone in sick. Agnes is sympathetic and tells me she hopes I feel better soon, and so for the remainder of that week, I hide myself away, crying for hours on end and wallowing in a feeling of total worthlessness. Life feels beyond bleak, and I can't imagine it ever changing. Devastated and distraught, I ignore my texts and leave the phone to ring, hardly eating a thing and getting through far too many bottles of wine before starting on Arian's most expensive brandy.

Torturing myself with memories, I go over and over the last five years in my head. How it all started, from when we met at Leo's to the first time we slept together. I remember it all too clearly. He loved me then, didn't he? Or did he? And what about buying our home and all the holidays we've been on? Trouble is, by the time I've dissected our years together, I've convinced myself that firstly, he never really loved me and second, that he's been having affairs for years. After all, with being away so much, how would I ever have known?

And then after a whole wretched week like this, somehow I summon the faintest notion of resolve and pull myself together. I have to. I'm not letting the rat ruin my life.

So, the following Monday, feeling more than a bit shaky, though on the plus side quite a bit thinner, I'm actually back in the office. The words *Arian's left me* play constantly in my head as if on a loop, followed by an equally dispiriting *divorce, divorce, divorce...* I do my feeble best to ignore them.

It's business as usual, I keep determinedly reminding myself as I get through the day feeling a little detached from reality. And it's a very long day. But I manage not to let on to anyone the events of last Saturday, until the vets have all left for the night, and I'm just going to get Elmer from the stables, when Agnes looks up from her desk and says gently, 'Louisa? *Dear?* Are you sure you're all right?'

The 'dear' throws me completely off guard and her kind concern makes me crumple. How can she *know*? But then Agnes has X-ray vision and a sixth sense, not to mention astonishing wisdom – she doesn't miss anything. I ought to know that by now.

Despite being the quintessence of efficiency and organisation, Agnes is a really lovely lady. It's like having a mum comfort me, except that mine would probably take Arian's side, which is why I still haven't told her. But after keeping my secret for yet another day, my nerves are frazzled. Tearfully, I tell her about Arian.

'Oh, Louisa, how awful for you. I'm so very sorry.' Agnes comes and puts her arms around me and I can't contain the sobs any longer. I cry for half an hour, wracking, self-pitying sobs, which leave me emotionally exhausted.

'Come and sit down.' Agnes pulls my chair near to hers, and unlocks the bottom drawer of her desk and takes out a bottle of whisky and two glasses. I'd always wondered what she keeps in there.

Her eye catches mine. 'Strictly medicinal,' she says firmly, as she pours an inch into each glass. 'Now, drink up.' Hers remains untouched as she watches me slurp mine.

'So, have you told your family yet?'

I shake my head and blow my runny nose. The whisky's good. It helps.

'Don't you think you ought to? I know if my daughter was going through something like this, I would want to know.'

Oh. I didn't even know Agnes had a daughter.

She is right of course. Only problem is that my family lives miles away, and I can just imagine my parents will want to come and stay, if only to satisfy themselves that I'm all right. And then there's my mother, who with her accusing ways and her unconcealed adoration of Arian, isn't exactly the person I need right now.

It would do my head in. For now, I need to be alone. I explain this to Agnes, who nods understandingly.

'I still think you should tell them, Louisa. But you could also say that you are staying with a friend for a while. And actually, you know, you'd be very welcome?'

I'm so touched by her offer I almost cry again, only Mrs Boggle arrives on her motorbike, then stomps in carrying her helmet.

'Good evening, Mrs Boggle. How are you?'

She shakes her head and sighs. 'Not so good.'

Agnes and I exchange glances.

'I know I shouldn't say it,' says Mrs Boggle, making our eyes glaze over because we know she's going to say it anyway. 'But I just knew them Forresters were a bad lot. Been banged up, he has. She has an' all too, and all them poor kids... Social services are all over 'em. Told you, didn't I...' She shakes her head and heads in the direction of the men's loos.

I stare at her, suddenly terrified that my life is over and I'll end up miserable with yellow hair, just like her.

As it is, I drive us home, me and Elmer. I call in at the village shop on the way and search the dusty shelves, sparsely and depressingly stocked with its uninspiring range of goods labelled 'basic'. They probably have about as much nutritional value as cardboard, but in any case I gather some unexciting staples like plastic bread and tins of cheap beans, telling myself I need to eat, even if I don't want to. And I pick up some more wine.

At the checkout, I stand for ages while the spotty young shop assistant finishes what appears to be a terribly important phone call about someone called Tone, only to fix me with her beady eyes.

''Ave you got your own bags?' she challenges me.

So I glare back. She can clearly see I haven't so she very sullenly produces one of those nasty thin ones that tears if you put more than two things in it. It promptly splits, of course, as soon as I lift it off the counter, so I stagger out to my car, a bottle of wine under each arm, scattering tins and bread behind me and drive home.

Home. For how much longer. Because however much I fight him, Arian will doubtlessly want his share of the house we have shared for the last few years. And of course, it's his salary that's paid for most of it. And of course too, we have no children, to sway the legal process in my favour.

Now I've left work, my mind is full of Arian again. When I get home, I collapse on our bed and cry some more. To be honest, it's more like howling than crying, but I think that right now, I'm entitled to.

About two hours later, when that's all over, my topsy-turvy emotions flip back to angry again, which is much healthier and much easier to deal with. Then I entertain fanciful thoughts of revenge. After all, hell hath no fury and all that. I fantasise for a brief glorious moment. He's an airline captain isn't he, a tall, dashing figure in his uniform, striding all-powerfully through airports around the world... If only I could sneak on board and get my hands on that PA system.

'Ladies and gentlemen, welcome on board this flight to Lisbon. Your captain today is Arian Mulholland, who incidentally is having it off with your First Officer Karina X, much to the consternation of his wife Louisa, who has a thoroughly worthwhile job looking after sick animals.'

Okay. So maybe the last bit wasn't so good, but the rest of it... It would be most gratifying. I bet his passengers would love to know how easily led he is – by his penis.

I shut a slavering Elmer in the utility room with her food. It's a spectacle I prefer not to watch. Taking Agnes's advice, I decide the time has come to call my parents. Steeling myself for what I know must follow, I first pour a large glass of wine. And take a very, *very* deep breath.

* * *

'Oh, Louisa, I *can't* believe it,' cries my mother, just as I expected, as though it's my fault that Arian's had an affair. God! She could be right. I hadn't thought of it like that. Maybe it is *all my fault*.

Dad is a little more sympathetic. 'Very sorry, darling,' he says gruffly, not quite sure what else to say. Dad's always a bit uncomfortable with these sorts of things. 'Stupid bugger,' he adds, unexpectedly, sounding angry for a moment. Then quite affectionately, 'Sure you're all right?'

I manage to persuade them not to come hotfooting it over here, telling them I'm extremely busy at work and mythical 'things', promising to go over there for lunch next weekend by way of a compromise. Phew. It's with a sense of relief that I end the call.

I wonder if Arian's told Pete? I pick up the phone again, and fortunately it's Leonie who answers. This time my composure cracks, and I break down when I tell her what's happened. Ten minutes later, my good friend appears on my doorstep with a wine bottle clasped in each hand. Apparently she was in the middle of painting her nails when I rang. Sure enough, only three nails are a particularly vibrant shade of turquoise. Her beautiful face is etched with worry and her long hair is still damp – dear Leo didn't even finish drying it before rushing over to my rescue.

'Oh, Lou...' She hugs me and I cry for a bit. I love Leonie. She's the best. Then I have to tell her what's been going on under my nose for the last year. She's astonished. Like me, she can't believe none of us guessed.

'I wasn't going to say anything, but Pete's hardly seen Arian lately, except when we all get together of course. It seemed strange, when they've been friends so long, but I just thought well, we all have busy lives, don't we? And sometimes you and I don't see each other for ages either...' She was silent, thoughtful.

'I just can't believe it, Lou. I mean...,I'm sorry, but he's a shit. You're married, for God's sake.'

I could almost hear her imagination working overtime, wondering if she'd notice if Pete were playing away. The shock waves of Arian's behaviour are rippling through our friends' lives too.

It's surprising me though, how I'm pulling myself together again, but then self-pity's never been my thing. Just as well in the circumstances.

We drink too much wine and slag off Arian some more. Call him every name under the sun we can think of. Leo's good like that. Has an absolutely first class vocabulary. Somewhere in the world, his ears must be on fire by now, if not completely incinerated. Then we start on Karina. *What sort of a woman preys on another woman's man*, we ask each other. *What a complete bitch*, we cackle hypocritically to each other. What a pair of old crones we are. Leonie vows to blank Arian from here on. Hmm. I appreciate the show of solidarity, but that may not be so easy, seeing as she's married to Pete.

Ages later, Leonie's had too much to drink to drive herself home. She calls Pete, and I don't hear the exchange that follows.

He doesn't stay long, but somehow, I get the feeling that something's not quite right. Might Pete have had an inkling that Arian was up to something? He hugs me anyway, asks me if I'm okay, and I don't see the look that Leonie gives him. I'd always thought Pete was my friend too, but clearly boys code and girls code don't overlap. You know where you are with girlfriends, but men? Maybe they just stick together, no matter how appallingly one of them is carrying on.

* * *

Word has quietly filtered around at work, and though no one says anything directly to me, I am aware that everyone knows. Later, when I'm mucking out a stable, Emma comes to find me.

'I'm so sorry, Lou. Are you sure you're okay?' She sees the look on my face, and adds hastily, 'Of course you're not. How could you be.'

Unexpectedly, she hugs me. She smells like a horse.

'Come round for dinner tonight. I'm not on call and I'll cook.'

Gratefully, I agree, thinking how brilliant my friends are. Agnes too is keeping an eye on me – more than usual at the moment. And work is a wonderful distraction, with all these beautiful horses coming into the practice. Agnes sees to it that I'm busier than ever and from the moment I set foot through the door in the morning, I don't stop. But being busy is exactly what I need and she's a slave driver – only I know she's doing this for me.

I've even started considering that perhaps it would be a good time for me to think about getting another horse, now that the opposition that Arian always posed has disappeared. Yes, a gentle, loving horse would be infinitely less trouble than any man.

This morning, however, there's an added distraction, in the shape of our new vet. And in one glance I just know the female clients are going to just love him. I definitely don't. He's too cocky, too smooth and far too sure of himself. I would imagine he's probably encyclopaedic about girls and sex. Oh, and did I mention he's extremely good-looking in a George Clooney kind of way? He's tall, with brown hair and deep brown eyes, and Agnes has already dispatched him off to Henderson's to look at the warty horse. She gave me such a look when she saw what was in the diary. Honestly, it's not *all* my fault. Emma was in on it too. Emma can't stand Henderson or his beastly horse. It's only right to share him.

No matter. Marcus is back from his baptism of fire in double quick time, warts efficiently dealt with and, more impressively, he's managed to extract a cheque from Henderson, which is nothing short of miraculous. Even I have to admit to being impressed. Agnes most certainly is. She apologises to him about Henderson, saying it was supposed to have been Emma's call, and gives him nice clients for the rest of the day as a reward.

Man-radar on red alert, Paris has already appeared to suss out the new talent. I'm sure she must sit in her bedroom, her eyes glued to her binoculars. This morning, as she sashays across the yard, all male eyes turn to stare. And with good reason. Her usually dark brown hair is peroxide blonde, her huge eyes are kohl-rimmed à la Katie Price and she's wearing the tightest jodhpurs imaginable as she lolls outside one of the stables eyeing Marcus up and down with no subtlety whatsoever. She obviously likes what she sees, which means poor Miles is off the hook.

Marcus's eyes are out on stalks as he reluctantly allows me to drag him back into the office.

'Who the blazes is *that*?' he asks in rather shocked tones, his eyes still pulled in the direction of Paris.

'Jailbait,' I tell him firmly. 'Sixteen years old, bored out of her brain cell and goes by the name of Paris Mankly-Talbot, locally known as PM-T. She lives up the road in that little hovel with twenty-six bedrooms, with Mummy who's extremely high maintenance and called Amanda and Daddy, who's a super-rich hotshot lawyer in the city – and is called Dick,' I add helpfully. And then snigger.

* * *

We all go for a drink that evening, to officially welcome Marcus to the fold. Our local is the old pub in the village, and it's called the

Hope and Anchor. Sam calls it the Dope and Wanker, which always makes me think of Arian. There's a big garden, in what used to be an apple orchard and it's well within staggering home distance – at least for me. They don't mind dogs either, so Elmer and Eric do their worst, scrounging shamelessly from all the other customers, while we pretend not to know them.

There's blossom on the apple trees, and though there's a chill in the air, it's a wonderfully sunny evening. We all drink the deliciously chilled cider that's a house speciality, except for Miles, because it's his turn to be on call tonight. And after a glass or two, it seems that Marcus might not be so bad after all. He certainly has a glowing recommendation from his last practice. Actually, he's quite a glowing sort of person altogether, which rather begs the question: if they loved him so much, why the devil has he left them?

After Miles's phone bleeps and he rushes off to tend to a horse that's tangled in a barbed wire fence, the rest of us order some food. By the time Elmer and I get home, it's late. There's time only to put a machine load of washing on, before I have a bath and climb into bed, so it's not until next morning that I notice the message light flashing on the answerphone. Bloody Arian, no less. Wanting to discuss the house. My poor, battered heart sinks through the floor.

Of course, I knew it would happen, but losing our home seems unbearable. My home. I've come to love quaintly named Plum Tree Cottage, with its crooked doors and ancient timbers. The three large bedrooms, in that imagination of mine, were for the baby Mulhollands I'd always envisaged would turn up at some point and all around there is space I imagined we'd grow into. It was for ever – like my marriage.

But sadly, there's no way in the world I can afford the mortgage. Arian arranged for a smarmy estate agent to value it last week, without even telling me – the bastard still has his door keys – and so smug Martin, with his designer suits and quiffed hair, has been poking around my home and taking measurements without me even knowing. Martin drives a big, expensive car and is always unnaturally tanned, even in December. He clearly makes a *lot* of money... His surname ought to be Slime, not Syme and yes, he really is that bad. Worse even. I should know. He was in the year above me in sixth form.

I wonder how many of his customers know about his little property-developing habit? About his little way of snapping up bargains before they're even on the market, no doubt at a knock-down price as he sweet talks the old dears into almost giving their homes away to him, only for him to re-advertise them a week later at eye-watering prices... Definitely a secret millionaire for all the wrong reasons, our Mr Slime.

I can just imagine him sucking up to Arian, man to man, having a secret, smug laugh about how the little woman doesn't know what he's up to.

'Oh, don't worry about a thing, sir. This kind of thing happens all the time, ho, ho... We'll sell this in no time. Marvellous little family home like this will be snapped up...'

To say I'm furious is an understatement. I'm so seething I'm almost incandescent. Worse, someone is coming to view it this morning. More strangers sniffing around my home. I ought to be tidying everything, according to Martin.

'Mrs Mulholland, you really do need to de-clutter,' he told me most pompously. De-clutter? Isn't that what those TV makeover shows tell you to do? To make the home I don't want to sell more appealing. Actually, I really don't care that there's a pile of my knickers on the kitchen table, and that last night's dishes are lying unwashed in the sink. My empty wine bottle collection is quite impressive too. After all, I am that woman spurned. Hopefully no one will like my cluttered home and I can stay here forever.

I get a call from Smug Martin during my lunch break.

'Mrs Mulholland?' he says in that smarmy voice of his, sounding far too horribly pleased with himself. My blood runs cold.

'Good afternoon, Mr Slime,' I say, on purpose, my heart sinking as I listen.

Bloody bloody wankers, him and Arian. I hate them more than ever. The first people he showed round have offered the asking price. I didn't think that kind of thing ever happened. So to add insult to injury, now I'm homeless.

I can't help feeling oh *so* sorry for myself, as yet again, I'm consumed by emotion. First my husband announces he's leaving me, and as if that isn't enough, he rips my home out from underneath me. My eyes are prickling again, and inside I'm screaming, silently, at the unfairness of it all.

'It may not be a bad thing, Louisa,' says Agnes most sensibly, when I put the phone down and start wailing. 'It's not going to be easy to get over Arian while you're living in the house that you shared.'

I snivel a bit longer then dry my blotchy face. I know she's right, but it's just too much, too soon. I'd rather wait until I'm feeling stronger, but Agnes has other ideas.

'It may be quite good timing, you know. Now, a friend of mine has a holiday cottage that she's thinking of renting out long term. It's only round the corner from here, too. I think she's fed up with the constant stream of people in and out of it, and would rather just not have the worry. Would you like me to have a word with her on your behalf?'

My mouth drops open. Agnes is truly a miracle.

'Please... if it's not too much trouble. There's Elmer of course too. Do you think your friend would mind her there?' My voice quakes. I can't possibly lose Elmer, now of all times.

'Leave it to me,' says Agnes briskly. 'I'm sure it won't be a problem.'

I feel instantly reassured, knowing that if Agnes says it won't be a problem, everything will be fine. And so I end up pulling myself together and being most sensible, agreeing with her that this somewhat fortuitous development might indeed be quite a good thing after all.

* * *

In the event, after umpteen costly meetings with solicitors, Arian agrees, most magnanimously, to split the equity down the middle. Oh, how generous of him. He and Karina of course, with their combined pilot mega-salaries, will be able to afford a huge mansion with knobs on. On my meagre wages, I'll be lucky if I can find a pigsty. I resign myself to my new lowly status, which is apparently no less than I deserve.

In the end, it's all settled remarkably quickly. He doesn't want any of our furniture, and actually, neither do I. After all, everything in our house that we chose together now feels tainted, and nor do I want anything that reminds me of HIM. The only exception is an ancient table that used to belong to my granny.

He leaves another message, telling me he'll be collecting his clothes and old flying manuals. Too late, that woman spurned re-emerges and wishes she'd thought to burn them before he got here... Or at least unpicked all his crotches. Far more subtle than cutting them up. How funny would it be if he found himself in the middle of Heathrow Airport, a fine figure of an airline captain basking in all these admiring looks, suddenly aware of a howling draught around his privates. I find the idea childishly appealing.

The Impossible Search for the Perfect Man

Sadly, I'm deprived of the opportunity. He comes in while I'm at work and also takes the mower. Well, it's hardly as though he'd forget *that*.

So then it's house clearance and that's it. All done. And here I am feeling surreal, as I stand in the middle of my house looking around at the emptiness. All that remains is a collection of boxes and a very large, battered table. It's all happened scarily quickly. Good old Miles is coming over with a horsebox to transport me, Elmer and the table to Agnes's friend's cottage, which I decided to rent while the dust settles, so to speak. Actually, I didn't know what else to do. It's smaller than Plum Tree Cottage, but just perfect for one newly single woman and her weird dog. It's quite near the Hope and Anchor, and it's furnished. There's even a paddock behind, I couldn't help noticing. Which just so happens to be empty... But, best of all, I can't help thinking, with relief, is that with any luck, now this is all over and done with, I really have no reason to speak to Arian ever, *ever* again.

4

But in spite of everything that's happened, my new home works a kind of magic on me. Surrounded by fields and beech woods, the huge trees catch the wind, and the air is full of the sound of birds. The peace and quiet is shattered only occasionally by the roar of a passing car or tractor – a definite advantage of living out the back end of beyond.

And there's the paddock... Fringed with hedges and knee high in shimmering grasses, it really does need a horse in it – just to keep it tidy, you understand.

Most mornings, it's a five-minute walk to the practice. And already, I'm hurting less. Or maybe it's just the change, because Agnes was absolutely right, and relieved of the clutter of my joint life with Arian, and trying to look on the bright side of being a complete failure as a wife, I do feel rather liberated.

Emma lives quite nearby, in a snazzy barn conversion, and as she's single too, we soon start seeing lots more of each other. She's an amazing cook as it turns out and I'm a more than willing guinea pig for her mouth-watering recipes. If she hadn't been a vet, my multi-talented friend would undoubtedly have been a winner of

Masterchef. What I don't understand is why she isn't fat as a pig. Out of her work clothes, Emma dresses simply but stylishly, and she's thin as a supermodel. If I cooked the way she did, I'd be eating all the time. My favourite skinny jeans are already on the tight side, which I need to do something about. Turning into a lard arse is hardly going to improve my self-esteem. I'm flabbergasted when she tells me after a few evenings spent together, that she, too, was married. And is now divorced. My mouth literally drops open.

'No one else knows, Lou,' she tells me hurriedly. 'I'd rather keep it that way too. I met him before vet college, and after I graduated we got married.' Then she adds sadly, 'I was so stupid, and well, young, really. It never could have worked. He wanted to settle down and have a family, and I wanted my career. I didn't study all those years to stay at home and have babies – well, not straight away, anyway. So a year later we were divorced and that was the end of it.'

Just as I'm thinking, *What a bastard*, she adds, 'He wasn't a bad person. We just made a mistake.'

'Oh, Emma, I had no idea...' I say inadequately, the wind completely taken out of my sails by her honesty. Then more bluntly, 'You don't look old enough.'

She raises her eyebrows at me. 'If I'd been older, I might have been a little wiser...' she says soberly. 'Anyway, it's history and not a mistake I'll make again in a hurry.'

And there's more to gossip about when I find out that Emma has fallen for a client, which isn't generally considered a good idea, but after her divorce, I doubt she's interested in anything serious. I've met him briefly and actually I have to agree, there's lots to like. Ben is very handsome in a serious kind of way and has a big horse (of course). Well, several actually – it's how they met. There's a horse at the heart of everything around here. He's even asked her out to dinner, but unfortunately for Emma, she was on call.

I've been so wrapped up in myself, it's passed me by that I don't have the monopoly on busted marriages. The realisation makes me ashamed, especially when everyone's been so supportive.

Another thing bothers me too, because Leo's gone quiet. She was often here when I first moved and spent many evenings devotedly keeping me company and helping, most therapeutically, to dissect Arian's shortcomings. But lately, I haven't seen her. I'm sure she's just busy, but all the same. Something niggles at me and I make a mental note to call her.

Tonight my mood is buoyant. Agnes is coming for supper, maybe Emma too, if she's not dashing around saving horses. I never try and compete with Emma's superlative talents in the kitchen, just keep it simple. Tonight we're having salad Niçoise, which ought to be within even my modest capabilities, with a freshly baked loaf from the pub.

But earlier than expected, there's a knock at the door. It can't be Agnes, because she's always spot on time, so I'm expecting it to be Emma, only it isn't. I open the door and it's Leo.

I'm thrilled that she's here, and as I pour my friend a glass of wine, she glances around admiringly.

'It's lovely here, Lou. I can't believe how settled you look, I'm so happy for you.'

Then she's uncharacteristically quiet.

Something doesn't ring true, because right now, Leonie doesn't look as though she could be happy about anything. Something's clearly wrong.

Then she asks, carefully, in a very subdued voice, 'Lou? When you thought something was going on with Arian, what was it exactly that made you suspicious?'

I look at her, dumbfounded. Surely not them too? Not Leonie and Pete, the greatest love story among all my friends I've ever had?

'What's happened, Leo? Is something wrong?'

And suddenly my fear is back, only this time it's for my friends.

She sighs. A very heartfelt sigh indeed and suddenly I notice that there are shadows under her eyes that were never there before.

'Oh, Lou, I don't know. Pete just isn't himself. He's distant. Bites my head off at the drop of a hat. All he wants to do when he's home from work is read or sleep. And he won't talk to me. Not about anything, and we've always talked, about everything, until now... I just don't know what the matter is. I really think it must be me. He seems fine with everyone else...' Her voice tails off.

I truly don't know what to say to help her. She's right. It doesn't sound like Pete at all.

'Just hang in there, Leo. It might be some work thing on his mind... A base check or an arsey training captain? We both know what these pilots are like...'

Only too well, in my case.

She raises huge brown eyes to look at me. 'If that's the case, why doesn't he tell me?'

'Maybe he's a bit under the weather Leonie, I don't know. Have you tried to get him out? Or maybe just spend some time together?'

None of which, of course, made a scrap of difference with Arian.

Leonie shrugs. I can tell I'm way off the mark here. We're not really getting anywhere with this.

'Stay for supper?' I offer. Agnes would know what to say. 'Agnes and Emma are coming round. There's plenty for four...' I try to persuade her. And it might take her mind off things for a while.

But Leonie shakes her head. 'Thanks, Lou, but I think I'll go. I don't think I'd be great company.'

* * *

Supper with Agnes and Emma is always fun, though tonight I can't quite shake my concern for Leonie from my mind.

Away from the office, Agnes lets her hair down just a tiny bit, and listens to me and Emma gossiping with an indulgent smile, as though we were her babies. When Emma and I start cackling about initiating Marcus though, Agnes is a touch disapproving.

'That was just a tad unfair of you, girls. If I'd spotted it, you would have got Henderson, Emma.' Her tone is slightly reprimanding, but there's the faintest ghost of a smile there too.

'Oh Agnes,' we both crow. 'It was *funny*. Emma's dealt with that horse loads of times. And Henderson actually paid. Result!' Emma and I high five each other.

Agnes has the good grace to smile properly then. 'On this occasion, you're off the hook, girls. But don't do it again. Really, that poor boy...'

Poor boy my arse. There's nothing poor about Marcus. He's obviously already reeled Agnes in, hook, line and sinker, along with all the other admirers, female of course, that are queuing up for his services, veterinary and otherwise, no doubt.

I've also, just recently, discovered Emma's guilty secret. Don't we all have one? Anyway, Emma's, it seems, is that she is addicted, quite seriously I'm finding out, to horoscopes. 'Astrology', she'll tell you, because she thinks it sounds more intelligent. Can you imagine? She's clever, educated, accomplished in her career, very pretty, and yet relies on a twat like Jerome Castello– 'astrologer to the stars', as he describes himself – to tell her how to live her life. I ask you. Even with my three and a half GCSEs, I'm not as daft as that.

Emma has updates regularly texted to her mobile during the day, and pretends to whoever she's with, be it client or colleague, that it's an urgent update on a patient. It must cost her a fortune. She is unreservedly and worryingly hooked, and I've decided it's my mission to cure her. Well, someone has to.

Jerome Castello must be laughing all the way to the bank. There are probably millions of Emmas who get sucked in via his website, and before they know it, they can't function without subscribing to his super-duper overpriced premier service. He's a con man. He must be. I plan to do some research and find out more about him. I don't like seeing my friends ripped off.

Halfway through the evening, there's a bleeping noise from Emma's direction. She leaps to attention and grabs her phone. It could be a call out from a client, or maybe it's just Jerome with an update. She stands there, listening, uttering the occasional 'erm' or 'I see'. Then hangs up. Definitely Jerome then.

'Okay?' I smile brightly at her, holding her gaze just a little longer than necessary.

'Fine.' Just like Beamish. It must be catching. But she's looking guilty. Ah-ha. She knows I know.

Agnes looks quizzically from one of us to the other. This must be the first time in the history of the world that I know something she doesn't.

Then Emma's phone bleeps again, and I look at her, annoyed actually, that she's going to let some stupid astrologer interrupt our evening for the second time. But this time it's a bona fide client, and after taking some details in a highly professional manner, Emma's off to save someone's precious horse. She exits very speedily, knowing full well that she's only putting off the inevitable, and that I'll be addressing her problem at the next possible opportunity.

* * *

It's funny really. My new home isn't far from where Arian and I lived, but life has changed beyond recognition. But it's crept up on me that it's better – a realisation that wasn't entirely welcome at first, but it's true. For starters, I have such great friends, I've realised, now I no longer take them for granted. And for the most part, I feel really good. There have been the occasional blips when I've forgotten myself and reverted to a bawling, snot-nosed wreck, but I always hate myself so much afterwards, I've tried to stop myself, because it's a simple fact that my marriage is over, and no amount of self-pity will change that. Shit happens, and not just to me, as I'm finding out.

But tonight's the first night I've been unable to sleep in ages. I ditched those hideous 3 a.m., gremlins when I left Plum Tree Cottage and have slept like a log ever since. But tonight, for a change, it's not about me. I can't stop thinking about Leonie, and wonder what's going on with Pete. They have always been so utterly devoted to each other. I can't in all honesty believe they're headed the same way as me and Arian, but how can I be sure? I didn't see that coming, after all.

Leonie adores Pete, loves him with every fibre of her being. I admire that kind of love. And I'm a little envious if I'm honest. I'm not at all sure I *ever* felt that way about Arian, nor did I invest the tireless, unselfish, unconditional effort that Leonie so generously does. It's not a welcome thought, but maybe our relationship wasn't as great as I'd assumed. Maybe, like Emma, I too made a mistake. I mean, far from falling apart, I seem to be managing just fine without him.

On that less than comfortable note, I fall asleep.

5

The next morning is clear and sunny. The kind when you'd like to pause for a moment and believe that summer is just around the corner, but today – no way. From the word go, it's so hectic there's barely time to think. It all kicks off with Miles, who was summoned to a riding school at the crack of dawn to a horse with a suspected fracture. For a horse, that's life threatening and the owner will be worried out of his mind. Meanwhile Emma has spent most of last night sitting in a stable with an in-foal mare in a very sorry state and has had about an hour's sleep, if that. And now, just to top it all, Beamish has phoned in sick. Gastric flu, he says, sounding extremely sorry for himself. Hmm. It might just possibly have been the whisky. So, while Emma is catching forty winks in an empty stable, it's just Marcus and a rather full diary.

'Okay,' he starts. 'Let's sort this out. This yard here.' He points to the first entry. 'It's all vaccinations and other routine stuff. Can you phone them and say I've been called out to an emergency and will be over this afternoon? Miles can cover this one.' He points to the next entry in the diary. 'It's just down the road from where he is now, and I'll get started on the rest. Think I'll take Sam, it might speed things up a bit. Give Emma another hour's sleep and ask her to call me.'

And with that, he's striding out of the office, wasting no time at all. Gosh. How jolly masterful. I feel ever so slightly inadequate. Uncharacteristically quiet, Agnes raises her eyebrows at me.

The afternoon gets better though. A very pretty Shetland called Lucy comes in for an ultrasound, and we all spend ages making a huge fuss of her. She's followed by a very shouty little pony with an equally gobby owner, who's unfortunately in no hurry to leave. Paris cruises by (cerise jodhpurs and classic Ray-Bans, hair screwed up in a sort of pineapple thing on top of her head) but stays all of about ten seconds once she's sniffed out the absence of testosterone.

Miles has sorted out his fracture, which ended up in the nearest equine hospital and which, being Miles, he's frightfully worried about. Emma by now is fully revived and perky as ever, after an hour's sleep on a bale of hay. How do vets do that? Mind you, pilots do it too. They can sleep anytime, anywhere it would seem – particularly in my ex-husband's case. But keeping my mind firmly focused on work, I've no doubt Beamish will be back in the morning, right as rain, and we'll be back on track. Marcus, to my surprise, is working his socks off. I'm not easily impressed, but, dare I say it, without him today would have been a nightmare.

Just before I leave, there's the roar of a very expensive-sounding engine from outside, followed by the clip-clop of very high, very pointy heels as Amanda M-T makes her way into our office for just about the first time ever.

'*Hellair*,' she says in that silly way that posh people do, as she flips her highlights over her shoulder. 'Do I need to register? Not me personally of course...' and she giggles in a girly way as if no one's ever said that before, which they have, of course, gazillions of times.

Agnes steps forward. 'Good evening, Mrs Mankly-Talbot. Can I take it you have a horse that you'd like us to look at?'

It transpires that Amanda and Dick have bought Paris a little show-jumper. Only a little one. And it only cost thirty-five thousand, she tells us, because after all, Paris does still have the sweet little horse she won at Hickstead on last year, but apparently this new little one was too good to miss. She waves her braceletted wrists around as she gesticulates flamboyantly and then I notice. I can't miss them. Because Amanda may be stonking rich and drive an extremely fast car, but she also has massive calves. And I mean whoppers. As well as a husband called Dick. I try not to snigger. It just goes to show, doesn't it, that absolutely nobody has it all.

* * *

When I get home, I make myself a cup of tea and settle down to call Leonie. I haven't been able to get her out of my mind. But it's Pete who answers. Not sounding his usual self at all. I try to draw him out, but, to be honest, I haven't seen him in ages – not since Arian and I went our separate ways – and my efforts are far from successful.

'How are you, Pete?' I ask brightly. Not that I expect him to tell me.

'Um, Fine. Thanks. And you? Leonie says you're doing well in your new place?' His words are slow, as though his brain is floating in glue.

'It's lovely. Come over with Leonie sometime, I'd love to see you.' I genuinely would like to see him. Them. And slightly selfishly, I think it would be even better if he reported back to Arian that I'm doing absolutely just fine on my own...

'Oh. Yes,' he says absently, not sounding like Pete at all. This is very odd. He sounds tired, rather than disinterested. And he's clearly not in the mood to talk.

'I'll ask Leonie to call you, okay?' he says.

'Great. Thanks. Bye then, Pete.' But he's gone before I even finish talking.

No sooner have I put the phone down than it rings again. It can't be Leonie already, can it? It's not. It's Marcus. You could have knocked me down with a feather. Marcus? Calling me at home? *I must have messed something up*, is the first thought that comes to mind. I can't imagine in a million years why else *he* would be calling *me*.

'Hello, Lou.' Tired, but definitely friendly. I breathe out cautiously.

'Hi, Marcus. This is a surprise.'

Then immediately think, *Oh shit, he's found out that it was me who set him up with the warty horse.*

There's a brief silence. 'Oh. Is it? Actually, Lou... oh look, are you busy, or could I come over?'

I'm flabbergasted. I'm not sure what's going on here. We've never spoken about anything outside of work – until now. So either I've done something wrong or he thinks I fancy him, which I most definitely do not. He's not my type. At all. But caught by surprise, I'm not quick enough.

'Erm, okay,' I say, not terribly enthusiastically.

'Great. See you in a minute then.'

Oh fuck. Okay, so I do not fancy him, I remind myself, but nor do I want Marcus in my cottage in its current state. He'll think I'm a complete slut. Like a dervish, I whirl around stacking magazines, plumping cushions and stacking the dirty plates more tidily in the sink so it looks like there's fewer of them. Then, just as the doorbell rings, I catch sight of my flustered reflection in the mirror. Excellent. My normal 'been through a hedge backwards' look. Still, it's too late to do anything about it. And it's only Marcus, after all. Smoothing my hair, and with a deranged Elmer barking excitedly, I open the door.

It's okay, I tell myself. It looks as though Marcus has come straight from work anyway. He's quite scruffy, but actually, I like that.

'Hello,' I say brightly, at the same time he says, 'Hi,' then we just stand there, smiling self-consciously at each other. Awkward doesn't even begin to describe it and I've still no idea what he's doing here.

'Um, would you like a drink? Coffee? Wine?' I offer.

He looks tempted. 'I could murder a beer if you've got one?'

Beer. Of course. And well, no. I don't have any. I shake my head.

'I'm sorry.'

He looks slightly embarrassed at having asked. 'Wine would be good?'

I go to the kitchen where there's quite a nice Pinot Grigio in the fridge. He follows, making approving comments about the cottage and asking things like how old it is. I get the feeling he's as ill at ease as I am, which amuses me because I've never seen him anything other than ultra-confident and in control.

I pour two glasses and pass one to him.

'Cheers.' We clink glasses and sit at my battered table. Elmer lays her bedraggled head adoringly on his lap and drools. Fickle bitch.

'How are you settling in?' I ask chirpily. A nice, neutral question.

'Great, actually. I'm loving it! You're nice people to work with.'

Oh. I suddenly feel terribly guilty. About Henderson's bloody horse.

'Have you worked here long?' he asks.

'It feels like forever,' I answer honestly. 'In the best possible way. It's actually only been about two years. Since my old horse was put to sleep.'

'Oh.' He frowns. 'Do you have a horse now?'

I shake my head. 'My husband wasn't keen. Said it was too much of a tie if we wanted to go away...'

Then I stop because I don't know what to say next. That my husband ran off with a tart, so I shouldn't have listened to a single word he said, or the current version, which is that actually, I'm thinking about getting another one. Horse that is, not husband.

Marcus surprises me. 'I did hear about your husband. And I'm sorry. Er, actually I do know what it feels like. Well almost. I wasn't actually married, but someone really messed me about. I have an idea what it's like.'

I find myself smiling at him. He's being very nice and it's very odd. I have to remind myself about how the female clients are always phoning and asking for him in breathy, girly voices, as if they've got nothing better to do with their day than play horses with the dishy new vet.

I gather myself. 'Well, I'm okay now. It could have been worse. And actually, I'm probably better off without him,' I add for good measure, sounding far more of a hard-nosed bitch than I'm feeling.

Marcus shrinks back in his chair, looking most uncomfortable. Ha. Somehow it's quite gratifying. He was probably thinking that poor, pathetic Louisa, still mourning the loss of her wayward husband, would be so very glad of his concern.

By now though, Marcus has clearly thought twice about coming round here. He drains his glass rapidly and stands up. 'Right. Well, I'm glad you're okay.' He gives me a quizzical look, which makes me feel rather dishonest. 'That's great. It's good you're doing so... fine. Erm, I'll see you at work then.'

And then he's gone, leaving me more nonplussed than I've ever been in my life.

6

Another week or so ticks by, and with each passing day, life gets easier. People stop picking their way so carefully around me as they realise, unexpectedly, that I really am just fine on my own. I'm starting to like that word. After all, I don't need a man to define who I am. And then something else truly amazing happens.

Miles comes trudging into the office one morning, looking even more unhappy than usual and before long Agnes drags out of him what the problem is. It takes her all of about thirty seconds.

'Flaming Daisy Mitchell is the problem, if you must know,' he says glumly. 'She's got this horse – well several, actually. They're all beautiful animals, but this particular one keeps going quite lame. He's not a youngster, and he's a bit creaky, but in between times, he's fine to go hacking. And today she told me she wants him put to sleep. Doesn't want the bother of an animal that's anything less than straightforward.'

Miles looks really upset and pissed off. Unfortunately this kind of thing happens sometimes and it's probably better than the poor horse being doped up and sold on to an uncertain future, but even so.

'Oh dear,' says Agnes. 'You really don't look happy about this.'

Miles is frowning. 'Trouble is, he's a nice old horse with plenty of life in him. It just doesn't seem right. He's not even that old. He's just an inconvenience as far as she's concerned.'

We're all silent. None of us like the sound of this. Then Agnes speaks.

'Well, it's perfectly obvious isn't it?' she says, quite matter-of-factly, as if we were all completely stupid or something. 'Louisa should have him.'

My jaw drops wide open. Did she really just say what I thought she did?

'There's an empty paddock behind your cottage. Louisa. You know perfectly well. And even an old stable in the far corner. Old Charley Peach owns it. I've known him for years. Leave it to me.' All spoken so firmly that none of us dare utter a word.

She dispatches Miles off up the drive to visit Paris's new horse. After all, a despondent vet is the last thing we need moping around the office when we have so much work to do. And at least he's safe from Paris, who still has a massive crush on Marcus.

Agnes should be prime minister. I'm beginning to wonder if at the very least she's a witch, but at any rate, she's definitely extraordinary. Just a couple of hours later, she tells me that Charley Peach would be delighted to let me have it for a pittance of a rent and Agnes has already decided that the vets can keep an eye on Horace (the horse) if he needs them.

And so the next day, when I get home from work, there is this huge gentle creature, mooching peacefully around in the long grass behind my cottage. Apparently Daisy Mitchell was delighted to wash her hands of him and so now it would seem, he is mine.

* * *

Horace is lovely, a real gentleman, with the most impeccable manners. He's dark bay with big, kind eyes and likes nosing gently in my pockets for sweets. How anyone couldn't want him is unfathomable. It is absolutely love at first sight, as far as I'm concerned. Not so for Elmer, who's extremely jealous and snarls at him. Then she eats his droppings.

My days are getting busier. Seeing as it's summer, Horace is turned out in the paddock day and night, but I like to go and spend time with him before breakfast and in the evenings, after work, I catch him up and groom him and in no time it's as though he's always been here.

Emma loves him too and is quite envious. I've told her she can ride him whenever she likes, but she works such long days, she hardly ever has time.

It's one evening when we're leaning on the paddock fence, waxing lyrically about how brilliant Horace is as he ambles around up to his knees in grass, that I broach my concerns about Jerome, the con-man astrologer. Emma, as I fully expect her to be, is instantly on the defensive.

'Have you ever read his website, Lou?' she asks. 'Only it's quite uncanny how accurate he can be. It's like he's talking specifically to *me*... You should take a look sometime.'

Perhaps I might, but I'm not telling her that.

'And what about the times he gets it wrong then?' I add confrontationally and more than a touch scathingly. 'Don't tell me – he's always so accurate...'

'Well,' Emma is pensive. 'Usually it relates to something that's going on. I don't know. It's sort of helpful, honestly...' She pauses. 'You know, when my marriage went wrong, it was kind of a comfort. Everything he wrote seemed to confirm to me that I was doing the right thing, when I was finding it hard to be sure.'

So that's how it started. Jerome hooked her when she was at

her most vulnerable. Poor Emma, if her only source of support was reading her stars. I can see I need some more ammunition. I'm determined to expose Jerome for what he really is, which is a crooked shyster who preys on defenceless women. I don't why I think women particularly. Nor do I know why Emma is so vulnerable.

'Why don't you try a whole twenty-four hours without tuning in to Jerome, including deleting those ridiculous texty things before you read them?' I suggest brightly.

Emma goes pink. 'How do you know about the texts?'

I give her a look. I mean, it's just *so* obvious.

'Maybe. I'll think about it,' she says, meaning well, but I know she won't. She's an addict, after all.

I give up. But only for tonight.

* * *

Miles comes over to check Horace. Or so he says. I think it's just an excuse to come and admire him.

'Nice old chap, isn't he?'

We hang over the paddock fence again and gaze lovingly at my beautiful horse. I do a lot of that these days. Terrible time wasters, horses are.

'I'm so glad you've taken him. Any time you're worried, just let me know. He does have his moments.'

Miles really does get *far* too attached to his patients.

That evening, I get another surprise visitor, only this one hasn't come to see my horse. It's Leonie, looking pale and haggard, with dark circles under her lovely eyes. I feel a flicker of alarm.

After I've made a pot of tea, we sit in the garden, so I can turn my chair and gaze lovingly at Horace.

'So how's Pete?'

Leonie sniffs and a tear rolls down her cheek. I'm shocked. I can't remember the last time Leo cried.

'Terrible,' she says, miserably. 'Something's dreadfully wrong, Lou. I even got to the point where I came out with it and asked him if he was having an affair. He went ballistic and threw his coffee mug at the wall. It really frightened me. It was his favourite one, too. Honestly, Lou...' Her huge brown eyes looked so sad. 'It's like he hates me. He can't stand me being anywhere near him.'

She picks up her mug of tea and sips it, trying to collect herself. 'There's another thing. He's off sick from work. Apparently he semi-collapsed down route somewhere, and they had to fly him home as a passenger.'

I sit there blinking at her. Blimey. That's serious in the airline business, which is a most unforgiving environment. Poor, poor Pete. And poor Leonie too. The whole company will know by now. But, far more important than that, there's something seriously wrong.

'At least one thing's come out of it.' She sniffs into a tissue. 'The fleet manager wants him to see one of their doctors. He's absolutely refused until now, but this time it looks as though he doesn't have much choice. If he doesn't go, he's out of a job – it's as simple as that. But he's said he will and I'm glad. If someone can just tell us what's wrong, then at least we can do something about it.'

'When's the appointment?' I ask, hoping it's soon.

'Next week. Not too long.'

But nor is it soon enough.

Horace chooses that moment to wander over and obligingly place his great head close to Leo so she can stroke it. Very therapeutic, horses are. He doesn't mind the tears rolling onto his nose one bit and just stands there with his eyes half closed, being comforting, while neurotic Elmer growls jealously from her lowly place at my feet. He ignores her. When you're as wise and noble as Horace is, a scruffy dog with a loose screw isn't a threat.

Poor, poor Leo. What can possibly be wrong with Pete? Physically he seems quite okay, that's what Leonie says, anyway. So what on earth can it be?

7

Oh my Lord. The parents are coming for Sunday lunch. Today. I've put it off as long as I can, and I'm steeling myself for the recriminations I know will be all too forthcoming from my mother. Dad will probably – and wisely – drink a little too much wine and fall asleep in the garden. I'd like to do the same. My mother isn't easy at the best of times.

I'm cooking leg of lamb, locally farmed, with Jersey royals and asparagus. Mum's bringing pudding. She insisted and I know better than to argue. It's probably sherry trifle made from a packet, the only sherry, most likely, being in its title.

Still, I tell myself. In a few hours it will all be over. For a few more weeks, or even months if I'm particularly lucky and maintain my air of elusiveness.

Elmer barks ferociously when she hears their car. My mother's never been a fan, but Elmer's oblivious to this. She grabs hold of Mum's skirt and wags her whole body delightedly before they're even through the door. My mother brushes her off distastefully.

'Darling. It's not as nice as Plum Tree Cottage, is it?' she says sharply, her beady eyes glancing critically around in her search of something to slate, even though I spent a large part of yesterday cleaning and tidying.

'Hello, poppet.' Dad at least looks pleased to see me. 'Nice place you've got here. I like it.'

Mum hmmphs her disapproval. I kiss the cold cheek she proffers.

'Come through to the kitchen and I'll pour us some wine.'

Already I'm tense as anything and they've been here precisely thirty seconds. I haven't offered a guided tour, nor do I intend to. She'd take it as an opportunity to rip my new surroundings to shreds. For some unknown reason, my mother can rarely find it in her to say a good word about anything.

'I see Arian let you keep the table?' is the first thing she says, as she looks around the kitchen. I instantly rise to the bait.

'Mum. It was always *my* table. Granny gave it to *me*, remember? He didn't even like it.'

There's a warning note in my voice. Mum just adored Arian. I've tried to work out what it was, exactly, that endeared him to her so. Was it his glamorous job? His salary? His swanky car? Probably all of the above, thinking about it. And the fact that he cheated on her only daughter seems neither here nor there, because my mother, as I concluded some time ago, is an out and out snob.

'Come and see the garden,' I suggest, taking me safely out of reach of the newly sharpened carving knife lying temptingly within reach on the worktop.

We walk outside. The garden's looking pretty. Arching boughs of roses are in bloom and there are clumps of herbs which release their scent when you brush against them. None of it's my doing, of course. I don't know the first thing about gardening. But the air is fragrant and it's peaceful, so I show it off proudly nonetheless.

'And this,' I add as Horace nickers at us and wanders over to the fence, 'is Horace.'

Dad smiles from ear to ear. 'So glad you've found yourself another one,' he says quietly, stroking Horace's soft nose gently. I know he'll pay for it later. Poor Dad's horribly allergic to horses, but he's never able to resist them.

Mum stares at me. 'Arian wouldn't have approved. He always said it was difficult to go away if you kept horses.'

'Well,' I say, stroking Horace myself to keep from exploding. 'Arian isn't here, is he? He's somewhere else, shacked up with the trollop who shares his rather questionable morals, so I think I'm entitled to my horse.'

I kiss Horace's nose and storm back into the cottage, leaving my mother standing there speechless.

No one mentions Arian after that. Not for a while, at least, as Mum whinges on about Margaret at the WI who wants to change where they go for their Christmas lunch this year, and moans about absolutely everything. She tells me the lamb is overdone and that it should be pink in the middle, even though I've never known her serve up any meat that isn't so dry it practically chokes you. But she eats every last thing on her plate and even manages seconds, so it obviously isn't too bad. Dad, as predicted, drinks too much red wine and nods off, absolutely the only way he's stayed married to my mother for so long. As he begins to snore, right on cue she starts again. She just can't help herself.

'Darling? Have you tried calling Arian? You have to work at marriage you know. Maybe you should try counselling?'

I sit at the table resting my head in my hands, wondering how much more of her insensitive comments I can take.

'Men can be fragile creatures you know. They do expect certain things...'

Oh no. *Please no*. Do not let my mother be talking to me about sex. That just about does it, and it's like the top exploding off a pressure cooker. This time, I don't mince my words.

'Look, Mum, I know I'm not perfect, but none of us are. And you seem to have conveniently forgotten that it was *Arian* who chose to have the affair and *Arian* who chose to leave. Without any attempt whatsoever to communicate my shortcomings to me, or any attempt to put things right. I'm not sure you've really grasped this at all, because the conversation we're having is clearly one you should be having with Arian, don't you think?'

I think she's got the message, as that's the final word – thank God. It's nice to know who you can rely on when the chips are down.

By the time they leave, I'm drained. I slump down on the sofa, utterly exhausted, in my lowest mood since I moved in here. Even Elmer's picked up on the vibe and she's exhausted too, lying flat out, twitching slightly and producing blood curdling yelps as she dreams about murdering small mammals, not even waking when I accidentally tread on her.

Later on, when Emma calls me to suggest going out for a drink, I nearly say no, until I decide not to let my mother ruin my day. And a nice girly chat is probably just what I need. I agree to meet her at the Hope and Anchor in about an hour.

In an effort to raise my flagging spirits, I run myself a bath and pour in what remains of my most expensive bath oil while turning up Owl City loud enough to have Elmer fleeing for her bed. But it has the desired effect, and half an hour later, I'm feeling human again and looking forward to seeing my friend.

But when I walk in to the pub and see Marcus there as well, I nearly change my mind. Then I see that the Ben that Emma fancies is there too. *Oh bugger*. They've seen me.

I pin on my brightest smile and join them. And actually, after a large glass of wine, it's quite an enjoyable evening, marred only by the fact that Marcus is there. The trouble is, he's still too good-looking and confident. And way too good at everything, even at being nice like when he came round to mine the other evening. Men like that make me feel like a blob. After all, I'm five foot four of not terribly slim, not terribly accomplished, mouse-haired, soon-to-be-divorced woman, while he's done so many awfully interesting things, which he tells Ben about now, in depth, as they have a man-conversation about extreme sports and who won the footy last weekend.

I tell Emma all about today's visitation. She's suitably horrified.

'Honestly, Lou. Your mother could have been a little more supportive, don't you think?'

I explain to Emma that I've always had the feeling that until I married Arian, I had been a constant source of disappointment to her.

Emma's thoughtful, then says wisely, 'I shouldn't take it too personally. It sounds like your mother is inherently incapable of approving of anything.'

'Exactly,' I agree. 'Except for my wonderful ex-husband of course, whose arse, for some reason, the sun shines out of...'

Emma and I get a little bit tiddly and giggly. Oops. I really shouldn't have had that fourth glass of wine, but it has been an exceptionally tough day, even by current standards.

Marcus keeps giving me odd looks, as if I've got a bogey on the end of my nose. I keep checking it just to make sure. And predictably, Emma's mobile bleeps one of Jerome's poxy, over-priced updates at her, which has her jumping out of her chair, then dashing outside to analyse its deep and meaningful message in private.

Which leaves me, Ben and Marcus. Marcus goes to the bar to get another round of drinks in, leaving me and Ben, who's very handsome and looks like Brad Pitt, with gorgeous eyes and a lovely smile. Lucky Emma. I gaze at the lovely smile a bit. Then he says,

'Erm, I don't know Emma that well yet, but she seems to do that rather a lot...'

I like the 'yet'. I make a note to self to tell Emma he said that. I'm guessing he's referring to her disappearing act.

'She does, doesn't she?' I say bluntly. 'Has she told you why?'

He looks at me quizzically, but then Marcus comes back and neither of us mentions it.

'How's your horse, Louisa?' he asks me. A nice safe topic of conversation. Hopefully I can manage not to say anything to scare him off this time. It seems I'm developing rather a talent for it. And it's something I'd rather not become known for. If I'm not careful, I'll end up being one of those mad old women who people cross the road to avoid. *Scary Louisa? Ooh, I wouldn't talk to her if I were you... she's a bit of a funny one you know...* as if I had two heads and fangs and barbecued adulterous ex-husbands.

I tell Ben all about Horace and how he's ended up living with me. And then I discover he used to go out with Daisy Mitchell and knows Horace really well! He must know Daisy pretty well too in that case, so I better watch my mouth. This horse world is far too jolly small, I can tell you. I need to become more like Agnes and learn to be supremely discreet. That would surprise everyone – but my thoughts are interrupted as Emma rejoins us. Looking rather worried.

'You okay, Em?' Marcus asks her, concern showing on his face. If only he knew why she looked like that.

'Fine,' she says vacantly. Ben clearly doesn't know what to make of these unexplained absences. He probably thinks she's on drugs or something. Right at this minute, she looks like it. Not surprisingly, after that, the evening goes rather flat.

Although my home is the nearest to the pub, I don't invite everyone back for coffee. After all, tonight I am a girl on a mission.

Alone with my flatcoat and my computer, I lock my door and get to work.

To start with, I google Jerome Castello. There are endless listings for the man, aside from his daily predictions. He's been published, it seems, in just about every newspaper imaginable and is quoted all over the place. What I'm looking for is some personal information about him, but there's hardly any to be found. I spend a whole obsessive hour, at the end of which I'm on page thirty-three of the search listings about him. And then I stumble across something rather interesting.

It's actually a forum, and the entry I read is written by a man whose wife was just like Emma. Addicted and dependent, unable to make the most basic decision on her own. Interestingly, this man found Jerome's home address somehow and wrote to him. Give him his due, Jerome actually met with the man and his wife, and after that, things got better.

Perhaps that's the answer for Emma.

I decide that's what I'll do. I keep googling and then on page fifty-four of the search listings, bingo! I hit gold. Jerome's postal address, and hang on, he's not called Jerome Castello at all. His real name is Jimmy Crook. Ha ha! How apt. I put together a letter, diplomatically addressed to his famous name of course, about how my poor misguided friend needs his help, and put it in an envelope ready to post.

8

It's Monday morning. Beamish has called a meeting of all of us, not just the vets. Only Mrs Boggle is allowed to be excused. I wonder what's up?

'Um, it won't take, er, long,' he assures us. Just as well. There's a mammoth list of calls and the phone keeps ringing.

He clears his throat.

'Erm, I'd like you all to know that after a long deliberation, I've, um, made a decision to, er, partially retire.' We all look at each other in astonishment. The only person who looks unsurprised by his announcement is Miles.

'As you all know, um, my health hasn't exactly been, well, perfect, lately...' *So it's not just a whisky habit then.* '... and the old, er, quack has advised me to slow down. So, um, seems I don't have too much choice in the matter.' Poor old Beamish looks rather forlorn. What a bummer.

'Um, Miles, I'm delighted to say, has agreed to, er, take on the role of senior partner and in my, um, absence, he is at the helm.' Everyone looks at Miles, who smiles awkwardly, lanky legs stretched out in front of him, looking uncomfortable. 'You will however have the pleasure of my company on Mondays, Wednesdays and Fridays. So it's very much business as usual. Erm, that's all.'

Except it's not, is it. Oh, I can see we're all thinking the same thing. We'll never cover the workload. We're going to need *another* new vet.

After Beamish's bombshell, we're all shell-shocked. But actually, it turns out he's sixty-five, which is much older than he appears. It probably won't be long before he retires altogether. This clinches it, I decide. Emma *has* to sort herself out, because one thing this practice doesn't need is a vet with personal problems. I'm not entirely sure she'll share my enthusiasm. And nor does she know that my letter's winging its way to Jerome as we speak.

Agnes goes out for lunch with Beamish. Probably a rather swish one, I imagine, as they're gone a jolly long time. *Hmmm... maybe they've gone to that little French bistro for an intimate five course dejeuner followed by café and cognac... Or that new Italian I really like which serves the most divine antipasti, all washed down by a bottle of Montepulciano...* But my daydreaming is interrupted as the phones keep ringing and there's general firefighting to be done. I'm just putting down the phone when Marcus comes in briefly. He's got an X-ray due in shortly.

'Bit of a shock, wasn't it?' he says thoughtfully, about Beamish's announcement. 'I wasn't expecting that at all. Trouble is we're flat out already. I'm not sure how we're going to cover everything.'

My guess is they'll do what they always do when we're a vet short, and end up working dawn till dusk.

I agree with him, tentatively suggesting that possibly we'll need a new vet before long.

'I just hope Emma isn't going anywhere,' he adds, 'only I've been wondering about her lately. She does seem quite distracted.'

I'm saved from avoiding an explanation by the timely arrival of his client, a pretty female one, naturally, with fair hair who looks like she's just stepped out of a salon, which she probably has and all in preparation for her vet appointment. Her equally pretty show pony prances along beside her.

Agnes arrives back at a quarter to four, cheeks slightly flushed and looking very smiley, all things considered. Seems they had a jolly nice lunch in the jolly expensive, traditional old English Wheatsheaf. Lucky Agnes. Beamish has gone home, so it seems we're into the one-vet-down thing right away. And we'll have to break the news to some of our longer-standing clients, who've known Beamish right since the beginning. Perhaps I'll impress Agnes by putting together a very official-looking newsletter we can circulate to our clients, with a nice smiley picture of Beamish and an authoritative one of Miles – if there is one.

* * *

One of the first clients that the Lower Shagford horse fraternity grapevine connects with is Sylvie Williamson. But of course. I would expect no less. She arrives at the practice in her enormous brand-new supercharged, super-shiny Range Rover, elegantly dressed in a linen suit, and bearing a large, embossed envelope, which she entrusts into the safe hands of Agnes.

'We're having a little party at the stud,' she tells us, 'and I thought, in the circumstances, it might be rather lovely if all of you could join us.'

My ears prick up. What, all of us? Even me? And Mrs Boggle? The large embossed envelope, addressed to 'all the staff', contained an equally large embossed invitation, to a summer party at the Amberley Stud, Sylvie's pad. Golly. I bet it's not a 'little party' at all. Probably the social occasion of the year, if not the decade.

The Impossible Search for the Perfect Man 65

How exciting! I've never actually been there, though I've heard so much about it, I feel I know every inch of the place.

I commit the date to memory. Easy. It's the fourth of July, American Independence Day. I'm not missing this one for anything. I feel excited already! Agnes senses my reaction, and gives me one of her looks.

'Thank you very much, Sylvie. I'll see to it that *everyone* is made aware of your kind invitation.' The *everyone* is emphasised, so that Sylvie goes away satisfied that Beamish will definitely be informed. I'm sure he'll be there too. Even he can't wriggle out of this one.

Agnes is so clever. Wonderful with the clients. I can't wait to tell Emma, though one of the vets will have to be on call, I suppose. I hope it's not her.

'Louisa? Could you photocopy this and make sure there's one for everyone?' Agnes asks me. 'Oh, and could you let me have an extra copy to give to Beamish? I could drop it in to him on my way home.'

That makes me sit up. So Agnes 'drops in' on Beamish does she? Hmmm... how interesting. My imagination races away with me. I've absolutely no idea if there is or has ever been a 'Mr Agnes'. Or maybe she's never met *the one*. Then another thought wallops me between the eyes. *Golly... perhaps she and Beamish are secretly dating and share romantic moments when none of us are watching... Maybe they'll get married and I can help her plan the wedding...*

'LOUISA?' Agnes's stentorian voice brings me abruptly back to the present.

As I work the photocopier, for a fleeting second I entertain the idea of leaving Marcus out. Then I decide I'd never get away with it. Everyone will be talking about Sylvie's party. Best just hope it's him that ends up on call.

Then there's another bombshell. I call Leonie, just to see how things are, and they're not. She's having a total meltdown and, on the other end of the phone, is in pieces.

'Pete saw the doctor this morning. Oh, Lou, I just can't believe it,' she wails. 'They say he's suffering from depression... I don't know what we're going to do. People who get that never get over it, do they? He won't be able to work, we won't have any money and we'll lose our house...' and there she is, sobbing her heart out.

I try to take in what she's telling me, because I'm having trouble getting my head round this. Ever since I met Pete, without fail, he's always jolly old Pete with a ready smile and a joke. He *can't* have depression.

'What happens now? What does Pete think? And where is he?' All these questions come into my head at once.

'He's upstairs, lying on our bed, gazing miserably up at the ceiling, refusing to talk to me. He did say that he has to see a specialist the day after tomorrow, but that's about all. Oh, Lou, it's the first time in all the years we've been together that he's pushing me away. I can't bear it...' She's sobbing again.

I think fast. I'm not sure what to say to her. I've never really come across depression.

'Why don't you ask if you can see the specialist with him? Tell him that way you won't need to badger him with questions...' I suggest hopefully. It might work, who knows.

'And if all he's doing is lying on the bed, why don't you come and have supper with me tonight? It might do you good to get out for a while.'

She's silent, then says, 'Thanks, Lou, I know you're probably right, but I think I'll stay at home. I don't really want to leave him, even if he isn't speaking to me.'

I kind of guessed she'd say that because that's Leo all over. 'Well, would you like me to come over to you?'

'Thanks, but can we leave it? He'll go mental if he knows I've said anything. Honestly, he's a different person, Lou.'

It certainly sounds like it. And I wish I could help – but I've no idea how to help them.

'Leo,' I say in the end, meaning every word. 'Call me, won't you, any time, day or night, if you need me. Okay?' Then I add, 'I'll call you tomorrow, okay?'

I rest my head in my hands, knowing that however worried I'm feeling, Leo's feeling a hundred times worse. I go to my computer again and type 'depression' into the search bar. Lord. Look at the number of pages here. I don't know where to start.

9

Later that week, I'm still thinking of Marcus as the new boy, when I catch Agnes drafting an advertisement for another vet. Then I wait for the onslaught that will inevitably follow, because no matter how strongly you emphasise that all applications should be made by post only, there's always the smart arses who insist on phoning or, worse still, 'popping in because they happen to be just passing'. Anyone who says that is lying, because absolutely nobody just passes the back end of beyond that is Lower Shagford.

Agnes, a master of patience, tolerance and all things virtuous, says the same thing to all of them, albeit a trifle wearily – could they please be kind enough to submit their application in writing, just like everyone else. If I were her, I'd be keeping a black list, or better still, file the smart arses' applications in the shredder.

She, Beamish – and this time round Miles – then spend long evenings perusing the many and varied CVs. Some of the applicants are known, at least by name, to Beamish, and he soon narrows it down to a handful, which I am then given the dubious pleasure of contacting, to invite to a formal interview. When I call them, one or two of them sound more than a little barking. This might be quite amusing after all.

* * *

When interview day arrives, fortunately we're not too busy, which means that Miles is interviewing too. Miles seems to be moving swiftly up the echelons in the practice and looking less and less happy about it. Anyway, it's good, because with the extra clients for Marcus to see, he spends less time hanging around here making me feel inadequate.

Never one to miss an opportunity, Paris is loitering with intent. I've come to the conclusion that instead of a brain, she has man-radar, and it's fully homed in on the imminent arrival of our would-be vets. Her hair is pink this week and she's wearing some rather flash leopard-print jodhpurs teamed with a tight, boob-hugging top that only a sixteen-year-old can get away with. Next to her, I look like a middle-aged spinster.

But I have to admit to finding it all hugely entertaining – much to Agnes's disapproval. She knows exactly what I'm like. Fortunately for me though, she's also in the interview room, so it's my job to welcome the candidates and give them tea or coffee, then usher them through at the required time. And so I sit quietly at my desk, pretending to be concentrating extremely hard on some rather important paperwork, all the time watching out of the corner of my eye, as the would-be vets, not ordinarily used to wearing suits, sit there most uncomfortably wiping their sweaty palms on their thighs before they are invited through to be interrogated.

After the first six, Agnes comes out. It's nearly lunchtime anyway. She stifles a yawn.

'Louisa, Beamish thinks we've probably seen enough,' she says wearily to me. She sighs. 'He thinks he's found the one.'

She nods back at the closed door, behind which candidate number six, a very sensible-looking woman in brogues, is enthralling Beamish and Miles with her impressive range of experience. Paris has already vanished, of course, no doubt disgusted by their choice.

'You mean...?' I nod at the room too, slightly disappointed if I'm honest. There are another four lined up for this afternoon, one bonkers one in particular who I was rather looking forward to meeting.

'So it would seem,' Agnes says firmly and won't be drawn further.

And before long, a beaming Beamish and relieved looking Miles step out, with the very sensibly dressed candidate between them.

'Ah. Louisa. I'd like you to meet Stella,' says Beamish, looking mightily pleased with himself. 'She will be joining us for, er, three days a week initially. It'll, um, take the pressure off all of us, no doubt you'll agree?'

I nod my head and hold my hand out to Stella, who grips it very firmly indeed with her sweaty one and almost crushes it.

'Good to meet you,' she says, looking more than a little hot in her rather tight tweed jacket, which is a jolly close match for Beamish's. Knowing Beamish, that's probably why he chose her.

Beamish takes over. 'Stella? Miles? How about we grab some lunch?' Stella daren't say no and nor does Miles, so off they all go to keep Beamish company while he has a little snifter or five.

'Honestly,' says Agnes in a low voice. 'He always does this. You do think he'd at least bother to see all of them. Now we have to hope we can reach the others and put them off. They're probably on their way here, and will have taken the day off specially.'

The Impossible Search for the Perfect Man

She's sounding most disgruntled, which is quite out of character. All we have to do now is to stand by for calls from the other vets, who will all be dying to know who their new colleague is. Marcus no doubt will be delighted to hear that there will be another female in the practice for him to exert his charms on, and when he calls in, I innocently tell him, 'Oh yes, she's really lovely, Marcus. Yes, that's right. Just like Emma…' He'll be imagining another blonde bombshell, not a forty-something sensible lady who's sturdy and wears tweeds.

* * *

After Stella joins the ranks, it doesn't take long before we realise she's quite a force to be reckoned with. She's extremely forthright, thinking nothing about putting a client very straight this morning when they made the usual mistake and assumed Sam was the vet and Stella the vet nurse. It happens to Emma all the time. That really got her blood up and she made quite a fuss about it. I've decided that to avoid getting on the wrong side of her, she'll escape being initiated with Henderson's horse's warty dick. Actually it wouldn't be much of an initiation. Marcus, it would seem, has that one admirably under control.

So we kind of settle down, our newly extended (again) practice family, and after a few little hiccups, things are okay. Stella might be ferocious, but apparently she's massively accomplished and has worked alongside some of the greatest horse experts there are. Agnes soon keeps her for the more troublesome clinical cases, where her bedside manner, or rather the lack of it, is less of a handicap, because Marcus and Emma are brilliant at client relations, and even Miles isn't bad. I guess the practice can carry one cantankerous old bat if her veterinary skills really are so mind-boggling. Elmer, however, weirder than ever, has decided that she absolutely adores Stella. She's probably just terrified of her, but she obediently does whatever Stella tells her, all the time wagging her tail most ingratiatingly and giving me smug backward glances.

Purely by accident, Stella's timing was good. She gets to be invited to Sylvie's party, though, as the newest recruit, she's volunteered to be on call that night. Double bugger! That means Marcus will definitely be going to the party. I resign myself to the fact that I won't be able to avoid him.

Emma says I protest too much and that secretly I fancy him. She must be mad. I don't, of course. It's obvious. Anyone can see that.

And eventually I hear from Jerome, though I haven't told Emma yet. But it's a nice letter, which surprises me somewhat, because I wasn't convinced I'd get any response at all. He explains that what he writes in his predictions is the most likely outcome at any given moment in time. But he goes on to say that there are always choices, and we have freedom to choose whatever we like. He expresses concern at Emma's obsession and says that, if after talking to her I'm still worried, to get back in touch. It's not at all what I expected, but Jerome's gone up just the tiniest notch in my estimation.

That night, as we're having supper together at hers, my most favoured place to eat for many reasons, I broach the subject. Emma splutters her Thai chicken curry all over the table when I tell her what I've done. She's not very happy at all.

'Look, Ems,' I say pointedly. 'If you had a friend doing something that you were really worried about, would you just ignore it? Because I bet you wouldn't...'

That got her. Very caring, Emma is. She wouldn't be able to ignore a friend in need any more than I can.

'But I've told you, Louisa. It's not even a problem in the first place.' She takes another mouthful.

'Okay,' I say calmly. Ha. Time to play the trump card. 'So what if I tell you that Ben thinks you're on drugs and Marcus thinks you're about to leave the practice.'

'Ben thinks what?' she frowns.

'Every time your mobile bleeps with one of those starbursts or whatever Jerome calls them, you just jump up, whatever you happen to be doing or saying, and hotfoot it out of the room. It's really noticeable, Em. Ben's noticed and thinks you're nipping out for another fix, and Marcus thinks you're very distracted and looking for another job. So don't you agree that it might just be time to try and get this... this THING under control?'

Emma looks extremely downcast by now. 'What did your letter say?' she asks in a small voice.

'Jerome simply explains that a horoscope is not an actual forecast, just the most likely set of outcomes if you don't take into account a person's ability to make a choice. I guess you could say it's like a weather forecast, and you know how often they get those wrong...' I pause, quite pleased with the bit about the weather forecast.

'Here. You can read it if you like.'

She sits and reads. Her Thai chicken curry goes cold. What a waste, I think, looking longingly at it. It was sublime.

Then she looks at me. Sheepishly. 'I have let this get a bit out of hand, haven't I?'

I nod exaggeratedly. 'But luckily you have a good friend like me to sort you out.' Then I say more seriously, 'Em, you will stop being so hung up on it all, won't you?'

She nods. 'I'll try, it's got a bit silly, I admit that. But I'm glad you told me about Ben – and Marcus. I had no idea.'

Result. But I'm watching her. I know what these addicts can be like.

We change the subject. The next most burning topic of conversation, after Stella's arrival, which we've exhausted for now, is Sylvie's party. And the rather pressing issue of what to wear.

'We should go shopping,' says Emma suddenly. 'I haven't bought clothes for ages. We could go this Saturday if you like. I've got a whole weekend off.'

Excellent. I can keep an eye on her phone habit too, while we're at it. Suddenly, I'm looking forward to this. Sylvie's party will be my first big public outing, if you don't count the pub, as a newly post-Arian single person and I can't wait. I'm going to find myself a frock to die for, glam myself up and have a truly fabulous evening.

10

It's Saturday, and I spend a glorious morning riding Horace. I love my new life, I've decided, and Horace is the best thing that's happened to me in ages. I adore him. He really is my perfect male, I can't help thinking. Gorgeously handsome, affectionate and unquestionably loyal. Even better, he doesn't answer back and lives in a field.

This morning, we amble up the lane to the bridlepath that leads down to the river. You can ride for miles along the flat, grassy bank and today we canter, his feet pounding rhythmically. It's bliss, I tell you, just me and this beautiful horse.

After, I hose Horace down and then he mooches happily in the shade of an oak tree while Emma and I go shopping.

Even though we go into what must be every dress shop for miles, Emma can't find a thing to wear. I buy my outfit in the third shop we go into, but Emma is being very blonde and indecisive. It gets so bad, I almost suggest that she asks Jerome, but bite my tongue in the nick of time. By the end of the day, there's just one shop we haven't looked in yet, and I'm determined to make her buy something if it kills me.

The price tags are astronomical, but Emma doesn't appear to mind, or maybe she hasn't noticed. Luckily for us both, she finds a dress that's been worth waiting for – a beautiful, flowing Grecian-style gown, which is dead posh and transforms her from grubby vet into total goddess in the blink of an eye. I resign myself to looking my usual inadequate self beside her on the night, while she pays the extortionate cost without batting an eyelid.

At last! We hurry back to mine to find out what havoc Elmer has wreaked while we've been shopping. Actually, apart from a well-licked butter wrapper on the floor, she hasn't done anything diabolical. I let her out in the garden and put the kettle on.

Emma rarely talks about herself and I'm realising how little I know about her life before we worked together.

'Em? How long have you lived here?'

She's looking extremely relaxed sitting in my garden. 'Oh, about two years now. I bought the barn after my divorce came through.'

Golly. I didn't know she owned it... She reads my thoughts.

'I'm lucky, Lou. Well, in that respect anyway. Andy was extremely wealthy. It's probably at least part of the reason I persuaded myself we should get married. I mean, I know everyone says money doesn't buy you happiness, but honestly? After my student days, I can tell you, it certainly does help.'

I can't help but be impressed by her honesty. But it brings a lump to my throat, as once again, I imagine sweet, insecure Emma disentangling herself from a loveless marriage to a total bastard and left all alone.

'He didn't do anything wrong, Lou,' she reminds me softly. 'I left him in the end. One of us had to do something. I knew he wasn't happy either, but he hung on and hung on... In the end I had no choice.'

Oh dear. It's still terribly sad but not at all as I'd imagined. And actually it's struck a bit of a chord. Maybe I made a mistake marrying Arian in the first place. Did it for all the wrong reasons, just like she did. And it's starting to make me wonder just how Arian would tell his side of the story.

Then Emma goes home, and we arrange to meet in the pub later. Suddenly I think, I haven't seen her look at her mobile once.

* * *

The pub is busy when we get there, but then it is Saturday night. And actually I'm feeling good, even next to Emma. My skinny jeans fit me again, and I've pinned up half my hair in a scruffy-sexy updo. Ben's already there, and his face lights up as soon as he sees Emma. And oh blast, why does Marcus have to be here too? Shouldn't he be on call or something? Uh oh. It looks like he might have one of his girly admirers with him tonight too. A small, pretty one with big boobs, spray-on jeans and half a ton of mascara. For some reason, I'm not comfortable with this at all.

Emma and I buy a bottle of white wine and wander over to join Ben. Then we all go outside because it's a glorious evening and the sun is still warm. It seems a waste to spend it sitting inside a gloomy bar. Emma has so far survived without her mobile bleeping once. I'm impressed. Hopefully she can keep this up. Ben is looking more relaxed too, now that she's not jumping up and down every two minutes.

And here comes Marcus. Hmmm... On his own.

'No lady friend?' I enquire coolly, looking at him from under my eyelashes.

He gives me a look. 'She's a client, actually. She was just giving me an update on her horse.'

Oh, I bet she was, I think crankily, not liking one bit that I'm beginning to sound jealous. *Jealous?* Why would I be? I don't even particularly like him.

He sits down on the chair next to me, which makes me stiffen. Noticing, he shifts slightly away from me. We chat for a bit, the four of us, mostly about Sylvie's party, which is next Saturday. Ben is going too, of course. I don't think I know anyone who isn't.

After a while, I make my excuses and leave, saying Elmer's been on her own all day and I should get back. I don't want to cramp Emma's style, and she and Ben seem to getting on like a house on fire tonight. Nor can I particularly be bothered to make conversation with Marcus, who stands up at the same time, yawning. I notice for the first time how tired he looks.

'Think I'll join you,' he says, regretting it when he sees my expression. 'Not, you know, I didn't mean...'

We leave together, stiffly, careful to avoid any physical contact with each other as we walk out to the car park.

'Like a lift?' he says gruffly, no doubt waiting for another of my typical overreactions.

'Um, thanks, but I'm only over the road. I can walk,' I say.

'Okay.' he heads over to his enormous Land Cruiser, then stops and turns back towards me.

'Um, Louisa, have I, er, done anything to upset you?'

I'm dumbfounded. I don't actually know what to say.

'Only you seem quite abrupt, so I just wondered...' he adds.

'Um, am I? I don't mean to be,' I say.

He stands there a moment, just looking at me. 'Oh. Well, I'll be off. Sure you wouldn't like a lift?'

I shake my head, mostly because I'm stubborn, but as he turns to get in his car, I'm left in a dither. I don't know what it is, but something about him throws me completely off my guard. For a brief moment, I consider walking after him, but then he speeds away in the Land Cruiser.

I walk quietly home, alone.

11

When I arrive at work on Monday, everyone is running around like headless chickens. It transpires that Marcus has been up all night with some poor horse who has colic. Seems he was on call after all. The horse has taken a turn for the worse. It's in acute pain, and everyone's agreed that as a last-ditch attempt to save it, they're going to operate. Stella's doing it. She wouldn't normally even come in on a Monday, and she's already been here for two hours. Apparently she's done these before. Miles is assisting and Sam's in there too. Marcus and Emma are off on calls, and Agnes is making a cup of tea for the owner, who's sitting outside, white as a sheet. I go into the office where the phone is already ringing.

Agnes soon follows.

'Poor Mrs Kilburn. It's her daughter's horse, Parsifal. They bred him apparently. She's out of her mind with worry.

I can well believe it. I shudder to think how I'd be feeling if it were Horace in there and I've only had him a few weeks.

The surgery goes on for hours, or so it seems. From time to time, Agnes or I go out and sit with Mrs Kilburn for a bit, or take her more tea. For once in her life, Elmer is being useful and has attached herself to our client and is being most companionable.

'Are you sure she's not being a nuisance?' I ask for the fourth time. Elmer gives me a look, which I return.

'Oh no, she's lovely,' says Mrs Kilburn. Elmer? Lovely? Oh well, I suppose Mrs Kilburn is having a particularly bad day. 'Flatcoat isn't she? Such brilliant dogs.'

In my experience, anyone who thinks that about flatcoats needs their head examined. If you love flatcoats, either you've never lived with one or else you're as batty as they are.

'I had one once. A long time ago,' she says fondly.

Ah, that explains it then. Time's a wonderful healer. Fades the most painful memories. But for once, Elmer is proving quite useful.

Just then, Stella comes out, with Miles following close behind. Just in case Stella makes one of her faux pas, I should imagine. Her bedside manner continues to be unpredictable, but today she's under control and though a trifle brusque, she efficiently gives Mrs Kilburn an in-depth description of what they've done to Parsifal's insides, telling her that they'll know more later in the week. But with luck, hopefully he's out of the woods. Parsifal, however, will be staying with us for a while yet, being kept an eye on round the clock. At times like this, Sam moves in and just lives here. He's a marvel. It means there'll be no party for him next Saturday, but he wouldn't have it any other way.

A guardedly positive start to the week then. I cross my fingers that Parsifal will be okay. Mrs Kilburn has gone home and is coming back later with her daughter.

After that bit of drama, the rest of the day is straightforward. I keep popping in to see Parsifal, who comes round remarkably quickly, though he's looking a little sorry for himself. He's quite appreciative of some sympathetic nose stroking, and the ever attentive Sam is never out of earshot. Stella's gone home, and the other vets are buzzing around in various parts of the county attending to their respective clients.

Which leaves me alone with Agnes, who takes advantage of a brief lull in the telephone ringing, to ask me how I am.

I think carefully before answering.

'You know, I'm good. I didn't expect to feel like this,' I tell her. 'My heart's been broken and I've lost my home, but actually, I'm fine.'

I'm struggling to believe it myself, but it's the truth. Agnes looks at me.

'It's early days you know, dear,' she says kindly. 'Don't be at all surprised if it yet catches up with you. You've been through rather a lot, Louisa. Any time you need a friendly ear, you know where I am.'

I can't help the tears slightly welling up again. Nor can I believe how understanding Agnes is. So much more so than my own mother, who just finds it all an embarrassing inconvenience – and still thinks it's all *my* fault.

'Thank you, Agnes. I really appreciate what you've just said,' I say inadequately.

Then the phone rings. Usually it would be my duty to answer it, but Agnes turns to take it, giving me a moment to recover my composure. I wish I could tell her how supportive she's been to me. But I'm not much good at expressing that sort of thing, and I'd probably start to cry again, so I don't say anything at all.

Mrs Kilburn arrives later that afternoon, to check on her darling, who's thankfully looking a little brighter. Her daughter's with her, in floods of tears. I take them a fresh box of tissues.

That evening, I go round to see Leonie and Pete. I call first, not sure that this would be the right time to just pitch up uninvited, the way I used to.

Two very wan faces greet me. But at least they appear to be talking to each other – even if it is strained and awkward. Leonie pours the two of us a large glass of wine. Pete's drinking orange juice. Contrary to what I'd imagined, it seems that alcohol is not a good thing if you're suffering from depression.

Conversation is stilted. In the end, emboldened by the wine, I think, I've known Pete for years. I can ask him a direct question. I mean, it's not as though he *has* to answer it.

'How are you Pete?' I ask cautiously. 'Only Leo said you'd been to see a specialist...' Oops, was that a bit *too* full on?

Pete sighs and looks really miserable. 'I've got to go to this place where they specialise in treating headcases like me. A remedial school for nut jobs...' He attempts a sardonic laugh. His eyes have a haunted look that never used to be there. The poor man looks completely exhausted.

Leonie places her hand on his arm. 'The specialist says that he's sure they can help Pete. It won't be an instant cure, but he'll be okay.'

I'm not entirely sure who she's trying to convince here.

Pete raises his eyebrows. 'We'll see, won't we?' is all he says, before changing the subject.

'Leonie says you've got a horse.' He tries his best to sound interested.

I tell him about Horace, then get the distinct feeling that it might be better if I left them to it.

Leonie hugs me goodbye. 'He's going to be okay,' she says quietly. But very firmly. Made of strong stuff, is Leo. Her jaw is set in that way it always is when she's determined about something.

I hug her back. 'I know. Of course he will. I'll see you soon.'

Boy. I hate to admit it but I'm relieved to leave them. That was seriously hard work. Pete, Leonie, Arian and I used to talk animatedly into the wee small hours, and have to force ourselves to call it a night. We've never been short of conversation, be it putting the world to rights, or the men bitching about the usual work-related issues. In fact, it was usually time that we were short of.

In fact, by the time I get home, I'm quite maudlin. I don't know whether it's what Pete and Leonie are going through, or the conversation I had with Agnes earlier.

Probably a combination of both, I decide, but by the time I close the front door of my cottage, tears are rolling down my cheeks.

Elmer grabs my T-shirt in her jaws and does her usual neurotic wagging, accompanied with an attention-seeking whine which is utterly different to the noise that normal dogs make. Tonight, however, I'm grateful for anyone's attention, even if it's a flatcoat, and I allow her to curl up on the sofa beside me.

Feeling truly dreadful, I sit there and sob, extremely sorry for myself. It should have been me and Arian who went round tonight, together, to offer support to our (joint) very good friends, I think miserably to myself... However, one thing transpired while I was there. It would appear that Arian hasn't been anywhere near for weeks. What sort of a self-obsessed, crap friend is *he*, I ask myself, wiping away my tears. That thought alone is enough to make me furious.

* * *

Oh my gosh, it's Friday already. That means it's Sylvie's party *tomorrow*. My melancholy mood of last night has evaporated and I'm actually really excited, probably because this is the poshest party I've ever been to.

I asked Agnes earlier what she was planning to wear. She gave me one of her looks, before saying she hadn't decided yet. Perhaps

she has an expansive wardrobe of elegant designer evening wear...
I expect she just thinks I'm mad, but today I really don't care.

Parsifal, the sick horse, has made incredible progress under Sam's tender loving care, plus that of the Kilburns, who have practically lived here this week. We virtually have to push them out of here at night. They arrive first thing, armed with body brushes and carrots, very thinly sliced to aid his fragile digestion, and they take him out for very careful walks. Parsifal looks as though he's loving every second of it.

Since Beamish announced his semi-retirement, Miles has been looking stressed and lankier than ever, I would say. He's lovely, Miles, but definitely a bit too sensitive. I'm not convinced he's cut out for the additional honour and glory not to mention pressures of joint-senior-partnerdom. He's a fabulous vet and all that, and his clients love him for how conscientious he is, but that's precisely why I have my doubts.

Marcus is the same as ever. Busy, and oh so incredibly super-efficient. Agnes simply loves him. Worships him. In her eyes, he's everything a vet should be. Honestly, you would have thought Agnes was beyond such idolisation and old enough to know better. He also seems to have become rather friendly with Stella. They're forever discussing complicated cases when they're both in the office. And it's funny, but since Stella's joined our ranks, I've hardly seen Paris at all.

The only person I can have a sensible conversation about the party with is Emma, who's as excited about it as I am, and on Friday night, she comes round to mine for a glass of wine. We gossip about whether Agnes and Beamish will be going to the party together. Emma too has picked up on the possibility that something might just be going on between them.

Both of us are quiet as we consider the prospect of Agnes and Beamish as a couple.

'God. They'd be a bit formidable, wouldn't they?' Emma's astounded.

'But, they've known each other forever...' I add. 'Maybe they've had a thing going on for ages and they're being incredibly discreet. Either that or we're all too thick to notice.'

We sip our wine.

'What about Miles?' I ask curiously.

'What do you want to know?' replies Emma, amused. 'Oh Louisa, you don't fancy *him* do you? You'd be wasting your time. Miles is already married – to the job. Every girlfriend he has lasts all of about a week, once they find out that they'll always be less important to him than someone's manky old horse. I mean, put yourself in their shoes.'

I can, and frankly it's not appealing. Not that Miles is the tiniest bit fanciable – he's a bit like a daddy-long-legs.

'Oh, Emma. I don't know how you can even suggest that. Anyway,' I say, 'it's not as though I even want to meet a man. Not now. A man is the last thing I need. I mean, I'm not even divorced yet, am I. I'm still married.'

Emma just looks at me.

'Not for much longer,' she says – very firmly. 'And, if your perfect man just happened to materialise right in front of you, don't tell me you'd turn your back on him, because I don't believe for one minute that you would.'

Maybe she's right. If he actually exists, which is not very probable at all.

12

It's Saturday! The day of the party! God. I'm sounding like a teenager. What is wrong with me? I need to get out and socialise more, preferably with people other than vets.

I've already decided that I'm going to have a gloriously self-indulgent day which means Horace, of course, is part of it. After all, what better way to start the day can there possibly be than some relaxed meandering around the countryside on the back of a beautiful horse?

This morning, the sun is shining brightly through the trees and the soft, warm air smells of summer. I forget my cares and because Horace is now fitter, we venture a little further, through open fields and shaded woods, cantering along a grassy path until suddenly, he stumbles and sends me flying.

I leap up, unhurt, but when I look at Horace, my precious horse is standing holding his off-foreleg pitifully. Talking to him gently, I try to coax him forward but he refuses to put any weight on it. And okay, so I work at a vets', but with my own, beloved horse suffering in front of me, I go straight into panic mode.

Emma's the first person I call. Her bloody phone is switched off. It's pointless leaving a message because I need someone NOW if not sooner. I try Miles. Ditto. What is going on? So I call the practice number. A calm, recorded message in Agnes's voice tells me my call is being forwarded to the vet on call.

Oh please hurry... I'm willing someone to pick up. Poor Horace hasn't moved and I'm terrified it's the lameness that Miles warned me about, back with a vengeance.

At last. A vet answers. It's Marcus. Of course. Crisply, he asks me where we are.

I haven't a clue how to explain.

'Er, past my house, up the lane, about half a mile down the first bridlepath on the left, then right into an enormous field...'

There's silence, then he says wearily, 'I'll come and find you. Just keep your phone switched on, okay?'

Horace and I wait for what seems like ages. My poor horse still hasn't put his sore foot to the ground. My cursed imagination is working at warp speed, as I contemplate all sorts of hideous possibilities like broken legs and pulled tendons, or even the worst-case scenario, which is that no one can help him and there's only one thing we can do.

Eventually, I hear my name being called. Very distantly. *Marcus*. I jump up and down and wave my arms just a bit. Not too much though, I don't want to startle the patient. Fortunately he sees me. He strides over, carrying, I notice with relief, his vet bag. Slowing his pace, he approaches Horace quietly and strokes his shoulder. Horace responds with a throaty whickering noise.

'What have you done to yourself, old fellow?' Marcus asks him gently, and by now I can't hold back the tears.

Horace is looking very sorry for himself.

'Right,' Marcus says. 'Can I take a look?'

Gently he runs his hands down Horace's leg and lifts up the foot that Horace is nursing.

'Louisa? Have you even looked at this?' His voice is just a little exasperated. 'Your poor horse has trodden on something. It's cut into the sole. No wonder he's sore.'

Sure enough, when I look, there's an indentation and what looks like a thin slice into the sole of his foot. Marcus puts the hoof down.

'I'll tape something round it, just to get you home and I'll give him a shot, just in case there's any infection. He'll be lame for a bit, but he'll be fine.'

He fiddles around in his bag and the injection is over with before Horace has even noticed.

'I can't believe you didn't even have a look...' he says, more than a little accusingly. 'Still, the main thing is he'll be okay. Just keep it poulticed for a few days, and I'll take another look next week. Are you okay to lead him home from here?'

I nod. As usual, Marcus has managed to make me feel utterly inept. But, to be fair, this time I've screwed up all on my own. If I'd exercised some common sense and kept my cursed imagination in check, instead of freaking out I could easily have dealt with Horace myself.

'Right. I'll be off then,' he says brusquely.

It's only late morning when Horace and I get home, but it feels hours later. I fuss over him and poultice the foot and wrap it in loads of bandages, with Horace loving every minute of it.

After all the drama of the morning, I skip lunch and think instead about this evening, looking forward to wearing my new dress. It's fitted, with a shortish skirt, in a soft, sage green, and I found some girly sandals that look great with it, because on heels I wobble precariously.

After a cup of coffee, I'm just putting my feet up for five minutes, when there's a knock at the door. It's Marcus.

'Um, I just thought I'd check on the patient,' he says, sounding a lot less arsey than earlier on. I'm still wearing my filthy jodhpurs from this morning. My T-shirt isn't much better.

'Come and see for yourself,' I say, and we go to find Horace.

Gratifyingly, Horace whinnies at me. At least, I assume it's at me and not Marcus. No matter, he wanders over to us, only marginally lame now.

Marcus climbs over the fence to inspect my poultice.

'Not bad,' he says. And actually smiles slightly at me.

'Oh,' I say. 'Jolly good.' I never say 'jolly good' about anything.

Then he says slightly apologetically, 'Um, sorry if I was a bit abrupt this morning. Actually, I was as relieved as you were that there was nothing seriously wrong. Well, better get on,' he adds, climbing back over the fence. 'See you at the party tonight?'

'Um, yes. And thanks, Marcus.'

* * *

The afternoon is more relaxing, and later on, I run a hot bath, and soak in it for absolutely ages until I notice that my fingers are looking rather prune-like. Hmmm – glamorous prune is not quite the image I'm seeking to cultivate this evening. I'd been thinking more along the lines of wowing my work colleagues and everyone else for that matter, revealing my as yet undiscovered beauty, so I hop out, wrap myself up in my fluffiest towel and collapse in front of the TV for an hour or so with my nail varnish. Then I forget the time and end up in a mad rush. But for the first time in my entire life, my make-up goes on just how I want it to and my hair doesn't look too bad, even considering its mousiness. My gorgeous dress feels as good as I remember when I tried it on in the shop, ditto my shoes and with a generous spray of my favourite DKNY, I'm ready to go half an hour ahead of schedule.

Emma's come round, looking breathtakingly stunning in her

floaty Grecian dress, her long blonde hair in shiny waves hooked behind her ear. A glass of champagne as we giggle together before leaving for Sylvie's seems like a perfect idea. I'm getting more excited by the minute.

It's not always great having a friend who looks like she ought to be on the cover of *Vogue*, but I love Emma and I've long resigned myself to being forever in her shadow. And Ben won't be able to take his eyes off her.

* * *

The Amberley Stud is everything I've been told – and more. Hidden behind vast wooden gates, tall flaming torches flank the drive as our taxi sweeps round in front of the house in all its glorious magnificence.

Emma and I follow the flow of guests around the side of the house onto the lawns – and it's hard to know where to look first.

It's all so glamorous, like setting foot into a parallel universe that's not remotely connected to everyday life. All around us there are beautiful people, in Dolce & Gabbana, or Balenciaga, drifting around, sipping champagne out of crystal glasses and sampling caviar proffered by attentive waiters. Okay. Maybe I'm slightly exaggerating, but there's definitely an other-worldliness.

Emma nudges me with her elbow, and points. There's PM-T, looking like a porn star in a tight low-cut red dress and surrounded by a crowd of equally gorgeous young things, mostly staring at her boobs and as expensively kitted out as she is. What *are* her parents thinking of?

And look. Aha! We were right. Agnes and Beamish, looking very much a couple. She's holding his arm in a most proprietorial manner and their heads are bent towards each other as they talk quietly. For whose benefit is that? I wonder, as Emma and I exchange glances. Is this to fob Sylvie off or is there something going on? Goodness, Agnes does look glam – as does Beamish – and they really seem quite at home.

It's a perfect evening, the air balmy with the scents of jasmine and honeysuckle. A lilac-tinted sky hints at a glorious sunset to follow. No doubt Sylvie arranged that too. Invisible lighting shows off the garden like a film set, except I know with certainty that it's utterly real, that this is how she lives and no one will come in tomorrow and dismantle it.

A handsome young waiter offers me and Emma champagne. He winks at us, which makes me think he's probably enjoying this as much as we are. And it's turning out to be such fun.

Emma and I amuse ourselves by watching the throngs of guests and it's not long before we find ourselves being chatted up by two very public school types. They're tall and dark and not my type at all, but Emma is loving the attention, so I sneak away and leave her to it. Only I don't get far before a familiar voice says quietly behind me, 'Louisa, you look lovely.'

Marcus. That was funny. For a split second, I had a delicious warm feeling when I first heard his voice. Until I remembered how I feel about him, that is. Champagne does odd things to me. I must pace myself. I turn around to find him looking quite James Bond-ish in his dinner jacket and bow tie. I wonder which floozy's with him tonight?

'How's Horace?'

'He's fine, thanks. And I didn't thank you earlier, did I, for coming to find us this morning. I think I panicked a bit. But I really appreciated it.'

He smiles at me. Properly.

We're still standing there, smiling back and forth at each other, when Beamish joins us. And, of course, it's only a matter of time before Sylvie's there too. She's probably been planning this moment for months, if not years. Oh my golly gosh... Where on earth is Agnes when she's needed?

I can see Beamish looking around agitatedly, before making his excuses and bumbling off again. But Sylvie seems remarkably reconciled to the idea that he's not available and barely even looks in his direction, as instead she turns towards me.

'I'm so glad to see you,' she says, most surprisingly. 'I particularly wanted to introduce you, and Emma too...' we both look around but Emma's nowhere in sight '... to my daughter. You see she's only recently moved back here, and doesn't really know many people.'

Goodness, I'm not at all sure about this. Going on past experience, when a stranger thinks you'd be the perfect friend for their daughter/son/niece/cousin, generally it's a terrible idea and doomed before you even meet.

Then Sylvie nods towards a girl walking towards us. She's not at all what I expect. More understated than her mother, she looks as though she'd rather be anywhere than here. It isn't helped either, by the beautifully cut dress she's wearing which looks a couple of sizes too small.

Sylvie looks at me. 'Er...'

'Louisa,' I chip in helpfully.

'Sorry. Of course it is. Louisa. Karina's probably a similar age to you...'

As the girl pauses to talk to someone, my mind does a double backflip. Suddenly I feel extremely dizzy. *Karina*. Oh. My. God.

Because I can see immediately from her slender frame and delicate cheekbones that Karina isn't plump at all. Without any shadow of a doubt I know she's pregnant. I feel very short of breath all of a sudden, and then horribly light-headed, as everything spins around me and, a moment later, my legs give way.

13

When I come round, I'm slumped on the ground with a most concerned Marcus on his knees beside me. Apparently Sylvie's gone to get me a glass of water.

I've been out for several minutes, Marcus tells me, looking most anxious.

'I'm fine.' I try to smile reassuringly at him, then at Agnes, who's materialised beside him. Though actually I do feel a little odd. 'I just had a little bit of a shock.'

And then I remember. *Karina*... Oh bollocks. Not a little shock, at all. My mind obviously just decided it couldn't cope and zoned out.

Five minutes later, though wobbly, I'm back on my feet and Agnes and Marcus between them lead me to a cushioned bench in a quiet corner of the garden. Mercifully Sylvie doesn't find us. I've no wish to explain what her daughter's been up to.

'I'm going to get you some tea.' Marcus strides off, leaving me with Agnes. How does he know that bizarrely, that at this party with free-flowing champagne, all I want is a hot cup of tea.

'It's her, Agnes,' I tell her urgently, when he's gone. 'The Karina Arian's having an affair with. I know it is...'

I try to stand up again, but my legs are feeling shaky. All I want is to go home.

'Sit down, Louisa,' says Agnes, calmly as ever. 'You've had quite a shock. But how can you be sure it's the same Karina?'

She has a point, but nevertheless I'm absolutely certain it is. It's an unusual name, 'Karina'. And she's pregnant. And just moved back home. And she didn't exactly look like a radiant mother-to-be, as though something wasn't quite right and I'd convinced myself that it was simply a matter of time before she saw Arian for the selfish tosser that he is. I know I'm right.

Agnes waits with me until Marcus comes back carrying a bone china mug, then she goes off to find Beamish. Marcus sits down, close enough that I can feel the warmth of him against me.

'To my rescue for the second time today...' I joke feebly, still a little shaky.

'Are you sure you're all right? Only for a moment there, you had me worried,' he says looking anxious still. No hint of cockiness or arrogance. Just kind concern.

'I'm fine. I just had a shock.' I sip my tea, which is strong and sweet, feeling calmer and less light-headed. 'I mean, you don't expect to meet the woman your husband's left you for, not at a party...'

Marcus stares at me, trying to work out whether I'm joking.

'She's called Karina,' I explain. 'His bit on the side is, I mean.'

'You know.' He frowns. 'It's possible it's not the same one.'

I give him a look. Honestly. Men have absolutely no sixth sense where such things are concerned. Can't he just see that I *know* she *is*?

'Okay,' he says soothingly. 'So let's say you're right. Now what? Would you like me to give you a lift home?'

It's tempting. Collapsing into my warm, comfortable bed seems very appealing at this moment, but hold on just a cotton-picking moment. I've been looking forward to this party for too long. I decide that I'm not letting anyone ruin this evening. That I can handle this little *inconvenience* and that 'Karina' might live here but as it happens, I'm still a guest.

'You know what? I'm going to stay, Marcus. I'm fine now.' Marcus is looking a bit unsure as I get up. 'Come on,' I add with more certainty. 'Let's go and join the party.'

Marcus glues himself to my side as we circulate. Not entirely relaxed, as we take care to avoid Karina. At one point, Sylvie sees me and immediately comes to check that I've recovered.

'I'm fine,' I say, losing count of how many times I've said that.

'Really. I think she was just a little, erm, overcome...' adds Marcus.

Nice choice of words, Marcus. Now she just thinks I'm a pisshead.

'Well, as long as you're sure... I don't know where Karina's gone, but I'll try and find her...'

'Don't worry now – we'll look out for her,' says Marcus.

Sylvie looks doubtfully from me to Marcus, who gives her a reassuring nod, and then disappears into the multitude of dazzling guests again.

I have quite a good time after that. Marcus and I dance for a bit, then he takes my hand and leads me off the dance floor. I'm feeling odd again, but not at all like earlier when I fainted. No. This time it's more like a lovely warm, floaty feeling, from my heart pounding a little faster Somehow, my hand ends up in Marcus's and we walk across the garden, which in the darkness has an ambiance of pure romance.

There's a silence between us, but for once it's comfortable rather than awkward. I'm just about to tell Marcus that actually, in spite of what went on earlier, I'm having a lovely evening, when out of the corner of my eye, among the hundreds of people that are here, I spot Karina again. The opposite side of the garden this time, over by the bar. She's definitely looking unhappy. And she's talking to someone I can't quite see because his back is towards us. But then he turns and his face is caught in the uplighting, so that I can make out his profile, perfectly silhouetted against the house. Unfortunately it's one I know well and for the second time this evening, a dizziness comes over me.

It's Arian.

14

At that point, I grasp Marcus's hand and march him agitatedly in the opposite direction. I'm sure he must be thinking I've gone mad.

'I have to go home,' I tell him, more than a hint of desperation in my voice. There are limits after all, and I'm really not ready to confront my ex-husband and his squeeze, particularly in front of all my work colleagues and an entire party of hundreds of posh guests. Gosh, wouldn't that give them all something to talk about.

Ooh, see that girl over there, the one that got pissed and fainted? She's only gone and given Sylvie's daughter a piece of her mind, and at Sylvie's party too... I ask you... You'll never guess what, but she says she used to be married to Sylvie's daughter's boyfriend... I think she's a bit mad, or maybe it's the champagne, you know, gives some people delusions... can't think why Sylvie invited her...

I don't think so. On this occasion, I would utterly prefer not to be the topic of people's gossip, and it would most definitely be more dignified to slink home quietly, unnoticed.

'Louisa? Louisa? Are you okay?' Marcus is sounding worried again.

No, I'm not okay at all.

'Can you tell Emma for me?'

'Look, I'll text her. I'll drive you. You look terrible.'

It's not what I want to hear. But he's probably referring to the ashen whiteness that I can feel stealing over my face. For once, I don't fob him off. I'm actually very glad to allow him to propel me in the direction of the Land Cruiser, where I sit quietly while he drives me home. It turns out he's hardly had a thing to drink. Mostly my fault, I suppose, because he's spent most of the evening babysitting me.

'So, Cinderella,' says Marcus, once we're away from Sylvie's, 'what *was* all that about?'

I sigh. Having dragged him away like that, the least I owe him is an explanation.

'It was my ex. Definitely. With Karina.'

'Ah.'

'And don't ask me if I'm sure,' I snap rattily at him. 'Because I am. I could hardly mistake him, could I? We were married for five years.'

'Hey, Lou. It's okay, I believe you,' he says calmingly, as if to one of the horses that he's about to stick a big needle into.

We drive the rest of the way in silence.

Marcus comes inside with me and I make us tea. Not really a night bird, Elmer staggers out of bed to greet us and then collapses snoring on my feet.

'I'm so sorry I ruined your evening,' I say guiltily to Marcus, as we sit down on my sofa.

'You haven't,' he says firmly. 'And anyway, these things happen. You're getting over your marriage breaking up. It's hardly an easy time for you.'

'But I'm fine,' I wail pathetically. 'At least I thought I was. I definitely don't want Arian back. I don't know why I feel like this.' And then once I start, the tears won't stop.

* * *

I don't know how much later it is when Marcus hands me a neatly ironed handkerchief. 'Here.'

I blow my snotty nose and wipe my eyes, and look at him. He takes the handkerchief from me and gently wipes under my eyes, where no doubt my redistributed mascara has made me look as if I'm impersonating a panda. Then gives it back.

'Look,' he says gently. 'I know you think you're *fine*, as you keep saying. But it takes a little longer than a few weeks to get such a huge betrayal out of your system. One thing I do know though, is that next time you see either of them, the shock will be less. The first time was always going to be the worst. Louisa, you really will be fine, you know.'

I've never heard a man say anything like that before. And so masterfully... I'm flabbergasted. How does he know all that stuff? I look at him quizzically.

'Did something like this happen to you?'

He laughs. Sort of. 'Kind of. But we were never married, thank God. My girlfriend shacked up with the bloke I thought was my best friend – after we'd been living together for three years. I'd been about to ask her to marry me. I'd even bought the ring.' He laughs again, more hollowly.

'Oh.' I'm shocked. That's almost as bad as what's happened to me. I'm nosy too, and then I realise, 'So that's why you came to work with us.'

'I'm afraid it is. I needed a change of scene. Laura and I worked together. I didn't have much choice in the matter. I couldn't see the point in giving myself a daily reminder that she preferred my mate to me.'

I put my hand on his arm. Poor Marcus. I know exactly how that one feels.

'Anyway,' he continues. 'It was months ago, and I really am okay now. Fine, in fact, to use your favourite word. But I'm also tired.' Looking at the simple, heavy watch he wears, he yawns. I like the watch. It's classy. Far more tasteful than the mobile phone type contraption that Arian used to strap on his wrist.

I look at my clock and realise we've been talking for ages. It's nearly three o'clock in the morning.

He gets to his feet and I walk with him to the door. Just before he leaves, he turns and looks at me, before kissing me on the cheek, taking me completely by surprise. He lingers slightly, as if wondering whether to do it again, then obviously thinks better of it and walks away.

15

I wake up later that morning. My bedroom is bright with sunlight and my watch says ten thirty. I'm about to leap up when I realise that, actually, it's Sunday and I don't have to. So I lie there for a bit, and go over the events of last night.

So Karina is Sylvie's daughter! What are the chances of that? Marcus is right though. Even today, the thought is less upsetting. *And Arian was there too*. It was the last thing I'd been prepared for, though the shock has worn off and I'm okay with it. At least, I think I am.

Then I remember Marcus again and how nice he was to me. And the kiss goodnight. Okay. I have to admit it. *Louisa Mulholland, you made a mistake. Marcus is not the arrogant womaniser you had him down as at all. He's really nice.*

Eventually, I get up and go to see Horace whose foot needs rebandaging, so I sort him out first and then Elmer and I go for a lovely relaxing walk by the river, the sun beating down on us. Well, it's relaxing until we pass a scruffy-looking teenage boy loitering along in the opposite direction, with a rather mothy-looking dog in a bling-encrusted collar. At that precise moment, Elmer goes into savage-attack-trained-pit-bull mode, nearly pulling me over in the process. She can really be a pain in the arse.

The boy glares at me malevolently.

'Oi, missus, you ortta train that effing dog a yours...' he shouts aggressively at me, as he reassures his trembling mutt. Cheeky bugger.

'Sorry,' I yell back, knowing it was all Elmer's fault and dragging my vile dog away, before she does anything else.

When I get home, Emma's there, talking to Horace. We have *loads* to gossip about. It'll take us hours to get through everything.

I lock a disgraced Elmer up in solitary confinement. Then we sit outside in the warm sun with cold drinks, and Emma tells me everything that happened with Ben. It doesn't take much to work out that this girl is *in lurve...* Apparently they drank champagne and danced until sunrise, and then he came home with her... Wow. Did he? Sleepover? I mean did they... Emma's smiling like the Cheshire cat from *Alice in Wonderland*.

'Oh, Lou, it was just amazing! Incredible! He is the sexiest guy...'

Oh. Well. Of course I'm happy for her, but it's too much information for me today. Especially after last night.

I tell her that I too had a memorable evening and that I almost met Karina and collapsed in an undignified heap on the grass in a dead faint, and then, after I'd seen Arian was there, Marcus took me home. But he didn't stay, I say pointedly. He went home. Her smile vanishes.

'Karina? Not Arian's Karina? What was she doing there?' she says incredulously. 'I'm so sorry I abandoned you... What a nightmare.'

'It's okay,' I assure her. 'Marcus was with me all evening, actually. He was great.' Emma does a double take. She's used to me slagging him off, not singing his praises.

'You,' she says, 'and Marcus...' and a grin slowly spreads across her face.

'It's not like that,' I say crossly. 'Focus, Emma. I'd just been told that the tart my ex-husband is shagging is to be my new best friend. By the way, I forgot to tell you this bit, Karina just happens to be Sylvie's daughter...'

That shuts her up. I tell her how Marcus took me home. I omit to tell her about him kissing me.

'I've arranged to meet Ben in the pub tonight. Do you fancy coming along too?' Emma says to me.

I think about it and how I'd quite like to see Marcus, who's usually there on a Sunday evening.

'Okay,' I say, in spite of feeling exhausted. 'I'll be there.'

* * *

It turns out that for once, Marcus isn't. He's on call. Of course. I think I knew that. Emma and Ben are like two lovebirds, so I quickly down my drink and leave them to it. There's a Land Cruiser pulling away from my cottage as I round the last bend in the lane. Aha, I know who that is. I wave at it.

It stops for a moment and reverses back. Marcus gets out.

'It's the first time my phone's stopped ringing, so I thought I'd drop in and see how you were.'

Goodness. This is rare. Once word gets out that it's Marcus on call, that's usually a cue for all the girly clients who fancy him to start inventing urgent problems that he simply must come and attend to immediately. But then, I contemplate delightedly, he had a brief lull *and he's come over here to see me.*

'Quite an evening, wasn't it?' he says, ruefully. 'How are you today anyway?'

I decide I've been overusing the word 'fine'. 'Good, thank you.'

Marcus raises his eyebrows at me.

'I think it really was just the shock last night,' I say. 'And thank you again, for rescuing me twice in one day.'

'My pleasure, madam,' he replies half-jokingly.

'So, don't you have endless pretty girls and their horses to attend to?'

He laughs at me. 'Trying to get rid of me again, Louisa?'

Oh. No. So he's noticed. I really wasn't, actually. Not this time. He sees my discomfiture.

'No. It's all quiet. There's some football match on. It's surprising how non-urgent some cases can suddenly become, you know. It happens when Wimbledon's on too, especially the men's finals.'

'I've just been to the pub with Emma,' I say.

'Back early, aren't you?' says Marcus.

'Well, Ben was there and it was all a little bit cosy,' I explain. 'You know, two's company and all that.'

He nods. I don't add that I'd hoped to see him there too.

Then his mobile goes off. He has to go. Somewhere, there's an equine that needs him.

'See you at work, Lou,' he says. I get another kiss on the cheek as he leaves.

* * *

A little later, Leonie calls me, and tells me that Pete's started something called Cognitive Behavioural Therapy.

'At least he's agreeing to go, but he's got weeks of it ahead of him,' she tells me. 'I was half expecting him to back out after the first session, but he says he's going to give it a proper try.'

Then she pauses. 'And it's really weird, Lou. Only a few weeks ago, he could barely bring himself to look at me, let alone speak to me, but now he's forever wanting sex...' She sighs.

What with Emma and Ben, Leo and Pete, Arian and Karina, it seems they're all at it like rabbits. Just not me.

It's great news, I tell her, that Pete is slowly on the up and I'm really, really pleased. And I'm sure she'll cope with the sex bit, even though I agree with her that three times a day does sound rather excessive.

'But take it from one who knows,' I tell her, 'too much is better than none at all.'

Then I tell her about the events of last night. I can almost hear her jaw hit the floor at the other end of the phone.

'Lou!' she says, quite shocked. 'How dreadful for you! What did you say to him?'

I tell her I didn't, seeing as it wasn't the place and how I'd been somewhat shocked to find him and his slapper at Sylvie's, of all places, when he's always been positively scathing about anything horsy.

'Marcus took me home,' I tell her. 'I just couldn't face them.'

'I don't blame you,' she replies sympathetically. 'Poor you...'

Then she adds, 'Pete had to go in to work, to see his manager, and while he was there, he bumped into Arian too. I wasn't going to tell you, Lou, seeing as you're just getting yourself together again. But it seems all is not rosy with him and Karina. By the way, Pete told him he was an arsehole. I thought you'd like to know that bit, at least.'

I make a mental note to thank Pete, but I'm wondering if Arian's thrown his marriage away for some short-lived fling, which only weeks on is going up in smoke too? What an idiot. I can't manage to feel the tiniest bit sorry for him. I'm not even clutching at the hope that he'll come back to me. Because one thing has just become even more abundantly clear than before.

I really do not want him back.

16

I'm relieved to get back to the normality of work on Monday, so much so, I'm early. I'm craving routine and something other than Arian/Karina to think about, and Agnes, bless her soul, comes right to my rescue.

'Morning, Louisa,' she says briskly, looking briefly, carefully at me for a second. 'I've decided that it's time we updated all the old customer records, to see who is and isn't current. They're mostly in that cupboard over there.'

My heart sinks. Okay. I need to absorb myself in work but I simply loathe filing. I've seen the cupboard. It's a mess. This will keep me busy for days, if not years.

'Most of them are on the computer, but can you check as you go, and keep a pile of those that aren't? Thank you, dear.'

Then she's back to organising the vets' calls again. Agnes calls me 'dear' quite often now.

* * *

Actually, once I get started, it's not too bad a job and what with answering the phones as well, it keeps me occupied. Miles pops in, looking worried as usual, and Marcus and Emma have been out on calls since first thing. Beamish turns up half an hour late. It seems he's taking semi-retirement quite seriously.

'Morning, Agnes.' He beams at her. Then he notices me. 'Ah, Louisa. Um, feeling better I hope?' Then not waiting for my answer, he absently says, 'Good, good.' Then, 'Um...' before he looks around vacantly and wanders off again, completely in his own little world.

* * *

Parsifal, our inmate horse who had surgery, is doing really well. I don't think Sam's been home since that horse arrived. There's evidence, however, that he may not have been alone *all* weekend... I found some rather skimpy pink knickers in the hay store earlier, which I carefully disposed of when no one was looking. A model of discretion I am, these days. Elmer found them actually. She's always had a penchant for underwear.

Back to Parsifal, he'll probably be home by the end of the week. His insides are working just fine, if the amount of mucking out I'm doing is anything to go by.

The next call from a client however, chills me. It's Ben. One of his event horses has been taken ill. Apparently he's called Emma, but she's up to her ears in something miles away and he doesn't think the horse can wait.

'Could you get someone out here as soon as possible?' He's clearly desperate.

'No problem,' I say. 'Someone will be with you in twenty minutes.'

Beamish. After all, he's wandering aimlessly around at this

minute, doing absolutely diddly squat. It's high time that man did some work and so I hunt him down in his office, where he's quietly perusing the pictures on his wall.

'Are you busy, Beamish?' I ask him a little impatiently, because he's clearly not. 'Only it's Ben Mavers. He's really worried about one of his event horses. I said you'd be over right away. I hope that's okay?'

Beamish gives me a fatherly smile. 'Er, call him back will you, Louisa, and tell him I'll be there in ten minutes.' I call Ben and tell him five. Beamish drives like a maniac. Then cross my fingers for his horse.

Then it's back to the contents of my lovely cupboard.

By the end of the day, I'm more relaxed. And quite tired. And very relieved to have got through twenty-four hours without a drama of some description, because my personal life seems to have turned into a soap opera.

* * *

A few quieter days are just what I need, while my brain churns the whole Karina thing around again, looking for a way to make it feel less shocking. The whole time she was just a name in my head, I could deal with it – just about – but somehow, having seen her and where she lives, has dredged up the old feelings of betrayal. And although Marcus is right and it does take time to get over trivial little things like busted marriages, I've since discovered that what doesn't kill you makes you stronger – and life is okay.

Ask me again in thirty seconds: *did I actually say that*?

Someone's knocking on my door. I'd planned a quiet Friday night watching *Friends* on TV. Emma's out gallivanting with Ben, and I'm not expecting a visitor. Least of all, this one, because when I open the door, it's Arian.

I stand there and just stare at him. And the first thing that hits me is that I honestly don't feel anything. Whether I'm numb, or whether it's shock again or maybe I'm over him, I couldn't tell you. And what the devil is he doing on my doorstep?

He looks terrible, I'm pleased to notice. Older, greyer, more haggard. Not handsome at all. There are dark circles under his eyes and his shoulders look stooped. His clothes look awful too.

'Hello, Lou,' he says, looking very uncomfortable. 'Do you think I could come in?'

I stand there a little longer. I'm not sure I want him in my home, sullying the Arian-free surroundings that I've grown rather comfortable with.

'Do you know, Arian? I don't think you can.'

Watch out, buster, this worm has definitely turned.

I'm about to tell him where to go, but then I see his face and something in me relents – God knows why. This is the man who betrayed me after all. Instead of turning him away, I take him round the back to my little garden where Horace nickers at me.

'You've got another horse?' He sounds surprised, and stands there looking not very pleased.

'Yes, Arian. He is indeed a horse. You know I've wanted to do that for some time,' I say patiently. *And didn't because of you.*

There's a silence – I've nothing to say. I'm just intrigued to know why he's here.

'Why is it exactly, that you're here? Our divorce is going through, the house is sold, there isn't any other business between us now.'

I must be an idiot even giving him the time of day. But then, we *were* married, I suppose. Sometimes I'm too reasonable for my own good.

He's looking very downcast, and more than a little nervous, fiddling with his fingers, not at all sure where to start.

'I'm sorry I spoilt everything, Lou,' he says at last, quite earnestly. 'More sorry than you'll ever know. I think I just got carried away.'

That's one way of putting it, I think to myself, staying incredibly civil as I let him continue.

'You see, Karina and I had so much in common.'

The 'had' doesn't go unnoticed.

'We shared the same lifestyle,' he continues. 'Enjoyed the same interests.'

'Interests?' I say very calmly. 'Oh I see, like sex, Arian, was that it? And aeroplanes maybe? Or was there something else?'

My self-control is astonishing me. I'm quite proud of myself.

We're interrupted by another car arriving. A big one by the sounds of things and then Marcus appears around the side of the house, carrying a bottle of wine. Bit presumptuous of him, isn't it? He didn't even phone to see if I was free. Arian's none too pleased to see I have a visitor. Especially a male one carrying a wine bottle. Marcus isn't looking too thrilled either. I stand up. I suppose I ought to introduce them.

'Arian, this is Marcus. We work together. He's a vet. Marcus, this is the wanker I told you about, my adulterous ex-husband, Arian, the one who's shagging Sylvie's daughter.'

Actually, what I really say is, in an exaggeratedly polite manner, is, 'Marcus, this is my *ex*-husband, Arian.' I emphasise the ex for both their sakes.

They actually shake hands, then stand and glare at each other, neither of them saying anything. This is *so* not how I planned my evening.

'Marcus, sit down and join us,' I say firmly.

But Marcus hedges. 'It might be better if I come back another time, Lou,' he says and turns to leave.

I walk round with him to where his car is.

'I'm so sorry,' I say to him. I don't know why I'm sorry, it's not as though *I've* done anything.

'It's okay,' he says abruptly. 'Go on. Maybe there's unfinished business between the two of you. You were married, after all.'

Which is annoyingly decent of him when really I'd rather he stayed.

I watch him drive off, with a niggling, irritated feeling gnawing at my stomach, wishing with all my heart that it was Arian leaving instead.

Arian is staring at me when I go back round.

'A *work* colleague?' he says sarcastically, looking thoroughly narked.

'Yes,' I say equally sarcastically. 'Just like you and Karina. Actually, not at all like you and Karina, not that it's any of your bloody business. Now for goodness' sake, get on with it,' thinking the sooner he tells me why he's here, the sooner he can leave.

'I was trying to tell you about Karina. That it's over.'

And so I ask him, 'And exactly what, Arian, has that got to do with me?'

He winces. Clearly I'm not responding the way he'd been hoping.

'I've realised what an idiot I've been, walking out on our marriage like that, Lou. Without even trying.'

I'm not sure I like where this is going. He continues. 'And I wanted to ask you, very humbly, if there was any chance at all that we could try again.'

It's too much.

'I think you better go,' I tell him, my eyes blazing. But he's not giving up.

'Promise me one thing, Louisa. Think about it, okay? Because we are at this moment, technically at least, still married...'

That does it. I'm fuming.

'Get the fuck out of my house and never come back,' I scream at him. Why am I screaming? I thought I was *so* over him. 'Go away, Arian. I want nothing more to do with you. Not ever.'

Thank God I don't have neighbours, though I should think everyone within a two mile radius heard my outburst.

At any rate, he gets the message and leaves.

Horace is staring at me over the fence. I go over and kiss his lovely nose, and instantly feel soothed as he soaks up all my stress. Then I go over the conversation with Arian. *Damn him*. How dare he come here like that. The bit that sticks in my head though, is about still being married, which, theoretically, I suppose we are. But he blew it big time, didn't he, when he shacked up with Karina. What reason could I possibly have for giving him a second chance?

And then it dawns on me, only rather than a dawn, it's more like a dark cloud descending on me. My flipping marriage vows, that's why. I'm not overly religious, but I made those vows from the bottom of my heart. I promised to stay with him for better and for worse. And if this bit is the 'for worse', does that make me as bad as he is, if I refuse to give him a second chance?

17

Thank heavens it's the weekend, because I really need a breathing space. Luckily Horace is sound again and the men in Lycra are out in force, appearing noiselessly behind us as we amble down the lane. He goggles at them as they speed past on their super whizzy bikes. And we meet the scruffy chav with the manky dog again. Fortunately I don't think he recognises me without Elmer.

I feel my tension disappearing the further we go into the countryside. We're out for two hours in the end, just walking, listening to the birds, both of us loving every second of it. Then as we're heading back, my mobile rings. It's Marcus.

'How are you, Lou? I wondered if you'd like to go out tonight?'

Gosh! A proper date! With Marcus!

'Okay,' I say. 'Thank you. I'd really like that.'

There's a brief silence. But then he's not used to me being enthusiastic about spending time with him. 'I'll pick you up at eight then. Okay?' He sounds as though he's smiling.

'That's great!'

Horace and I plod home, and suddenly I'm really looking forward to this evening.

***

Marcus arrives bang on eight. Luckily I've been ready for ten minutes. Yes, I've actually made an effort for him and he smiles approvingly when I open the door. He looks as though he's a bit spruced up too. I get a peck on the cheek and catch a hint of something spicy on his skin.

'You ready then?' he asks.

We drive to a pub I haven't been to before. It's called the Pig and Whistle and is very olde worlde, with a thatched roof and a lovely garden. Marcus finds us a table in a quiet spot and goes to get us some drinks. The sun is warm, and it's blissful to sit back and enjoy this wonderful place he's brought me to.

Marcus returns with a chilled bottle of wine, two glasses and a menu. As we peruse it, we discover a shared love of seafood and order delicious platters of prawns, mussels and langoustines, fragrant with garlic and herbs. Squeezing lemons over, we share them.

It really is just about perfect. I've just realised how much I'm enjoying myself, when Marcus goes and ruins it.

'So how did it go with your ex on Friday?'

He might as well have thrown a bucket of cold water over me, as in a split second, my carefree mood is replaced by a particularly thunderous one. Just thinking about Arian does that to me.

'Do you know,' I say to him crossly, 'I was really enjoying myself until you asked me that.'

But Marcus isn't smiling either.

I sigh. I actually feel quite despondent. I tell Marcus the gist of the conversation with Arian.

'Trouble is, he's actually made me think I have a duty to give our marriage another try.'

Marcus is silent, then says neutrally, 'So how do you feel about that?'

Truthfully, I reply, 'I'm not at all sure. I mean it's not that simple, is it? In my heart, I don't love him. I've completely fallen *out* of love with him. It honestly doesn't bother me if I never see him again. But in my head, there's something telling me that I made a vow and that's the bit I happen to think still matters.' I hold my head in my hands, because this is really, really hard. 'I wish it didn't. But you know, it's that bit, "for better, for worse". Well, what's going on now might be the "for worse" bit,' I try to explain to him. Then add slightly nonsensically, 'After all, what's the point of marriage if you run off at the drop of a hat?'

Marcus looks thunderstruck. 'Louisa. You don't owe that wanker anything. He's the one that ran off anyway. Can't you see? He knows you too well. He obviously wants something and he's playing on the honourable side of your nature to take advantage of you.'

Goodness. How illuminating. So Marcus thinks I have an honourable side. I'm quite flattered. But it's not helping my muddled thoughts one bit.

'If I'm completely honest with you,' I say slowly, 'then I think I'm going to have to arrange another meeting with him. At least, to hear what he's got to say.'

Not surprisingly, it kind of kills the evening. Marcus is looking quite furious and we go home shortly after that. I ask him in, but he refuses, coming up with an excuse that is plainly just that. He's suddenly distant, just when we were getting on so well. But sadly, there's nothing I can do. Except what I think I *ought* to do, which is to call Arian and invite him over to talk.

I badly need a woman's take on this. It doesn't seem right to burden Leonie at the moment with everything that's going on with Pete, so I call Emma and, for once, she answers straight away.

'Can you come round, Em? Only I need your advice, wise vet friend,' I say.

'Of course, Lou. Is about half an hour okay? See you then.'

* * *

Emma's reaction is a bit like Marcus's, only what she actually says is, 'So he's managed to screw up your marriage by cheating on you, and now, just as you've scraped yourself together and are getting back on your feet as a more or less happy single person, you're going to let him come waltzing back in to screw that up too.'

Then sits there looking at me as though I'm certifiable.

And actually, she *almost* convinces me. But there's still my conscience whispering away in all its misguided wisdom, *But you're still married, it does make a difference, remember the vows...*

'It's not quite like that, Em,' I try to explain, but clearly she thinks I'm off my rocker.

* * *

In spite of all well-meaning advice to the contrary, I call Arian. With some trepidation. Best to get it over with, I decide.

'Louisa!' He sounds more like his chirpy old self. 'How are you?'

'I'm calling you, Arian, to ask you if you want to come over this evening. Just to talk, nothing more,' I emphasise firmly.

'Yeah! Great! What time?' He sounds far too delighted. Not one bit like a penitent Casanova and I'm already beginning to regret this.

'Er, six thirty?' I say.

'Okay, see you later.' He's gone. Just those brief words of conversation have left me tense and needing some air.

* * *

Arian is early. It makes no difference. It's not like I was going to any effort for him.

He leans forward to kiss me on the cheek, and I immediately think of Marcus.

'You better come in.' I lead him through to my kitchen, indicating a chair at my table.

'Beer, wine?' I offer.

'Wine would be nice.'

Even Elmer is cool with him and glues herself loyally to my side. Then we sit across the table from each other and I try to explain my line of thought.

'I've thought about this a lot, Arian, since you came round before. The bottom line is, you've completely destroyed our relationship. Smashed it to pieces. There's no love and certainly no trust. I'm not sure I even like you any more.' I can hardly believe what I'm saying. 'The only thing left is the piece of paper saying we're still married. That, and this voice in my head that I honestly wish would shut up, telling me annoyingly and illogically, that even though you didn't, I ought to honour the vows I made.'

Arian's face lights up most inappropriately. How can he be smiling when I've just told him that I don't love him? Did he even listen to what I said?

But he's taken my hands, telling me that I won't regret it, that I'm a wonderful person and in the next breath how he's never stopped loving me.

I snatch those hands back. 'Hands off, mate. I haven't agreed to anything. Weren't you listening? All I said was I'm having an argument with my conscience.'

'Oh,' is all he says, looking like a sulky little boy again.

'However, as a compromise, I think we should try dating. See how it goes. But only for now, that's all.'

Arian looks a little more sober. Good. He's realised at last that I don't feel the same enthusiasm he does.

'So, it's over to you, Arian. Those are my terms. Take it or leave it.' Hoping he'll just walk away.

'Okay,' he says slowly. Reluctantly. 'It'll be very odd though.' Then in a rush he adds, 'Couldn't we just move back in together and carry on where we left off?'

But he sees the expression on my face, and rapidly adds, 'No, of course not. Sorry.'

He goes after that, more subdued than when he arrived, and I'm unashamedly relieved to see the back of him.

18

The filing takes up most of the next week too. I decide I need the opinion of someone wise and sensible, like Agnes, on the burgeoning problems that my love life is posing.

At the end of the day, as I'm tidying up the office and before I go and get Elmer, I ask her, 'Agnes, do you have a spare ten minutes, only I've got a real dilemma going on...'

'Of course, dear. Now. Just let me switch the answerphone on. There. Now, what exactly is it?'

'It's complicated, Agnes, and I'm not at all sure I'm doing the right thing.'

I fill her in on everything, including my friendship with Marcus and how everyone except me thinks I must be crazy to even give Arian the time of day.

When I finish, Agnes is looking at me intently. 'Louisa. I think it's commendable that you're prepared to go to such lengths to honour your wedding vows.'

I look at her, surprised. 'Don't look so surprised,' she continues briskly. 'So many people give up far too easily these days. It doesn't matter what your friends think, or what I think either. Only that you do what *you* think is right. It's true that your ex-husband totally disregarded his vows and it may well be that you don't have a future together at all. But at least this way, you'll never look back and regret you didn't try.'

I consider what she's saying. I haven't thought of it quite in those terms before. Interesting. And I think I know now, what I have to do.

'Just one thing,' she says, looking at me with such kindness. 'You do know, don't you? That whatever you do, it will work out for the best.'

* * *

Arian calls that evening, to invite me to dinner on Thursday and I accept. I wouldn't exactly say I'm looking forward to it, but I've decided that it's the right thing to do. I wonder what it will be like, going on a date with the man I used to share my life with? Quite possibly like putting on an old coat, only to find the sleeves have shrunk or someone's sewn up the pockets, I suspect, but I tell myself that there's no point if I don't keep an open mind.

We go to the Italian in the nearest village. Arian has an advantage in that he already knows what I like plus the food is always good here. Conversation, however, is a little stilted.

'How are your parents?' he asks, really scraping the barrel here. He didn't even ask when we were married.

I splutter into my wine, and tell him that my mother utterly blames me for his adulterous behaviour. 'Oh no, she really does,' I tell him. 'I nearly stabbed her with the carving knife.'

'Oh,' he says, more soberly. 'I suppose at some point, I ought to go and see them.'

'Maybe not just yet, Arian,' I suggest. 'Let's see how things go.'

It's a terrible idea. I can't have him getting my mother's hopes up, only for them to be dashed when we break up again. Arian doesn't have to cope with the fall-out.

'So, where do we go from here?' I ask him. 'If we're going to try to resolve our problems, don't we need a plan? Think back, Arian. There must have been a reason why it didn't work between us. Haven't you ever noticed how little we ever talked to each other?'

But Arian's hmmphing impatiently at me. 'Don't be silly, Louisa. Of course we talked. Every day. We lived together, didn't we?'

'Arian. I don't recall us ever having a conversation of any substance unless it was over a bottle of wine with Pete and Leonie, until the night you told me about Karina. I think at the very least we need counselling.'

'Look, it wasn't anything you did, it was me,' he says resignedly.

I think about it for a moment. But actually, the more I look back at our marriage, there are gaping holes all over the place.

'Nice of you to say so, but I'm not sure it's that simple,' I say with a hint of sarcasm. Then suggest, 'Perhaps we should go to Relate...' Looking at his face, you'd think I'd suggested eating witchetty grubs.

'Up to you,' says Arian grumpily. 'Look, I feel like I'm on trial here, Lou. Can't we just get on with it and see how it goes for a bit?'

This isn't at all what I imagined. I'm getting the feeling that he's not at all prepared to make an effort. For someone apparently so intent on making amends, it's just a little bit *strange*.

'Well, I think for both our sakes, we should give it a time limit, at the end of which we make a decision,' I say. 'I was thinking of about a month.'

Gosh, I'm being impressively matter of fact here. He's not looking thrilled.

'Where are you living?' I ask him.

He's vague. 'Oh, I'm lodging in another pilot's house for a bit – until I find somewhere to buy.'

And then, because I'm downright nosy, and because she's the reason our marriage broke up in the first place, I ask him about Karina. And to my great surprise, find I've opened a whole can of worms.

Arian is trying not to show that he actually is quite upset about the whole business.

'We haven't worked out what we're going to do when the baby arrives. I mean, it's not as though I can share looking after it when it's tiny, but as it gets older, I'll be able to get more involved.'

He doesn't sound convinced, but then Arian has never been keen on babies. I can't help wondering if he's one of those men who can't stand not being the centre of attention.

'For goodness' sake, Arian. The baby will be wonderful!' I tell him firmly. 'Don't you think it's miraculous that half your genes will make up that tiny little person?'

Just as long as the poor mite doesn't get the unfaithful ones.

'You're going to be a daddy!' I add enthusiastically. 'And just think, he or she's bound to end up being a pilot!'

And this time, I'm not taking the piss. Why can't he wake up to the fact that it really is an amazing experience that lies ahead of him and that he's lucky? It's a miracle that's happening, only he doesn't see it.

And I'm curious, because he hasn't told me yet. Why he and Karina broke up. Eventually, I winkle it out of him.

'No particular reason,' he says unhappily. 'We were getting on each other's nerves, I suppose. Both stressed out with work. It got worse when Karina had to stop flying. She loves it and I think she resented me still going off to work as usual. She's been having terrible morning sickness.'

I can just imagine how sensitively he coped with that. Probably just told her to man up and stop being such a girl, while she retched over a toilet bowl. And Arian meanwhile is the one who takes offence. How do I find the words to explain to him that he's behaved like a first class moron.

'Arian. Have you tried to put yourself in *Karina's* shoes? Let's see. She's worked as hard as you have, in a testosterone-driven environment, to get the job she's always wanted. You, an *unavailable* married man, whisk her off her feet, impregnate her and then, when she's unable to do the job she loves because *your* foetus is making her as sick as a dog, *you* are the one who feels hard done by and *you* run out on *her*.'

I'm feeling quite defensive on her behalf which is utterly bizarre. I certainly didn't expect to be sitting here giving marriage guidance to my ex-husband.

'Oh.' Arian looks up, quite shocked as he registers what I've just said. Then his face takes on a look of utter confusion. 'Do you really think that?'

I roll my eyes at him. For a relatively intelligent man, at times he can be a complete dimwit.

'Arian,' I try again wearily. 'Listen. Imagine you are Karina.' I say it slowly, as though he is particularly thick. I'm beginning to think he is. 'How would you be feeling right now?'

At last the penny drops. 'Oh God. I've been an idiot, haven't I?' He drops his head into his hands.

I'm sitting there nodding my head.

'Um, Lou...do you think, well...' He's too embarrassed to ask me if I mind if we call it a night.

'You want to go? What a shame. I was rather looking forward to dessert,' I say brightly. Well, why should I make it easy for him. He doesn't deserve it. He's a rat.

But I relent. Now that he's come to his senses, I've no desire to spend any longer than necessary with him.

He drops me home, earlier than expected, and fortunately doesn't come in.

'Good luck,' I say. He looks at me, puzzled. He just can't fathom how I'm suddenly fine about his extra-marital relationship. 'I mean it, Arian. Go on, you've got some making up to do.'

* * *

Well, that was the last thing I expected. I'd imagined I'd have a problem keeping Arian at arm's length. Ha. I'm obviously not that irresistible. But one very good thing has come out of this evening and that is that I have most definitely laid a ghost. And hopefully silenced my irritating conscience for good.

But the best thing is that a huge weight has lifted from my shoulders, as Arian has proved to me, once and for all, just how unreliable he is and how utterly clueless when it comes to relationships. When he picked me up this evening, he was intent on worming his way back into favour with me. Only two hours later, and he's scuttled off to try and patch things up with Karina. I wonder how she'd feel if she knew what he'd been up to.

Agnes was right. I need to tell Emma too that she needn't worry. That all is resolved. That I've seen the light and Arian's gone back to Karina. The only regret I have is about Marcus, who now thinks I am utterly unreliable and flakier than ever. How do I convince him I'm not?

19

Frustratingly, I don't see Marcus on Friday, nor the whole of the following week. It seems he's taken a few days off. He didn't mention anything before he left, but I can't help wondering if it's something to do with what happened between us – or rather didn't. Agnes isn't giving anything away and Emma doesn't know where he is either. Or so they tell me. I'm disappointed that he isn't here to share my news with. To make up for his absence, Stella is working full time and no one seems able to tell me for how long.

'Never mind, Lou, why don't you come out with me tonight?' Emma asks me, sensing my peculiar mood. 'I'm meeting Ben and some friends of his later on. Only in the pub. How about it?'

Seeing as I'm not doing anything else, I think unenthusiastically, I suppose I might as well.

* * *

In the event, it turns out that it's me, Emma, Ben and half a dozen of his mates, all male except for Samantha, who runs his stable yard.

'She's been seeing Sam you know,' whispers Emma in my ear, none too quietly. Sam and Samantha. I wonder if I should mention the pink knickers.

Samantha's fun actually and so are the guys. One of Ben's friends, Oliver, seems to be trying to chat me up.

'So you work with Emma,' he says. He's a nice enough guy, but with an air of intent that's seriously scary.

'Mmm,' I say half-heartedly in response, my eyes glancing around the pub for Marcus.

'Ben tells me you've got Daisy's old horse – Horace isn't it?'

That gets a more enthusiastic response. 'I have, he's fabulous,' I say. 'I completely love him.'

Oliver tells me about a horse of Ben's that he rides quite a lot. I think he's waiting for me to suggest that we go riding together, but I won't be doing that. I'm rather possessive about my outings with Horace. They're not for sharing, being strictly for the two of us.

He must sense that I'm not really interested, because he gradually wanders away to try his luck elsewhere. I have to admit, I'm finding I'm quite preoccupied with thoughts of Marcus tonight. And not just tonight, actually. Just to emphasise my complete and utter failure with him, Emma and Ben are practically glued together. They become more inseparable with every passing day.

I go home early in the end. So early it's still light. And I'm sober, which is just as well, because the instant I walk through the door, the phone rings. It's Leonie. And she's distraught.

'Lou…' she's sobbing. 'Please can you come over? Now? It's Pete…' In the background I hear the sound of glass smashing. 'He's drunk and he's completely lost it…'

'Okay, Leo, calm down, I'll be right over.'

I think for a moment and then can't believe I'm doing it. I'm calling Arian. Thank God he answers.

'Louisa! What a surprise!' but I cut him short.

'Arian, get over to Pete and Leonie's NOW. Please...' I beg him. Somehow I think a drunk and out of control Pete is going to be more than just Leo and I can deal with.

'Arian, this is *really* important. Pete's smashing the house up as we speak.'

'Okay, *okay*. I'll be there.'

* * *

For once, I can honestly say my ex-husband is a godsend. Pete most eloquently calls him a two-timing shithead and tries to punch him on the nose. The alcohol hasn't completely numbed his brain then. He misses of course and falls over. Arian just tells him he's a meathead and steers him out into the garden. Eventually, he gets him sitting down, and the next minute, Pete's aggression has evaporated and he's crying pitifully in Arian's arms.

Leo looks like a nervous wreck. The weight has just fallen off her since Pete's been ill and her familiar sparkle has all but disappeared.

'Thank you, Lou. And I mean it. That was an inspired idea. He'll be okay now.' She makes as if to go to join them, but I catch her arm.

'Leave them for a bit,' I say. 'This might be good for both of them.'

Leo stands beside me and we watch them.

'I didn't know you were in contact with Arian,' she says at last.

'I wasn't,' I tell her, 'but Karina kicked him out and he wanted us to give it another try. That was last weekend. We went on one date, and he told me about all his troubles with Karina. I ended up giving him marriage advice. Me of all people! As far I know they're back together now, though I haven't actually asked...'

'You what?' Leonie turns huge dark eyes to stare incredulously at me.

'You wouldn't believe the half of it,' I tell her. 'How didn't I know how crap he was? Pregnant girlfriend and somehow he holds it against her. Truly.'

'You're extraordinary,' she tells me with astonishment.

But I know I'm not. 'Do you know, this is the first time in months that I feel anything remotely positive towards that man?' I say, feeling something curiously akin to affection as I watch Arian cajoling a smile out of Pete. There's a male bonding ritual going on out there. I doubt that either of them is saying anything particularly intelligent, but at least they're communicating. They've lost time to make up. They've been friends for twenty years, far too long not to get over their differences.

'Shall we put the kettle on?' I suggest. A nice hot cup of tea would be good for all of us right now, especially Pete, with all that surplus alcohol buzzing around his veins.

We take a tray of mugs outside to join them. Poor Pete is looking embarrassed, but more sober than earlier and definitely in control again.

And strangest of all, it's almost like old times as we sit there together.

'I've told Pete we need to spend more time together,' Arian tells Leo. 'I'm not away much at the moment, even with frauds like you off sick,' he ribs Pete. 'So there's no reason not to, is there.'

Oh my golly gosh. Arian's actually thinking of someone other than Arian for a change. Maybe there's a shred of decency in there after all.

* * *

We walk out together. To our separate cars.

'Thank you,' I say to him. 'For coming over so quickly.' I give him a kiss on the cheek.

'I can't believe I didn't know what's been going on,' he mutters, looking guilty. 'I wish someone had told me.'

'Problem is, Arian, you've been too wrapped up in yourself by half,' I say, maybe a little *too* honestly. 'When was the last time you called Pete and went for a beer with him? You've been so self-obsessed, that you've cut yourself off from the best friend you've ever had. Please make sure you *do* phone him. Believe it or not, he needs you.'

Brutal – but true. With that, I get in my car and drive off up the road. When I glance in the driving mirror, Arian's still standing there with his mouth open.

20

I've long finished all that confounded filing that Agnes gave me. I found out some interesting snippets though. When I came across the volumes that comprised the Amberley Stud, I skimmed through them and found Karina Williamson owned a black stallion. Maybe still does. Ha! So Arian hasn't escaped the dreaded horse habit at all. Karina's probably as potty about horses as I am. She'd have to be, brought up in a place like that. We'd probably be quite good friends in different circumstances.

Marcus has returned, but he's super-busy and other than when he whirls into the office, I've hardly seen him. I'm beginning to think he's avoiding me. Hmmm... I'll have to formulate a plan. This can't go on. We were getting on so well until Arian stepped in and ruined it. Correction: until I let Arian step in and ruin it.

And I've a sneaky suspicion that Emma's up to her old tricks. Only much more furtively than before. She's set her mobile to vibrate for one thing, so only she knows when there's an update and she's more disciplined about how frequently she answers them. But I'm watching. And she knows I am.

***

Life has gone relatively quiet, as a result of which I'm on my guard, waiting for the next problem to materialise on my doorstep. But for once, none does, thank goodness. Pete is slowly on the up, Arian has kept away, which is very good news, but so has Marcus which is not so good. On the plus side, I have more time with my adored horse.

Summer's most definitely over and the woods have taken on a distinctly autumnal look. The colours are incredible this year. Rich russets and golds, all the more vibrant after the heat of recent months. It's October, but still quite warm and a perfect temperature for riding. Now that his hoof has healed, Horace loves cantering through the fallen leaves along the bridlepaths. I've cleared out his stable too, ready for when the weather turns. My precious horse won't be slumming it out in the mud all winter. Oh no. He'll be cocooned in layers of cosy rugs, with a big haynet of the sweetest meadow hay and up to his knees in straw. It's all there now, ready and waiting for him. Nothing's too good for my beloved Horace.

Later that week, at the end of the day, I go to remove my dog from its stable and come face to face with Marcus, who has obviously miscalculated because no way can he avoid me this time. But as his brown eyes meet mine, I notice how strained he looks.

'Hi,' he says, and just stands in front of me.

'How are you?' I ask brightly. 'I haven't seen you for weeks. Well, you know, not properly...'

'Um, I'm okay,' he says. 'Fine actually.'

Fine. That word. I snort. He looks surprised.

'Well, I am,' he says, a touch defensively. 'How's it going with your ex-husband?'

'Um.' I think. How exactly do I put this. 'Well, he took me out for dinner, and I suppose you could say I helped him to see the light about Karina.'

'Oh.' Marcus looks downcast. 'Well, I wish you well, Lou. You really deserve to be happy.' And he turns to go to his car.

'We're not back together,' I say to his retreating back. Sod it. Why do I care what Marcus thinks anyway. I bend down to clip Elmer's lead on her collar.

But when I stand up, he's still there, looking quizzical.

'What I meant,' I say slowly, because he's being a bit thick here – I think it's a man thing, 'is that I made him see that he shouldn't be running out on Karina. Helped him see her point of view, I suppose you could say.'

'You did?' Marcus looks incredulous. I can see he's having trouble grasping this one.

'Well, just because she has morning sickness, because she's pregnant with *his* child, and is miserable because she can't go and fly her big aeroplanes, doesn't really give him reason to walk out on her, does it?' I say heatedly.

Marcus is looking at me as though I'm mad. Then he runs his fingers through his hair and says, 'Look, shall we go for a drink sometime and you can tell me about it? Properly? Like maybe tomorrow night? If you're free?'

'Okay,' I say cautiously. I know he's a vet, but I'm seriously wondering about Marcus's cognitive abilities. He's mighty slow on the uptake where relationships are concerned.

* * *

So, on Saturday night, I'm feeling a strong sense of déjà vu because haven't I been here before? Getting smartened up for a date with Marcus, only the last time, it all went desperately wrong.

Arian's fault? Actually, all mine.

Marcus is looking very gorgeous, in faded jeans and a check shirt. He's tanned and he smells nice too. He's obviously made an effort – for me?

There's no kiss hello. In fact, he's still a bit cagey. He drives us to another hidden-away country pub I've never been to before, and this time orders a warm, oaky Shiraz, which we sip at a small table outside.

'You know, I still don't really understand what you were telling me about your ex,' he eventually says, as I knew full well he would.

Duh...

'There's not much more to tell,' I say. 'You know I'd decided that because Arian and I were legally still married, I felt obligated to at least attempt to give him a second chance. Even if only so I didn't regret it in the future,' I add, thinking of my conversation with Agnes, all those weeks ago.

'We went on a date. Just the one, as it turns out. I don't think he ever really wanted to get back with me – not for the right reasons. I think what he needed was somewhere to stay, which he certainly didn't find with me,' I add hastily seeing the look on Marcus's face. 'So I asked him about Karina. And then it transpired that he was being completely useless and not thinking at all about what *she* was going through. I made him think, I suppose and when the penny dropped, he couldn't get away fast enough.'

'Oh,' Marcus looks nonplussed. 'So were you okay after that?'

I look at him impatiently. He just doesn't get it, does he? 'I told you ages ago, Marcus, that I don't have any lovey-dovey feelings towards Arian. At All. Okay?' My voice is rising in exasperation. 'He's history. I've filed for divorce, on grounds of adultery. Can we talk about something else, *please*?'

My failed marriage and failed attempt at resurrecting it aren't my proudest moments. They've happened and they're part of who I am, but it's time to move on.

'Sorry,' he says. 'Somehow I thought you still had feelings for him. It wasn't making sense after what he did to you. And I didn't want to get in the way.' But yet again, Marcus has killed the mood. We don't have much to say after that. After finishing our drinks, he drops me home.

I'm not sure what it is with Marcus. And just as our friendship was drifting into something more romantic. After all, when he thought I was unhappy, he was the epitome of kind and caring. But he doesn't seem to believe what I'm telling him, that Arian belongs firmly in my past.

I'm not really up to any more complicated relationships. Right now I don't need them. I have good friends, okay, even if one does have a screwed-up husband and the other a horoscope habit. Not to mention an ex-husband who I'm counselling about the girlfriend he left me for. There you go. So I certainly don't need anyone else with problems at the moment. It would be nice, I fantasise, to go out with a straightforward man, who isn't remotely screwed up and have some nice, straightforward fun. Nice, straightforward sex too. Now there's a thought... Well, it's okay to dream isn't it? For a short while I'd imagined that such a possibility existed with Marcus. Seemingly that's not the case. Of course, it doesn't even occur to me that he might have issues of his own.

21

I am now officially sworn off men. Probably not for good, but at least for a very long time. I invited both Leonie and Emma over last night, as witnesses and as I told them both, after all that to-do with Arian that he blew sky high out of the water and the nearly something with Marcus that he insisted on mucking up, it's too late for the pair of them. I am now off limits.

Emma just snorted disbelievingly at me and Leo got the giggles. I was most disappointed with both of them. Not much of a show of solidarity is it, when the friends you've been bolstering up over the last few months fall over with hilarity the minute you ask for their understanding.

So I left them to it and went outside to talk to Horace, who was much more sympathetic. Eventually, they came out and apologised, but I could tell they didn't really mean it.

And here we are again. Another Monday morning and a brand spanking new resolution, because I'm going to be extremely brisk and efficient in my dealings with Marcus from now on. I'm not falling for the 'understanding male' act that he nearly sucked me in with. He's clearly *not* that understanding at all.

I've dressed accordingly too. Tailored black trousers which are very smart and not at all suitable for mucking out, but today I don't care. My hair is pinned back in a French pleat. I look extremely business-like and more than a little Miss Moneypenny. Marcus does a double take when he sees me, which this morning I completely ignore. I let Agnes give him his list of calls and busy myself with putting an order together for all the drugs and other stuff that everyone gets through so much of.

But by lunchtime, I'm worrying about Agnes. She's been very quiet and didn't even comment on my unusual (for me) attire. Her face is pale too – not just pale, but kind of drawn, as if she's in pain. So, for once, our roles are reversed and I'm keeping an eye on her. When I get a chance, I'm going to have a word with her.

Then I rapidly change my mind. I'm not waiting. She's doubled over, and looks dreadful.

'Agnes? Are you okay?'

A small moan comes from her. Clearly she's not. 'Agnes?'

Then her eyes half close, as though she's about to pass out. 'Agnes?'

She doesn't answer. Then I realise. No one else is around. It's just me and all I know is Agnes is a tough old boot. I've never known her have as much as a headache in all the time I've worked here, which means something's seriously wrong.

I grab the phone.

'Hello? Ambulance please... Yes. It's the lady I work with. She's collapsed. No. No health problems I'm aware of. Look, please can you hurry? She's really ill. Oh, yes, the address...'

It feels like an eternity as we wait, though by now, Agnes is out of it, hardly moving. Her eyelids fluttered shut a few minutes ago and the only sound she utters is the occasional faint moan. I'm letting the calls for the vets' go to answerphone, because there's a full-blown human emergency that needs me more.

I want to move her, though I'm not sure where to. But I can't and then, oh dear, she sounds like she's about to throw up. In the nick of time, she stirs and I place the wastepaper bin in front of her. Not a moment too soon.

When they get here, the ambulance men are jolly amazing. So nice and friendly and unbelievingly efficient – just like Marcus. They check her over, then within minutes she's on a stretcher and being lifted into the ambulance. I want to go with her but obviously I can't. Agnes makes this whole practice happen. It's not going to be at all the same, but without her here, the realisation suddenly hits home that everything's down to me.

Once the ambulance has left, I slump onto a chair and think for a moment. Who I should tell. And, of course, the first person to call is Beamish. Not just as her employer, either. His phone rings for ages and when he answers, he sounds very relaxed, his voice positively soporific until I explain.

'Beamish? Are you sure you can hear me okay? Only you sound miles away. Did you get that? About Agnes? She's been rushed to hospital in an ambulance... Yes... Winchester General. Sorry? Did you say you're going straight there? Thank God. Please can you let me know what's happening the minute you get there?'

I put the phone down. I have his mobile number and I know where Agnes has been taken. One way or another, I'll keep tabs on whatever's going on.

Suddenly I remember that Agnes has a daughter. I don't even know her name. And then shame rushes over me as I think I've worked with this wonderful person for two whole years. She's held my hand through my marriage break-up and I've never even asked her about her daughter.

But now isn't the time to dwell on it. I have to try and do all the stuff that Agnes so effortlessly does, day in, day out, no matter what.

It's not long before Miles calls in, wanting Agnes to order specific drugs for a complicated case he's treating. He's shocked when I tell him what's happened. Then he gives me the list and asks if it's okay if I sort it out. Of course it is. Surely it can't be that difficult.

Oh bloody hell. It's not that it's complicated, it's just that I don't *how* Agnes does these things. It takes me hours to get to grips with her computer. In the end, Sam comes to help me. Between us, we work out what we need to do, but it's about 10 p.m. by the time everything is done. In the meantime, Mrs Boggle comes in and when we tell her what's happened, she sighs heavily. She loves a bit of drama, especially something like this. Then surprisingly, she tells us about Agnes's daughter, who's called Rachel, but even she doesn't have her phone number. Much more sighing than usual goes on, no doubt in sympathy with Agnes.

Elmer is very pissed off when I go and get her from her stable. It looks as though she'd resigned herself to spending the night.

I'm exhausted when I get home. It's beans on toast for both me and Elmer, I give Horace a few carrots and then fall in to bed. I'll need to get up earlier than usual tomorrow, otherwise I'll be behind before I've even started.

22

I get to work at seven, filled with determination to make Agnes proud of me. I will keep everything ticking over as usual in that office if it kills me. But, oh my gosh, there is so much to do.

First, I look at the diary. Is this what faces Agnes every morning? There's a list of calls as long as your arm, and somehow I have to assign them to each vet.

Okay. I take a deep breath. I know some of these. The rest I'll have to look up. Then I group them geographically, and then try to consider which ones will take the most time. By the time the vets pitch up at a quarter to eight, there's a shambolic sort of list awaiting each of them.

After reading through with much raisings of eyebrows, they go on their way, more quietly than usual. No one's even questioned me! It's only when they've all gone, that I realise that I haven't taken any notice whatsoever of Marcus. In fact I was so preoccupied, I barely even registered he was there.

Actually, in a funny sort of way, I'm enjoying the challenge. So far, I've managed to keep on top of everything, and though I'm working much longer hours, it's good to know I can do this. I miss Agnes terribly though and I'm going to see her tonight, after work.

I try desperately hard to get ahead. Ha! Last week, I was a lowly assistant, now I seem to think I can run an office single handed and even manage to get away early! Stupid, Louisa. In the end, I get away at seven thirty and go straight to the hospital, leaving Elmer to night-stop with Sam.

I negotiate the network of hospital wings and wards with difficulty. I'm just not used to them. Actually, I don't think I've been in one since I was born. After asking half a dozen highly efficient nurse types exactly where Agnes's ward is, once I manage to get to it I stand there uselessly looking for her, until I hear a weak voice saying my name.

I turn round and lying in a bed that looks enormous with her tiny, frail body in it, is Agnes. I'm deeply shocked. Since when did she get so small? I go and sit next to her and, by accident, find myself holding her hand.

I've been there all of three minutes when Beamish comes in, looking a little pale himself, I notice. But determinedly keeping the old pecker up.

'Ah. Louisa. Jolly nice of you to visit. Um. Fancy a little walk?'

I tell Agnes I'll be back in a few minutes. As we walk out of her ward, Beamish has stopped trying to look as though everything's okay. Clearly it's not.

'Peritonitis.' He says it quietly. 'She's about to go in to surgery any minute.' He looks at his watch, then adds, 'If you'd been five minutes later, you'd have missed her. They've had her on antibiotics since she came in, but she's, er, not so good. But chin up, old girl. I'm sure she'll be, er, fine.' Then he lapses into silence.

I don't have anything to say either, so after Agnes is taken to theatre, we sit and wait together. Shock slowly seeps over me. I mean I knew Agnes was ill, but if Beamish is to be believed, it's serious.

Then I remember. 'Beamish. Agnes has a daughter. Rachel, Mrs Boggle said. We have to tell her what's happened.'

He pats my arm. 'Don't worry, old thing. All under control.'

An hour later, we're joined by Miles. And half an hour after that, Emma. Marcus is out in the dark somewhere, in a field with half-a-dozen firemen and a horse that's stuck in a ditch.

We keep our vigil in silence, losing track of time until a surgeon comes towards us through double doors, looking serious.

'Family?' he asks. We all shake our heads. Maybe Beamish slightly less so.

'Um, work colleagues,' he says, standing up and squaring his shoulders. 'And, um, extremely good friends.'

The surgeon surveys our motley little band suspiciously, then for some reason decides that we're genuine.

'Well...' he starts. 'She's out of the woods. For now. A particularly vicious peritonitis. I'm not quite sure how she kept going. She must have been feeling terrible for quite some time.' He shakes his head. 'She hadn't seen her doctor?'

But out of all of us, I'm the one who completely gets it, and I feel terrible. If you have a job like Agnes's, it's impossible to take time off when no one else knows how it all works. Especially if your assistant is me.

'It may be best if just one of you visits tonight...' he adds. 'She's very drowsy still, and on medication for the pain. And hopefully by tomorrow, she should start to feel a little better.'

Beamish stands up, then sits again. It's obvious this has really knocked the stuffing out of him. He looks at me.

'Er, why don't you pop in, Louisa? She'll want to see you,' he says gruffly. 'Give her love. Er, from all of us. I'll come back in the morning.'

When I see Agnes, she's very drowsy, but already starting to come round. She tells me that the pain has gone. I crouch down by her bed, relieved to see her looking marginally less awful than earlier.

'They're all outside,' I tell her. 'Except Marcus. He's in a ditch,' I explain, and the eyebrows rise weakly.

'They all send their love. Beamish says he's coming back in the morning.' I'm not sure how he'll swing that one by the ferocious-looking sister who monitors all incomers. Visiting hours are strictly 3–7 p.m. There's a big sign on the wall that says so.

I bend over and kiss her pale forehead. 'Hurry up and get better,' I whisper. 'We need you.'

Then I take the hint from the nurse who's glaring at me and leave.

Out in the corridor, I report back to the others. And tell Beamish about visiting hours, but I don't think he's listening. There's unanimous agreement to find somewhere for a drink and a quick bite to eat – not because we feel like celebrating, it's just none of us particularly wants to go home just yet. We're used to any number of sick horses, but one of us being ill, least of all Agnes, that's another matter altogether.

* * *

The next morning I start work earlier. When I arrive at the practice, Elmer ignores me. Clearly she's decided that I'm superfluous to her needs and that it's much nicer living with Sam.

So I check the answerphone, read the emails and compile the lists of calls. Stella's in today, so I try to give her clients who are least likely to be upset by her. Okay, so where are the vets? *Gosh. It's only 7.30 a.m. I'm actually doing rather well.*

My next job is to compile another list of supplies that need ordering. But then I notice someone wandering around in the yard. I finish scribbling down what I'm in the middle of, then go outside, to find Sam has beaten me to it.

I recognise the figure immediately. It's that chavvy boy. The one whose skanky dog Elmer went for – I'd recognise its blingy collar anywhere. She's out there now, sat, by Sam's side, growling menacingly, but doing exactly what Sam says. He's obviously a dog whisperer too.

The skanky dog's looking very sorry for itself. It's hunched up, and shivery, with saliva drooling from its mouth. Sam crouches down, and strokes it gently, all the time talking quietly.

The boy glares at me. His worn jeans are hanging off his backside in that way that only teenage boys can carry off, exposing boxers and an expanse of lilywhite flesh. 'Please, missus, can ya keep yer dog away? Only he's well sick, is Beckham... Fink me stepdad's gone an' poisoned 'im...'

I grab Elmer by the scruff and drag her away to a stable, while Sam talks to the boy. When I come back, Sam has things under control.

'I think Zac could be right about poisoning,' he tells me, then turns to Zac. 'But don't worry. One of the vets will be here any minute and they can look at Beckham straight away. Do you want to bring him into the hay store?'

The boy gently encourages his mutt to stagger feebly across the yard, following Sam, as right on cue, Marcus pulls up.

'What's going on here?' he asks me, looking at Zac and Beckham.

God help us. Marcus is being thick again. Just when I least need him to be.

'It's a sick dog, Marcus,' I say, nice and slowly. So he understands.

'But we only do horses.'

'Does it matter? If Beamish were here, he'd be over there looking at it himself,' I say firmly. And ping. A light goes on.

'Yes. Right. Of course,' says Marcus, and grabbing his bag, he's safely back into superhero-mode as he lopes across the yard after them.

Marcus quickly confirms that the poor dog has indeed been poisoned, even though the rest of us already know that.

'How do you think it happened?' he asks Zac.

'It's me stepdad,' he says sullenly. ''E's a right fuckin' tosser. 'E 'ates Beckham. Says he's a manky old fleabag.' Then he adds, ''E 'ates me too.'

I can see Marcus looking quite angry, probably thinking that he'd like to get Zac's stepdad prosecuted, or at least give him a good thumping, but it's first things first, which in this case means attending to Beckham.

'Okay,' he says. 'First we have to make him vomit up whatever it is he's eaten. And then I need to give him charcoal to stop him absorbing anything that's left. Now, I need to go and check on dosages because I'm a little out of touch on dogs, but it won't take long and I'll be right back.'

Leaving Zac sitting on the floor beside his poor dog, panting and looking most uncomfortable.

'How old are you, Zac?' I ask him, trying to be friendly.

'Sixteen,' comes the sullen reply, muttered under his breath as he shoots a look of pure hate in my direction.

'Where are you from?' I try again, trying not to make it sound as though I'm interrogating him.

There's a pause, then under his breath he says, ''Evverside.'

I know exactly where he means. Heatherside is one of those God-awful council developments. Not one of the nice ones, as the name might suggest, with properly laid out quiet streets and gardens, but more like a mish-mash of the ugliest houses you've ever seen, all crammed in, with the least desirable, most troublesome tenants concentrated into just three streets. It ought to be called Hell's Bottom. And it's miles away. Well, on foot it is. Way further on from where Arian and I used to live, which makes it at least five miles away.

'Here we go.' Marcus is back masterfully wielding various syringes, and hearing the phone start to ring, I bolt back to the office.

When the other vets turn up, Emma takes Marcus's first call, so that he can concentrate on the dog. Fortunately it's not a busy morning.

Marcus stays with Zac and his dog for quite a while. It even looks like they're chatting. Then Marcus walks off and makes a call on his mobile, before coming back again. Leaving Beckham in the capable hands of Sam, he brings Zac into the office.

'Louisa. I've just been speaking to Beamish. About young Zac here. It seems that he'd like to do some work. To, um, earn Beckham's treatment...'

Zac turns to him. 'I don't want no charity, mister,' he says sullenly. 'And I ain't goin' fuckin' 'ome neither.'

'It's not charity, Zac,' says Marcus quietly, and very firmly. 'Louisa will tell you that we're one man down at the moment. Normally, there's two people in this office and she spends part of her day out in the yard, helping Sam. So, my thinking was, that if you helped Sam, Louisa would be free to concentrate on the office. What do you say?'

There's a begrudging "Kay.'

Great. Terrific, even... He sounds *so* enthusiastic. So now, not only do I have Agnes to worry about, there's the delights of a bolshy teenager too. I wish Marcus had run it by me first.

But Sam's horse-whispering skills work like a charm on Zac. Before long, he has him out sweeping the yard and then together

The Impossible Search for the Perfect Man 147

they scrub down an empty stable or two. He even gets him to pull his jeans up slightly, so there's less of the boxers on show. And every so often, one of them checks on Beckham, who Marcus is absolutely certain is going to be just fine.

I'm so wrapped up in everything that's going on out there that I keep forgetting that I'm not just a lowly assistant at the moment. In Agnes's absence, I'm actually *running* this office – and if I don't get some bills out, none of us will be getting paid.

Since Agnes has been in hospital, which is only a couple of days, I can't believe how quickly time is flashing by. What with calls, orders, paperwork, bills, odd things like Zac and Beckham thrown into the mix, there truly aren't enough hours in the day.

So the afternoon finds me sitting behind the computer, cursing. The confounded stupid contraption which should have been updated years ago, is playing up yet again. The trouble is it's Beamish's pride and joy. He honestly believes we have a state of the art office, even though it's more state of the ark, with a computer you can only describe as vintage.

My loud *bugger* catches the attention of Zac, who wanders in, still looking at me as though I'm the least trustworthy person on the planet.

"Sup...' he mutters, staring at his trainers, obviously reluctant to even share the same space as me, owning as I do, the most evil and dangerous of all flatcoat retrievers.

'Oh. Nothing,' I say. Then, 'D'you know, actually it's this stupid machine.'

'I could 'ave a butcher's...' Zac shrugs, then stands looking utterly disinterested. Suddenly I remember very dimly that schoolchildren are all computer whizz kids these days.

'You reckon?'

He shambles over and leans down to look at the screen. 'Wot you tryin' to do?'

I get up and explain what I'm trying to do, and in no time, he's sitting, his fingers flying around the keyboard, and two minutes later, the job is done.

'I fink your 'ard drive's well shit,' he says. Then he gets up again.

'Wow! Thanks!' I say, impressed.

'Actually I fink yer 'ole computer's...'

'... well shit?' I finish for him. 'I agree with you, Zac. Unfortunately, the boss does not, so if you have any bright ideas...'

'Dunno,' he says reluctantly, then shrugs and swaggers out, shoulders slightly squarer than when he came in.

I just hope he doesn't go out and nick one.

Thanks to Zac though, I manage to finish my bills and get to the hospital to see Agnes, dropping Elmer home on my way, to make sure Beckham isn't attacked again.

I make my way to the same ward where we saw Agnes last night. Looking down the beds, I can't see her anywhere. I check again, and a bossy-looking nurse comes up to me.

'Excuse me? Are you lost?' she says, in a most unfriendly manner.

'I'm looking for Agnes,' I say. 'She was here last night. I saw her...' I'm starting to sound a little crazed. The nurse's expression becomes more sympathetic, and she takes my arm and leads me gently out of the ward.

Oh God. Agnes isn't dead is she? Suddenly I'm light-headed and my heart is in my mouth, because being here for Agnes is so much more important than the office. As my mind runs away with me, I barely register what the nurse is telling me, which is that Agnes has been moved to intensive care. That there are complications.

On the one hand I'm thinking, *Phew, thank heavens she's okay*, and then suddenly I realise what the nurse was saying. Intensive care. Complications – which doesn't sound okay at all.

* * *

I find it eventually. It's a strange place, with loads of electronic lights and bleepings, and other strange noises. Agnes is looking tinier than ever, lying back with tubes and lines coming in and out of her arms and nose.

'Louisa...' she just about manages when she sees me.

'How is everything, are you managing...' she murmurs slowly, and so quietly I can hardly hear her. Her eyes are half closed. She looks drugged.

'Sshh, Agnes. Don't worry. Everything's fine. We can talk tomorrow when you're feeling better,' I say gently, and like last time, I sit and hold her hand until her eyes close and she's asleep again.

And suddenly I'm terrified.

23

That night I do *a lot* of thinking. It's one of those 3 a.m. lying-awake jobs again, as I worry about Agnes and whether the practice will survive being at the mercy of my modest assistant-rated skills. But then, I remind myself, no one's actually complained. Not vets, or clients. At least, not yet.

And then my brain's whirring about Pete, and Leo of course, by which point it's only a matter of time before Arian's back in my thoughts as well, and before I know it there's a regular maelstrom going on in my head. I think it's out of sheer desperation more than anything else that my poor brain shuts down at this point, giving me just about an hour of oblivion before the alarm goes off for yet another brand-new day.

* * *

I wake up feeling as like I've just flown back from Australia. I switch my radio on to the rousing sound of Blur's 'Woo Hoo', which has the desired effect and gets me out of bed to make some extremely strong coffee, which I take outside to drink with Horace.

Lucky for me horses are such forgiving creatures, because it feels as though I've hardly been at home. But he bears no grudge for being neglected these last few days, just touches his velvet lips to my cheek and blows gently.

His beautiful shiny coat is growing thicker, a clear sign that the nights are getting colder and that for the end of October, these unseasonably warm days are lulling all of us into a false sense of security. I've ordered him a rug for the winter, like a weatherproof duvet for horses. His stable is full of straw and he's looking really well for a horse consigned to death row. He munches the carrots I give him, and then just hangs around, being companionable. Horace is a total darling and I love him.

* * *

Not surprisingly, I'm not at my most sparkling this morning. Beamish arrives shortly after me, which I'm not expecting as he's not supposed to be in today. He spends ages talking to Zac, then looking at Beckham. Beamish loves it when we get different animals in. Then he fiddles about for a while, and has serious vet conversations with Marcus and Miles when they come in. Emma's already been called out on an emergency.

Shortly before nine, when the others have cleared off, he comes in to find me. Standing there awkwardly, he shuffles his feet then clears his throat. He really looks most uncomfortable. What the blazes is he going to say, I wonder, my imagination of course already ten steps ahead of the game.

Er, Louisa, terribly sorry, I'm afraid we're going to have to sack you. You haven't been doing an awfully good job since Agnes was taken ill... Frightfully sorry old girl...

My imagination, as always, is a curse. I'll end up having to get all the other vets on my side to back me up – and maybe some of the clients... I'm reasonably popular so some of them are bound to. And I'll just have to prove to Beamish that actually I haven't been doing too bad a job, at all. My anxiety is clearly showing on my face at this point, because Beamish asks, 'Er, Louisa? Are you all right?'

'Um. Fine,' I tell him, trying to put my imaginings out of my head.

'Excellent. Well, I have some jolly good news. Um well, yes.' And he stands there, with his chest puffed out, suddenly looking extremely pleased with himself.

What is it, Beamish? Agnes is better and coming back to work?

'Ah. Well, I have to say you've been doing a damn fine job since poor old Agnes was taken ill. Yes, damn fine job indeed... Hmmm...' He stands there, still looking very happy.

For God's sake, man, I'm thinking. Get it over with.

'Yes, Beamish?' I say, a trifle impatiently by now.

'Ah. Yes. Well, I've found you some help. Only while we're without Agnes, of course.'

Oh fuck. My heart sinks. Into my boots and out through my heels. He thinks I'm useless. Incompetent even. *Oh buggering hell.*

'Um, now I don't want you to think that you're not doing a good enough job. No, no. It's not that at all. But a friend of mine has a daughter, who's, er, um, let's say, a little out of sorts at the moment, so I've offered her a part-time job giving you a hand. Jolly good eh?'

Great. So as well as a stroppy chav, I have a troubled girl. Probably a pregnant teenager with hormones coming out of her ears. Who's been done for shoplifting or granny-bashing and who I'll have to keep an eye on every second of the day.

Beamish interrupts my thoughts. 'Ah. Just the ticket. Here she is.'

He turns to look at the door, and following his eyes, so do I.

She's pregnant all right, but she's no teenager. In fact, I can't believe this is happening.

You could have knocked me down with a feather. Quite literally. To be fair, Karina looks as uncomfortable as I feel.

The first thought that comes to mind is, what the fuck is she doing in my office? Don't up-the-duff lady pilots get given terribly specialised 'ground duties' in one of their flight report centres or uniform stores or something? Or cleaning loos maybe.

At the party where we almost met, I'd been out cold before I could register that far from being the Scandinavian blonde of my frenzied imaginings, her hair is a similar shade of mouse to mine and she's my height too, but that's where the similarities end. This girl has stunning, model-type facial features, eyelashes like a Jersey cow and exudes, in spite of everything, a quiet confidence.

My bumbling boss chooses this moment to make his exit. Maybe he's not as daft as I thought.

'So, well, erm I'll leave you two girls to it, shall I? Um, jolly good...'

And when I look round, he's gone. As if vapourised into thin air.

I've never had to think so quickly in my life, because whether I want Arian or not, having Karina here in my office is definitely weird.

I hold out my hand. 'I'm Louisa.'

Karina holds out a beautifully manicured hand that obviously hasn't had too much to do with horses lately.

'Hello,' she says, in a very posh sort of voice. Slightly stand-offish but at least slightly, if reluctantly friendly-ish.

'Well, this is a bit of a surprise,' I say, buying myself some time while I figure out how to deal with this.

There's a deathly silence which is so heavy, you can almost see it.

'I mean, I take it you know I was married to Arian? Before, you know...' I nod my head towards her stomach, which looks pregnant, but quite small still. No point in beating around the bush, I've decided very quickly. This is *my* territory, after all.

She looks somewhat discomfited. 'I had a feeling it was you.' She's silent, then adds, 'This wasn't my idea. Just so you know.'

'Oh.' I know I no longer care about Arian in *that* sense, but this still feels supremely odd. It's like making a huge mistake that you'd rather forget, only to find that just as you do, some joker's tattooed it across your forehead while you weren't looking. So, okay. Maybe I'm exaggerating again, but this really is deeply strange.

'Well,' I eventually say, because whatever she's done, there is a mountain of work we need to get to. 'I better show you what needs doing round here. Apart from flying big aeroplanes, what other experience do you actually have?' Slightly more sarcastically than I intended.

Karina obviously notices and doesn't answer straight away. There's an awkward silence. 'None.'

I immediately jump in with, 'Well, it's only an office. No added complications of rudder pedals. Or joysticks...' I just can't help myself. 'Got to be easier than flying. Here. We need to check if these invoices have been paid.'

It would probably be quicker if I just did it myself, but I have to give her something to do. Painstakingly, I go through what's required.

'It was actually Beamish who asked my mother if she knew of anyone who might be able to help out for a while,' Karina says stiffly, in an attempt to justify her unwanted presence. 'I have to say I wasn't exactly happy when she told me. After all, I should have had a ground job with the airline.'

Why is she telling me this? I didn't ask and I don't need to know. So I add a week's worth of filing to the pile of invoices on her desk and point her in the direction of our client records.

Once she's got the hang of it, I leave her to it. It's hardly rocket science, after all, and she can't be stupid. She's a pilot isn't she? Just like my ex-husband. And then I realise the irony of my thinking.

It's even more ironic when Marcus pops in mid-morning, because, honestly, he just never does that. Mostly he's out from dawn to dusk and I never see him. And so I take great pleasure in introducing them.

'Ah, Marcus. I'm *so* delighted that you're here.' From which he'll immediately guess I'm taking the piss about something.

'I'd like to introduce you to Karina. She's, um, helping out while Agnes isn't well. Isn't that kind of her?'

God. I sound just like Beamish. Karina, meanwhile, is giving me the evils.

Marcus looks at me, for a split second longer than is strictly necessary, then turns to Karina with a beaming smile.

'Delighted to meet you,' he says, very nicely. With one of his loveliest smiles. Oh, ten out of ten, Marcus. Very well done indeed.

Then as he's walking out of the office, he glances back at me and says casually, 'Oh, Louisa, could you come with me for a moment. Only I'm in a hurry and I want to fill you in about some calls I need you to make for me.'

'*Terribly* sorry,' I say to Karina, over-apologetically, and scuttle out obediently after him. Relieved for the chance to escape if I'm honest and thinking, *Thank you Marcus*, for once inordinately glad that he's around.

'What on earth was all that about?' he asks incredulously as soon as we're out of earshot. 'What the blazes is going on?'

'One of Beamish's great ideas,' I reply bitterly, grateful that he's concerned because I have a burning need to unburden myself to someone and if nothing else, Marcus is very good for unburdening on.

'As if it's not enough that I'm without Agnes, he has to dump this on me too. Thinks he's being helpful.'

'Oh God,' says Marcus. 'Are you okay?'

'Fine,' I say impatiently, because it's the first word that comes to mind.

But I'm forgetting for a moment that Marcus is a man. The stupid arse actually believes me, then looks at his watch and gets in his car, leaving me standing there feeling abandoned as the Land Cruiser cruises purposefully out of the yard. But, of course, horses take priority over everything.

* * *

Karina and I get as far as lunchtime, being frightfully polite to each other. But no further, because by then, I'm bursting with stuff I absolutely have to say to her.

I start quite cautiously. 'Um, so, Karina, did you know Arian was married when you met him?'

By the time the words are out, I already can't believe I actually said them.

Of course, she's gobsmacked. Literally. Her mouth is wide open. When she's got over the shock, she appears to consider her reply.

'When I first met him, no. That's the truth,' she says.

Ha. Okay. So then what?

'We got to know each other a bit,' she continues cautiously. 'I have to say, Louisa, that when I found out he was married, I was shocked. I told him it was over. I'm not in the habit of stealing other women's men.'

But you went ahead anyway, I think triumphantly. *You betrayer of the sisterhood, you husband-stealer.*

She sighed. 'Truth is, I found out I was pregnant before I found out about you.' She raises earnest eyes towards me. 'I'd like you to believe me, but in your shoes, well I understand. I'd probably feel the same. And then, well, he was very persuasive and I wanted my child to have a father. He told me you never wanted children, so it seemed that I was giving him something you couldn't.'

I'm speechless. It's no secret that I've always wanted children. Somehow containing an explosion of indignation inside me, I make myself stop and think, because two things are jumping out at me. More than ever, I don't want Arian back, but secondly, however much I don't like it, I'm believing every word she says.

At this point, it seems only right that I enlighten her and so I tell her that actually, he's been telling both of us porkies.

'Actually, Karina, I *did* want children. Funnily enough, that's why we moved into a three-bedroom, family-sized home complete with family-sized garden. Don't be too sure that you can believe everything that man says to you.'

Karina leaves shortly after that. Thankfully Beamish has only asked her to do mornings.

After my last outburst, all she says is, 'I'll see you in the morning,' in a quiet, dignified sort of voice, as she walks out of the office.

I feel a little deflated when she's gone. Truth is, I honestly *don't* want Arian back. I know I keep saying it and it sounds like I'm trying to convince myself. But nor can I let her off scot-free either. It doesn't feel right.

Without the added stress of Karina lurking in the background, I manage to catch up on a huge volume of work, and am amazed to find that by five thirty, I can actually go home, but not before Mrs Boggle makes an appearance. It looks as though the pudding basin hairdo has had a tweak, and from under the mid-forehead fringe, she gives me one of her deeply sympathetic looks. From that I assume that she knows all about Karina, especially when she does one of her deeper sighs and asks me how I am.

'I'm fine, Mrs Boggle, thank you for asking,' I reply, a trifle surprised to say the least, because mostly all she ever says is, 'Evenin', lovey. I'll lock up, all right?' before walking off to the men's bog with her bucket.

I've hardly seen Zac, who Sam appears to have taken completely under his wing. Paris has been down to check him out. Canary-coloured jodhpurs, long suede boots (new ones) and Katie Price hair again. She changes its colour so often it's a wonder it doesn't drop out. The man-radar's obviously in good working order though. Not that Zac fits her normal category of victim. Or maybe she fancies a bit of rough. Zac didn't look too impressed. I caught him muttering something about 'stuck-up bitches' under his breath when he thought no one could hear him – unless he was talking about me.

Beckham has been mooching around the yard, still looking sorry for himself, but definitely on the mend. He's out there now, so before I go and collect Elmer, I go over and stroke him. He quivers slightly, like a little cat purring, but doesn't move away. He's quite a sweet dog, no trouble at all, which is more than I can say for mine. I can hear her now, whining jealously in the stable.

Zac comes over. He's caught the sun, and looks only marginally less distrustful as he stares at me.

'How are you getting on?' I ask him. 'Hope Sam isn't too much of a slave driver?'

'S'okay…' he says, after thinking about it. 'Sam's a good bloke.'

He snaps his fingers and Beckham's at his side in an instant, tail wagging feebly in spite of his woes.

I'm impressed, and I tell him.

Zac looks embarrassed. 'S'trainin', s'all,' he says, and he and Beckham slope off together in search of Sam.

When Elmer and I get home, I call Beamish for news of Agnes. There's no reply so I leave him a message. Then I go and tell

Horace how much I love him and kiss his noble face, and then a car screeches to a halt on the road, and there's the sound of male footsteps as they stomp round the side of my cottage.

'Louisa!'

Arian. And what is he sounding so cross about?

'What's this rubbish you've been telling Karina? You've upset her terribly. I really would have thought better of you.'

Oh. He's *such* an arsehole.

'Okay, Arian,' I say calmly. 'What rubbish would that happen to be? Oh, I know,' I say, suddenly pretending to be enlightened. 'You mean, about me not wanting children? But that's your rubbish, not mine. I think you're getting confused, pal. It was you who told her the rubbish, not me.'

He stares at me, looking really pissed off. Not a pretty look. And to think I used to think him handsome.

'I suspect it's you who's upset at being found out, rather than her. Are there any other lies I should know about?' I say coolly. 'As Karina and I are going to be sharing an office for a while, it would seem. We've plenty of opportunities for nice girly chats.'

Arian clearly knows he's in the wrong. As he turns to leave, I shout after him, 'And don't forget to go and see Pete.'

I hear him slam his car door so hard it's a wonder it doesn't fall off. Serve him jolly well right if it did.

After that little interlude, it's definitely time for a glass of wine. Tonight, I tell myself, I deserve it. And then Emma's coming over for supper. I've made pumpkin soup. And I also need to check the state of play where Jerome is concerned.

Emma turns up late, tired. Apparently she went straight to the hospital when she finished her calls. Just like I was, she's shocked at Agnes's appearance.

'She looks so frail, Lou. Really poorly. Apparently the peritonitis has resulted in blood poisoning and it must be quite severe.

They're treating her with antibiotics, but her organs are affected. It's really bad.'

Then she tells me Beamish was there, looking very anxious. He was still there when she left, too. And apparently Agnes's daughter had visited, so that's a good thing.

I tell Emma about my day.

'Beamish breezed in bright and early with a little surprise for me,' I tell her. 'He's found me someone to help out in the office.'

'Oh that's fantastic,' says Emma. 'At least it will take the pressure off you a bit.'

I raise my eyebrows and give her a look. 'Erm, not exactly, Em. You see, of all the people he could have found, it just so happened that he picked Karina.'

'NO...' Emma can't believe it. Her face is a picture. 'Not, THE Karina... Oh, Lou...'

'It's okay, Em. I coped. The bit that really pisses me off is finding out about the lies Arian's been telling her. Latest one is how I didn't want children. And goodness knows what else. I'll probably find out in due course.'

Then I crinkle up my face as I realise that for some bizarre reason, I'd be more inclined to believe Karina than Arian. Obviously he's a pathological liar as well as a two-timing, philandering rat. I'm well shot of him. I'm quite glad in the circumstances, that it's not me having his baby after all.

'Lou...?'

'Oh, sorry, Emma. I was miles away. Just adding bloody liar to my list of Arian's less desirable personality traits, just in case I'm ever tempted to feel sorry for myself. How's Ben, by the way?'

Emma beams beauteously at me. I don't think I've ever felt that mushy about anyone – except maybe Horace...

'It's wonderful,' she says serenely. 'We're just so well matched! I don't want to harp on, you know, but I'm *so* happy...'

I glug a huge mouthful of wine and wait for it to take the edge off the cavern of emptiness I suddenly feel inside me.

'I'm glad for you, Em,' I say, truthfully. And I mean it. Emma and Ben will be joining the ranks of the smug marrieds before long, I can see it coming. *Emma resplendent in flowing white, her blonde locks crimped into pre-Raphaelite curls and Ben, tanned and handsome in a grey morning suit. They'll walk out of the church together holding hands, and ride off into the sunset, man and wife, on two of his beautiful horses...*

'Lou?' she's asking again. 'Are you *quite* sure you're all right?'

Damn, that soup's boiling, it'll be ruined.

'Fine, honestly. Just tired. And hungry. Shall we eat?'

We have walnut bread with my soup, which turns out not to be ruined after all. Then Emma's phone makes a funny little noise which makes her jump and as she looks over at me to see if I've noticed, she goes just slightly pink.

I look straight at her. 'Emma! You're not still getting them! You promised you'd try.'

Then I add for good measure, 'Ben will think you're on drugs again...'

And he'll call the wedding off. No galloping off into the sunset for Emma with the scrumptious Ben. Oops. Nearly forgot. There isn't actually a wedding – as yet...

After supper, she leaves early. It's just as well, because after Karina, then Arian and now Emma's problem resurfacing, I'm exhausted.

I'm sound asleep by ten o'clock. No midnight gremlins for me tonight. If they come anywhere near, I'll set my dog on them. But I don't need to worry. I awake only when my alarm shatters my blissful dream, in which I'm riding Horace through miles and miles of woods and fields. And I lie there for a moment, wishing if only real life could be that simple.

24

Early starts are now my new routine. I'm determined to gather my wits about me before Karina's arrival, so I whizz through the diary, then check the answerphone before organising the calls.

Zac's in the yard, laughing at something with Sam. Gracious, is Zac sleeping here too, I wonder with astonishment. And Beckham's out there too, looking much stronger. And as the phone rings, Karina walks in and I'm instantly back on my guard.

She's wearing a soft jersey top that clings in all the right places, even with her bump, and expensive-looking jeans. Even pregnant, she makes me feel like a frump. We steer away from controversial subjects this morning. As she quietly gets on with the work I give her to do, I answer the calls that are coming in relentlessly. There's a brief lull, fortunately just as the vets appear, but as they leave, it rings again. This time it's Beamish.

'Ah. Louisa. Thought I should let you know the old girl's out of the woods. Yes, hmmph, turned a corner...'

Then obviously confused by my silence, he says, 'Agnes, Louisa. Um. Er, she's going to be fine.'

But I'm too overwhelmed to speak and tears of relief course down my cheeks.

'Just thought you'd like to know,' he adds gruffly, before ringing off.

I sit there with my back to Karina, oblivious to the phone ringing again or to her answering it, until she taps me on the shoulder, then sees my face and says into the receiver, 'Could I ask her to call you back in just a few minutes?'

Then she comes back over to me and puts her hand on my shoulder.

'Louisa? Are you all right?'

I take a deep breath and mop my face, and find I'm looking into gently concerned eyes. The only snag of course being, that they're Karina's.

'I'm fine,' I say, sniffling and wiping my nose and gathering myself together. I attempt a watery smile.

'Actually, it was good news. You must know about Agnes, that's why you're here... only she's better, she's going to be okay, and for a while there, I wasn't so sure...'

Oh bloody hell, the tears start again, and Karina's being all sympathetic, which is most disconcerting.

'I've been so worried about her,' I say, before finally dissolving into a weeping mess. Karina pushes a wodge of tissues into my hand and then I hear her putting the kettle on.

Once I've stopped snivelling, we sit there drinking hot sweet tea. She tells me I need it because I'm getting over a shock, even if it is a good one, and she needs it because it stops her feeling so disgustingly nauseous. We actually both laugh together, genuinely, for the first time ever. Then she sighs.

'I'm not much help to you, am I, Louisa. It would be easier for you in many ways if I wasn't here.'

And in a way she's right – only there's the practice to think about and I can't do everything on my own.

'Nonsense,' I tell her. 'There's tons to do. Have you finished the invoices?'

I indicate a pile about a foot high that she hasn't even touched yet. She glances at it, pauses, then without a word, goes back to her desk.

'By the way,' she remembers, 'that was a Mrs Brazier on the telephone for Agnes. I told her you'd call her back.'

It really is one of those days. When I call Mrs Brazier back, she is not very happy. Actually she's mightily pissed off. I've never met her, but I understand she's a fairly abrasive kind of woman, who looks after her horses barely adequately. That's to say they're never thin enough or manky enough to intervene or call the RSPCA, but absolutely only just. Apparently the mighty Stella has just visited because one of them had ripped itself to shreds on the terrible fencing. And it seems she was unable to stop at just treating the animal. Yes, you've guessed it, she went on to give the delightful Mrs Brazier a large piece of her mind.

'I really *do not* appreciate being told I don't look after my horses properly,' splutters Mrs Brazier most indignantly. 'Nor being threatened by *that woman*...'

'Threatened?' I ask cautiously, thinking *threatened* isn't good at all. 'Um, what exactly do you mean by that, Mrs Brazier?'

And she's off again. I really wish I hadn't asked.

'That vet told me that unless I look after my horses better, she would not be prepared to treat them in the future. She even told me to re-fence my field. Does she think I'm made of money? I told her, by the time I paid your flaming bill, it would be quite some time before I could afford a new fence. I really think I might change to that new vets' that's started up. Perhaps they'll be more appreciative of my custom.'

Nice one, Stella, I think to myself. Why didn't the silly woman just keep her mouth shut, do her job and leave? Mrs Brazier might not mollycoddle her horses, but I know for a fact that there are far worse out there.

Eventually, I pacify her and persuade her not to change vets by offering her Stella's visit on the house. I almost suggest she spend the money on fencing, but decide against it. It seems to take the wind out of her sails, and slightly mollified, she rings off. I decide that I urgently need to talk to accessible-joint-senior-partner Miles, seeing as Beamish seems to be in another world. We can't have Stella charging around like a loose cannon, losing us customers – even if they are like Mrs Brazier.

As it is, the way things turn out, it's me who sees Stella first. She pops back to the practice to pick up some drugs.

All I say to her, rather pointedly is, 'Mrs Brazier phoned in. She wasn't very happy.'

Stella raises her eyebrows, but clearly isn't prepared to discuss the matter with a mere office minion such as myself, which suits me fine too. I'm more than happy to let that little task rest with Miles.

When she leaves, Karina says to me, 'Is she always like that? Only the other vets are all so personable, and Stella doesn't have quite the same manner, does she…'

'You could say that,' I agree, 'but apparently she has amazing surgical powers and all this extraordinary experience that seemingly no one else has.'

Like maybe at bullshitting.

We raise our eyebrows. There's not much else to say.

* * *

Later on, Karina says, 'I know I don't know all the ropes yet, but if you want me to stay on one afternoon so you can visit Agnes, I'd be quite happy to...'

'Thanks,' I say, quite surprised. Actually, that would be good. Really good. At the moment, if I go to the hospital after work, I don't get home until at least 8.30 p.m.

'That would be great. Thanks, Karina.'

So the next afternoon finds me taking her up on her offer, and after lunch I make my way over to Winchester General. It's about a thirty-minute drive, mostly wooded country roads until you get near the town, and I turn my music up loudly, put my foot down and enjoy it.

When I get there, Agnes is sitting up in bed with a little more colour in her pinched cheeks than last time I saw her... I kiss her on the cheek and give her the flowers I brought for her – cornflowers I think they are, mixed with lavender and something else that smells nice. Well, I liked them when I saw them, and Agnes does too, burying her nose in them to inhale their delicate scent.

'How are you feeling?' I ask her.

'Oh, I'm doing fine.' She gives me a small smile. 'Just weak as dishwater. It's a darned nuisance. I hate being laid up like this.'

Now that sounds much more like Agnes.

'Now, Louisa. Tell me how things are at the practice.' That sounds even more like Agnes.

Do I tell her the truth? But then it's pointless not to. This is Agnes we're talking about. She has special powers that enable her to see through absolutely anything.

'It's all absolutely fine,' I say firmly. 'Well, apart from you not being there. Stella managed to upset Mrs Brazier yesterday, but I think I did a reasonable job of pacifying her. And the usual percentage of invoices has been paid, and...'

'How are you coping with Karina there?' asks Agnes quietly.

I sit there blinking. I didn't know she knew.

'Oh, Beamish told me,' she said wearily. 'How he convinced himself it was a good idea is beyond me,' she adds resignedly. 'Sometimes men can be unbelievable. I'm so sorry, dear, that you've had that added pressure too.'

I'm silent, then decide to tell her the truth. 'It *was* a shock at first. I couldn't believe it either, but actually we're extremely civil to each other, and it's okay. She even offered to stay on this afternoon so I could come and see you.'

Agnes raises her eyebrows and says nothing, no doubt impressed with my new powers of tact and diplomacy. But before we can say anything else, both of us spot Marcus, looking very spruced up and carrying a bouquet of flowers. Actually, what really happens is that we both spot this massive elaborately wrapped bouquet making its way towards Agnes, behind which we catch a glimpse of Marcus. Of course, this serves to make my little bunch of flowers look pathetically inadequate.

'Marcus! How lovely! Oh, you shouldn't have...' Agnes looks slightly embarrassed.

'Hello, Marcus,' I say, without much enthusiasm, getting up to leave. 'I better get back to work, Agnes. Don't go overdoing it,' I say to her, just as another visitor arrives.

Gosh, Agnes is popular today. This girl is petite and extremely pretty, like a little Barbie doll with chestnut hair, a button nose and sparkling eyes.

'Oh I'm so glad you've come, darling,' says Agnes, a smile positively lighting up her face, as the Barbie doll flings her arms around her and kisses her lovingly on both cheeks. Radiantly, she turns towards me and Marcus.

'Louisa, Marcus, this is my daughter, Rachel.'

Ah. So this is the famous Rachel... I stand there feeling mousier, dumpier and more inadequate than ever in the combined presence of Marcus, his bouquet and this little bombshell, who smiles brightly at us both and holds out her dainty hand.

Marcus is looking rather silly with his chin nearly on the floor. Get a grip man, I think, watching him. But I don't need anyone else adding to my inadequacies and I leave them.

25

That evening, I catch up with Leonie and Pete. I've invited them for supper and they're actually coming, which is great news because I don't think Pete's been anywhere much lately – apart from to see his therapist. He's doing well, Leo's told me, and is at last receptive to the idea he can be helped. Apparently that's half the battle, she tells me, because until recently, he was pretty much in denial that he had a problem at all. So it's great news all round and knowing that Agnes is on the mend too, my heart feels lighter than in ages.

I've splashed out on a farm shop speciality – steak and mushroom pie – to have with red wine and crusty bread and salad.

Leonie and Pete are both looking better. Less pale and haggard and weighed down with stress, I'm relieved to notice, as they hug me on the doorstep.

'Nice place.' Pete nods approvingly. Gosh. I'd forgotten he hasn't been here before. He's looking trim and slightly tanned.

'Pete, you look really good,' I say. He looks slightly embarrassed.

'Pete's taken up cycling,' says Leonie proudly, by way of explanation. 'Apparently exercise is really helpful if you suffer from depression, so he decided to get a bike.'

Pete's shifting uncomfortably by now, clearly finding the topic of his illness a difficult subject of conversation.

'Used to race as a teenager,' he mumbles.

Oh my golly gosh. So Pete has joined the ranks of the men in Lycra has he? I'll have to watch out for him when Horace and I are on our Sunday morning travels. And I'll have to stop my eyes being drawn to the tightest bits. Ew... this is Pete, after all.

'Come and meet Horace,' I say to Pete, partly to deflect the attention away from his illness and the thought of all that Lycra, and partly because I want to show off my beloved horse.

Pete tells me he's seen quite a bit of Arian, but neither of us mentions Karina directly.

'You called him a two-timing shithead,' I remind him admiringly.

'Did I?' says Pete wonderingly, sounding quite pleased with himself. 'Good.'

* * *

We actually have a good evening in the end. Lower key than in the past, but enjoyable nonetheless. Leo drags them away early.

'Pete needs his sleep at the moment,' she says protectively, and Pete doesn't argue.

Elmer and I stand at the door and watch them go, my dear friends. At least they're sticking together through probably the hardest time either of them has ever known. I can't help but wonder if the same thought has crossed Arian's mind... somehow, this time, I can't imagine it.

26

Suddenly another week's flown by, and it's Saturday again. Horace and I get a soaking while we're ambling through the woods, and then my mobile rings in my pocket. It's Emma.

'Fancy going to see Agnes together this afternoon?' she suggests.

Which is perfect, because I haven't seen Emma properly in ages, because she's spending more and more time with Ben.

But she's a little quiet as we drive to the hospital.

'How's Ben?' I ask, never suspecting for a minute that the fairy tale department that is her love life would be anything other than just that.

'Okay,' she says, with a fraction of her usual enthusiasm. Then nothing.

I wait a while, then ask, 'Is something wrong, Em? Only you don't seem your usual sunny self.'

'I'm fine,' she says tersely. I get the message and back off.

* * *

Agnes is looking better today. Rachel is already sitting at her mother's bedside and they both give me a big smile.

'Hi,' she says. 'It's nice to see you again! Mum's been telling me how you had her whisked away in an ambulance, and how you stepped into the breach at work. Thank you,' she says more soberly. 'I hate to think what might have happened if you hadn't acted so quickly.'

Golly gee. I only did what anyone would have done, which is what I tell her.

Then I remember Emma is standing beside me.

'Emma, this is Rachel, Agnes's daughter. Emma's one of the vets,' I explain to Rachel.

And after that, we're all chattering while Agnes assumes her usual long-suffering expression.

Then Rachel says, a little cautiously, 'Um, why doesn't one of you fill me in on Marcus? Bit of a dish isn't he?'

Her words are like a blow to my stomach and Emma catches my eye. But hold on. I stuffed up with Marcus – I can't blame it all on him. So doesn't he deserve a chance with someone else?

'He's lovely,' I say. 'Very good-looking, yes, as you've no doubt noticed, and charming and a genuine, nice man.'

Emma looks at me oddly. So does Agnes. Rachel sits there beaming.

'Oh, cool!' she says excitedly. 'Only he's asked me out for dinner.'

* * *

When we drive home, this time Emma and I are both quiet. I'm mulling over how I go about becoming a nun and Emma, well, I've absolutely no idea what she's thinking. She's giving nothing away.

'Fancy meeting at the pub?' she asks. 'If I don't get any calls?'

But I shake my head. 'No thanks, Em. Not tonight. I could do with a quiet evening at home to catch up on stuff.'

Besides, I don't feel much like bearing witness to the latest development in Lower Shagford's great romance (Emma and Ben) nor do I feel like risking running into Marcus and stunning Rachel.

I have a pleasant enough evening. I clean Horace's saddle and bridle, do some ironing and eventually settle in front of the TV flicking through every channel half a dozen times before settling for a rerun of *Friends*, with a large glass of wine. And just the one, I think virtuously, instead of the three I would have got through if I'd gone to the pub with Emma.

* * *

I'm woken too early by the phone on Sunday morning. It's Emma, sounding very wobbly and upset. Seems I'm about to find out what was bothering her yesterday.

'Can I come round?' she asks in such a small voice, I can't find it in me to say that actually, no, it's too early and normal people are still in bed snoring.

Five minutes later, she's at my door. I'm still in my pyjamas but I've hurriedly put some coffee on to brew and she comes in looking as though she's been up all night.

'Emma? You look like you've hardly slept a wink... what's wrong, my friend?' I ask her, rather concerned.

She struggles to find the words and then it all comes out in a rush.

'Ben broke up with me.' And she dissolves into tears. I hug her tightly and then get her some tissues. Then I pour her some coffee and make her drink it. When she's calmed down, I make her tell me what's happened. It can't be that serious, not really. After all, I was almost planning my wedding outfit.

'Okay,' I say, now that she's calmer. 'Tell me what happened.'

'It's true,' she says, a picture of abject misery. Then to my surprise, she lifts up her tear-stained face and says, 'If only I'd listened to you, Lou. None of this would have happened. *It's all my fault.*' And she's off again.

Still none the wiser, I put my hand on her arm. 'What is it Em? You still haven't told me what it is.'

'Oh, those stupid texts,' she wails, dissolving again. 'I'm such an idiot. I had to see what Jerome said. I really thought Ben might be about to propose...'

I have to say I did too.

'He asked me why I kept running off. Asked what was so important that it couldn't wait. He told me I was secretive and that he couldn't have a relationship with someone who kept secrets from him. Oh Lou...' Her voice was getting higher and higher. 'He said he really loved me... but... then he said... it was over...'

And she's sobbing her heart out, devastated, her hopes and dreams shattered into tiny pieces. And don't I know how that feels.

'Emma,' I say firmly. 'Stop crying. Look, have some more tissues. Now, listen. If Ben loves you, you need to talk to him and explain you have a problem. A problem you're trying to solve, but you have to tell him the truth. No more fobbing him off, okay?'

She wipes her eyes and looks at me. 'I can't... What if he won't listen to me?'

'Well, you've nothing to lose have you? You can at least try. And the other thing is, I am writing to Jerome today and I'm going to set up a meeting. And come hell or high water, you, my friend, will be there. Get it?'

She looks at me again, and doesn't dare to say no.

'Okay,' she says, in a very subdued little voice. At long last, she's desperate enough to do something.

27

Yet again, I'm glad it's Monday morning. Even though that means Karina. I wonder if Marcus has been on his date with Rachel yet and if he took her to one of those lovely pubs he took me to? Or if he kissed her? On the cheek like he did me or on the lips, I wonder, with a flare of jealousy that I can't ignore.

This morning I do my best Miss Moneypenny hairstyle and I'm wearing my favourite boots with heels. Which, with my smartest, tailored trousers next to Karina's expanding middle, have got to make me look at least a *bit* sylph-like. Anyway, with Zac looking more and more like a permanent fixture, I don't get to do much mucking out these days. And I'm quite enjoying my new image.

Beamish is the next to arrive, smartly dressed as ever in his usual checked shirt and tie, and a waistcoat under his jacket now that it's getting colder.

'Um, Louisa. Jolly good. Just the person I wanted to see actually. Now.'

A feeling of dread descends on me, because I remember the last time he did this and, seconds later, foisted Karina on me.

He clears his throat and looks around while he pontificates

about what he's going to say to me. Then he sits down opposite me and looks at me directly.

'Um, now, tell me honestly,' he says. 'Er, what do you think of, um, Stella?'

Oh my gosh. Shouldn't he be asking one of the vets? Or Agnes? Oh, but she's not here and lucky old me, I am.

'Well...' I start, very cautiously, thinking just how I put into words that while she's a jolly good vet, or so I'm told by all and sundry, when it comes to clients, she's more like a human bulldozer.

'She's a good vet, isn't she? Um, and very, very experienced...' I emphasise. 'But, you know, maybe she could possibly do with just the tiniest bit of well, *coaching*, I suppose you could say, with the customer relations side of things, if you know what I mean?'

I pause, hoping that will be the end of it. Beamish looks at me sideways and nods his head. Then he says, quite succinctly for him, 'Hmmph. Thought that might be the case. Um, have you er, heard anything Louisa?'

'Oh no, no,' I say, shaking my head. 'Well, that is if you don't count Mrs Brazier last week, who was just a little bit unhappy, but I calmed her down, and she was fine, Beamish, so don't worry about that.'

'Hmmph. Er, anything else?' he asks.

Bugger.

'I think it might be best if you have a little chat with Miles,' I suggest, smiling encouragingly at him.

'Miles? Hmmph. Yes, jolly good idea. Good. Well. Thank you, Louisa. You've been, um, jolly helpful.'

He carries on sitting there, then adds, 'Now, about that, um, boy out there...Zac isn't it? Quite a useful little chap I would think...'

'Yes, he is,' I reply, realising it's true.

'Excellent,' says Beamish and with that, he's off, to wait for Miles I presume.

Oops. Sounds like Stella's in the pooh. I wonder exactly what else Beamish has heard? I don't have to wait long to find out. Beamish and Miles both look extremely serious after their little confab and they ask me to call Stella to see if she's able to come in for a meeting later today.

Karina's very quiet this morning.

'You okay?' I ask her. Well, she was nice to me last week, wasn't she?

'Yes, thank you,' she replies, and carries on with the mountain of filing I've given her. Actually, if I wanted to, I could totally abuse my position of authority here and give her the most God-awful jobs I could dream up. So she's quite lucky it's just filing.

So, it's all fun and games here today. Even more so, when Stella appears for her meeting with the mighty joint senior partners, and after a heated exchange, which the closed door fails to muffle, storms out ten minutes later with a face like thunder.

I catch Miles and ask him what's going on. After all, I need to know, now that I'm running this office.

'We had to give her a warning,' he says, 'about how she speaks to the clients. Which is perfectly reasonable in the circumstances.' He sighs unhappily. Poor Miles is not cut out for these little confrontations. 'Then she told us that there was no way she would compromise her standards and keep her professional opinion to herself where a horse's welfare was at stake, and told us, and I quote, "we could poke our lousy job".'

Actually I'd heard that bit. Stella's quite loud. Miles, however, is looking worried. Even though she's been a liability, Stella's eased everyone else's workload no end. Until now.

'So,' he says. 'I'm afraid it's back to square one.'

Oh bloody hell, I'm thinking. I was afraid that was coming. That whole recruitment palaver all over again.

'I hate to ask,' he continues despondently, 'but is there any chance you could unearth Agnes's last advert? Oh, and maybe contact the candidates we never got round to interviewing last time... You never know, one of them might be right for us.'

But he's not sounding convinced. I try to imagine what Agnes would suggest.

* * *

When I go to see Agnes later, the news has reached her ahead of me and I'm most gratified to see that Marcus's super-duper ultra-expensive bouquet has already wilted, while my cheerful little flowers are still going strong.

'I was beginning to wonder about her,' she says knowingly, about Stella. Then she adds, 'Why don't you ask Marcus, Louisa? See if he knows of anyone who's looking for a job.'

I open my mouth and then close it again, like a goldfish. Okay, I will – and no doubt let him make me feel useless as usual. But only because Agnes has asked me to.

'How much longer are they keeping you in?' I ask her, to change the subject. It feels like it's been ages.

'They say at least another week, possibly two. And then they want me resting at home for a good while. But don't worry, Louisa, I'll be back at work as soon as I'm on my feet again.'

'Oh no.' I say it very firmly. 'No, Agnes. You'll do exactly what the doctors tell you. And everything at work will be fine. I'll make sure of that, I promise you.'

I don't know if that reassures her – she lies her head back and sighs.

* * *

I breathe a sigh of relief when I eventually get home to my cottage, which feels like a refuge from the multitude of problems pervading my life at the moment. I want to lock the whole world out, as I brush Elmer's coat – which I never do – and tell her she's lovely, which I absolutely never do. And then I go outside and hug Horace and kiss his nose, and adjust the expensive new rug he's wearing.

But typically, as fate would have it, just a short while later, one of my problems materialises right before me. Emma. And oh... dear... *bugger*... she's with Ben, and they're both looking extremely serious.

'I hope you don't mind, Lou,' she says most apologetically, but with a hint of determination about her. 'But I asked Ben to come with me, so you could tell him that what I'm about to say is true.'

Nice of you to warn me, Em. Just when I was beginning to unwind, too. Oh well, they're here now. Best just get this over with.

'Come inside and I'll put the kettle on.' I give Emma a look and smile at Ben, who has no idea what's going on.

We sit at my table, and Emma explains to Ben that she's addicted to astrology. He looks baffled.

'Horoscopes,' I chip in helpfully, just to make sure he follows. Then I add, 'Ever since her marriage broke up, they've become a crutch and Emma's become utterly reliant on them. Emma is an addict.' I spell it out. 'She knows that, don't you, Emma?'

I give her another look and she glares at me. 'But more importantly, she's doing something about it. Aren't you, Emma?' I look at her again, and this time she nods her head frantically.

'Oh yes. I am, Ben... And I'm not on drugs or anything, I promise you.'

Oh God. I rest my head, which is starting to throb, wearily in my hands. Now why did she have to mention drugs? Ben's looking at her as though she's mad. I'm almost inclined to agree with him.

Eventually, he agrees that they haven't broken up, but says that from here on, she absolutely has to talk to him about it and, more importantly, she has to get some help. In pure desperation, she agrees – I think she'd shave her hair off if Ben asked her to – but, hallelujah, it seems that he's succeeded where my best efforts have failed. I'm very glad when they leave, holding hands, albeit sheepishly.

My life is suddenly going mad, I realise, as I remember my promise to Agnes – now I have to talk to Marcus.

28

Karina's in a very funny mood this morning. Probably hormones. She's bitten my head off already and I daren't let her answer any phones. In fact, she's showing worrying signs of becoming a Stella.

Marcus comes in, looking very chirpy and well, handsome I suppose. Very clean and scrubbed for a vet in the middle of the morning. How come he's so late? And looking so chipper?

'Ah, Marcus,' I say in my best Miss Moneypenny voice. *I really need some of those tiny glasses so that I can peer provocatively over the top of them at him... Hmmm... And maybe a tight skirt or a different hairstyle.*

'Yes, Louisa?' He waits patiently for me to stop my mental ramblings.

'Ah, yes,' I say, suddenly remembering what I wanted to talk to him about. 'Well, you know we're going to need another vet, well, I was talking to Agnes about it and, well...'

He's starting to look less patient.

'She wondered if you knew anyone who might be interested?' I finish brightly. And preferably male, good-looking and single would be good too.

'Actually I might,' he says thoughtfully. 'Leave it with me – I'll make a couple of calls.'

And I resign myself to the fact that Marcus will undoubtedly dredge up an uber-glamorous she-vet or two, just to make me feel more inadequate than ever.

'How's Rachel by the way?' I say to his retreating back.

He stiffens slightly but pretends he didn't hear me. Moments later, I hear the Land Cruiser roar off out of the yard. But, true to his word, he calls later and asks me to pass on a message to Beamish and Miles.

'Mate of mine from Cirencester,' he says. 'Chap called Will Farley. Says he's looking for a change, so can you give them his number for me?'

Will Farley... Sounds dreamy... I bet he's tall and dark... athletic rather than muscular, quite serious and deeply, disturbingly sexy... It's amazing how much you can tell just from a name. I have a feeling this Will Farley is going to be most interesting.

My attention is soon drawn back to Karina, however, who looks mightily pissed off. In the end I ask her what on earth is the matter, if nothing else because she's creating a really bad atmosphere.

'Karina? Obviously there's something wrong, so why don't you tell me what it is? You never know, maybe I can help?' I say doubtfully.

She snorts derisively at me, which rather takes me aback. After all, I'm genuinely trying to help the girl...

'Oh, I suppose HE'll tell you sooner or later so I may as well fill you in,' she says bitterly. 'I chucked Arian out.'

Oh God. *Not again.*

'What happened *this* time?' I ask, a little wearily. Cancel all aspirations about seducing Will Farley. It's honestly far simpler to be single.

'He's useless,' she says heatedly. 'Unsupportive, unhelpful, un-anything else you can think of...' she says angrily.

'Like unfaithful?' I suggest. She ignores me.

'He doesn't understand that I'm working too, even though I'm not flying. He treats my job here like something I do for fun. He has no idea how tired I get, and expects me to do his washing and cook supper every night.' Then she looks at me.

'I can't believe I'm talking to you, of all people, like this,' she says, shaking her head with disbelief. 'You should hate me.'

Truth is, I honestly don't. I'm fully cleansed and abluted of all carnal feelings towards Arian. Have been for ages, as I told Marcus. It's hardly my fault if no one believes me.

'Karina. It truly doesn't bother me in the slightest, you talking like this. More than anything else, I think I understand better than *anyone* what you're talking about, don't I?'

She thinks, then giggles. 'This is weird.'

It is. Deeply weird. 'The trouble is, you and Arian are the parents of that baby you're carrying. Isn't it worth at least *trying* to make him understand? To see things from your point of view? Believe me, it's never been one of his strengths, but you'd be doing him an enormous favour – even if you do still break up with him...'

She says stroppily, 'I'll think about what you've said. But I'm too angry at the moment.'

Then she adds, 'Thanks.'

'You're welcome.'

* * *

It's almost as though Agnes is back in residence as miraculous things start happening all over the place and a tall, muscly and extremely attractive man wanders into our office.

'Hi,' he says loudly, in broad American. 'I'm Will. Will Farley.

Old mate of Marcus. I was just passing, so I thought I'd call in and introduce myself.'

Oh. Wow. Just this once, I'll ignore that 'just passing' line that usually has me spitting blood. This man is drop dead gorgeous. I was right, wasn't I? I just knew he'd be handsome. Okay, so the dark, athletic part was a bit out, but who cares? And that accent...

'I'm Louisa,' I say, holding my stomach in and giving him my most beaming smile.

'Oh, and that's Karina over there,' I say, nodding in her direction. It's absolutely pointless *her* trying to hold her stomach in. Ha. But she doesn't need to, because even pregnant, she's stunning.

Will positively beams at us. 'Gee. Great to meet you both. Hey, do you know if Beamish is around? Or Miles isn't it, the other guy?'

'I'll find out for you,' I say, being very efficient and determined to make a good first impression. I call Miles on his mobile and tell him that Will's here about the job. It turns out that Miles is already on his way, so I relay this back to Will.

'Hey,' he says. 'That's cool. Okay if I wait here with you?'

Karina and I look at each other and shrug. Her cheeks have flushed the most delicate shade of pink, making her even lovelier than ever.

'Of course,' we reply in unison. How could we possibly object to this gorgeous American brightening up our little office.

'Say, how did you two get to be working here?' he asks jovially. Just being friendly. We tell him, and explain about Agnes.

'So do you guys go out after work then?' he asks.

'Some of us,' I say, just as Karina says clearly, 'No.'

Will raises his eyebrows at us.

Karina looks at me and seems to be trying not to giggle again. She's definitely in an odd mood today.

'Just tell him, Louisa. That I'm pregnant with *our* ex's baby...' and with that she screams with laughter and collapses on her desk.

'Don't worry about her,' I say calmly. 'It's probably just a mood swing. She's hormonal.'

But Will's looking highly amused by now. And he's obviously intrigued.

'Holy cow,' he says. 'You girls share an ex?' His eyes are like saucers.

Holy shit, I think. He better not go getting any weird ideas about me and Karina. Things are already weird enough.

'Yes,' I say firmly. 'One Arian Mulholland, serial philanderer and misunderstander of all women, especially pregnant ones.'

Will's tickled. 'Gee,' he says, grinning widely. 'This Arian guy sounds a real card. I'd like to meet him!' Then he adds, his eyes lighting up, 'Say, do you guys come as a pair?'

I think this is the point when, looking at my expression, he realises he might have pushed his luck a tad too far, because he rapidly adds, 'Hey, just kidding...'

Fortunately for him, Miles arrives in the nick of time, and Will hotfoots it out of the office to meet him. Shortly after, there's the sound of another car pulling up outside. A Land Cruiser, I do believe. Marcus.

29

As Karina correctly predicted, it took Arian just two days before he turned up on my doorstep. Again.

'To what do I owe this unexpected surprise?' I say, utterly unsurprised to see him there.

Give him his due, he does look quite dejected.

'Can I come in?' he asks. 'Only I think I could do with some advice.'

Blimey. I'm beginning to wish everyone would keep their problems to themselves – or else I should charge.

I look at my watch. 'You can have twenty minutes,' I tell him. 'Then I'm going out.' Ha. Good thinking. I'm not, of course, but he doesn't know that. Maybe that's the way to play it. Allocate all of them twenty minutes, then chuck them out.

'Karina's thrown me out,' he says miserably.

'I know,' I say. 'And to be honest, Arian, I don't blame her.'

Instead of trying to bluff, he sighs. Maybe he's finally getting the message that as far as women are concerned, he really is worse than useless. I do feel just a tiny bit sorry for him – after all, he doesn't seem able to get very much right at the moment.

'You know,' I say, 'perhaps if you were to try and understand what Karina's going through, you might be a little more tolerant and considerate. Like, do you know that she has terrible indigestion? And that if she stands for too long her ankles swell? And that carrying the baby means her body is working twice as hard as usual? She gets tired, Arian, in a way you've never experienced, even after a whole week of night flights.'

I let my words sink in and give him plenty of time, because after all, this is Arian we're talking about. Then I carry on.

'What Karina needs is someone to take the load off her. To do the ironing, the shopping and the cooking... help with the housework and make her peppermint tea, which she can drink while she sits with her feet up to stop her ankles swelling, and who tells her how radiantly beautiful she looks, even though she just feels fat and whale-like... She is beautiful, Arian. You should tell her.'

'Oh. You think so?' He sits there looking perplexed. 'Anything else?'

'Talk to Karina,' I say firmly. 'Not me. You're with her now, remember?'

I make a point of looking at my watch, and fortunately he takes the hint.

As he leaves, I ask, 'How's Pete?' and to my surprise he smiles.

'He's good,' he says. 'We're spending more time together. He says he's starting to feel better.'

So Pete's crawling out of his depression. I am so pleased to hear that. It's been worth putting up with Arian just to hear that.

'Bye, Arian,' I say firmly. 'Go and talk to Karina, before she's whisked off her feet by the sexiest American that ever was.'

That got him. His face looks thunderous.

'Thanks,' he mutters at me, and shambles off.

* * *

'Whatever did you say to Arian last night?' Karina asks me as she comes into the office the next morning.

'Oh, not much,' I say airily. 'Why? Did he come grovelling back with his tail between his legs?'

'Actually, he didn't so much grovel, as come in with a car load of food shopping muttering about peppermint tea and how I really ought to put my feet up when I get back from work. By the way, I can't stand peppermint tea, Louisa. And he's bought packets of it. Would you like some?'

Then she adds, 'He also muttered something about a sexy American. You wouldn't happen to know where he got that idea from, would you?'

'I can't imagine,' I say innocently and quickly give her a mountain of filing.

So, bliss is restored in that household, at least temporarily. I wouldn't bet on it lasting.

Will Farley is indeed our new vet. After our dodgy start, I decide that he's harmless enough and he works hard, which is exactly what we need. Paris's man-radar is fully activated and she duly appears, sporting newly Titian hair and emerald green contacts, which make her eyes look like a cat's. She leans decoratively against Will's car, eyeing him sideways as she pretends to smooth the non-existent wrinkles in her jodhpurs.

'Are you the new vet?' she lisps coyly, her lips pouting as she looks at him. 'Only I'm Paris. I live just up the lane.'

Will just stands there and gawps. I give him a warning look.

'Say hello nicely to Paris, Will. And then come inside please. I need to give you some addresses.'

Will still doesn't manage to speak, but tears himself away to follow me in.

'What a honey,' he eventually manages, looking completely gobsmacked.

'Will,' I say sternly. 'She's a sixteen-year-old nympho and does that to all the new vets. Now, I don't know what rules you go by where you come from, but she is most definitely underage and off limits. Now get a grip and concentrate.'

* * *

Will and Marcus are very good mates, it turns out. No doubt they'll be double dating with Barbie-doll Rachel and one of her teeny-tiny girlfriends. I can imagine it – two big husky vets and their dainty dolly birds, going to all those lovely hidden-away pubs that Marcus knows where to find. It's so not fair.

Thank God Karina isn't tiny. I'd end up changing my name to Louisa the Blob – which rolls off the tongue rather too easily. And *I* wouldn't mind going on a date with the husky American. I wonder if they kiss differently to English men...

And that evening, Will actually does ask me out. Be very careful what you wish for, Louisa Mulholland. I'm forgetting about the strange and powerful magic we have round here. All I'd done was think it would be nice to go on a date with Will, and abracadabra... here I am on a date with Will.

Will drives an awfully nice great big Toyota. It's twice as big as Marcus's Land Cruiser and very swanky with electric absolutely everything including heated seats, he tells me with one of his overly suggestive looks. He's a complete tart. I'm starting to wonder, just a tiny bit, why these men have to drive such enormous and impressive cars – after all, you know what they say.

We spend a lively evening at the Swan and Tadpole, which I've never been to before. It wouldn't be Marcus's kind of pub at all. There's live music and I soon find out that Will fancies himself as a bit of a groover. He's not half bad actually, and so we whirl around for a while to Danny Devonshire's Rock and Rollers, which is jolly good fun and quite exhausting.

Then, when we sit down for a rest, he starts asking questions again. Is insatiable curiosity an American quirk, or is he just nosy?

'Say, you must know Marcus quite well then,' he starts in that gorgeous accent which I could listen to for hours. 'He talks about you one hell of a lot.' Then he frowns. 'Seems he don't have so much time for this Arian guy you were talking about...'

I smirk. 'They don't really know each other,' I say, 'but let's just say they got off to a bad start.'

Meaning they'd like to lock horns or stamp on each other's heads.

'So, does Marcus have a girl?' he asks innocently.

'I believe he's seeing Rachel,' I say. 'Tiny, beautiful... daughter of Agnes...'

'Oh.' Will looks confused. I think maybe American men are even slower on the uptake than English ones.

'Well, I guess you should know, babe...'

I'm flummoxed. Is or isn't Marcus dating Rachel... and if not, why not?

Will and I actually get on really well. I still think he's incredibly good-looking, in a large, slightly oafish way though. Something about him reminds me of a fair-haired Jeremy Clarkson – with more hair – and his personality is scarily similar too. Only there's one major snag, which is nothing either of us can do a thing about. And that's chemistry. He's like a big kid, larking and joking around; pulling my leg like I'm his little sister. This bonhomie continues in the office, and it's not long before we get noticed.

'Bit cosy aren't we?' Karina's the first to comment. Slightly archly, but she's obviously curious. 'You and Will? Could he be the man of your dreams?'

She and Arian seemed to have reached a new understanding

and I think she'd love that, for me to meet *the one*, as then my threat level would be reduced to zero. Even though I am no threat at all, even in my current incarnation as a sad single person.

Beamish too makes his characteristic fumbled attempt at giving our non-existent union his blessing.

'All I'd like to say is, um, yes, well, I'd be very happy... Yes, most happy indeed...' I assume he's talking about Will and me?

Even Mrs Boggle notices. 'Oh dear, are wedding bells in the air, Louisa? I always cry at weddings I'm afraid,' she tells me unhappily, the corners of her mouth already quivering in anticipation. I hasten to reassure her that she is way off the mark.

'Actually, you've got it completely wrong,' I say. 'He's more like a brother than anything else.'

'Oh, dear, that's such a shame,' says Mrs Boggle.

Honestly, there's just no pleasing some people.

***

Conversation with Marcus is minimal, sadly. If we meet, we're terribly polite, talking about the weather or Elmer, once we run out of work-related stuff. He's impossible to read, but then he's a man. Chances are even he doesn't know what he's thinking.

30

Absolutely the best, most fantastic news ever. Agnes is out of hospital! I can't wait to see her and I intend to give her a very stern lecture about resting properly and not overdoing things.

I ask Beamish where Agnes is staying. He huffs and puffs more than ever – then he tells me.

'Um, Louisa. Yes. Um. Well. Um...' which goes on for about five minutes or so, with a few 'jolly goods' thrown in for good measure, until he actually manages to stutter out that 'Um well, thought she shouldn't be on her own.'

I have to say I'm mystified. So she hasn't gone home, but he still hasn't told me exactly where she *is* staying. With Rachel maybe?

'So where exactly is Agnes?' I ask, very patiently, knowing that the way things are going this may take a while.

He clears his throat. 'With me,' he mutters quietly under his breath.

I do a double take. 'Oh, that's such an awfully good idea,' I say, trying to look completely un-astonished. 'Yes. Um. Very good indeed.'

Beamish nods his head and carries on looking at the ground.

'Um, would it be okay with you, Beamish, if I, er, just popped over to see her? I promise I won't be there too long...' I shake my head to reassure him.

'Um, yes, jolly good idea,' he says. 'Um.'

* * *

'I rather imagine the cat's out of the bag now,' says Agnes when I call round to see her. She's looking tons better, and is putting on a bit of weight at last too.

I rather imagine it is.

'I don't know what you mean,' I say, a model of tact, such as I am these days. 'After all, here you are, just staying with a very good friend until you're better. What's to know?'

Agnes fixes me with a look that I haven't seen in a very long time.

'Beamish and I,' she says, quietly and deliberately, 'have been having a relationship for ten years. I think we've done quite a good job of keeping it a secret – until now,' she adds ruefully.

'But why, Agnes?' I ask her.

'What, why Beamish, or why the secrecy?' Then she laughs at my expression. 'Oh, Louisa, I'm no spring chicken. It suited us both that way. But the funny thing is, well, since I've been ill, it's made both of us view our friendship differently. I've realised that I'm not immortal and Beamish has had quite a scare. So we've made a decision.'

When she looks at me, her eyes are quite misty. 'You have to promise to keep this to yourself, just for a day or two. I haven't even told Rachel yet, but she's coming over later today so I will do. But, Louisa, dear – Beamish has only asked me to marry him!'

'*Oh Agnes!*' is all I can say. How lovely, lovely, lovely. I swoop over and hug her as tight as I can without hurting her.

'It's truly wonderful news,' I say, a tear in my own eyes by now. 'If that's what you both want, I think it's completely fantastic. Congratulations!'

'Thank you,' she says, looking a little overwhelmed by my response. Agnes is not used to being the centre of attention, but she's going to have to get used to it. I mean, she's got a wedding to plan, a dress to choose, an enormous guest list to compile, oh and invitations, and there'll be all eyes on her on the big day...

'Louisa, we're planning just a *tiny* wedding,' she says warningly. Sometimes I think Agnes knows how my imagination works better than I do. 'Just a handful of close family and friends – and that's all,' she adds firmly.

'But, Agnes,' I can't help butting in. 'You can't! You and Beamish have so many people who would want to be there to wish you well.'

'Louisa,' she says, persuasively. 'We will have a big party, don't you worry. Maybe you could even help me to plan it? And Rachel too? Your organisational skills, after all, have somewhat come into their own, whereas mine... well, let's just say I'm a little out of practice.'

Wow. I beam at her. 'Agnes, I'd be honoured.' And I would, even though teeny-tiny Rachel makes me look the size of a house.

It's terribly difficult keeping such an exciting secret to myself when I get back to work. Karina gives me very odd looks, and eventually asks me why I've got such ants in my pants. I'm sure she thinks it's to do with Arian. She's terribly suspicious.

Eventually I spot Beamish out in the yard, so I shoot outside and catch him on his own.

'Agnes told me,' I whisper excitedly. 'It's so exciting, Beamish. I just wanted to say *congratulations*,' I add, kissing him on the cheek.

He puffs his chest out and looks highly embarrassed. 'Um. Thank you, Louisa. Yes, well, um...'

Marcus knows instantly that something's up, which is quite illuminating given that he's a man. In between discussing this complicated case with Miles, he gives me very questioning looks. Miles is completely unaware, being totally oblivious to anything unhorsy and clearly having higher things on his mind. He's looking upset again, which can only mean one thing. A horse in need. And exactly which horse that is, I'm just about to find out.

'What's wrong Miles?' I ask, if only because he looks as though he's about to tell me anyway.

'Don't suppose you'd like some company for old Horace?' he says glumly, looking a lot like Eeyore. 'Only it's Mrs Winkle's Wurzel. She's got to go into hospital and she's got no one to have him for her. She's worrying herself sick about him,' he adds dejectedly.

Then he adds, 'It won't cost you. You can have all her hay...'

'What's wrong with her?' I ask, hoping it's not serious. I like Mrs Winkle. She's a sweet old lady and always makes us the most delicious Christmas cake.

'Cancer,' says Miles, and sighs. My blood chills in my veins. 'Not quite sure how serious yet. That's why she's going into hospital.'

Oh bugger. I *can't* say no. And actually, I don't mind. Not at all. Wurzel's a small, elderly Welsh Mountain pony and I know he won't be any trouble. And I'm sure it's only a rumour that he's good at climbing out of fields and going off adventuring.

'Okay,' I say. 'Of course I will, Miles. Please tell Mrs Winkle I'd love to have him.'

'Tell you what,' he says. 'Why don't you come with me to pick him up?'

***

We go the next day and I'm quite shocked. Poor Mrs Winkle's not looking at all well. She was never big, but she looks shrunken and her skin looks too big for her. Whatever it is has clearly made her lose a lot of weight. She offers us a cup of tea, so we follow her into her kitchen, which is sparsely furnished but immaculately clean, and she produces one of her cakes.

We sit there eating the huge slices she cuts for us – and it's delicious – only I have to admit I'm not enjoying it. I've a horrible feeling and it gets worse when she fetches Wurzel from the paddock at the end of her garden, then pauses for a moment and hands his lead rope to me.

'Thank you so much for having him,' she says to me. There's a tear in her eye. 'I can't tell you what a relief it is to know he'll be cared for. He's a little darling and taught all my grandchildren to ride. He's old you know, but tough as old boots.'

She stands there stroking the furry little neck and pats his shoulder for ages.

When we load him in the horsebox, the way she says goodbye to him, I wonder if there's something she's not saying. And as Miles pulls out of her driveway, I turn and wave out of the window, and she's just standing there, at the side of the lane, looking small and frightened and alone.

* * *

It's just two days later when Mrs Boggle starts on one of her favourite subjects and drops a bombshell.

'She's dead, duckie. Didn't no one tell you?' Making all these tutting noises as she heads for the men's loo with her bucket and mop.

'Now hold on a moment,' I say, rather alarmed. 'Just exactly who are you talking about here, Mrs Boggle?' My blood running cold as instantly I think of Agnes.

'Mrs Winkle, lovey. Only bin and gone and died, inn't she.'

Oh, poor, poor Mrs Winkle. I can't believe it... I only saw her two days ago. And gosh. It strikes me that I've just inherited an escapologist of a Welsh Mountain pony.

* * *

While on the one hand, everyone is celebrating the fact that Beamish and Agnes are getting married, the edge is most definitely taken off things by the death of poor Mrs Winkle. Miles and I go to her funeral, which is a simple service in the village church. Black rather suits Miles, who's more long-faced even than the coffin-bearers. However, in spite of the sadness, the sun shines brightly and it's the most gloriously sunny day for early November. It's a fitting tribute to Mrs Winkle, because she loved the countryside and today it's at its radiant, autumnal best for her. Loads of people turn out to bid her farewell and the little church is packed. I leave a simple bunch of daisies outside the church with the other more elaborate flowers, and a note:

Wurzel and I will miss you, Mrs Winkle, Louisa x

31

Karina's become enormous. I'm beginning to wonder if she's having twins... or triplets maybe... Golly! How funny would that be. It would freak Arian out completely! But, on a more serious note, I have to admit I actually like her... and feel for her a little bit too. After all, the poor girl is massively eight months pregnant and can't walk any more – she waddles. And she's all but hitched to the loser that used to be my husband.

Work is busy as ever, but when I get home in the evenings, things can sometimes be fairly exciting too. It's dark now by the time I finish at the practice. Usually I switch on my torch and go out to the paddock to check my horses. Note the plural... Horace, bless his heart, always nickers as soon as he even hears me and just follows me into his stable. He's more darling than ever. Wurzel *usually* just follows along behind. But last night... Well, there was Horace, reliably in the same place as always, patiently waiting for me, but there was no sign of Wurzel anywhere. I put Horace to bed, then traipsed around every inch of the field with Elmer. There was no Wurzel to be seen. Not anywhere.

I ended up walking all around the village before I eventually found him, feasting contentedly in the allotments, the little blighter. Oh yes, I can safely say that there's absolutely nothing wrong with Wurzel's night vision. He'd homed in on Mr Jones's prize carrots no problem, and Mrs Percy's cabbages and God knows what else. I didn't like to look as I sneaked him out. But he did leave rather a lot of hoof prints all over those precious vegetable gardens and everyone must have heard us clip-clopping up the road. And there aren't *that* many ponies round here, not ponies with reputations like Wurzel has.

Then at work this morning, round about elevenses time, Rachel pitches up.

'Hi, Rachel,' I say. 'You looking for Marcus? Only he's out for the rest of the day.'

I carry on whirling around looking very busy, but out of the corner of my eye I notice that she's frowning, and then she says, 'Er no. Actually I wanted to see you. About Mum's wedding.'

Oh gosh. Stupid Louisa. I stop whirling and give her my full attention.

'Isn't it just the best news?' I say.

'Yes, it's great,' she says warmly. 'And Mum was wondering if you could help us with the planning? You probably know they don't want anything too fancy, but it's still special. So... what do you say? Should we get together and see what we can come up with?'

'Okay,' I say, slightly cautiously. Then add, 'Of course. I'd love to help, Rachel. If you want me to.'

And I mean it, I'm just wondering if Marcus will be 'helping' too.

* * *

Next morning, I say to Karina, 'Isn't it about time you gave up work? You don't want one of the vets forced into practising their midwifery skills on you – or do you?'

She raises her eyebrows and looks most put out. 'Are you trying to get rid of me, Louisa?' she says in peeved tones.

'Don't be silly,' I say. 'Of course I'm not. But that baby could appear at any time now. And shouldn't you be putting your feet up and taking it easy?'

Isn't that what you're supposed to do when you're about to have a baby?

'In case you haven't noticed,' she replies a bit testily. 'I am actually quite useful here. I do loads of things in this office which you don't have time to do. What will you do when I stop?'

About the furthest I think ahead at the moment is to the end of each day and she's absolutely right. Karina has ended up working much more than just mornings now and she's become quite useful. There's going to be far too much for just me to do, once this baby arrives.

'We'll need to get a temp,' I say decisively, in my best office manager voice. 'To do mornings, like when you started.'

Karina's silent for a moment, then she says carefully, 'Have you thought about asking Zac? You said yourself, he's a whiz with computers, and I'm sure you could teach him the ropes... You taught me after all, didn't you?'

Golly. Zac the chav? Well, it's certainly a thought. I can't say I'm ecstatic about the idea, but at least if things were quiet, he could bugger off outside and hang out with Sam like he does at the moment.

'Maybe,' I say. 'Perhaps I'll run it by Beamish first. It might work,' I add, not sounding convinced.

Silly me. I just don't learn do I? Yes, I mention to Beamish about Karina's idea about Zac, and instantly Beamish and Zac are standing here in front of me waiting to discuss it. Just like that. As if by that magic again.

Though I have to say that Zac doesn't look too convinced either.

'Wotcha do in 'ere, then,' he asks indifferently.

Beamish clears his throat and steps in to the rescue.

'This, my fine young man, is the nerve centre of our veterinary practice. And Louisa is right at the heart of it.' He coughs and looks at me expectantly.

Oh golly. Am I? Then I feel a flicker of pride as I realise that actually, I am.

'And your, um, job, if you'd like it, would be in the, um, mornings, helping with the, er, organisational side of things. You know, like sending out the bills, putting everything where we can find it.'

'Filing, Beamish,' I interrupt efficiently. 'It's, um, actually called filing you know.'

Beamish looks baffled for a minute. 'Um, er, is it? Well, bless me...'

Then he carries on. 'And what I, um, thought, young man, is that if you, er, start studying for your, um, you know, veterinary nursing exams, we'll give you the time off for your course, as long as you er, do a bit of hard work for us in return.' He fixes twinkling eyes on Zac, who looks as though he's been zapped with a cattle prod.

'And who knows...' Beamish is still twinkling most jovially '... at the end of it, there may even be a job going. So. Um. Jolly good.'

'Blimey,' says Zac incredulously. 'Fanks, sir, really fanks. I'll make you well proud...'

Beamish is nodding and smiling like a proud grandfather.

'I've no doubt you will, my boy. Now, um, run along and give, er, Sam a hand, there's a good chap.'

Oh dear God... whatever next? We could have Mrs Boggle assisting in the operating theatre perhaps. Or maybe I could go out on calls while Beamish and Agnes go on their honeymoon, with a spare vet bag and a really big car. Hmmm. I'm beginning to wonder if Beamish is losing the plot.

I catch up with Emma that night and fill her in about Zac.

'That's brilliant, Lou. If Beamish didn't give him the chance, Zac would probably end up back at that ghastly housing estate, living with the evil stepfather who beats him up and who poisoned Beckham. Beamish has thrown him a lifeline. And he's good with animals... there's no reason why he wouldn't make a great vet nurse.'

I'm still thinking, that yes, it might be jolly good and all that, but it's me who'll have to train him in the office, as I tell her.

'I've just trained Karina. She's really useful and now she's leaving,' I moan. 'And now I've got to do it all again.'

Emma stares at me. 'You didn't even want Karina, remember? So presumably you won't mind that she's leaving. And you'll have to train someone. So, it may as well be Zac.'

My friend can be *so* unsympathetic.

'How are things with Ben?' I ask, switching the spotlight from me to her. Ha. That will fix her. But Emma's very cool.

'Good thanks. He came to see Jerome with me.'

I nearly fall off my chair. 'He what?' I splutter.

'Don't look like that, Louisa,' she says. 'Actually, Ben's being most supportive, and we really are getting back on track.'

I know he took her phone away and made her buy a new one with a new number, so none of the texted horoscopes could sort-of accidentally on purpose get through – I had to circulate the new number to everyone at work under the pretext that she'd dropped her old one down the loo.

'That's really good, Em,' I say. 'I'm so pleased for you... And well done for dealing with your gremlins,' I add for good measure. 'Shall we go and get some fish and chips?'

Perfect timing. The chippy closes in ten minutes. It's run by Gilda, a bohemian-looking girl who has the most admirable attitude and incredible shiny black hair, which reaches in waves all the way down to her rather ample backside. It must be a nightmare washing the deep-fried smell out every night. Her eye make-up is a piece of artwork, and I can never stop myself studying it while we wait for our fish and chips.

The food is the exact same version that they sell in the pub, but cheaper. Plus it comes in these rather pretty boxes. But the best bit is that when it gets to closing time, she screeches out at the top of her voice, 'Closin',',... then waits for a few seconds, then says, 'Now,' pronounced 'Noo'. Then she slams the window shut, and sits, filing her nails which are as amazingly painted as her eyelids, as all the starving masses exit the pub having waited all evening for the cheaper version of the fish and chips. She delights in telling them that they shouldn't be so tight and 'It ain't my fault loverrr, it's yours innit,' and how they should have got their arses over earlier on, because she has a licence and no customer ain't worth breaking no rules over.

Tonight we're in good time, and she serves us without any objection, except to tell us that if we'd been any later, we'd have been shit out of luck. Emma and I go and sit across on the green, and wait to laugh at all the customers who are about to find that they are indeed 'shit out of luck', as Gilda so eloquently puts it.

I tell Emma about the exploits of Wurzel, and she giggles. 'I had a pony that was like that,' she says. 'It didn't matter how many volts you rigged up to the electric fence, somehow or other he got out.'

Which doesn't give me a good feeling. But tonight little Wurzel stays put. Or maybe he's much cleverer than I give him credit for and he sneaks out in the middle of the night, but comes home before I wake up. Only I know as well as everyone else – ponies aren't that clever.

32

Karina's had a brilliant idea which I should definitely have thought of first.

'Why doesn't Zac work alongside me for a few days?' she suggests. 'Then, when I disappear, he'll already know some of what I've been doing to help you.'

Which sounds like a jolly good idea.

'And by the way, Karina, have you decided when you are finishing yet?'

'Well,' she says. 'I thought the end of the week, if that's okay. On Friday...' she clarifies.

I know when the end of the week is. Just because I'm not a pilot doesn't mean I'm stupid.

'Oh,' I say, then, 'You teaching Zac, that's a good idea. Thanks.'

* * *

Miles and Beamish are having one of their little confabs in Beamish's office. I'm straining my ears to listen, but they're talking in low voices. It's not at all like when they had Stella in there. That time, I could hear every word. Mind you, so could the whole of Lower Shagford.

Oh, the door's opening.

'Leave it with me, old chap,' Beamish is saying. 'Um, don't worry. Er, I'm sure we'll think of something.'

How mysterious. Miles looks even more down in the mouth than usual. What could it possibly be?

'Er, Miles?' I say, once Beamish has gone. Very cautiously because he is looking rather fragile, I ask, 'Are you okay? Only you seem, well, a little...' I'd been going to say *troubled*, but instead I settle for 'well, just a *little* out of sorts...'

He gives me what for Miles passes for a smile. I give him one of my most understanding smiles in response. He's definitely one of life's worriers, is Miles. Takes on the cares of the world. What he needs, I've decided, is a thoroughly good woman to make a fuss of him and love him absolutely to bits. But if Emma is to be believed, he can never bring himself to be interested in them. Which is to say, of course he likes them, but puts so much energy into his work, there's none left for anyone else. He needs to meet another vet as dedicated as he is, so they could exchange worries, shed the odd tear together, agonise over their more worrying cases... Or maybe not. It would probably make him worse.

Then I have this great idea. Miles needs some fun. I will enlist Emma's help on this one and, between us, we will take him out and make him laugh. Golly. Suddenly I'm stunned to realise that I've never, *ever* seen Miles laugh. Not once, which is deeply disturbing. Not laughing is like not drinking. I don't know how anyone can possibly survive like that. It *can't* be normal. And actually, I'm starting to wonder if maybe he's yet another example of one of these jolly fine young men, forging ahead in the career of his choosing, only to reach the pinnacle and get knocked viciously off it by the black dog itself – depression. Like Pete. The very thought makes me shiver.

Meanwhile, I have my own black dog to attend to. She may be demanding, as she is right now, howling like a wolf in the stables as she waits for a lunchtime walk, but at least she doesn't completely ruin my life.

* * *

With Karina's baby imminent, I decide to organise a card for everyone to sign, and buy her a present. I add it to my growing to-do list. I'll have to go shopping after work tonight. Late-night shopping somewhere after I've dealt with my horses. Maybe Emma will come along too.

But Emma is cosily ensconced with Ben tonight. It seems that all is back to normal on that front. Do I dare to start thinking about my wedding outfit yet?

So I'm on my own in Marks & Spencer, looking at the cutest little baby clothes I've ever seen. Kind of pretty and cuddly-looking, in the most gorgeous array of colours. There are all these little blankets, the softest you've ever touched, oh, and the toys. I didn't even know there were toys for newborns.

It's a whole new world to me and I have to admit to the teeniest bit of envy, when I think about what lies ahead for Karina. I mean, a baby... Isn't that the reason we're put on this earth after all? To go forth and multiply? Maybe some of us more than others.

Whatever happens between Karina and Arian, she'll have her baby to nurture and care for and give the best of herself to. She'll be a mother. I'm not at all sure how Arian will cope with that, playing second fiddle while it's tiny. Knowing my ex, I see trouble looming.

I wonder if I'll ever have children? And then I decide that actually, I will, even if I have to go and bribe some fine specimen of manhood like Will for his sperm, so that I can artificially inseminate myself. And actually, wouldn't it be a whole lot easier to have just the children and no husband? And I can't imagine Will would take too much bribing. It's certainly a thought.

* * *

I awake in the middle of the night certain that I can hear the faint clip-clop of hooves, but when I lie there listening, there's nothing. And next morning, Wurzel's grazing harmlessly in his paddock – but, who's that marching up the lane? Oh. It's Mr Jones. Not looking happy at all.

He knocks on my door and I open it, mystified as to why he's here.

'Morning, Mr Jones, how are you this morning?' I ask brightly.

'Now look 'ere. Right sorry, miss, but it's that dang pony out back. It's bin in my carrots again. Little bustart pulled 'em all up by the green and ate the 'ole flaming lot.'

And from behind his back he produces a handful of carrot tops that some creature has indeed eaten the bottoms of. Some creature, and quite a clever one at that, which has left very horse-like teeth marks behind.

'But, Mr Jones,' I say soothingly, 'it can't possibly have been Wurzel. Look. He's out in the paddock, just where I left him last night, though thinking about it, I woke up at some point and heard hooves. But it can't have been Wurzel. Like I said, he's been in that paddock all night. It must have been someone else's horse...'

"E's that Mrs Winkle's pony, isn't he, God rest her,' says Mr Jones, most disbelievingly. 'I know 'im. 'E's a regular 'Oudini that one. You mark my words. It were 'im all right.'

After Mr Jones has left, I go out to my horses. Wurzel's little ears are pricked and he's a picture of innocence. But wait a moment. There's something on his headcollar. It looks ever so slightly like a bit of carrot top. I stare at Wurzel, and those unblinking brown eyes look knowingly back at mine. Just a touch too knowingly. Maybe Mr Jones was right after all and the little sod goes out for midnight jaunts, getting home before anyone's the wiser. Mr Jones is obviously no fool. Quickly, I remove the evidence and grind it into the mud.

* * *

Karina is making fine progress with Zac. He's razor sharp and remembers everything she tells him straight away. I had a devil of a job with her to start with, but then I suppose she had pregnancy-brain at the time. And as far as all things computer-related go, Zac is quite clearly a whiz – which gives me an idea. Seeing as he's so chummy with Beamish, maybe he'd like to suggest to him that it's about time our office ditched our ancient PC and moved into the twenty-first century.

* * *

Rachel is popping over tonight. We're going to talk about the wedding. I've been thinking and thinking about it, and had this absolutely inspired idea. Okay, so Agnes and Beamish only want a tiny wedding, but who said anything about afterwards? I mean, no one's said anything at all about not having a little bit of a party...

It's not a nice evening when Rachel pitches up. It's cold and raining, and sounds like it's blowing a gale out there, which, with all the curtains drawn and logs burning merrily in the fireplace, makes my cottage feel even cosier.

'Hi,' she says, when I open the door. 'What a night!' Even in her enormous coat, she's still tiny.

'Come in, Rachel, and I'll open some wine.'

'You know, I was quite surprised, when Mum told me,' she says. 'I'd kind of guessed, you know, that something was going on there, but even so. Still, it's nice isn't it? I mean Beamish is very fond of her, isn't he?'

'Emma and I had kind of guessed too,' I tell her. 'And I agree. It's lovely for both of them.'

'So,' says Rachel. 'About this wedding... You know my mother has this ludicrous idea that it's just going to be a small affair. Like me, you and everyone at work, and Beamish's brother and sister-in-law. Mum has a couple of good friends she wants to invite too...'

'How many is that then?' I do a quick calculation. 'Less than twenty, isn't it? That's awfully small,' I add doubtfully.

'But she says that's what they want,' says Rachel. 'And a party later on. But I don't know. It just doesn't seem quite right.'

She's quite right. It's not. Beamish and Agnes are wonderful people and stacks of people absolutely love them. And it really isn't fair to deprive all their friends of a jolly good knees-up.

'You know what we *could* do.' I tell her the plan I hatched earlier and her eyes go like saucers. Then she grins.

'It's fab!' she says enthusiastically. 'Perfect! Oh, Louisa, this is going to be such fun.' Then she looks more sober. 'We will have to keep this absolutely secret. No slip-ups, not a single one. Or, knowing my mother, she'll probably run off and elope. She's a devil to keep things from, you know.'

Oh gosh. I'd forgotten for a split second that Agnes always knows everything that's going on. How do we keep something like this under wraps? If she found out, it would ruin everything.

'Okay,' I say. 'Shall we meet up at the weekend? Saturday afternoon? Come round and we'll draw up our battle plans.'

***

Will's been flirting outrageously with Karina again. Rather too outrageously. I think he's rather keen on the whole pregnancy thing. And she looks as though she's loving it.

'Well, I think you're absolutely gorgeous,' I hear him say to her, rather admiringly and none too quietly, and weary though she is with being eight months plus pregnant, I can tell she's flattered. Then he swoops down and kisses her on the cheek and she blushes.

Will winks at me as he leaves. 'See ya later.'

'Ha, ha,' I laugh delightedly at her, when he's gone. 'Now do you believe that there's nothing between me and Will? You never know, if Arian doesn't pull his socks up, you've got an ardent admirer there, ready and waiting in the wings.'

She doesn't say anything, just throws me a look like daggers.

Then before I know it, it's Friday. Karina's last day.

I've secretly organised everyone to call in to the office at as near to lunchtime as they can manage. They're all out in the yard with Sam right now, waiting for me to wave them in. If she's guessed something's afoot, she hasn't said.

Beamish comes in first, in his usual fumbling fashion.

'Ah. Um. Karina. Um, any chance you could come with me a moment?'

And while he whisks her away under the pretence of something work-related, the others scoot in with a cake and some very low alcohol champagne, so that when she comes back in, everyone shouts 'surprise' and claps loudly. There's an ear-splitting wolf whistle which comes, I imagine, from Will.

'Well, we just all wanted to say er, thank you,' says Beamish. 'And, er, well, good luck!'

There's more clapping and then I give Karina the card and present from all of us. She looks as though she's going to cry.

'Thank you so much,' she says quietly. 'I've really enjoyed being here.'

Just before she leaves, I give her another present. This one is just from me and it's one of those super-soft baby blankets in lemon yellow. I couldn't resist.

'Thank you,' she says, looking really touched. 'And I'm sorry, Louisa, about everything. You've been really good to me.'

Oh golly. There are tears in my eyes now.

'Don't be,' I say and give her a hug. I mean it. 'Everything really has worked out for the better.'

And I never thought in a million years I'd say this, but I'll miss her.

33

On Saturday morning, Horace and I brave the elements. It's grey, cold and windy again, and it really feels like December. I'm bundled up in a waterproof jacket, which is the most unflattering garment imaginable, and Horace has a blanket thrown over his rump, just so he doesn't get cold.

I can't believe that Christmas is just around the corner. All I've been thinking about is Karina leaving, Wurzel escaping, flirtatious Americans and now the wedding. And it doesn't really feel like Christmas. My parents are expecting me so I can't imagine getting out of it. But at least they don't want me to stay the night, thanks to my mother's aversion to Elmer. There are times when being the owner of an unhinged dog does actually work in my favour.

After lunch, I head over to Leonie's. We've a lot of catching up to do. She's working hard at the moment too and I don't think she likes to leave Pete for too long when she's home.

But when I get there, she's on her own. Pete, it transpires, has joined a cycling club. He is now not only a man in Lycra, but hangs out with a whole crowd of similarly tightly clad enthusiasts.

'Actually, Lou,' says Leonie, 'between you and me, I think he's become a bit obsessed. If he's not on his bike or cleaning it, he's online looking at cycling websites or finding out what latest gadgets he's convinced he needs to buy.'

Then she frowns. 'He spends a small fortune at the moment,' she says anxiously. 'I mean, that's okay for a bit, but really, Lou, I mean *a lot* of money... stuff like different bike pedals. The latest padded Lycra shorts because they're more efficient at wicking moisture away or some crap like that.'

Padded Lycra shorts that wick moisture away... I have to say it's never crossed my mind before that such a thing even exists.

'Well,' I say, sensibly, 'he's come a very long way from where he was three months ago. When does he go back to work?'

Her brow furrows as she thinks. 'Not until the New Year,' she says. 'They're going to be quite kind and start him back in gently, or so they say. I guess we'll just have to see how it goes.'

'Are *you* okay, Leo?' I ask sympathetically, only because I know she's had a rough time of it lately. And had to carry on working full time, while Pete fell apart at the seams.

'I am now,' she says honestly. 'I'll tell you what though, there have been days where I've felt like screaming – or falling apart myself. But we've survived! I'm just hoping that when Pete goes back to work, everything will be back to normal again.'

I hope she's not overly optimistic. Pete's better, definitely, but I'm not at all sure if depression works like that.

* * *

Gosh, what a jolly busy social time I'm having. I've rushed home from Leonie's to put my horses to bed. That now includes Wurzel, who gets locked up every night with Horace, just in case he gets it into his head to go on another of his midnight jaunts down to the allotments. And Rachel is due round any minute to talk about wedding plans. Perhaps we might go to the pub after. I'll wait and see how huge I feel when she gets here.

Rachel and I, I've decided, are a dynamic duo when it comes to wedding planning.

'They're thinking about spring at the moment,' she says. 'To give Mum a bit more time to recuperate first. At a push I think I can persuade them to go for May, which was really warm this year and then it's all systems go with your idea. I don't think it should be anything too big or formal, just a party, so people can come and go. But we need to decide where. And honestly, Lou. If you'd heard them last night, talking about Winchester Registry Office followed by a fish and chip lunch at the Hope and Anchor...' She screws up her face. 'Nothing against the Hope and Anchor, or fish and chips for that matter, but really, for your wedding day...'

'I think we can do better than that,' I say to her. I've been thinking about this quite a lot. 'There's a bloke called Les who does a mean spit roast. He's not commercial or anything, so he's quite cheap and Beamish is his vet, so I'm sure we could do a deal.'

'A pal of mine works in the wine trade,' says Rachel excitedly. 'She's offered to help us on that score.'

'And music,' I interrupt. 'Will's the person to ask about that. He'll know someone. He's quite into his dancing, is Will.'

'Oh, is he?' All of a sudden Rachel sounds coy. And her cheeks have flushed pink. Suddenly I'm confused – I thought she'd been dating Marcus.

'Um, Rachel,' I ask cautiously, 'I thought you were going out with Marcus?'

There. I've done it. Now she'll think I'm a nosy old cow, which I suppose is exactly what I am.

'We went out for dinner. Only once – and he's really nice, but not my type. He's quite well, *intense*, isn't he?'

'He is?'

Is he? Her comment leaves me slightly mystified. I suppose he is a bit. Not like Miles, who does full-blown intense to the extreme.

'So are you seeing someone else?' I say nosily, because girls *are* supposed to share this sort of information.

'No,' she says, a bit cagily. 'You?'

'No,' I say shortly. Then, because I suddenly realise that she probably doesn't know about the whole Arian-Karina-pregnancy-divorce saga, I give her a potted summary of the events of the last few months, including about how I've been out with Marcus a couple of times, but we just didn't quite hit it off. Well, sort of did but sort of didn't too.

'Funny,' she says afterwards. 'He talked about you quite a lot when I went out to dinner with him.'

Very funny. That's almost exactly what Will said about him too. My stomach starts doing that fluttering thing.

'He also told me about his ex. Seems she was a prize bitch, and when she dropped him for his so-called best mate, not only was he on his own, but because they'd worked together, he had to move jobs because she wouldn't. You can't blame him, really.'

Golly gee. That would explain a few things. *What if Marcus is secretly in love with me, but terrified that I'm on the rebound? That we'll start this mad passionate affair, only for me to come to my senses and go running back to Arian, only because we work together, it'll be just like the last time his heart was broken and he'll have to find yet another job...*

'Louisa? *Louisa...*' Rachel's waving her hand in front of my face. 'You were miles away. What on earth were you thinking about...'

'Oh nothing,' I say, then seeing her face, I add, 'Okay. It was what you said about Marcus. I think that probably you're right and he has baggage in the shape of his bitch-vet-ex-girlfriend.'

I have to say that Rachel's remark has made me think. I'm still thinking, much later, when we go to the pub, by which time we've both decided we'll drink lots of wine and she can sleep over at mine.

We brave the elements, buffeted by the wind and rain for all of about four minutes, then make a bit of an entrance that absolutely no one can miss as the wind slams the door closed behind us.

Then I notice Marcus. And Will. I nudge Rachel in the side. Good grief. Miles is here too – and Emma. It looks like there's a serious vet conversation going on, because they haven't even noticed us. Then I spy Paris M-T over by the bar, in designer jeans and a boob tube, with a glass of what could be lemonade but is more likely vodka, sending unsubtle, sultry looks in Will's direction and daggers at us as we wander over to join them.

'Hey, can I get you girls a drink?' Will, ever the gentleman, is on his feet and gets a round in. It looks as though they could do with it. It's a very sombre gathering at the moment.

'Hey,' Rachel says to me. 'Isn't this just the perfect time to fill them all in on the wedding?'

I grin at my co-conspirator. 'Most definitely.'

After making each one of them swear on their life not to utter a word to anyone, we tell them what we're planning.

'Just one snag...' says Marcus. 'Where are you going to hold it and how will you get them there without giving the game away?'

'We'll think of something,' I say confidently. After all, it's months away isn't it?

'Well,' says Will, stretching out huge, muscly, denim-clad legs which I can't help but gaze at. 'Just let us know the date when you've got one. I could probably ask a pal of mine to cover calls, don't worry about that. He owes me a favour...' He grins broadly to himself about something that he's obviously not telling us about.

Ben arrives, much to Emma's delight. Will keeps dropping Karina's name into everything, then tells me he thinks Arian's a dimbo if he doesn't hang on to her, and that maybe someone should have a word with him.

I tell him he's got it exactly right. That Arian is indeed a dimbo, that all his brain power goes into flying aeroplanes and breathing and things, and that it's a waste of time anyone trying to talk sense into him.

'I should know,' I say wearily. 'Lord knows I've tried.'

Someone's put Nickelback's 'Rockstar' on the jukebox and suddenly I forget our serious conversation and collapse helplessly with laughter.

'Hey? What's the joke?' asks Will. 'It's a great song, this...'

Ha. Of course, don't all blokes love it? To be fair, I do too. I just find it funny.

'What's funny is that it's the soundtrack to Arian's life,' I try to say through my giggles. 'Really! Nickelback wrote this song just for my ex-husband, with all his deluded notions of what real life is...'

Oops. I think I've just shattered one of Will's illusions – he's looking most disappointed, and saunters off to chat to a client he's spotted by the bar for a minute. Then from behind me a guarded voice asks, 'So what exactly is the soundtrack to *your* life, Louisa?'

I stiffen, and as I turn to face Marcus, I'm thinking, do I give him an honest version or the censored one.

'Oh it's got to be "Ironic", hasn't it,' I say cryptically, thinking quickly to distract myself from the sudden racing that my heart seems to be doing. 'Wouldn't you agree? Or maybe "Free Bird"?' I'm quite pleased with that. This is quite fun. 'And I'm quite partial to a bit of "The Boys of Summer" too...'

Marcus is smiling. Phew. You can never be sure that Marcus won't take the strangest things personally.

'Okay,' he says. '"Ironic". That's good... Now what about that American friend of ours? What would do for him?'

'Easy,' I say promptly. 'Nickelback again, "Feelin' Way Too Damn Good". Your turn. How about our two lovebirds over there?'

We both turn to look at Emma and Ben.

'"Two Hearts"?' suggests Marcus. 'Phil Collins?'

'Hmm, not bad,' I say. 'Or Oasis, "Let there Be Love..."'

And not one of us has noticed Miles. And Rachel. Deep in conversation and totally oblivious to everything around them. Heads together as they talk. I wonder what on earth *about*?

'There's a very lame horse in the car park,' I say in a loud voice, as a test. Nothing. Miles doesn't even so much as twitch in my direction.

'Leave them alone, Louisa,' says Marcus. 'Now, how are you getting on with Zac?'

'I think he'll be fine, once he stops glaring at me. He works hard enough, that's for sure.'

'He just doesn't trust people,' says Marcus. 'He's been through too much for someone of his age. Just give him a chance...'

'What exactly is it with Zac?' I ask. Why is everyone so keen to give him a chance?

Marcus looks at me for a moment, then says, 'I suppose it's okay to tell you. I mean, you'll keep it to yourself, won't you? Only his stepfather is a vicious thug. He's done time and he's knocked his step-kids around a fair bit too. Including Zac – and Beckham.'

'God.' I'm shocked. I mean, my parents might drive me insane, but just the thought of Dad lifting a finger against anyone.

'Poor Zac. But what about his mother? Surely she wouldn't put up with the stepdad if he goes around doing that...'

'Apparently she spends most of her time in the pub, and always sides with her husband,' says Marcus. 'Plus she's more concerned with Stace, who's Zac's fourteen-year-old sister and has just had a baby.'

Oh. I know teenage pregnancy happens, but it's just so dismal, because with role models like that, what chance does the baby have?

'I know,' says Marcus quietly. 'It's depressing. And there's nothing any of us can do about it, which is why it's so great that Zac at least has got a chance of breaking away from it all, and it's all thanks to Beamish.'

I am so glad he's told me all this. I mean, it's ghastly, but like everyone else, I too am now going to do my best to help Zac make a go of this. He *can't* go back to those awful, terrible people and end up like his vile stepfather.

'Where's he living?' I ask Marcus. 'Surely he can't be back at his mum's every night...'

'He's bunking at Sam's. In a little box room. Beamish supplied a bed, I took him home to collect his stuff, and well, that's all there is to know.' He stops for a moment, then adds, 'Actually I had the pleasure of meeting the delightful parents. She started screaming at me that I was kidnapping her baby, and she'd see to it that I was put on the paedophile register, and then *he* came out, yelling obscenities and looking for a punch-up.'

My jaw drops.

'By then, Zac was on his way back out again. So I told the stepfather that next time he tried to poison anything, he'd have the police to contend with, and not just about cruelty to animals either. Then we left.'

Golly. I'm in awe. He's a bit of a hero on the quiet. What with Beamish coming up with a spare bed for Sam's box room and Marcus dealing with the wicked parents, I really do work with some wonderful people.

Then changing the subject, he says thoughtfully, 'You know, I think you coped really well with the whole thing with Karina. It must have been quite difficult for you, especially to start with.'

Well, it was. Bloody difficult, as I said to Agnes, but to be truthful, I've forgotten the worst bits.

'I've ended up really liking her,' I say honestly, half wishing that she was here this evening too. Only the snag is, of course, she'd have Arian with her.

It's one of those evenings where everyone is on good form and the time just flies. And when we finally get kicked out of the pub, Marcus, Miles and Will troop back to mine with me, Rachel and some beers.

As I rummage in the kitchen hunting for glasses, I'm suddenly aware of someone behind me. I turn round and it's Marcus – and he's frowning.

Just as I'm thinking, *what have I done this time*, he comes and stands quite close.

'Lou?' he asks, sounding not at all sure of himself. 'I know you and I haven't exactly managed to spend much time together without me putting my foot in it or you getting uppity...'

'*Me? Uppity?*' I say incredulously, completely outraged. 'Well, thanks very much, Marcus. Looks like you've just put your foot in it yet again.' I glare at him.

He looks most contrite when he realises what he's said. 'I'm sorry. Really. Look, calm down, I didn't mean it like that. It's just that whenever I ask you anything personal, you go off at the deep end.'

'And do you know why, Marcus? Well, I'll tell you. Because you have this incredible, unerring talent for homing in on all my weaknesses and shortcomings, which I'm already fully aware of, thank you very much, and it makes me feel very small, inadequate and... and fat.'

Wow. Deep breath. That felt *good*. At last I've got it off my chest, because in a nutshell, that's exactly what he does, time and time again. I turn back to the sink.

'So, now that you've made yourself amply clear, do you want me to leave?' he says calmly to my back, as I start washing glasses.

'Yes,' I mutter, then 'No,' in a very quiet, pissed-off sort of voice.

He doesn't say anything, but I can feel him move even closer and this time when I turn round, he's there, right in front of me. Then somehow his arms are round me and the next thing, his lips are on mine.

We don't actually make a final decision. In fact I completely forget what we were deciding about. Marcus's kiss just about wipes every other thought clean out of my head.

'I've wanted to do that for a long time,' he says, when we stop. His brown eyes are looking so intently at mine, it's as though he's looking right into my soul. 'Just one thing, though – why do you always sell yourself short?'

'I don't,' I say, genuinely surprised. 'I mean, there's nothing to sell. I'm an unremarkable, mouse-haired newly divorced office worker. Plus I have a weird dog. And I'm completely inadequate, as you keep reminding me.'

Marcus looks astonished. 'You can't really think that?' He pulls me closer again, and this time he takes my face in his hands.

'I'll tell you what you are,' he says softly. 'You're strong. A brilliant friend. I've seen you. You cope with everything and everyone that life throws at you without complaining. You're also smart, wonderful and very pretty. Okay, so you have a weird dog, but none of us are perfect. Only you should also know...' he pauses for a moment '... that I want far more than your brilliant friendship...'

And this time, the kiss is far more urgent than before and I find myself kissing him back, just as passionately as the thoughts whirl giddily in my head.

Oh my God. If I chuck him out now, he'll think I don't want this. Which I do... but I'm not at all sure about the carnal knowledge part, not just yet, which is where this is clearly headed. I mean, it's a bit quick. I've only just found out how he feels and I have to admit that far from feeling strong, at this moment I feel quite scared... and definitely cautious. I mean, I don't want to risk the whole broken-hearted thing again. At least, not for a while...

I pull back just a little bit, and with great difficulty break away from him. But I have to say this.

'Marcus?' Oh dear. Just how do I put this into words...

It's my turn to stroke his face. It's a lovely, kind, caring face. I can't believe I ever thought he was arrogant.

'Hey. It's okay. Don't look so worried!' He laughs. Then says more soberly, 'Things were getting a bit, well, hot there for a moment, weren't they...'

I look at him, trying to gauge just where he's going with this.

'Very,' I say. Followed by 'Positively steamy where I was standing actually,' nodding behind me at the sink of hot, soapy water. It lightens the mood.

'Oh, sorry, I hadn't noticed.' Marcus perches on the side of my old kitchen table and pulls me to him again. This time the kiss is more contained.

'Well,' he says afterwards. 'Am I right in thinking that you're quite happy about this?'

If he means the kissing, then, oh, I'm more than happy with it. I nod.

'Look,' he says reasonably. 'I know you've only just got divorced, but how about we spend some time together – away from work? And just see...'

He's looking quizzically at me, waiting for a reply.

I think, but only for a second or two. It's a no-brainer.

So I say, 'Um, going out a bit, properly, is fine, Marcus. I'm definitely okay with that. In fact, I'd go so far as to say that just seeing would be fine too. Perfect, in fact.'

'So for the first time ever we are in agreement?'

34

It's far too late to gossip by the time Marcus and Miles eventually leave, so it's over a pot of fresh coffee the next morning that Rachel and I get down to the nitty-gritty of last night.

'You changed your tune quick smart,' I say to her curiously. 'I thought it was Will you had the hots for, not Miles!'

Her face turns beetroot. Ha! It's nice to see Rachel looking less like a perfect little Barbie doll and more like a normal human.

'Do you know...' she says in a most astounded little voice. 'I've never believed in that whole love at first sight nonsense. I mean, you can hardly fall in love when you don't even know someone...' Then she does one of those girly, breathy sighs like clients do about Marcus.

And oh my God... I have to say I'm gobsmacked.

'Only, the minute Miles and I started talking, it was like we'd known each other forever...'

'Well,' I say very sensibly, 'he has known your mother for years...'

Rachel gives me a look. 'What's that got to do with anything?' Then the soppy look comes back. 'Miles is quite possibly the nicest man I've ever met,' she says, looking utterly lovestruck. 'He's so lovely and unselfish, and so devoted to his work.'

'Rachel, there's something you really *ought* to know about Miles on that subject,' I say warily. Well, it's only fair that she knows the truth – sooner rather than later.

'He may *tell* you he's not married,' I continue, as a look of complete horror crosses her face. For her own sake, I have to be brutal. 'But he is, I'm afraid. Two hundred per cent. To his job.'

'God, just for a moment, I wondered what you were going to say there,' she says looking annoyed then relieved again.

'So what about you and Marcus?' she asks me, keen to change the subject. 'It took you a jolly long time to get those glasses...'

'Me and Marcus?' I say airily. 'Well, we talked for ages. Then if I hadn't extricated myself from his amorous advances, we would have ended up ripping each other's clothes off and having passionate sex right here on my kitchen table.'

Rachel looks uncertain, as if she's not at all sure I'm telling the truth.

'Well, it looks strong enough,' she says doubtfully.

* * *

Rachel goes to have Sunday lunch with Agnes and Beamish and at last I am alone. Did Marcus and I really actually agree that we'd sort of try going out again? Well, this time I'm going to get the full story of what happened with his ex. And as we're going to try going out properly, perhaps we should also try a bit more of that kissing while we're at it.

By the middle of the afternoon, I've decided that I'm not waiting around any longer. After all, there's no time like the present, so I send Marcus a text and invite him over for supper, then go out to feed my horses.

When I get out to the paddock, darling Horace does his usual nicker when he sees me, and mooches over to say hello. But there's no sign of Wurzel anywhere. Thinking, *I bet the little bugger's eating Mr Jones' carrots again*, I traipse across the field to see if I can find him. And then stop in my tracks. Because there, in the long grass right at the far end, is Wurzel, stretched out, not moving.

My heart is thumping in my chest, as I run over, at the same time reaching in my pocket for my mobile to call Marcus.

'Hi, Lou,' he says cheerfully. 'Just got your text...' but I stop him mid-flow with 'Oh Marcus, it's Wurzel.' And as I reach down to touch the cold, furry ears, I say tearfully, 'Oh, Marcus, I think he's dead...'

I'm so grateful to have Marcus here. He came over straight away. Once he'd confirmed that Wurzel was indeed dead, he got on the phone and arranged for the disposal people to come over right away. So while he deals with all that side of things, I'm in the stable with Horace, putting all his rugs on and crying into his mane.

I've no wish to watch the indignity of little Wurzel being winched into the knacker's lorry. I'd prefer to remember him as the feisty, cheeky, clever little chap that he was. I hope that somewhere, wherever it is he's gone to, he's reunited with Mrs Winkle. Somehow I think she'll be awfully pleased to see him.

* * *

It's not exactly the romantic evening I'd envisaged. I'm tearful, sad, and not much fun at all, but Marcus stays anyway.

'It was probably his heart, Lou. Especially if he was fine this morning?' he says. 'Just "bang". Quick as that. He wouldn't have known a thing.'

Small comfort, and it helps – a little. As does snuggling up to

Marcus on my sofa. But the trouble with horses, however small they are, they steal into your heart – then break it.

* * *

And of course, back in the office on Monday morning I now have a brand-new boy assistant. Zac, who comes in looking very spruced up, boxers *nearly* completely under cover and more than a little unsure of what to make of this new arrangement.

'Morning, Zac,' I say. 'I'm really glad you're here. Would you mind putting this lot away while I get started on the calls?'

''Kay,' he says, then turns and mutters, 'sorry 'bout your pony.'

Gosh. I didn't expect that.

'Um thanks,' I say, tears threatening to spill over again. 'Thanks very much, Zac.'

When I'm bent over the computer later, cursing and swearing, Zac comes over and fixes me with a stare.

'Wot the fuck you doin' to it? 'Ere... lemme do it...'

And in no time, his fingers are whizzing around all over the place.

'Do you give lessons?' I ask hopefully.

He sits back, stares at the screen and says, 'I don't get why you 'ave such a crap computer. A new one would make loads a stuff easier.'

Gosh, that's the most he's ever said to me.

'I wondered,' I say cautiously, 'whether you could help me explain that to Beamish, Zac? He might just listen to you...'

'Dunno,' says Zac, then, ''Kay. I'll try it.'

* * *

I go outside to make sure Sam is okay with Zac spending all this time in the office.

'Sure,' he says, those gleaming, green eyes of his twinkling bewitchingly at me like the devil he is.

'He's a good lad, Lou,' he says, nodding in the direction of the office. 'Sorry about your pony,' he says.

'Thanks,' I say.

Oh gosh, how do they all know already? Then just as I turn to walk back to the office, Marcus drives in to the yard.

'Hello, gorgeous,' he says, loud enough for Sam to hear. Sam gives me a wink.

'Hey yourself,' I say. 'How is your day?'

'Pretty shit actually,' he says. 'I've just been up to Sylvie's place. Well, you know I have. Anyway, I ended up having to put that mare to sleep. She was only young. One of those things you wish you didn't have to do.'

I put my arms round him and hug him. I know we're at work, but I can't help it. After all, he was lovely to me last night, about Wurzel.

He looks a little brighter. 'Anyway, got to get on. I just popped back to pick up something.'

'Of course. Actually, I also have work to do,' I say importantly and head back for the office. Behind me, Marcus shouts, 'How about dinner tomorrow? Pick you up about eight?'

'Lovely,' I shout back, catching sight of Sam making kissy faces at me from one of the stables. I poke my tongue out at him.

That night, when I put Horace in his stable, he's not himself. I think he's missing Wurzel. We both are. Maybe I ought to put the word around, see if there's a four-legged waif or stray somewhere that needs a field and a new mummy. Actually, now that I've as much as formed the idea in my head, and knowing how things go on around here, it will, I imagine, only be a matter of time before it happens. The magic, remember? I'll mark it in my diary and see how long it takes.

Horace and I have a long talk about all sorts of things and I groom him for ages by which time we're both a little less sad. Then I give him carrots, which makes us think of Wurzel again and before I know it, I'm howling into his mane. Horace is relatively unperturbed. After all, he's got rather used to emotional goings-on since he moved in. He carries on munching his hay and lets me get on with it.

And then, just when I could do with some good news, something wonderful happens. No, not a pony, not just yet, but when I go inside, the phone rings and it's Arian.

'Karina's had the baby!' he says sounding the most excited I've ever heard him sound. 'I'm a daddy! I can't believe it!' His voice is high-pitched and he sounds as mad as a hatter.

'Congratulations, Daddy!' I say. 'How is Karina?'

'She's great!' he says. 'Actually, for a while there, I did wonder... she was being rather strange...'

'What exactly do you mean, Arian?' I say, most concerned, because after all, oddly, I do now class Karina as a friend.

'She told me to fuck off and never come near her again. Karina never swears. And she kept making the oddest grunting noises and moaning...'

Ah. The penny drops.

'Arian, you idiot,' I say, then slowly, because after all, this is Arian, 'Karina was in labour. It hurts. *A lot.*' I think for a moment. 'Imagine if you can, just for one moment, you are trying to shit a football – or a huge melon.'

There's silence, then, 'Oh.'

'You haven't told me what sex the baby is,' I say, not only to break the silence but because I want to know.

'It's a boy,' he says proudly. 'I have a son and heir,' he adds ecstatically, sounding high-pitched and mad again. 'We haven't named him yet. Er, having trouble agreeing on that, but we'll get there.'

'Give her my love,' I say. 'And I'll pop in to the hospital to see her. Er, when you're not there probably. Which is when?'

Arian's far too excited to take offence and rings off to make some more calls. If I were Karina, I think I'd stay in hospital as long as possible and lie to him about the visiting hours.

35

The next morning I pin a notice on the door: 'Karina had a baby boy', with yesterday's date. Then I look at the date more closely. December 15th. It absolutely can't be. It's not possible. I knew Christmas was coming, but it's ten days away...

I've done no shopping, which means I'll have to go on a Saturday, with the rest of the heaving masses, and oh, just the thought makes my heart sink. It's the kind of shopping I loathe. But first I'm going to see Karina. Tonight. And I'm really looking forward to it.

* * *

The baby is tiny with Arian's dark hair. Karina looks tired but serene, with the baby nestled in her arms, making quiet little murmuring noises.

I kiss her and give her the chocolates I brought her.

'Thanks, Louisa. The food here is worse than airline food,' she tells me.

'Get Arian to bring you something nice,' I suggest. 'Would you like me to have a word with him?'

'He'd probably bring Mars bars and Doritos,' she says. 'Anyway, I think Mum's bringing me something later on. I'll be fine.'

When she asks me if I want to hold the baby, I hesitate – I've never held a newborn before. And this one's Arian's. Yet again, I think how weird this is. But then I hold out my arms and carefully take him. Isn't that why I came here?

This little person that's part Karina and part my ex, he's the most perfect thing I've ever seen.

'He's gorgeous,' I say truthfully, gazing enraptured at the warm bundle in my arms. Then I clock that he's wrapped in the blanket I gave her and I feel strangely touched. And I'm riveted as I watch each delicate movement, each tiny yawn, but when he starts to wail, there's nothing cute about that whatsoever and I hastily return him to Karina, who attaches him expertly to one of her enormous breasts.

'Blimey,' I must have said out loud.

'Don't stare, Louisa. Anyway, it's perfectly natural,' says Karina. She's right, of course, and actually, it's rather fascinating.

As I leave the hospital, I feel a hollow sensation inside. A strange feeling I've never felt before, almost like a yearning. But all thoughts about babies vanish, when rounding a corner in one of the corridors, I run slap bang into Arian. Honestly, he is *so* unreliable.

'You told me you weren't visiting tonight,' I say crossly.

'I wasn't, but I couldn't stay away,' he says, a stupid smile on his face.

'I've just been to see your baby, Arian. And he's beautiful.'

Arian beams. 'He is, isn't he? Everyone always tells you that life changes forever, but you just don't realise, until you have one of your own...' he adds, with uncharacteristic soppiness.

Then he looks at me more soberly. 'I'm sorry, Lou. That was really tactless of me, especially...' He breaks off and looks at his feet. Gosh. Has Arian finally discovered his sensitive side?

'It's okay.' I reach out to touch his arm. 'Really...'

'Erm, could I walk out with you? Only there are one or two things I wanted to say, and now's as good a time as any.'

'Er, okay,' I say slowly.

As we walk, he speaks. 'The thing is, Lou, I've realised it wasn't you at all. I wasn't happy at home, because I wasn't happy with anything. If I'd been around a bit more, we might have had a chance.'

Blimey, I think to myself. That's deep, especially for Arian. Fatherhood is going to his head.

So I say truthfully, 'Actually, Arian, I think it was purely sex between us, and when that burnt out, we were more like brother and sister.'

Then in his next breath, he astounds me.

'I've decided to look for another job. I want to make this work with Karina and if we're both away all the time, how can it? I know some people manage to, but I think we both know that I'm not cut out for a double life.'

Gosh again. I've always thought that Arian was one of those people who was defined by his job. I wonder if he realises that leaving flying will be far more life-changing for him than having a baby. Somehow, I doubt he's thought that far. There'll be no more admiring glances as he strides through international airports, no more posh hotels – unless he pays for them himself. No. I can't see this at all.

'That sounds wonderful, Arian,' I say dubiously. 'I wish you the best of luck. Look, why don't you go and see Karina? I think visiting hours are over soon...'

I get the briefest kiss on the cheek before he turns smack bang into the wall then almost runs back the way we've walked. I experience a moment's pity for Karina.

Life can be truly weird, I decide. I find Arian's new-found energy quite exhausting, so as an antidote I think about Marcus and immediately get a warm, fuzzy feeling inside.

* * *

The next night is my dinner date with Marcus and he takes me to an Indian restaurant on the outskirts of Winchester.

'Hope you like curry,' he says. 'I should have checked, but all the damn pubs have Christmas meals and Christmas parties going on, and to tell you the truth, one Christmas meal is more than enough for me.'

'Curry's great,' I say. 'I absolutely love it and I completely agree about Christmas,' thinking about my darling mother's overcooked, dried-out turkey, mushy sprouts that make you fart for days, gravy straight out of a packet and Tesco's value Christmas pudding.

'So what are you doing for Christmas?' Marcus asks, as we speed along in the Land Cruiser.

'Nothing special,' I say. 'I'll probably go to my parents – just for lunch.'

'That's nice,' he says.

'Actually, it's not,' I say. 'Not really, because I have a mad dog, so I'll only have one glass of sherry because I'll be driving home that evening. My mother can't stand Elmer. She'll also send everyone insane with her moaning, my father will get as pissed as a fart because it's the only way he knows to cope with her. I, meanwhile, will bite my tongue *most* of the time, try to eat the horrific meal she's cooked and stay sober enough to leave the first moment I can get away.' I smile sweetly at him. 'What about you?'

'Not sure,' he says shortly. 'My parents are away – as usual.

Even if they weren't, I'm not sure I'd see them. They live in Salcombe and I'm on call Boxing Day.'

Golly. Salcombe... How very posh. Hmmm. Do I dare invite him to join my weird family Christmas...

But fortunately he says, 'Actually, Emma and Ben have invited me for lunch. They've asked Will too, so I think I'll probably do that.'

Sounds much more fun than mine will be. I'm envious. Emma's Christmas lunch will be scrumptious.

'How about,' he suggests slowly, sounding quite pleased with himself, 'you and I have Christmas together on Boxing Day evening? The way *we* want to do it?'

'Oooh, that sounds fun,' I say, envisaging me and Marcus pulling crackers and drinking champagne by my fire.

'Tell you what,' he says. 'Why don't you leave it to me?'

* * *

I have so many presents to buy this year. There's Mum and Dad of course, Leonie, Emma, and Marcus and Agnes... and maybe something for Zac. And a box of chocolates for Mr Jones to make up for the carrots that Wurzel stole. So I forgo my Saturday morning ride on Horace, and head into Winchester, wishing I hadn't, because it's Christmas shopping at its absolute, bloody worst, with the traffic queuing for miles and queues for all the car parks. And to top it off, it's wet and windy, which isn't Christmassy at all.

By the time I've finished, I vow that next year all my shopping will be done online. I am never going Christmas shopping ever again.

But then something happens that absolutely makes my day, because I bump into smug Martin, that jumped-up little shit of an estate agent who sold mine and Arian's old home. Battling with the crowds in the streets, I try my hardest to avoid him, but he comes right over anyway and says as smoothly as ever, 'Mrs Mulholland! How lovely to see you again. How are you?'

As if I were a long lost friend or something, the git.

'I'm awfully well, thanks, Mr Slime,' I say, standing there in the downpour, water pouring down my face. 'Oh yes. Very good indeed. Oh how lovely, I see you're wearing one of those Value suits from Tesco... excellent aren't they? I mean, these days, no one can tell the difference can they? Must go. Happy Christmas!' and I walk away leaving him looking really stupid as he stands there with his mouth wide open. He's probably wearing Armani. Tesco's value is absolutely okay to me, but Martin's a complete snob.

* * *

We close the office at lunchtime on Christmas Eve, and Beamish and Agnes arrive with drinks and nibbles. What we used to do was have champagne and cut Mrs Winkle's delicious Christmas cake – not this year, though. But Agnes, bless her, has done us proud. It's not just nibbles at all. There's the most sumptuous array of delicious hot canapés, and tiny, bite-sized roast beef and Yorkshire puddings, so when all the vets get back, we have a party.

Mrs Boggle always comes in specially, wearing tacky earrings made of singing Christmas baubles, and always says something like 'Oh, I couldn't eat another bite,' as she stuffs yet another delectable morsel into her mouth. Zac's looking at it all as though he can't believe his eyes. He told me he's spending Christmas with Sam at Sam's sister's. I'm awfully glad he's got somewhere nice to go to, not just his lousy mum's.

It's lovely having Agnes back here, even if she's only passing the food around. For once, she's doing as she's told and taking it easy. Beamish is terribly protective of her, and even makes her sit down and actually passes some of the food around himself.

Marcus keeps giving me the loveliest of smiles, and Will's regaling Agnes with various outlandish tales that appear to have her in stitches.

'She's a great lady,' he says to me later.

I agree with him. 'She is. One of the best,' I say loyally. 'Actually, she has been the best friend to me this year. She's more like a mother than my own mother.'

'Wow.' Will is fittingly awed. He obviously realises how special she is.

And so I go home alone, but I'm meeting everyone later on in the pub, except maybe not Marcus who's on call for the rest of the day. He kisses me goodbye in the car park, which thoroughly baffles Beamish, who thinks he's given his blessing to my union with Will, which he still hasn't realised only ever existed in his imagination.

* * *

Ah well. So it's Christmas. That evening, everyone gets to the pub – including Marcus. When I walk in, they all stop talking at once and look over at me.

When I ask Marcus what it is they were discussing, he says, 'Nothing, Lou. Don't know what you mean.'

I ask Emma too. She gives me an evasive look and changes the subject. Suddenly I'm less than happy.

What am I not supposed to know? Secrets make me uneasy – there've been too many in recent months – and I can only imagine the worst, like I've done something terrible, or I'm about to be fired, or Marcus's ex is coming back to him...

36

I wake up on Christmas morning a little less paranoid. Horace has done surprisingly well from Santa this year. As well as a bulging stocking of carrots and apples, he has a lovely new headcollar from Emma and a soft, fleecy rug from me. It's bitterly cold this morning, so I put it on him. It's like thermal underwear, with his hefty old waterproof rug over the top and he looks very happy and cosy. I spin it out for ages before turning him out, because now, oh joy of joys, it's time for the parents.

* * *

My mother looks like she has a smell up her nose when she opens the door.

'Oh, how lovely, darling,' she says as we air-kiss. 'You're just in time to peel the sprouts.'

'How lovely, Mum. I can't wait.' I smile brightly at her. *Fucking blasted sprouts.* I hate the things. She completely ignores Elmer, who's had a bath and is wearing a red bow especially for the occasion.

'Happy Christmas, poppet,' says Dad, clearly already on the vino. Mum's obviously on form then.

'Auntie Lucy and Uncle Peter are coming for lunch,' she calls from the kitchen. 'I knew you'd love to see them.'

Auntie Lucy's okay. She's Dad's sister and I can't imagine how she puts up with Uncle Peter, who's a lecherous old pervert with an eye for a cleavage. I know Auntie Lucy's a little on the flat-chested side, but even so, I do my cardigan up to the top straight away, in case I forget later.

Then I have a glass of wine with Dad while Mum makes the gravy from a packet.

'How's it all going then, sweetheart? Still as busy as ever?' says Dad, looking a little mistily at me. Hmmm, it's only eleven thirty. *Better ease up on the wine, Dad.*

'Really good,' I say. 'Yes, work's good...' *And I have a gorgeous vet who wants to get my knickers off, my friend Karina's had Arian's baby, I've sorted Emma's horoscope habit and Pete is on the up again...* only my dad doesn't really know any of my friends these days, except Leonie, and he'd never get his head round the whole Arian–Karina thing.

'Yes. Thanks, Dad. Everything's great. Why don't I make us a cup of tea?'

But he shakes his head. 'I'll stick with this, thanks, poppet.'

But then he surprises me. 'I'm very proud of how you coped when that, that, you know...' *Ah, you mean the tosser-loser-wanker left me?* '... well, that idiot of a husband left you. Anyway, I wanted you to know.'

'Golly. Thanks, Dad.'

Oh God. The doorbell. Auntie Lucy... and Uncle Peter.

I kiss Auntie Lucy who's actually very sweet, and always reminds me a bit of Dad, but then they are related. They have quite a lot in common too, having particularly annoying spouses.

The Impossible Search for the Perfect Man

'You're looking mighty hot, young lady,' booms Uncle Peter.

I'm not sure if he means the gorgeous kind, or the damp kind. I can already feel sweat trickling down my back but no way am I taking off this cardigan with him hanging around for an eyeful.

'I'm fine,' I say sweetly. 'Absolutely fine, but thank you so much, Uncle Peter.'

This Christmas I'm lucky. Mum boils the sprouts until they disintegrate, so we agree, terribly sadly that we'll just have to throw them away and make do with the frozen vegetable medley that she bought when it was on offer in the Co-op. Fortunately, I catch her just as she's about to feed the pulped mush to Elmer, which would have been catastrophic. There's a chink in the clouds though, as even Mum can't ruin the sausages with bacon wrapped around them and though they're a bit crispy, they're edible. Thank heavens, I'm thinking to myself. I nearly inflicted this on Marcus. And then I remember that right now they're all sitting down to an Emma special, and it will be the best Christmas lunch in the history of the world. Filled with a rush of insane jealousy, I swiftly remind myself that I'm lucky to have my parents, who, in spite of their quirks, are in their own peculiar way still my parents.

My dear mother has wrapped tinsel around the napkins, which sheds glittery strands all over the table and everyone's plates, and she's bought these candles which were a bargain, only they've melted into puddles of wax even before we've sat down. But still. It's Christmas and this is my family. And as I stare at the plate in front of me, I remind myself – at least we've been spared the sprouts.

Dear Horace saves me though, because he's the perfect reason why I have to leave before it gets too dark. And as my parents' front door closes behind me, I unbutton my cardigan to let the air in and breathe a huge sigh of relief that it's over. Perhaps next year, I'll invite them over to mine, but blissfully, that's a *whole year* away at this moment and who knows, by then, anything could happen.

Dear Emma has stuck a Christmas card through my door. When I look more closely, I see it's not your average card. It's a photograph, clearly taken earlier today, of her, Ben, and Will wearing silly hats holding champagne glasses in the air. So where's Marcus? On the back she's scribbled:

Hope you had as much fun as we did, come over later? We'll save you a glass xxx

Ah bless. I might just do that. But by the time I eventually get there, I think perhaps that, actually, maybe I shouldn't have. I've never seen Emma so drunk. Ben looks very smiley and he's slurring all his words, and as for Will… either he's consumed a huge amount of booze or he's a complete lightweight. He goes to pick up his glass and misses. Then looks mystified as to what's gone wrong, so he tries again. Mainly because I'm hours behind them in the alcohol consumption stakes, I pick it up and put it in his hands.

'Noooooo,' cries Emma, a mad grin on her face. 'You've spoilt it. He's so funny…' and she collapses in giggles on top of Ben, who's practically wetting himself.

Will studies his glass with serious intent. I really don't fancy catching this lot up tonight, I decide, so I finish the drink that Emma gave me and wish them all a very good night.

'And don't forget to drink lots of water,' I tell them very sensibly, just before I leave.

It's only when I get home that I realise I completely forgot to ask them what had happened to Marcus.

And then Christmas is over and it's Boxing Day, which I love, especially this year, because tonight, Marcus and I are having our first Christmas together. And yes, I know it may be our only Christmas. So, I am going to look my most gorgeous and completely wow him.

I've still no idea what he's planning. He texts me that afternoon, telling me to be ready at seven. So I'm ready at six thirty, with his present wrapped. It's an ironic present, because it's the Nickleback CD we were talking about the other night, and I've also bought him a very nice bottle of wine. Well, I hope it's nice, because it cost me twenty-five quid.

Marcus arrives bang on seven. Almost as though he'd been sitting outside looking at his watch.

'Hello.' He grins and kisses me lightly on the lips. 'You ready? Why don't you bring Elmer?'

Needing no encouragement, Elmer's there in an instant, wagging her tail most ingratiatingly.

'Okay,' I say. 'But can you wait while Elmer brushes her teeth, only she wasn't expecting to be going out...'

Marcus has his arm round my shoulder as we walk out to his car. It's a lovely clear, frosty night and his body feels warm against mine. He opens the door for Elmer to climb into the back, then opens the passenger door for me. And there's no awkwardness – it's perfect.

Just ten minutes later, he turns off the road and pulls up in front of the loveliest old farm cottage ever. The lights are on inside and it looks so welcoming. There's even a candle burning on the windowsill.

'Welcome to my humble abode,' he says apologetically. 'I kind of thought that you'd be all Christmassed out by now, so actually, I thought I'd do the cooking rather than go to a pub. I hope that's okay?'

Oh, it most definitely is.

He unlocks the front door, and I find myself standing in this glorious cottage. There's bare brick and battered old timbers everywhere. The floors are wonky but there are logs burning in the fireplace, huge comfortable sofas in his living room, one bright green and the other mustard yellow, and a massive Aga in the kitchen, which is also crammed with high-tech gadgets everywhere I look. I wouldn't know how to use half this stuff.

Marcus goes to the enormous fridge and pulls out a bottle of champagne, which he uncorks noisily and pours into flutes.

We chink our glasses and say, 'Cheers.' Then I have to ask. 'Are you like Emma? A secret Masterchef in the making? Only, all this stuff...' I gesture around the kitchen.

That makes him smile. 'Not exactly...' Then the smile goes. 'It was my ex who was into cooking. I, kind of, dabble...'

Oh. That's made me feel a bit funny. So this house was *theirs*. Then I remind myself to keep this in proportion, because I have a history too.

'So did you miss Emma's Christmas?' I ask him. 'Only she sent me a picture of all of them completely off their heads and you weren't in it.'

'I spent yesterday in a muddy field with a horse that wouldn't move. When we eventually did get him to his stable, I had another call – a colic – and so on and so on... Someone gave me a turkey sandwich, but that was about it,' says Marcus, looking quite relieved that it's over. 'Not one of my better days... Anyway, I hope you're hungry. Don't expect anything too impressive but it should be edible...'

I actually can't believe how much trouble he's gone to. There's a rose on the table and a pair of tall candlesticks, and he's set it out so we're sitting opposite each other. To start, he's made a goat's cheese salad. Well, it's a large hunk of goat's cheese which he's toasted on the top, with some salad leaves and tomato. It's delicious. It's followed by salmon baked with herbs, and then there's lots of cheeses, and medjool dates and mouth-watering dark truffle

The Impossible Search for the Perfect Man

chocolates. And I haven't even mentioned the wine. We've long finished the champagne and now we're on this gorgeous velvety red which tastes of oak and vanilla.

I'm not quite sure how I'm going to get home, but then, as if reading my mind, Marcus says he'll call me a cab – later on. So everything is just perfect.

'Every bit of that was wonderful,' I tell him sincerely. I don't think Arian tried to cook for me once in all the years I knew him. 'You couldn't have chosen better... and best of all, not a sprout in sight,' I add, most happily.

'Well, thank you kindly,' he says, looking rather pleased.

Then he takes my hand across the table.

'You know, Lou, I've messed up most of the dates we've been on,' he starts. 'And I don't know if you realise why...' he says, a little awkwardly. 'Only it's because as well as living with Karen, I worked with her too... and...' He sighs.

Oh. I can't help prickling at the mention of 'Karen', but Rachel was absolutely right.

'And you don't want to make the same mistake again?' I say gently, because actually, I really do understand.

He smiles and takes my hands in his. 'Does it sound silly? I know you're not remotely like Karen, but after that, I decided I wouldn't rush into anything.'

'It's okay,' I squeeze his hand. 'I understand.'

When neither of us can manage to eat another delicious thing, we retire to his living room, where amazingly Elmer is stretched out by the fire, snoring. Kicking off my boots, I collapse on one of the huge sofas, while Marcus sits at the other end, lifting up my feet so they're resting on his lap. And quite simply, lying there, warmed by the fire and the wine, it's bliss. And I'm glad I shaved my legs because Marcus is stroking them and it would have killed it slightly, the sensuous feel of stubble poking through my tights.

'There's only one problem,' he says softly after a while. 'Lovely though your feet are, they're not the bit I want to kiss...'

So of course, knowing that, I have to wriggle myself round, so it's the other half of me that's resting against Marcus, and then he kisses me.

And this time – apart from a snoring dog – it's just us and the kissing becomes more and more passionate.

And then I decide that all this taking it slowly and just seeing what happens isn't such a great idea after all, because right now I know exactly what I want. It's abundantly clear that Marcus feels just the same, as he takes my hand and leads me upstairs to his bedroom.

* * *

The next morning, I lie in Marcus's bed feeling extremely satisfied in every conceivable way, gazing at his ceiling, wondering for a moment if this is real. Then I think back over everything that happened last night. It's a jolly long time since I had sex like *that*. Come to think of it, I'm not sure I've ever had sex quite like *that*.

Marcus looks so relaxed. He's lying there asleep, stark bollock naked with his hair all scruffed up. And oh... he has a lovely body, I think to myself. Not too lean, but gloriously hard, definitely in all the right places – I remember that vividly too.

Marcus is waking up, and when he sees me lying there looking at him, he smiles this sexy, sleepy smile, and pulls me to him. And oh my goodness me, even in the cold light of day and the absence of an alcoholic haze, as he kisses me with a growing sense of urgency, suddenly very much awake, it's every bit as good as the night before, possibly better.

Then later, as we lie there, I suddenly remember. 'Marcus, I got you a Christmas present. It's in your car.'

'Thank you,' he says, but with a glint in his eye adds, 'Actually you've already given me the best Christmas present...' and kisses me soundly again.

Then he says casually, 'I got you something too... but I'll give it to you later if that's okay?'

Of course it is. And gosh. How decadent we are, just lying here in bed for so long. Then all of a sudden I leap up.

'Horace!' I squeak. 'He's in his stable waiting for his breakfast! I have to go to him!'

Marcus grabs hold of me and pulls me back, saying firmly, 'Rubbish. Firstly, it's only eight o'clock in the morning, and secondly, Horace won't mind one bit if you're late because it's yet another cold day, and given the choice, he'd probably much rather stand inside eating.'

Which is probably true, in which case, we might as well stay in bed just a tiny bit longer, so we do.

After Marcus has made a pot of fresh coffee and cooked us scrambled eggs, he offers to drive me home. I go and get his present from the car, and he laughs when he unwraps the CD.

'I'm not quite sure what to think about you giving me the soundtrack to your ex-husband's life, Louisa,' he says after a minute. 'But thanks anyway – I think!'

And he's really pleased with the wine. And I can't help wondering what his present is for me.

But when we get back to mine, it's weird. Firstly, Horace is in his paddock. I suppose he must have escaped, having learned the necessary skills from the incorrigible and much missed Wurzel. But then I notice he's wearing his great big outside rug. I frown. I definitely put his stable rugs on last night. I remember putting an extra one on because it was so cold.

Horace nickers when he sees us and then I hear a second, unfamiliar little neigh. And behind him there's a walking hairball with tinsel round it's neck.

'Er, Happy Christmas, Louisa,' says Marcus from behind me. I can tell from his voice that he's smiling. 'This is Mavis, and she is my Christmas present to you and Horace.'

Didn't I say something like this would happen? Horace is very pleased, and Mavis, who's a small, black Shetland pony, is also a right little tart. She minces around flicking her tail in Horace's face, and squealing indignantly if he eats the wrong bit of grass. But as she comes up to me, and nuzzles my outstretched hand, her large black eyes studying me through her great mass of forelock, there's a sweetness and knowingness about her that I instantly take to.

Marcus tells me that she's about ninety-three in human years but will probably outlive Horace, no problem. 'Also,' he adds because he knows it will ensure Mavis's security with me forever, 'she's been chucked out by her family, who have been forced to move because the husband's lost his job.'

'You'll have to tell them they can visit,' I say sympathetically.

'I already have.'

'So who is your partner in crime,' I enquire, because he clearly didn't do this on his own, which means that at least one other person knows I spent the night with Marcus last night. The question is *which* other person.

'Emma. Aided and abetted by Ben. Actually it was Ben who found Mavis in the first place. And I think Miles went with him to pick her up.'

So they were all in on it. It's good that Emma knows what devious scheming her boyfriend is capable of. Then the penny drops.

'So that's what you were talking about! That night in the pub, when you were all being mysterious. I thought something terrible was going on – not this!'

'Sorry... But you do like her, don't you?' asks Marcus in wounded tones.

I look at him in astonishment.

'Of course I do, you silly. I love her already. Come here and I'll show you just how much.'

The week between Christmas and New Year goes in a blur, after that. Taking things slowly has gone by the wayside and Marcus and I spend a lot of time together, both in and out of bed, so much so that I'm beginning to wonder, very tentatively, if maybe we might have a future...

37

It's a bitch of a January, however. It's that damp raw cold that's slightly above freezing and permeates every inch of your being. There's not even a glimmer of sunlight for days on end.

Work is back into its normal routine, though not excessively busy, which is just as well because Will has gone home to the good old US of A to catch up with his family.

Then one morning, Marcus has a meeting with Beamish, from which he comes out looking most thoughtful. Then the next morning there's another meeting, only this time it's Miles in with Beamish, and the following one, all three of them are in there together. Now I'm sorry, but don't tell me there's nothing go on. I catch Marcus on his way out.

'Marcus, what's going on? Only Beamish hasn't said a word, and there's clearly something...'

Marcus gives me a questioning look, and leads me outside into the biting January gloom.

'Seems I may have been offered a different job. It's a huge step up, and more involvement in running the practice,' he says. 'Only having seen Miles struggle with it, I can't help but wonder if I'd be better off sticking with the day-to-day side of things.'

But I'm not really taking his words in. Can he really be thinking of leaving? Then he sees my face.

'Lou, don't worry about it. Look, I've got a lot on my mind. Can I explain later? I'm already late thanks to Beamish... I'll fill you in. Pub at eight?'

I nod wordlessly, suddenly hating the tumult of emotion I'm feeling. If Marcus moves now, I'll *really* miss him, I think to myself. And in a flash I'm whisked back to when Arian told me about Karina, only it hits me, this is far worse.

I hold it together all day, building it up in my head with every passing hour. Then I get cross because these meetings have been going on for a few days, and Marcus hasn't shared any of it with me until today. I imagine the whole flaming recruitment drive all over again. How I'll have to plan Marcus's leaving do and get a card for everyone to sign just like I did for Karina. And a present – like maybe nice shiny new emasculators. By the evening, however, the hurt has given way to anger.

So much so, that I think, bollocks. I'm not going to the pub. I'm standing him up. But I do change into my favourite jeans and pin my hair up artfully messily, just in case he calls round, which is sort-of what I'm hoping he'll do.

He texts me at eight fifteen which I decide to ignore, then at eight thirty there's a knock at the door.

'What happened to you?' says Marcus, looking ever so slightly put out.

'I was thinking,' I say determinedly. 'It's easier to think here than in the pub. Er, quieter, and things.'

'Oh,' he says. 'Okay. Er, anything I should know about, Lou, only you seem a little er, upset?'

'Well, no. Not really,' I say coolly. 'Except for the fact that you're job hunting and you don't think it pertinent to even mention it to me, even though I am just divorced and emotionally fragile and we've been shagging each other senseless for the last few weeks.'

Marcus is trying not to grin. 'Um, three weeks and five days actually,' he says.

Is it? I'm momentarily distracted. Even I didn't know that.

'Louisa... come and sit down and I'll tell you exactly what's happened, because I'm still not sure what to make of it myself.'

And then he tells me that Beamish has asked him to take on Miles's job as joint senior partner, and that all the meetings have been to make absolutely certain that Miles is happy about it and then about how to present it to our clients.

I'm speechless. So he's *not* leaving and I've wasted all that angst on *nothing*. Okay. Let's take a step back here. I'm clearly missing the obvious again. After all, I have to remember that Marcus is a man and there are some things that men are absolutely rubbish at, communicating being one of them. I take the opportunity to explain this to him.

'Congratulations, Marcus,' I say slowly. 'It's very good. But now, I want you to imagine for a moment that you work in an office – my office. I'm a vet and I've been acting weirdly and secretively, oh and I'm still your girlfriend by the way, in the make-believe thing. Are you with me so far?'

He looks a little confused but nods his head.

'One day, I come out of the last of a string of meetings, and as I'm rushing out, I tell you out of the blue that I may have been offered a different job, but oh. *So* sorry, got to dash, darling. Now think about it. How does that make you feel?'

He thinks about it, then says, 'It's fine.' Then adds, 'I like the "darling".'

I refuse to be distracted. 'What do you mean "it's fine"? How can it possibly be fine? Don't you care that your girlfriend may be about to disappear and hasn't bothered to tell you?'

'Er, you're forgetting something here, Lou. It's fine, because I trust you.'

'Trust me?' I say, frowning. 'Even though your ex-husband betrayed you and you never thought you could trust anyone again?'

'Okay. So maybe I should have thought about that,' he says. 'I rather assumed that because we're, er, together, that you would trust me not to hurt you.'

Which rather takes the wind out of my sails, because isn't that exactly how it ought to be?

'Don't you trust me, Lou?' he asks more seriously, coming over and putting his arms around me. 'Because there's no way I'd ever do anything to deliberately hurt you, when I love you so much.'

'You *love* me?' I ask, incredulous. When did that happen? '*You* love *me*?'

'Yes, now shut up,' he says and kisses me, and much later on after a whole lot of kissing and much, much more, I eventually tell him that I've thought about it carefully, and actually, I love him too.

* * *

This afternoon, Rachel and I are having another secret wedding-planning meeting. Karina's also coming over with baby Oscar. Seems she won on the name front then. Last I heard, Arian wanted to call the poor thing Montgomery. A few weeks into motherhood has transformed Karina, and though she's tons thinner, she's still all curvy and motherly, and without doubt one of that new breed of supermums.

She comes in with this enormous Mary Poppins-type bag which looks innocent enough from the outside, but holds the contents of an entire nursery. Oscar is looking very chubby, which is hardly surprising as he seems permanently to be attached to one of her boobs, which have got even more massive since she's had him.

'How's it all going?' I ask her, as I settle Oscar comfortably on my lap.

'Oh, it's fine,' she says airily. 'He's so easy, and as long as he's not hungry he just gurgles or sleeps. I can't understand what all the fuss about newborns is,' she adds, as she busies around in my kitchen making us some tea.

'The funniest thing is Arian,' she says. 'Because for a man who apparently didn't want babies, he is completely besotted. Did he tell you that he's looking for another job?'

'He did mention it. To be honest I find it hard to imagine Arian without his uniform... Not in that sense,' I add hastily, looking at her expression. 'It's just that he's only ever been a pilot, or training to be one...'

Then I have to ask her. 'Er, do you ever hear from Will?'

From the colour of her ears, I already know the answer.

'Why do you ask?' she says guardedly.

'No reason,' I reply innocently. 'Just that he's still very single, and if I remember rightly, he had a bit of a thing for you...'

She sighs then, but looks far from happy. 'He asked me out several times, if you really want to know. He's a great guy, and wasn't the slightest put out about my, er, baggage.' She glances at Oscar. 'In the end, I had to tell him that I'm a mother now, and I'd really like to give things a proper go with Arian. And if that doesn't work out, well, we'll see. But I'm not planning on it. Actually, Arian asked me to marry him, Louisa. I think I might say yes...'

Golly. That's brilliant. And positively enlightening to realise I truthfully don't feel anything other than happy for all three of them.

'I've been seeing Marcus,' I tell her. 'A *lot* of Marcus.' I raise my eyebrows at her to make sure she gets the drift.

'That's great, Louisa,' she says, looking relieved. 'He's so nice. You really deserve a decent man.'

I'm just wondering if Karina and I will ever be entirely comfortable with each other, when our cautiously heart-warming conversation is interrupted by the arrival of teeny Rachel, complete with an armful of wedding brochures.

'Karina, this is Rachel, Agnes's daughter, and, Rachel, this is Karina who's about to marry my ex-husband.' I really have to stop saying that, because Karina's looking most peeved again.

Rachel looks at us quizzically but she's not her mother's daughter for nothing and doesn't ask. We explain our plans to Karina, who I know is trustworthy and who looks really impressed. Ben's come up trumps by offering to host the party at his place. It's a huge old house, a bit like a small stately home.

'Can I do anything?' she offers. 'Only I know a few people who might help. Especially as it's for Agnes and Beamish. Transport, for one. Mum's got an old carriage horse who loves to go on the occasional outing... do you think they'd like that?'

'Perfect,' I say decisively. 'I was thinking in terms of Miles's old Land Rover with white balloons tied all over it, but a horse and carriage is much more classy. And you will swear your mother to secrecy, won't you?'

'Of course.' Karina gives me a look which suggests that I must think she's stupid.

After a couple of hours, Karina takes Oscar home and Rachel fills me in about Miles.

'It's the most intense relationship I've ever been in,' she says, looking slightly apprehensive.

'Miles is extremely intense,' I say reassuringly, 'about everything, I should think. He should probably work for the RSPCA or something.'

'Actually,' she says. 'I've suggested we go skiing. I thought it would give him something else to think about, and it would be fun, and believe it or not, he's really keen. We're planning to go when Will gets back.'

I can't help thinking that Miles, on holiday, does sound a little unlikely.

Then she tells me, 'Miles hasn't had a holiday for six years...'

Now that I can believe.

'This is all sounding jolly serious and, well, intense...' I say, catching her eye with a giggle.

'Don't take the piss, Lou,' says Rachel. 'He's a lovely man. He just needs to lighten up a bit, that's all. So, what's going on with you and Marcus?'

Where do I start. 'He's a lovely man. Just fine. Doesn't need to lighten up at all,' I can't resist. 'It's really good, thanks. He gave me an ancient Shetland pony for Christmas.'

I'm not sure Rachel gets that. I don't tell her about the 'love' bit. Some things are for keeping to yourself.

38

On Sunday morning, I get dressed in layers and layers of clothes, with tights and thermals under my jodhpurs, about five T-shirts under my thickest fleece and three pairs of socks. Marcus is lying in my bed trying to suppress his laughter, telling me I look about three times my normal size, which I do not appreciate one bit.

But it's worth it for a canter through the woods. Mavis was not impressed at being left behind, and her squeaky little voice followed us for ages after we set out. And though it's bitterly cold, at least it's dry, and so lovely to be out on my horse, I don't really notice the wind burning my cheeks. And when we get back, and Horace is rugged up and back in his field with Mavis, I go inside to find Marcus has coffee on the go, is cooking bacon sandwiches and has even been out to buy the Sunday papers.

'This is perfect,' I say through a mouthful of bacon. 'Just what a girl needs on a Sunday morning after a freezing old ride in the woods.'

He grins and comes over, grabbing my arms and pulling me to him. 'I think you might need some help getting all those clothes off,' he says mischievously, starting by peeling off my fleece. And my perfect Sunday gets even more perfect.

After lunch, Marcus goes home but asks me if I'll go round to his this evening. We are spending an awful lot of time together. But of course it's not awful, it's good, and so I say yes, of course I'll see him later.

This afternoon I'm going to see Leonie. Pete is off on one of his bike races again. Seems like biking is as bad or as good as golf, depending on your viewpoint. It can keep men occupied for entire days, which definitely has to be a good thing.

'It's great to see you!' says Leo, looking far more like her old self. Her face has lost its tired, worried look, and she's had her hair cut so it hangs in layers just past her shoulders. 'I've got loads to tell you about. Since the New Year, it seems like everything's gone a bit mad...'

'Has Pete gone back to flying?' I ask, because I know he was due to start this month.

'He did. Three weeks ago.' Leonie looks more serious.

'And?' I prompt. 'How did it go?'

'Not that good.' She sighs. 'Actually, calamitous, in the sense that Pete came to the realisation that he doesn't want to do it any more. He says the job is to blame – at least in part – for his depression.'

'So what now?' I ask, alarmed. 'I mean, he can't just do nothing, Leo. I know *you* work, but he has to do something...'

'He is...' she says, starting to smile. 'He's been really lucky and negotiated some part-time work flying for the next two months, after which he's leaving. For good. He's starting, well, started actually, an internet business sourcing and selling unusual bike parts. I know it sounds weird, but believe it or not, it's already taking off.'

'Golly,' I say, most impressed. 'There must be something in the water. I saw Arian just before Christmas, and he too was talking about finding something else to do.'

But Leo's jumping up and down now. 'Oh! Didn't I say? They're doing this together! Arian's flying part-time too and Sylvie, you know, Karina's mum, has an empty barn they can use for stock! So they're both ploughing in some funds and racing ahead with it! It's very exciting!'

No doubt it is. And also very weird, because however much I'd love to, I just cannot get shot of Arian. And now that Leo and Pete know Karina, and Sylvie too, it would seem my old life and my new one are to be thoroughly entangled for some time to come. So much for moving on.

Oh my giddy aunt. Here's Pete, all hot and sweaty, carrying a pointy cycling helmet and wearing incredibly tight Lycra. And particularly tight shorts that bulge in all the wrong places. I avert my eyes, and catch a waft of armpit and generally sweaty man. There's no avoiding the fact that Pete most definitely niffs.

'Hi, Lou,' he says cheerfully, as he kisses Leo anyway. 'I'll just go and have a shower. You look well,' he says, sounding just like the old Pete again.

'Thanks, Pete. Um, so do you,' I say doubtfully.

'Anyway, what were you going to tell me?' asks Leo. 'Quickly, before Pete comes back down.'

'Marcus,' I say smugly. 'We've been spending a lot of time together. Like most days, actually. And most nights.'

Leo looks at me anxiously, probably wondering what specimen of manhood I've hooked up with this time. She hasn't met Marcus.

'Is it love?' she asks quietly. 'I do hope so, only you look so sparkly and happy, and I couldn't bear for someone to break your heart again.'

'I think it is,' I say carefully. 'At least, he says he loves me.'

And then she grins and her eyes go all misty. 'About time,' she says.

*　*　*

Marcus is exceptionally affectionate this evening. We have soup and toast in front of a blazing fire, our feet up on the coffee table as we watch TV. Then we have a very early night, because actually we're quite tired so it's a very sensible thing to do. And then, later, as we're lying there sleepily he says, 'I'm beginning to get rather used to this...' and promptly falls asleep.

I lie there awake a bit longer after that, thinking about what he just said – because the truth is, I am too.

39

Emma is moving in with Ben! She's beaming from ear to ear and asking around to see who'd like her old sofa and it's all unbelievably exciting! She told me at work this morning, but has been rushing around ever since, so I made her promise under threat of death to come round to mine this evening.

'Oh, Lou, it's fantastic...' she says, positively glowing. 'We went riding on Sunday, and we rode over to the Stony Plough at Frampton.'

The Stony Plough is a tiny little pub in the middle of nowhere, even more out of the back of beyond than Lower Shagford, with no car park, just an old-fashioned paddock to put your horses in.

'Anyway,' Emma continues excitedly. 'When we went in, there was hardly anyone else there. You know what it's like. We sat at one of those rickety old tables, and then Ben said he'd just love it if I'd move in to his and we could just spend all our time off together like this, and what did I think...'

'So what did you say?' I ask, knowing only too well Emma's thoughts about marriage and commitment.

'Well,' she says, her eyes shining as she looks at me. 'The best thing is he hasn't mentioned marriage – at least, not yet, thank goodness – and he's just so relaxed about it all. There's no pressure, I just love being with him.'

I sort of get it actually. And being smug unmarrieds is the perfect arrangement for Emma. And who knows, in time I'm sure Ben will make an honest woman of her if that's what they decide they want. So all in all, it is *very* exciting.

Then I tell her how Marcus and I are spending nearly all our evenings together and how wrong I was about him being arrogant.

She's not even slightly surprised. 'I knew you fancied him, way back.'

'You couldn't. Because I didn't, Em. I didn't even like him. Not to start with.'

'Yeah, right,' says my friend most annoyingly.

Our gossip divulged, Emma and I head over to the pub; Marcus is already there with Ben, who has a bottle of champagne and pours us both a glass, before saying that he and Emma are actually indebted to me, and that if it wasn't for me, it would most probably be a very different story. Gosh. I feel quite strange. I mean Emma's my friend, so why on earth *wouldn't* I want to help her?

'What was that about?' asks Marcus, when eventually we have a chance to talk.

'Well,' I say carefully, because there's not really any need for Marcus to know about all that horoscope malarkey. 'Let's just say that Emma had a personal problem for a while. Only a little teeny one, but I helped her to sort it out, that's all.'

'Oh,' he says, looking at me. 'Just wondered, that's all.'

* * *

The miracle has finally happened and Beamish has allowed Zac to order a super-whizzy computer. How he got Beamish to agree, I'll never know, but the main thing is that he has. And when it gets here, Zac will be responsible for setting it up and teaching thickos like me how to use it.

Marcus is thriving in his new role as joint senior partner, and I must say, it suits him down to the ground. He doesn't mind all the meetings and dealing with complicated paperwork or any of the stuff that Miles loathed, while Miles is as happy as Miles ever can be, just being a regular, everyday vet wholeheartedly devoted to his beloved patients.

Will's back too, larger than life and twice as handsome. His first morning back, he marches in and sweeps me up in his arms and swings me round, before giving me a resounding kiss on the cheek. Oh, and is that Paris I've spotted, illegally speeding down the drive in one of her mother's cars?

'Will!' I shriek, but not too loudly because it's rather nice being swept off your feet by a gorgeous American.

'Hey, Louisa!' he says loudly. 'How's the old place managed without me?'

I fill him in about Marcus's promotion and Miles willingly being un-promoted, and about Emma moving in with Ben, which produces an expectedly enthusiastic response from him.

'And have you seen Karina at all?' he asks more quietly, frowning.

'I have, Will,' I say gently. 'Actually, you probably ought to know. Arian's proposed.'

'Beats me what she sees in him,' he says sadly. 'After what he did to you too. The guy just doesn't deserve her.'

'Cheer up, Will,' I say. 'With a wedding coming up, I bet you anything there is romance around the corner just waiting for you.'

'Yeah, well... in the meanwhile I guess I better do some work,' he says, peering into the diary. 'How's it going, mate?' he calls to Zac, who mumbles back his usual, "Kay.'

'You've got Daisy Mitchell first,' I say, 'who comes with a health warning. Ben used to go out with her and she has her horses shot when she's bored with them.'

Which makes him wince and rightly so.

'Then you've got a new client. Billie Lincoln. Don't know her at all, but she keeps dressage horses and one of them's slightly unsound. Here's the address.'

Will heads out just as Miles comes in, looking very long faced for a man who's about to go off on a skiing holiday. What on earth's the matter with him?

'Hey, Miles, what's up?'

It's probably another horse he's worrying about. *Oh no* – my field is full. At least for now.

'Er, you know Rachel quite well don't you?' he says miserably.

'Of course I do,' I say. 'Why?'

'Think I've blown it,' he says, looking utterly morose. 'I just can't go away on this skiing holiday she's got planned. I don't know... I keep thinking, what if there's a crisis and I'm needed here, or one of my clients gets sick?'

Oh honestly. Miles is *ridiculously* obsessive about his clients.

'For God's sake Miles, I'm afraid you are being ridiculous,' I say firmly. 'What could possibly happen that Marcus, Emma and Will couldn't cope with?'

'That's exactly what Rachel said,' he says, even more despondently. 'Then she said that I was married to my job and it was pointless us continuing our relationship.' He looks as though he's going to cry.

'None of us are indispensable,' I say to him gently. 'It's not healthy to let your job rule your life like this. You're a great vet, Miles, but aren't there other things you want too? Like seeing the world – or have a family maybe?'

He sighs. 'I suppose I've never been fussed. My job's always been enough for me. It's just that I thought Rachel understood and was okay with it...'

Oh God. He's done it again. Poor Miles, but this really is ridiculous. He needs help.

'I think you should talk to someone, Miles,' I suggest. 'This isn't normal. I'll get you the name of someone and make you an appointment – if you'd like me to.'

Miles raises shocked eyes to stare at me. 'You think I'm mad, don't you?' His eyes look terrified.

'A little bit, yes,' I say honestly. 'And would it honestly hurt to go and talk to someone who might be able to help you feel a lot happier? Think about it...'

Hmmm... Louisa Mulholland, personal counsellor, Louisa Mulholland, wedding planner... Never mind the day job at the *nerve centre* of the practice, as Beamish puts it. Life is going through one of those slightly uncontrollable phases again with all the stuff that's landing on my doorstep.

And this evening, sure enough, Rachel pitches up there too.

'I've given up with Miles,' she says resignedly. 'Did he tell you? I've tried so hard to get him out of his rut, but he refuses to budge, and he's dragging me down with him. It's a pity, because I think we could have had something really special. *I really liked him...*' A tear trickles down her cheek.

'Trouble is, Rachel, leopards don't change their spots,' I say sadly. 'Maybe you're better off without him.'

But it's a waste of a perfectly good skiing holiday...

'Sorry,' she says. 'I didn't mean to dump this on you, Lou.'

'Don't worry,' I say. 'And I'm sure things will work out for the best.'

And I've a funny feeling they probably *Will*.

Even though she's puffy faced and not at all in the mood, I drag Rachel over to the pub where we treat ourselves to the expensive version of the fish and chips, which is yummy. And then we're joined by Marcus and Will, who rally round and make a fuss of Rachel. She's much brighter when we leave.

'Didn't quite work out then?' asks Marcus as I stand at the bar waiting to pay.

'Erm, no, not really,' I say.

'Miles still married to the job?'

'You could say,' I agree.

'Fancy coming back to mine, gorgeous?' he whispers seductively in my ear and I giggle.

'I'd love to, but I think tonight, Rachel needs me rather more than you do...' I say regretfully.

'Don't be too sure about that,' he says darkly, kissing me on my neck.

Oh. I know where I want to go – but I haven't forgotten how it feels either, when the man of your dreams turns out not to be.

40

In the end, I talk to Pete about Miles's problems and he offers to have a bit of a chat with him.

'Are you sure he'll be okay with that, Lou? Only I don't think I'd have been too keen on any interfering, however well meaning.'

'To be honest, Pete, he's in such a bad way I think he'll just be grateful. Tell you what, I'll invite you both over to mine. It might make things easier.'

And believe it or not, it sort of works. After Pete has told Miles all of what he's been through over the last few months, Miles is regarding him with more interest and eventually agrees to go and see Pete's therapist, which is a better outcome than even I had imagined.

Then we all go to the pub and I introduce Pete to Marcus. It's very weird, because Pete and Leonie are part of my old-life-with-Arian and yet here's Pete slap bang in the middle of my new-life-with-Marcus. Of course they get on really well and talk about bloke things like men do. Including cycling.

So I leave them to it and track down Emma, who has far more interesting things to talk about and we decide I'm going to throw a dinner party, which will be a sure-fire success for one very good reason: Emma's promised to help me with the cooking. Marcus is coming, of course, and Ben, Pete and Leonie. Then I decide to invite Will, because I'm very fond of Will in a big-brother sort of way, and then I feel sorry for Rachel because of the whole business with Miles.

So, all in all, with a few ulterior motives thrown in, like Leo meeting Marcus, and bringing together two lonely hearts, it should be jolly good fun.

Saturday afternoon finds too many cooks in the kitchen, with my slavering dog lurking under the table, and with Emma's eagle eye on things, it's coming along just fine. We've dreamed up this fabulous menu, starting with Provencal fish soup, which smells absolutely divine, all fishy and garlicky, and I simply have to keep tasting it. Just to make sure it's okay. Then it's venison casserole, followed by vanilla cheesecake and an array of scrumptious cheeses. In fact, much to Elmer's joy, my kitchen looks every bit as exciting as the inside of a deli shop. Oh, and there's lots and lots of wine, and we thought we'd have a tiny little snifter of champagne now – just to help us with the cooking, you understand.

Marcus is first to arrive and finds the carnage in the kitchen quite amusing.

'Er, Lou, would you like me to help clear up while you get changed?' he suggests, a twinkle in his eye.

Emma and Rachel are already in my bedroom turning themselves into glamour pusses, but I'm still fiddling around with place settings in my grubby, horsy jeans with that dragged-through-a-hedge backwards hairdo that Marcus must be getting used to by now.

'S'fine!' I sashay over and plant a kiss on his lips. 'Is something wrong?'

'I think you might prefer to,' he says firmly, steering me towards the mirror at the bottom of the stairs.

Oops. He's quite right. Never mind the hair. I am truly a sight, with grease and cheesecake mixture spattered all over my top half and any remaining make-up smudged under my eyes.

This was not the impression I wanted to make at all, so I fly upstairs and turf Emma out of the bathroom. She's been in there ages and if she does any more glamorising, I might as well crawl under a rock in the garden. Between her and Rachel who's as perfect and dainty as ever, it's like they're the Cinderellas and I'm the ugly sister.

But actually, once I've tamed my unruly hair, repaired my make-up, and put on this flirty little number with my sexiest high-heeled boots, I feel quite good, even next to these two and Marcus whistles appreciatively when I go back downstairs.

It's a bit of a rowdy evening. Leo announces to all of us that she loves Marcus, Will slags off Arian and absolutely no one tries to stop him. Fortunately, no one is driving as they've all decided to splash out on taxis. I thank my lucky stars for mopey Miles, who's volunteered to be on call. He's much happier in a stable or field than socialising with the rest of us.

The food goes down a treat, as does far too much alcohol. I sit Rachel next to Will, watching developments out of the corner of my eye, most discreetly.

It's about one in the morning when everyone finally goes. Except Marcus, naturally. Even in her pissed state, Emma has most efficiently sorted most of the kitchen which is possibly why Ben asked her to move in with him.

'Nightcap?' offers Marcus tipsily, a half-drunk bottle of brandy in his hand.

''Kay,' I agree.

'I really like your friends,' says Marcus, as we collapse onto my sofa. 'It was a great evening. I haven't been to a dinner party like that in years.'

'It's because of Emma, you know,' I say. 'I can't really cook like that. She truly is superwoman in the kitchen.'

'You're doing it again, Lou,' says Marcus mock-sternly. 'Selling yourself short. I thought you'd agreed you wouldn't. Now listen,' he continues, pulling me over closer to him and slopping my brandy on his shirt. 'Never mind that. What I want to know is, are you happy? With me I mean?'

'Um, yes,' I say honestly, then seeing his face, add 'Very, actually. Can't you tell?'

'I thought so.' Marcus is very smiley. I think he's a little bit pissed too. 'Only, we spend so much time in each other's houses, Lou. To be honest, I can't imagine being without you.' And he kisses me like he really means it.

'Actually I...' he starts. Then stops.

'What?' I say, pulling back slightly. There's a strange look on his face. 'What, Marcus?'

'Nothing,' he says, which is most annoying of him, but that, for the moment, is that.

* * *

When I wake up in the morning, I creep out of bed so as not to wake him, wincing as I move my thumping head too quickly. After last night, I'm fragile and some nice bracing air is just what's needed.

A stable in the early morning really is one of the most peaceful places to be, and I stand for ages tickling Horace's ears and stroking his noble head, while he just cosies up and enjoys it.

We spend a lovely, lazy Sunday, then all too soon it's over and it's back to the fray. Monday morning is frenetic. It doesn't help that the new computer's delivered while Zac's on his first day of vet nurse training. But it will have to wait, because clients have been ringing in all morning. There have been a couple of outbreaks of strangles in the area, which is horribly contagious and very nasty, and means an awful lot of anxious horse-owners want their darlings checked.

I try my best to group the calls geographically but of course it doesn't always work like that. Some of the clients have their favourites: like Mrs Dawlish, who will only see Miles, as will the horse sanctuary, but the snag is these are opposite ends of the county, and so the vets are tearing all over the place. It's definitely one of those days. In the end, I call Beamish and ask him if there's any chance he could spare a few hours. After all, he never said he was retiring completely.

'You fine young people are doing a jolly good job without me,' he told us all jovially, just a little while ago. Secretly, I think he's too busy canoodling with Agnes.

Fortunately, when he answers my call, he says, 'Um, no problem. Um, be right over,' and five minutes later he's there. I'm not at all sure he should drive at that speed, but today it might be quite useful, so I give him the list of calls and then he screams off in his car like Lewis Hamilton.

That afternoon there's another panic-stricken phone call. I don't recognise the distraught voice at the other end of the phone, but eventually decipher the garbled words enough to establish that it's Paris. One of her multi-million pound show-jumpers has colic.

As I try to calm her down, Emma comes in. Holding my hand over the receiver, I call her over.

'Em, do you have time to whiz up and take a look at PM-T's show-jumper? Colic?'

Emma nods and heads off again.

'Paris. Emma will be with you in two minutes. I hope he's okay,' I add, not terribly professionally but I feel sorry for her. She's obviously really worried about her horse, but on the other hand, it is just the tiniest bit funny, that the one time she has a genuine excuse to see a vet, the only one that's free happens to be a woman.

***

I haven't seen Karina for ages. She's gone back to flying part-time, and Sylvie, I believe, has been enlisted in her capacity as granny, as unpaid childminder to little Oscar.

Now that it's March, the worst of the winter is behind us, or so I'm hoping and there are daffodils springing up all over the place, making Lower Shagford look even more picturesque than ever. But something else is looming – and rather too quickly. Beamish and Agnes's wedding.

Rachel and I are very busy bees as we cross all the Ts and dot the Is, suddenly aware of the enormous pressure of time. It's all coming together though and all we need to figure out is how to get them to their own party without giving the game away. In the end, we decide that the only way to do it is once the happy couple have left the church, we'll prime Will's vet mate to phone Beamish and tell him there's an emergency with one of Ben's horses and that it's all hands on deck. Beamish absolutely won't be able to resist it. Nor will he smell a rat when we all go charging after them.

Karina's suggested that Rachel and I take the carriage horse for a spin, just to check we think it will be okay for the wedding. I tell her I'd love to, but I've never driven a horse and carriage, and don't know the first thing about it, so Karina says she'll come with us.

'I'll teach you, Louisa. It's an absolute doddle,' she says scathingly.

Fine. Okay. So I don't mind Karina teaching me, at all. I'm

rather looking forward to it, in fact. But then, at the last minute, Rachel pulls out because she can't get away from work, and then, Karina gets called out on standby. I ask you. My friends are completely useless.

With all this time suddenly on my hands, I call Marcus, who suggests a picnic.

'Perfect,' I tell him. 'Only please, no talk about balloons and music and spit roasts – I need some serious, wedding-free time.'

'Fine,' he says briskly. 'I'll pick you up in an hour. And bring Elmer.'

It's a perfect day for a picnic. On the chilly side but sunny, with a few fluffy clouds in a pale sky.

'Where are we going?' I ask Marcus, as we head away from Winchester and into the rolling countryside.

'Wait and see.' He grins. 'Elmer's going to love it.'

'Have you a plan B?' I ask. 'In case it rains?' I'm looking at the clouds which are getting ominously darker the further we drive.

'Don't worry,' says Marcus confidently. 'It won't, Lou.' Then he changes the subject and witters on about this fancy bike Pete was telling him about.

When we pull up in a stony car park, I've no idea where we are, but Elmer, as predicted, is out of her mind with excitement and making mad squeaking whimpers from the back. Marcus lets her out, and when he closes the door, he's carrying an old-fashioned picnic hamper.

'Wow! A proper picnic!'

'Of course,' he says impatiently. 'What other kind is there? Here – can you carry this?' He passes me a folded rug. 'It's not that far from here. But it's a great spot – it'll be worth it.'

Suddenly, a large splat of rain lands on my head. But with a whistle to Elmer, Marcus strides off between the trees, oblivious to the fact that the sky is turning blacker by the second. But he's right.

In just a few minutes, the trees open out and we're faced with what ought to be a glorious view – usually.

'Oh.' Marcus looks disappointed. 'Pity. You can normally see right across the lake.'

I have to take his word for it, because it's now more like twilight than daylight. A monochromatic landscape stretches in front of us, painted in shades of grey. It's true – I can see the water, but only a short way before it blurs into the mistiness.

'Never mind.' Marcus takes the blanket and spreads it expertly on the ground, just as another drop of rain splats in my eye.

'Um, Marcus... Are you sure this is a good idea? Only it looks as though it's about to pour...'

'Nonsense, Lou. It's just a spot or two. It'll pass.'

He opens the hamper and it really is a proper picnic he's brought us. I forget the clouds and dive in – there's sliced ham and whole cheeses, with the Hope and Anchor's crusty bread. And there's strawberries too. Suddenly I'm starving.

'This is wonderful,' I tell him, fishing out the china plates that he's packed carefully in the bottom.

'I love it here,' says Marcus wistfully, clearly reliving some of his misspent youth – or teenaged fumblings – he doesn't say. I'm about to ask, but then two things happen. First Elmer appears from the lake and leaps on top of us. Then just as Marcus drags her off us, there's a flash of lightning followed by a clap of thunder overhead. And then, the heavens open.

'Let's get back to the car,' shouts Marcus, grabbing the rug and flinging everything back in the hamper as we make a run for it.

Elmer is loving every second of this, leaping into the air catching raindrops, then yelping at every crack of thunder as though it's bitten her. Safely inside the car, however, Marcus looks crestfallen.

The Impossible Search for the Perfect Man

'Don't worry.' I reach for his hand. 'You weren't to know. And it's like you said. It's only rain. It'll pass.'

He sits there, silent, then suddenly he leaps out of the car and strides round to my door, opening it and pulling me outside too. The rain has become a monsoon, soaking my clothes, slicking my hair to my head.

'Let go!' I shriek, half laughing at him. 'Marcus! We're soaked! What are you doing!'

But he pulls me into a clearing where we stand unsheltered beneath the sky.

'Okay... You said you were happy, Lou...' He's shouting, because it's raining so hard the noise is deafening. He's drenched – we both are – and I've still no idea what this is about.

'And proposals are supposed to be memorable, aren't they?'

Did I hear him right? My heart misses a beat and suddenly, I'm not thinking about the rain. There's another crack of thunder and a howl from the car, as there, surrounded by water, he goes down on one knee, holding my hand tightly, pressing something into it.

'I know you're right off weddings and it can be a small, simple one, I don't care, but, Louisa... will you be my wife?'

As he says the words, time stands still, paradoxically, not unlike it did when Arian left me. Only that was a lifetime ago and this couldn't be more different, because this is Marcus, who I love more than anyone in the world. His eyes are bright with excitement and the rain, and with hope, as he waits for me to say something. I look at him, then at the beautiful ring he's just given me, trying to scorch this extraordinary moment into my memory forever.

'*Yes!!*' I screech, flinging my arms up at the merciless heavens and twirling round, and as he gets up, throw myself into his arms.

* * *

As we drive home, the aroma of wet flatcoat filling the car, I'm the happiest I've ever been. I can't take my eyes off the ring and I keep touching it and twisting it slightly.

'Are you sure it fits?' Marcus asks.

'Perfectly,' I tell him. I don't think I'll ever be able to stop smiling. 'It's the loveliest ring. I can't believe you chose it.'

'What's that supposed to mean?' He pretends to be huffy. 'I have excellent taste.'

Then a bit later, he pulls over and turns the engine off, then pulls me into his arms.

'Did you really have no idea?' he asks.

'None,' I tell him. 'Whatsoever. You have been quite cryptic, though.'

'In what way?'

'Just saying things.' I smile at him. 'Nice things, though. So don't worry.'

'I'm not worrying. I'm just happy.' He kisses me.

'So am I,' I mumble.

And I am. I'd no idea I could feel like this. It surpasses all of my weird dreams. Then the horrific thought occurs to me that this is actually one of them and any moment, I'll wake up and be in my own little bed with a sad, empty feeling because I imagined it all... And then I'm returned to the moment by the smell of dog fart.

And, for once, there are no words.

41

I feel incredibly self-conscious, as if I'm wearing the crown jewels on my left hand. My beautiful ring is an antique, Marcus says, because he wants everything about our getting married to be different to my first time. *Hallelujah*! I can get married in pink or black or something I really love, with my hair blowing in the wind and my feet bare on the grass... And absolutely no bridesmaids of course, because then I'd have to ask Emma, and much though I love her, I'm not being upstaged by anyone on my wedding day. In the end, I decide I'm not going to tell anyone. I'll wait and see if anyone notices. But no one says a word, until later on, Karina calls.

'Well?' she says. I've no idea what she's talking about.

'Oh, for goodness' sake, Louisa,' says Karina irritably. 'Did you say yes?'

'Oh. That. Of course I said yes!' I say, then I'm suspicious. 'Was this a set-up? There is a carriage horse, isn't there? It's really important, you know...'

'Thank God!' she says. 'Of course there is. Don't worry, I'll take care of it. Look, congratulations. I'm sorry but Oscar's screaming – I have to go.'

Most disappointingly I don't see Emma the whole of the rest of the day. Sam gives me a wink across the yard, but not even Mrs Boggle comes in tonight to tell me how she always cries at weddings.

And now I've another wedding to plan. Mine and Marcus's. In spite of the lack of interest around me, I feel so zingy and happy, I could cry.

Marcus comes over to mine as soon as he finishes work.

'Haven't changed your mind, have you?' he asks teasingly, holding me close against him.

'No way not ever,' I say, and throw my arms round his neck.

'Have you fed those horses yet?' he asks.

'Ages ago,' I reply.

'Well, it's a bit early for the pub,' he says, looking at his watch.

So I take his hand and lead him upstairs, because after all, we have lots to do. And to start with, we need to decide whose house we're going to live in, and absolutely the best place to do that from has to be my bed.

There's yet another surprise in store when we get to the pub. As we go in, I notice that everyone from the practice is there, which is most unusual, and then they all yell, 'Surprise!'

I can't believe it. All the vets, Zac and Sam, Beamish and Agnes, Leonie and Pete, Rachel, even Karina, but fortunately she's had the good sense to leave Arian at home. That would have been just a little *too* weird. But nothing can spoil this evening for me.

It turns out I was right and the whole let's-go-carriage-driving bit was a complete set-up, right from the beginning. Rachel was in on it and Karina wasn't called out anywhere. Which means Marcus must have been feeling reasonably confident to tell them before he'd even asked me.

'My boyfriend can be just *soo* romantic, I had no idea...' I tell Emma very smugly, feeling warm and tingly again, now that I'm telling her about it. 'A picnic in one of the most glorious spots you've ever seen...' I omit the part about the thunder and my farting dog.

Will sweeps me up in an enormous hug and even Miles manages a wan smile. Then someone pushes another glass of champagne into my hand, and Beamish clears his throat and knocks on the table.

Oh no. Not one of Beamish's speeches. I hope everyone's sitting comfortably – this isn't going to be quick.

'Ahem.'

Here we go...

'I um, really am delighted you are all here tonight.' He beams round at everyone, looking highly pleased with himself as Marcus squeezes my hand. 'I'm sure all of you, um, would like to join me in a toast to, er, Marcus, who is a splendid, um, vet, and to Louisa, who, um, keeps our, er, practice on its feet... so without, further ado, a toast – to Marcus and Louisa.'

Phew. That's it. Marcus and I clink our glasses together and then everyone else want to clink glasses with us. I'm so happy I could fly – and it just keeps getting better.

By the time we wander home to mine, I'm floating, literally on air, my head full of plans for our future.

'You're quiet,' he remarks.

'Just thinking – about weddings, and where we're going to live, darling Marcus. Tell me where you would like to live.'

'Do you know, Lou, much though I like my cottage, I think I'd like to put it on the market,' he says decisively, making me float a little higher.

'So, why don't I move in with you and your animals, and we can just take our time deciding. What do you think?'

'Oh, Marcus,' I say, my heart singing because it's exactly what I want too. Then we'll have oodles of time to find ourselves a family-sized house with a paddock and stables for Horace and Mavis, and bedrooms for children... and then it strikes me. Oh my God. We've never even mentioned the subject of children... What if he's like Arian and doesn't want them? I'll have to give him back my ring and tell everyone the wedding's off and it will be even worse than when Arian left me.

Then he says casually, 'I suppose we ought to find somewhere with at least three bedrooms. I mean, *hopefully*...'

Then I come back a little to earth, because he stops walking and turns to look at me. 'Well, I sort of assumed we'd have children... you better tell me if I'm wrong... we haven't talked about it, have we?'

There's a brief silence as the hugest smile plasters itself across my face.

'I want loads and loads of children,' I say, flinging my arms around him. 'Well, at least two or three. If we can. And if not, we'll adopt lots of orphans...'

Marcus silences me with an absolute smacker of a kiss. I think I can safely say that we're in agreement on this one, too.

* * *

Oh, Lordy. I am now instrumental in planning *two* weddings, and am whirling around feeling madder than ever. Normal humans who do that are rather glamorous and called wedding organisers, so I've no idea what's going wrong.

Last weekend I took Marcus home to meet my parents. Mum was a bit sniffy to start with, but Dad was Dad, and welcomed him warmly to our family. Even Mum thawed in the end, especially when Marcus told her what a delicious lunch it was, which it really, truly wasn't, though thankfully she didn't cook sprouts.

Marcus can be very charming. He also said to them that seeing as it was my second marriage, it would be different this time and that though we weren't quite sure what we were doing yet, we would love them to be an important part of it, but we would be paying. So Dad said immediately that he'd like to buy the wine, and Mum wants to help me choose my dress – all this, even though we haven't set a date...

In turn, Marcus takes me down to Salcombe to meet his family, which is lovely but jolly scary. He says it's okay to take Elmer and we leave Horace and Mavis in the capable hands of Emma. Salcombe is gorgeous, but I'm too nervous to enjoy myself, even though Marcus's parents turn out to be lovely and his mum says she's so glad to see him happy after everything he's been through.

We take Elmer for some lovely walks, and Marcus tells me how when he was a boy, his father was hideously strict.

'You'd never know now,' he says ruefully, 'but I wouldn't say it was the happiest time. I don't want us to be like that with our children, Lou, I want them to have idyllic, carefree childhoods, if we're able to give them that.'

Gosh. So do I. In fact, I can't wait to get started on the children part of things. I can see them already – an adorable little pink-cheeked baby sleeping in an old-fashioned wooden cradle, wrapped in snuggly blankets like the one I bought for little Oscar. I can just see too, tangle-haired toddlers running around on the lawn with chocolate on their faces and an elderly, grizzle-faced Elmer as their nanny, and when they're older, having all their friends round for tons of parties that Marcus and I will moan about, because ours will be the kind of house where everyone wants to be.

'Louisa?' Marcus is saying to me. '*Louisa?* Did you hear me? You were miles away again...'

* * *

My state of bliss doesn't alter. I honestly can't believe how I feel and how incredibly, unbelievably lucky I am. Have I really found my happy ending? I have this wonderful man in my life who wants to marry me, all these fantastic friends and a job I absolutely love. It's as though everything in my life that has gone before was simply building up to this.

The past is just that – the past – and I don't feel even a tiny bit smug or self-deserving. I've learned the hard way that you can afford to take nothing for granted and so I just feel quietly, gratefully incredulous, as I wonder at the way things have turned out. And very slowly, allow myself to get a little bit used to it too.

It's one of those rare, fairy-tale interludes and I bask in every single second of it. It lasts for a few blissful days. And then I get home from work to find a message on my answerphone. As I play it back, reality strikes with a vengeance and my bubble well and truly bursts.

42

It's my mother, sounding very strained and odd, even for her. The first thing I do is call Marcus, but he's out on a call so I leave him a tearful message.

'My dad's in hospital... they think he's had a heart attack. Oh, Marcus, I'm terrified... He's in intensive care...'

I rush around my house in a blur, throwing some things into a bag, and leaving a message for Emma because she's not answering either. Then as I'm walking out of the door, my phone rings and, thank God, this time, it's Marcus.

'Can you hold on for ten minutes, Lou? I'll be right over and I'll drive you to the hospital,' he says most decisively.

So I sit down and wait, then get up and pace around because I'm desperate to be on my way. I can't help thinking, what if just ten minutes means I'm too late. What if Dad dies before I get there... It's the longest ten minutes of my life and all I can think of is that he's my dad and I don't know what I'd do without him.

Marcus is seven minutes, not ten. I know because I've had my eyes fixed on my clock watching every second tick by. He hugs me tight, then picks up my bag.

'Come on, let's get going. Elmer will be fine here,' he says firmly. 'Emma or someone will come and pick her up later.'

The drive takes an hour and a half. Marcus drops me at the hospital entrance, then goes off to park, saying he'll catch me up, so I belt along those corridors, plea-bargaining with God as I run. It feels like a race against time, to get to my dad before it's too late. Then I find intensive care and clatter through the swing doors, making all the nurses look up.

One of them comes over and says very quietly, 'Are you looking for someone?'

'David Sparks,' I say tearfully. 'I'm his daughter.'

'Follow me,' she says. 'Are you in the picture about what's happened?' she asks.

I shake my head.

'He's had a major heart attack, but he's responding well,' she says. 'He's on medication to thin his blood, and we need to monitor him for a few days, to assess the damage to his heart. But we're reasonably hopeful at this stage that he's going to be okay.'

I'm too relieved to speak, and in any case I can't, because the tears are pouring down my face again.

Dad's lying in a bed wired up all these machines. He looks pale and tired, and Mum is sitting beside him looking worried to death.

'What are you doing here, poppet?' he asks in a rather breathless voice.

'Oh, Dad,' I say and bend to kiss his stubbly cheek.

'Hello, Mum,' I say and she actually kisses my cheek for once, rather than the air.

'Your father's given all of us a scare,' she says, making a valiant effort at sounding bright. 'But fortunately, the early signs are that he should be fine...' She gives him a small smile and takes his hand. I can't remember seeing her do that before.

Then Marcus appears and I'm so glad to see him.

'Oh goodness,' says Dad, embarrassed now by the fuss he's dared to cause by having a heart attack. 'I'm not dying, you know...'

'Well, for a moment there, I wasn't sure,' says Mum, her voice cracking slightly. She must have been petrified. I mean, what must it have been like? One minute Dad's sitting there, right as rain, the next minute he has a crushing pain in his chest and he's struggling to breathe. I squeeze Marcus's hand.

'Do you know how long you'll be in here?' asks Marcus. 'Only I suppose they'll want to keep an eye on you for a bit, won't they?'

'Two or three days,' says Dad, looking less than delighted. 'Bit of a bloody nuisance,' he adds sounding much more like his old self.

But I for one am glad to hear it, and Mum looks quite relieved too – I think if he came home any earlier, we'd both be worried sick.

'Erm, can I get anyone a cup of tea or something?' Marcus asks.

'Oh,' says Mum, 'tea would be very welcome, thank you.'

'Same please,' I say and beam at him.

I have to say, that tea or no tea, having Marcus here makes all the difference in the world.

'I love you, Dad,' I tell him, when it's time to leave, which I haven't said to him since I was about thirteen.

He looks a little teary. 'I love you too, poppet.'

* * *

As we leave, I glance back over my shoulder. Lying there all alone, he looks very old and worried, now that he thinks no one's watching. And just like Agnes when she was ill, for the first time ever, my dad looks small.

Marcus and I take Mum home. I scrub the carpet for her, where poor Dad was sick when he collapsed and Marcus makes a pot of tea and beans on toast for us all. He's called both Will and Emma, who've agreed that he should take at least tomorrow morning off, so he's staying here with me and Mum. And my fickle hound's not the least put out – she's snoring on Emma's sofa.

Mum is very subdued. I guess she's just had a sneak preview of what it would be like to lose Dad for good. I think I can understand now, what Agnes said, about how her illness made her change the way she saw things, because this heart attack of Dad's has certainly given all of us a reminder that not a single one of us is immortal.

I'm amazed when Mum produces only one set of clean sheets, which are for the double bed in my old room. I'd fully expected Marcus to be shown to the guest room – it has a creaky old bed so everyone can hear what you're up to – and she comes up with a new toothbrush and a clean shirt of Dad's for the morning. Then she says she's tired and trudges wearily off to bed.

I rummage around in the drinks cabinet, and, buried at the back behind the gin and Bacardi and whisky, I find it.

'Aha,' I say to Marcus with glee, pulling out the half full bottle of Rémy Martin Louis XIII that I was sure was still lurking somewhere.

'Shall we?' I ask him wickedly. 'I mean, strictly medicinal, as Agnes would say...'

'Oh I think we ought to,' he agrees. 'If you're sure your dad won't mind. This stuff costs a fortune, Lou.'

'It was a present about five years ago,' I explain. 'So I think we can safely assume they won't miss it.' I pour us two large glasses.

'Nectar,' says Marcus after the first sip.

'Thank you for coming with me tonight,' I say, reaching to stroke his cheek with my spare hand.

'That's okay,' says Marcus. 'I could hardly let you drive over here on your own. It does make you think, though, doesn't it? I mean we all just carry on with our lives as though we'll go on forever.'

I wriggle nearer and kiss him. 'Even more reason to make the most of every bit of it,' I say, before moving in for a full-on snog.

The only problem is that, as we already know with brandy, just one little glass doesn't quite hit the spot and before we know it, we've finished the bottle.

'I'll never be able to drink brandy again,' says Marcus sadly, gazing at the empty bottle. 'Because it will never live up to what we've just drunk.'

'I know, we could call our first baby Louis,' I suggest, giggling, as we tiptoe up to my room so as not to wake my mother.

'Have you ever done it in this bed before, Louisa?' asks Marcus a little later, as his hands slide under my T-shirt to stroke my back in the most erotic way imaginable.

'Absolutely no way,' I say sternly. 'This bed squeaks like billy-oh.'

'Well then,' says Marcus huskily, as he pulls me even nearer, 'we'll just have to be quiet...'

* * *

'Darling, you didn't give Marcus that ropey old brandy did you?' says Mum the next morning when she finds the empty bottle. 'Oh, Louisa...' she says crossly, sounding much more her usual self. 'How could you? It's been there for so long, I've been meaning to throw it away for ages. Didn't you find the nice Bacardi and Cinzano?'

'Oh, it's okay, Mum, it wasn't too bad,' I say, giving Marcus an I-told-you look at the same time. 'I think he found it quite reviving...'

Marcus drives us to the hospital again after breakfast, and Auntie Lucy's coming over to see Dad later, so she'll give Mum a lift home. Apparently Dad has had a good night. He's looking slightly less pallid this morning and his mood is definitely better.

'I'll be over at the weekend Dad,' I tell him. 'So just do what these nice nurses say, will you and hopefully you'll be coming home.'

'You don't want to come all the way over here again, poppet,' he protests weakly.

'I do and I am,' I say firmly.

'I wouldn't argue,' says Marcus, with a wink at my dad.

I kiss my parents goodbye.

Marcus kisses Mum's cheek too, and then we transport ourselves back to the normality we left just yesterday, which now feels anything but.

43

There's a message waiting for me on my desk. It's from Karina. I call her straight away.

'I'm so sorry about your father, Louisa. If you need me to cover the office at any time, I'm not flying much and I'm more than happy to fill in.'

'Thank you,' I say, touched at her concern. 'But hopefully he's out of the woods.'

'I don't want to frighten you, but I lost my father from a heart attack,' she says soberly. 'He had high blood pressure, smoked too much and drank too much. His killed him outright. Your dad's lucky. Hopefully he can change his lifestyle so that it won't happen again.'

Oh my gosh. I knew Sylvie was a widow, but I'd no idea what the story was. Karina's right, of course. Dad will have to make serious changes. I mean, he certainly drinks too much wine and I don't think his blood pressure is exactly low, and he barely moves at all, except from his armchair to the dining table and back again.

'Thanks, Karina, that's really kind,' I say genuinely. Then it strikes me. I wonder if she's missing her old job – or possibly Will.

Then I notice an unfamiliar figure hanging around the yard. She looks about Paris's age and build. In fact, just like Paris, except the hair is an unremarkable, lightish brown colour and she isn't wearing any make-up. And the jeans aren't skin-tight and she's wearing an everyday, unflattering kind of sweatshirt. I do a double take. *Can it be?* As I peer through the window at this girl, she walks over to the office and tentatively comes in.

'Um, *Paris*?' I say disbelievingly.

'Could you give this to Emma for me, please?' The girl hands me an envelope. Her eyes have only the slightest hint of mascara, and the hair's in a messy Emma-style ponytail. 'Only she was so brilliant the other day - she practically saved Chelsea's life. I really love that horse – I was kind of hoping to see her to say thank you.' A solitary tear trickles down her cheek.

'I'm not at all sure when she'll be back,' I say gently. 'But don't worry, I'll make sure she gets this later on.'

'Okay. Thank you.' Very quietly, Paris wanders out.

And then I get it. I better warn her quick smart, because Emma is obviously the latest crush.

* * *

Marcus has started moving his clothes and other bits into my place and it's quickly becoming apparent that my cottage is a little bit on the small side for all our combined stuff. He's decided to put his furniture into storage (well, it's in a spare barn that Ben just happens to have knocking around) until we decide where our future lies. It's hardly a problem though, because we are just enjoying inhabiting the same space. Though there's nothing wrong with one or two ground rules.

'Now, Marcus, on the subject of loos,' I start firmly. 'As well as leaving the seat up, it has come to my notice, and this is not specifically directed at you, that males in general have problems with their aim, and that frequently they miss – and I for one, am not a Mrs Boggle. I do not enjoy cleaning toilets,' I add, waggling a finger at him.

'I'll have you know that there's nothing wrong with my aim and I'm quite good at cleaning too,' he says in injured tones.

'And the other thing, Marcus, is shoes, which live in wardrobes or in the porch. Not under chairs and tables and scattered all over the floor.'

'If I'd known you'd be such a nit-picky fusspot,' he says woundedly, 'I'd never have proposed. I'd have asked Rachel or someone instead. Maybe I better move back to my place...' he adds, with a sideways look at me.

'Oh no,' I say alarmed. 'You can't. And I'm not giving you back my ring, buster, so you just stay right here.'

'Well, I have only one rule,' he says, coming and standing very close in front of me, then bending his head to kiss me on the mouth.

'Mmmm?' I say, grinning up into those gorgeous eyes.

'Sex,' he says, picking me up and carrying me up the stairs, as if I was tiny like Rachel. 'And plenty of it. Starting now...'

* * *

I've just realised that Agnes and Beamish's wedding is only three weeks away. Rachel and I have lots of secretive conversations as we tie up even more loose ends and make sure that we haven't forgotten anything. Emma and Karina are coming to decorate Ben's with us the night before, because any sooner and Beamish would most definitely wonder where we all were and smell a rat.

Beamish is frightfully impressed with Sam and Zac, who have been spring cleaning like you wouldn't believe. It serves as an excellent distraction while the rest of us are being furtive and trying not to give the game away. Sam has an empty stable in which we can lock secret things and he's told Beamish he can't find the key. Karina's been in a few mornings to help out in the office, so it's been a bit like old times, except I no longer refer to Arian as my ex-husband; from now on, he's her fiancé – and she's more than welcome to him.

Dad's doing really well. Mum told me that he's got to start doing regular exercise. But first they're going to Devon, and Dad's going to eat more healthily and start walking, even on holiday. He has to start gradually, and she's going to join him, she told me, because it would be good for her too. Oh my golly gosh. I can see it now... my parents morphing into a couple of power-walkers, in matching shell suits, maps round their necks and those ski-pole things which for some reason power-walkers always seem to use, instead of just legs like normal people.

Rachel and I go to Emma's old place for a proper girls evening and because she likes to check up on it from time to time. When I get there, she's scooting around unlocking all the windows.

'I'm so happy at Ben's,' she says, her eyes shining with happiness. 'I think I'm going to put this on the market.'

'Weird, isn't it,' I say. 'How even six months ago, neither of us could have imagined we'd ever be anything other than single...' I giggle, because you'd think, wouldn't you, that after one disastrous marriage and a painful divorce, we'd have learned. And here's Emma flinging herself willingly into life with Ben, and me getting married after I'd sworn off men for good.

'Seen much of Paris?' I ask innocently.

Emma gives me one of her looks. 'Believe it or not,' she says, sounding rather impressed, 'she's asked if she can come out with me for work experience. She's thinking she might want to be a vet.'

I splutter with hilarity at the idea. 'She just fancies being around hunky males all day, that's all, Em!'

But Emma doesn't laugh. 'You are so immature at times, Louisa. She's actually quite a smart girl. You wait and see.'

When Rachel comes in, both of us quiz her mercilessly about Will.

'He's lovely.' She looks at us. I can hear the *but* before she says it. 'He's completely different to Miles... funny, larks around, like having this big buffoon of a brother...'

'That's what I thought!' I chip in. 'Does he remind you of Jeremy Clarkson?'

They both turn and look at me oddly.

Then Rachel says thoughtfully, 'I think it's just that he's *too* much the opposite of Miles. I mean, is he ever serious about anything?'

This time I keep quiet, because I know for a fact that there is a serious side to Will, but unfortunately too, it sounds as though he's still hung up on Karina, which is not good news.

But then we get on to the hot topic that we're all itching to talk about, because there's only a few days to go.

'I've written a list,' says Rachel, 'of everything I can possibly think of. So can you both just listen and see if you can think of anything else...'

And she runs through the list, consisting of transport, the vicar – who's booked and which we didn't have to worry about because Agnes and Beamish did that bit – then it's on to catering, which is the hog roast, the wine is all sorted, as is the music, the flowers...

'So that's about it,' says Rachel eventually. 'All we have to do now is wait for Friday and leap into action...'

* * *

Poor old Beamish. He wants to go on a bit of a stag do on Friday night. The task of telling him that none of the vets can go falls on Marcus, owing to his position of joint-senior-partner. He persuades Beamish that Thursday would be a far better night, so that he'll be rested and clear-headed on the Saturday, which fortunately Beamish agrees with. The reality is that Emma and I have roped in all the vets we can lay our hands on to help us on Friday night.

'Have you had any thoughts about *our* wedding?' asks Marcus that night, as we cuddle up in bed.

'To tell you the truth, the only wedding I've been thinking about lately is Agnes and Beamish's,' I say honestly. Then I stop, and prop myself up in bed so I'm looking over Marcus's face.

'That's terrible,' I say, gently kissing his lips. 'It sounds like I'm not that fussed, and I *so* am. I can't wait to marry you,' I tell him.

'I feel the same,' he says soberly. 'This might sound daft, but rather than get into some huge, complicated rigmarole of planning all the details which actually, as far as I'm concerned, don't even matter, why don't you buy a gorgeous pink dress, we'll have a small ceremony – a church, registry office, a field – anywhere! And then we'll have a party at the pub to celebrate!'

Oh! I am marrying such a clever man. I really don't care about the whole big white wedding thing. I just want to be married to him.

'We'll invite our parents, under the pretence of getting them together before the wedding,' I say excitedly. 'And we can book them rooms at the pub.'

I collapse back on the bed and gaze up at the ceiling. 'What I'd absolutely love is a tiny service round the corner in the church... do you think the vicar would agree? Just our parents there, no one else... and late afternoon, so we can all walk over to the pub like you said, where everyone will be taken by surprise...'

Marcus has a broad smile on his face and he absolutely agrees with me, so we decide that I'll pop over and have a chat with the vicar and as soon as it's organised, we'll go ahead.

* * *

Everyone is working flat out this morning, to get everything done in double quick time, because tomorrow's the big day. Will's come up trumps, supplying not just one, but two willing vet mates who are taking all our calls from five o'clock this evening. It's unheard of, all of us being off work at the same time, and with everyone in a holiday mood, it already feels like a party.

Rachel's here and Karina came over at lunchtime. 'Helping in the office,' was what we told Beamish when he showed up rather unexpectedly. I can't help noticing that there's totally unmissable chemistry still going on between her and Will.

Marcus and Miles have collected some beers from the pub, because this is jolly thirsty work and we'll most certainly need some serious refreshing before too long. For early May, the weather is perfect, and though the temperature's dropping this evening, it's been the most glorious spring day imaginable.

Dear old Will turns out to be a dab hand at all this. He's strung up miles of bunting in the garden behind Ben's house. Karina got hold of it and far from being the plastic village fete variety which I was expecting, it's actually Cath Kidston and really pretty. He's despatched Miles and Marcus to go and pull ivy off the trees to festoon the staircase with, and meanwhile, us girls are fannying around with flowers and fairy lights, as Marcus so eloquently describes it. Oh, and drinking some of those beers.

Sam's carrying piles of chairs inside, Zac's spreading white cloths on the tables and it's all starting to look quite amazing. And really, given one lovely old house, a few vets, a stunningly organised office manager (me) and a few more helpers thrown in, what more do you need?

44

It's nearly ten o'clock when Marcus and I get home, and poor old Horace has almost given up on me. He comes cantering up to the gate hungrily, followed by a moth-eaten Mavis, who's mid-moult and looking most peculiar. And when I go to bed, I look at Marcus's lovely suit hanging next to my very sexy dress, and get a warm fuzzy feeling at just seeing them together.

* * *

The wedding is at three o'clock in the village church. As expected, there's just a handful of guests, including all the practice staff and the few close friends that Agnes and Beamish have invited. She looks so elegant in a moss-green dress, and she's carrying the tiniest posy of lily of the valley, which I suspect has come from their garden. Beamish looks proud, and very dapper, in an immaculate suit that's a world apart from his usual hairy old tweed ones.

So, after months of waiting, here we are in the church. There's Marcus, me, Emma, Ben, and across on the other side, teeny little Rachel squashed between Miles and Will, hedging her bets I wouldn't wonder. Sam and Zac are just behind, and so is Mrs Boggle, complete with handkerchief, which is already very much in evidence, with a man who's a whole head shorter than she is. He, too, has a pudding basin haircut, and I can only presume that he's Mr Boggle, because he couldn't possibly be anyone else.

And as we stand, I link my arm through Marcus's and feel a thrill of excitement, as I hope with all my heart that it won't be long before we're standing in here for our own wedding.

* * *

In no time, the brief service is over and we traipse merrily out behind the happy couple to the sound of church bells, which is a bit of a giveaway, given that this is supposed to be a secret. Emma and I throw rose petals while Ben takes some photos. Agnes and Beamish look so happy... And then it's time for the tricky bit.

'We've arranged a little surprise,' I tell them vaguely, and immediately they both look wary, until they spot Terry the carriage horse, when their expressions change to relief, then as he pulls up in front of them, to complete delight. Terry's carriage is positively festooned with flowers, which I'm guessing is thanks to Karina.

We all stand and wave as they trot away – then it's time for the *really* tricky bit.

Marcus takes out his mobile. 'Wish me luck...'

There are a few tense moments, before Marcus gives us a thumbs up. Yes! Beamish has gone for it, and the driver has already turned the carriage around. We all get in our cars and dash over to Ben's so we get there first... Golly. Terry's no slouch – I can already hear him hoofing it down the lane behind us.

As we park out of sight in Ben's stable yard, Emma waits in front of the house for the carriage.

'I'm really so sorry about this,' she says, somehow managing to sound as though she really is extremely sorry. 'Quick, come through here,' she says, and takes both their hands in hers.

And of course there's a predictable cheer as they walk in through the front door, and oh golly, suddenly I'm worried. I hope this isn't too much for them. There are about fifty good friends and clients, and more promised later, plus some family that Rachel managed to winkle out. Everyone's dressed in their finest and raising their glasses to Beamish and Agnes, who just stand there, looking utterly amazed.

Rachel steps forward.

'We know you didn't want a big party, but so many people wanted to be part of your day,' she says, looking anxiously from her mother to Beamish.

'So many people helped,' I chip in. 'You wouldn't believe how important you two are round here.'

And still they say nothing. Then Agnes takes Beamish's arm.

'It really is rather something,' she says to him, looking around at how we've done up Ben's gorgeous old house. 'Do you know, darling,' she says to Beamish, 'I think this is absolutely lovely. Shall we go and mingle?'

And Beamish coughs and says, 'Um, yes, dear,' and arm in arm, off they go. I can't tell you how relieved I am. And what do you know, as they walk away, Agnes turns her head and winks at us!

Now that our mission's accomplished, I go to find Karina, who's come with Sylvie. Arian, I'm happy to report, is nowhere to be seen.

'The carriage looked fantastic,' I tell her. 'You did a brilliant job.'

'Glad you liked it,' she says, but sounds distracted. Oh. I see why. Will's over there. Correction, because actually Will's coming over...

'Wow, this is terrific,' he says enthusiastically. 'You girls certainly know how to throw a party.' Suddenly it feels like the moment to disappear, because their eyes are glued to each other. The attraction between them is palpable, even to me. I'm not sure where this leaves Arian...

'Oh, golly, I must talk to Rachel,' I say, wondering if I'm doing the right thing, leaving my ex's girlfriend with the American who fancies the pants off her. But surely, I think to myself, if I were in Karina's shoes, there'd be no decision to make.

Rachel's looking confused, but then she thinks she has a choice between a handsome American who she says is never serious, and a gloomy Englishman who she says is never humorous. Personally I think she should forget about both of them, and look elsewhere.

'Over there,' I tell her firmly, pointing to where Emma and Ben are standing. 'Ben's brother, I believe. Very hunky and nice mixture of big smiles and smouldering glances. How about him?'

* * *

The party is a rip roaring success. Well, how could it fail? The food is great, there's more than enough wine and beer, even for us lot, and Will's band impresses everyone. In fact, I'd go so far as to say it's perfect, as I tell Marcus.

'It is rather, isn't it?' he agrees. He does look dishy in that suit.

'I have to say, I wasn't sure to start with. And look... I think they really are having a good time.' He points to where Beamish and Agnes are dancing cheek to cheek, as the band alters its tempo from Latin American to smoochy.

Marcus takes my hand. 'Well, my future Mrs Fitzpatrick, shall we?'

* * *

Later on, I find myself accosted by Beamish, who's holding a glass of whisky and frowning, which makes me wonder what it is he's going to say.

'Um. Louisa,' he says as usual.

'Um, yes?' I say back.

'Um, now, no one else knows this, but Agnes and I, um, were thinking, well, you're doing an awfully good job, old girl. Yes...'

'Thank you very much, Beamish,' I say. After all, it's always rather nice when your boss gives you a compliment.

'Yes,' he says again. 'Um, think old Agnes might quite like to retire... what, er, do you think?'

What is he getting at here?

'Well,' I say, after considering his question, 'I think we'll miss her terribly. But I understand, Beamish, because she works so terribly hard. But we might need just a little bit of extra help you know.'

'Well,' he says jovially, 'can I, er, leave that with you? Only, um, as you're in charge now, seems the best idea, um, yes. Well. Jolly good. Glad we, er, got that sorted out.'

Then as he starts to walk away, he's still muttering. 'Damn fine party. Jolly good indeed. Well done.'

He goes off to find Agnes, a beaming smile on his face, leaving me none the wiser as to exactly what we've seemingly just sorted out.

* * *

We wave Agnes and Beamish off at about eleven thirty. I think we're all amazed that they've lasted this long, but they seem to have had a fabulous time. And when I finally sit down, I feel bone-achingly weary but it's been worth all the effort. Every bit of it.

'Do I need to carry you home?' says Marcus sympathetically,

the bow tie hanging loosely round his neck now that he's undone the top button of his shirt.

'I think you might have to,' I say.

Then he frowns. 'Had rather an odd call a little while ago. From the police. Apparently someone was seen hanging around the practice earlier tonight. Amanda M-T happened to drive by and thought she better call them. They've been over and everything looks in order, but it does seem a little strange.'

'Don't worry. It's probably nothing... Come on. Let's go home.'

On our way, we glance across at the dance floor. And oh golly gosh. Karina and Will are still smooching, ever so closely, her head blissfully against his chest, his arms protectively over her. And even though it's I'm-always-joking-Will, I have to say it all looks rather serious.

45

An enormous box of chocolates and a card is sitting on my desk when I get to the office on Monday morning. There's also a crate of champagne.

I open the card.

Dear Louisa,

We're both delighted that it's you taking over my job. Me in particular. You've proved yourself such an asset while I've been ill and we're both extremely grateful. I've enjoyed almost every day I've spent there over the last fifteen years, and I have a feeling that you feel much the same.

The chocolates are for you, and the champagne for all of you after putting on such a wonderful party for us on Saturday. Oh, and Beamish will be putting this in writing, formally with details of your pay rise.

Thank you, dear Louisa, so very much.

Agnes x

I sit down, feeling, I have to admit, stunned. So this was what Beamish was not getting at on Saturday. I now officially run this office. I sit and let it sink in for a moment, then suddenly, I feel euphoric!

Then it strikes me that with Marcus being joint-senior-partner, and me being office manager, we are pretty much holding the reins of this between us. Golly. Scary, or is it? Will it actually make very much difference, because at the end of the day when you take everyone into account, we have a fairly amazing team.

Right, I decide. My first important decision is coming right up, because I want Karina back in here regardless and if she doesn't want the job, then I'll have to look for someone else. And then I find myself thinking about her and Will, smooching – and it strikes me that on a purely selfish level, what I struggle with most is the ambiguity of our friendship, considering how I met her in the first place. Or is that in the past?

I call her.

'Hello, Karina. This is the office manager of Beamish's vet practice here, now also official head hunter.'

There's a silence. Then she says warily, 'Louisa, is that you?'

'Well, of course it is,' I say proudly. 'They've given me Agnes's job! It's official! As far as this office goes, I hire and fire too. So do you want your job back or what?'

There's another silence. 'Oh, Lou,' she says eventually. 'I do. Of course I do, but it's complicated. I'm really not sure...'

'It's Will, isn't it?' I ask her gently. 'Anyone can see there's something between you. Do you want to meet later? Come over for a drink. I think Marcus is on call, so we can have a good old chat and sort it out.'

'Thank you, Louisa,' she says, sounding so unlike herself. 'Oh, and congratulations.'

I just hope we *can* sort this out. It could be inordinately messy.

Then I call Marcus and give him the news.

'Hello,' I say proudly. 'This is the vet practice office manager speaking. Just doing a little checking up on you... How is your day?'

'Louisa,' says Marcus slightly impatiently. 'What are you talking about?'

'This,' I say. 'My new job. They've given me Agnes's job!' I reiterate because he's a man and being thick again.

'Oh,' says Marcus, the penny clearly dropping. 'Well done. I must say it makes sense, after all, you've been doing it for months. Look, I'm in the middle of something. See you later, okay?'

* * *

It's a very sober Karina who knocks on my front door that evening. Marcus has been in and brought me a huge bunch of flowers in recognition of my new official position. He's now gone out again, because I've explained that Karina and I need a bit of a girly chat. He raised his eyebrows and disappeared quite quickly. I wonder if he'll bump into Will.

'I honestly don't know what to do,' says Karina, once we're sitting down with a glass of wine. 'It seems so terrible to talk to you about this at all, when it was your marriage I broke up in the first place.'

'Look,' I say firmly. 'If I'm honest, at the time I was devastated and much more. But that was then. I am truly glad, from the bottom of my heart, that you did what you did, because I'd never be with Marcus if you hadn't, and honestly, I've never felt like this before about anyone. Least of all Arian. So please. Stop feeling guilty.'

She sighs. 'I really *am* glad it's worked out for you.'

'Thank you. So what's been going on,' I ask gently. 'Only you look so dreadfully worried.'

To my horror she begins to cry. 'Do you know what? I'll be completely honest with you too. I haven't even been honest with myself until now, but I've fallen in love. And it's not with Arian...' and she starts to sob again.

'Oh. Karina...' I say sympathetically. 'It's hardly as though you did it on purpose... and none of us can help our feelings. But what about Arian? What do you think you'll do?'

'I have to tell him, don't I? I can't live a lie. He ought to understand that well enough,' she adds wryly.

Oh my golly gosh. What's she saying? What goes around comes around or something like that? At any rate, it looks like Arian's about to get a taste of his own medicine.

'And poor little Oscar...' She sniffs.

Poor little Oscar will be just fine, with step-daddy Will just dying to get into his role, and a wonderful mother like Karina, and Arian around when it suits him.

'Little Oscar will be just fine,' I tell her firmly. 'He'll have you and Will, who will make a fantastic dad by the way, and Arian will still be in his life. Actually, once he gets used to it, it will suit Arian down to the ground being a part-time parent. And you have Sylvie. I'm jolly glad you didn't call him Montgomery, by the way. Terrible name.'

She manages a watery smile. 'Would have been ghastly for him don't you think?'

'Ghastly.' I nod.

'Lou, I think I better go and find Arian,' she says with trepidation.

'Good luck. If he's a nightmare, send him round to me,' I say resignedly.

* * *

Later, I take a call from the police. Just a follow-up from Saturday night, they tell me. I confirm that nothing seems to have been taken or damaged, and that's the end of that – or so it seems.

46

Surprisingly, after this latest episode with Karina, I don't hear from Arian. She told me later that he took it reasonably well in the circumstances. I'm not convinced, and it's Leo who updates me.

'God, Lou. I know he's upset, but I wish he'd leave. He's been here a week now, ever since they split up.'

Oh. That can't be much fun for Leo and Pete.

'How is he?' I ask, fearing the worst.

'He's okay, all things considered. He's had a few drunk and disorderly sessions with Pete, but he's starting to pull himself together. He's got to; the new business needs them both working on it. The main problem is that he hasn't anywhere to live. Karina and Oscar are in the cottage, of course. Which is why we've ended up with him here.'

'Oh,' I say. 'Well, he's a big boy. He'll just have to find somewhere, won't he?'

* * *

I wait for the opportunity to catch Will on his own, just to check he's up to speed with the goings-on between Karina and Arian. As suspected, he isn't.

'I haven't called her yet,' says Will thoughtfully. 'I mean, from what you say, she's only just got *him* out of there. I'm not sure she'll want some other guy blundering in before his half of the bed's gone cold.'

I'm not sure she would want any old some other guy, but in Will's case, she might make an exception. I try to explain this to him.

'Will... Don't you think she might be quite pleased to see you? I mean, I rather thought, after Agnes and Beamish's wedding, that you two were fairly cosy...'

'You think?' Will thinks about it.

Do I have to spell it out?

'Because it's only since then that she and Arian broke up.'

'I guess,' says Will, still not putting two and two together and making three.

I stand in front of this gorgeous great American and take his big Neanderthal hands in mine.

'Idiot. She likes you.' I stare up into his big unblinking eyes. Talk about a compromising position. I hope Marcus doesn't walk in.

'A lot, Will,' I reiterate.

A broad smile stretches across his face and he smacks a kiss on my cheek.

'You actually know that, don't you,' he says, grinning at me, and looking happier than he's looked in a long time.

* * *

A little later, Zac saunters in, looking quite pleased with himself. It's the first time I've seen that look on his face in all the time he's been here.

'Passed me exams,' he says, looking embarrassed and pleased at the same time. He actually speaks to me now, and not just to answer questions.

'Fantastic!' I cry. 'Congratulations, Zac!'

He looks bemused, and saunters out again.

Then Karina turns up, completely unexpectedly.

'The thick American was in a little while ago,' I tell her. 'You just missed him.'

'Oh,' she says. 'Will's not thick, Louisa. And actually it was you I wanted to see.'

'Oh?'

'Were you serious when you offered me my old job back? Only I'm flying so much that I'm finding it impossible to get enough time at home with Oscar. And then there are always delays, roster changes, you know how it is...'

Which I do.

'Wow,' I say. 'You mean you're leaving the Big Airline too? They won't have any pilots left at this rate. Of course you can have your old job back. I'd love you to!'

She looks relieved. 'I'm so glad you said that. I've already handed in my notice, because I couldn't have carried on anyway. But coming back here, well. Thank you, Lou. I really appreciate it.'

Then she says nonchalantly, 'Did Will say anything to you just now?'

'Oh,' I say. 'Not much. You know Will. He'll probably call round at some point, though,' I add casually.

Karina looks at me suspiciously. 'You haven't said anything, have you?'

'All I said was you probably wouldn't mind if he called you. Or something like that, I forget now.' I'm lying, but with only the best of intentions.

'Right,' she says, clearly not believing me at all. 'When do you want me to start?'

'Monday morning 8.30 smart,' I say in an efficient office manager-ish kind of voice. 'There's a nice big pile of filing already there just waiting for you.'

'I can't wait,' she says, only slightly sarcastically.

* * *

Marcus and I are going to see my parents this weekend. I haven't been down there since they got back from their holiday, and ever since Dad's scare, I decided that I'd make more effort. After all, you only have one set of parents.

'Darlings!' My mother air-kisses both of us. That's interesting – so Marcus is now a 'darling' too.

But she's looking relaxed and even has a slight tan.

Dad comes to the door, also looking a bit tanned, and trimmer and more upright than he has for years. Golly gosh. That heart attack really has well and truly shaken things up around here.

An imperious 'yap' comes from the direction of the kitchen. Mum looks mildly embarrassed and Dad says, 'Ah. I forget. You haven't met little Benjy. Benjy? *Benjy?*'

My parents have a dog??

Then out of the kitchen struts an elderly, moth-eaten terrier-shape, wagging its tail and baring what's left of his teeth.

'Good boy, good boy,' says Dad delightedly. Even my mother has a doting smile on her face.

'We decided that if we had a dog, we'd walk more,' explains Dad. Then on a more serious note, he adds, 'Chances are, if I don't keep up the exercise and eat more healthily, the old ticker might play up again. Got to be a bit careful.'

Lunch is also a revelation. My mother, previously a master of everything deep fried, overbaked and generally cooked to a mush, has prepared the most delicious bowls of salads I've ever seen.

'Mum!' I can't help myself. I'm completely astounded. 'This looks fantastic! I didn't know you could do this sort of thing.'

'Nor did I,' she confesses, but clearly quite pleased. 'Much healthier than what we used to eat, isn't it?'

Lunch is quite a jolly affair, but on the way home, I'm deep in thought. The magnitude of the changes to my parents' lives does not escape me. Which must mean that Dad had a pretty narrow escape and presumably it could happen again.

'You're quiet,' remarks Marcus.

'Just thinking,' I say pensively. 'About my parents, actually. I'd never in a million years have imagined that they could ever live with a dog and eat salads.'

Marcus smiles. 'It is surprising isn't it, how you can think you know someone so well and yet they can still manage to surprise you,' he says, cryptically.

He carries on smiling, which is odd. If I didn't know better, I'd absolutely swear he was hiding something.

47

I'm so glad that Marcus and I are having a small wedding, which reminds me, I still need to talk to the vicar, so after lunch I sneak over to the rectory, leaving Karina in charge of the office.

'Ah. Louisa Mulholland, I presume,' says the rosy-cheeked Reverend Wiggins. 'Come in, come in. Your young man not with you?'

'No,' I say. 'Well, not this time. He will be, of course, er, next time...'

'Jolly good,' says the Reverend, cheerfully. 'Now, take a pew and tell me what it is that I can do for you.'

I tell him how Marcus and I want a tiny, intimate wedding, no fuss or bother, but we'd like it to be in the church, and we only live around the corner. And how we'd like to do it soon, which seeing as it's only going to be a tiny affair, shouldn't be too much of a problem – should it?

'Hmmm.' The Reverend sounds unsure. 'Problem is, young lady, I'm going away for a month in July. We can't do it before, because there isn't time to read the banns and do the necessary paperwork. Unfortunately, it's quite complicated these days. So, the earliest we're looking at is round about the end of August. But hold on, I've got wall-to-wall weddings for at least three weeks after that. Mmm... So it will be the end of September I'm afraid,' he says cheerily. 'Shall I pop you in the diary for then? Before someone else books the date?'

I swallow my disappointment. I hadn't expected to wait three months.

'Um, yes please...' I say, feeling very subdued. 'Thank you.'

Then I wander back to work feeling deflated.

'What's up?' asks Karina, instantly noticing my mood.

'Oh. Nothing really,' I say, and luckily the phone rings and prevents her asking any more awkward questions.

Marcus isn't as disappointed as I thought he would be.

'Don't worry, Lou. We'll just wait. Or get married somewhere else. And anyway, you need to go and buy a dress. A really gorgeous one. Your mother wanted to help you, didn't she?'

My heart sinks even further, because no doubt my mother will want to see me squeezed into some ghastly, enormous meringue of frilled organza, or boned white taffeta in which one sweeps along – like a ship. I've set my heart on a green, flowing dress that would look just as perfect walking barefoot through the fields, with my hair blowing in the wind.

But it turns out that my mother has a few more surprises up her sleeve.

'Now, Louisa, Marcus has told me that you don't want a formal wedding dress,' she says, as we drive up to Windsor, where she assures me I'll find something I like.

'I don't,' I say. 'I don't want anything formal or the slightest bit traditional this time round. I mean, the first time, with Arian, it was an incredible wedding,' I say hastily. 'And I know now how hard you worked to make it like that. Thanks, Mum.'

'Nonsense,' she says, sounding just a little pleased nevertheless.

She even knows where to park, and then we trail along the high street, past windows of typical wedding dresses which are a million miles away from this picture I have in my head. I'm preparing to be very depressed. How can my mother, of all people, know how to help me find *the dress*? But give her her due, she doesn't even so much as glance in the direction of a single meringue as we pass. Doesn't even suggest, *We have to start somewhere, Louisa*, just leads me down a side street, and round a corner, and then looks at a scrap of paper she's taken out of her pocket and says, 'I think this is it.'

I look at the window in front of us – properly – and feel a flicker of excitement. The window is full of dresses that look like what the flower fairies might wear when they're all grown up. The colours are soft and muted, the fabrics ethereal and floaty and, believe it or not, there isn't a single meringue in sight. My heart starts to thump wildly.

'Mrs Sparks,' says my mother brusquely to the shop assistant. 'And my daughter, Louisa. We need a wedding dress.'

Now, if you'd told me my mother would find the dress of my dreams to marry Marcus in, I would have hooted with laughter. My mother's dress sense is traditional, unexciting, predictable, as befits a lady of her years – high-waisted trousers, nice little twinsets and pearls – you get the idea. And yet bizarrely, here in this shop she's brought me to, is simply the most divine collection of dresses I've ever seen.

I try on one after another... in moss green, lilac, even black, just for a laugh. Imagine, me and my mother laughing together about getting married in black. It actually happens. And then hanging in a corner all of its own, I find it. *The One.*

If someone had leafed through the pages of my imagination,

they couldn't have done better than this. The bodice is fitted and laces up at the back, but it's the delicate, floaty skirt that I fall in love with. It's made of overlapping layers of the sheerest tulle and chiffon, in soft shades of shell pink and oyster, which sounds horrible but is divine. It's pretty and funky at the same time, and you could definitely walk barefoot through the fields in it. The second I put it on, I can feel it. This is the dress I'm marrying Marcus in.

Even my mother is quiet as she looks at me in it.

'Beautiful,' is all she says, just as I wait for the torrent of criticism to pour forth. But there is none, which is most unlike my mother. Luckily, she insists on paying for it, because it's the most expensive dress in the shop.

After she has been so amazingly wonderful, the very least I can do is take her out for lunch. But narky Mum is back and picks holes in everything our waitress brings us. The coffee is bitter, the juice isn't fresh and she'd have found a better sandwich in the Co-op.

'Honestly, Louisa. I can't believe you're not going to send that back… and such a ridiculous price for a salad…'

Oh yes, situation completely normal.

* * *

I entrust my dress to no one. I can't give it to Emma because she'll start asking nosey questions about the wedding which I won't want to answer. I don't want to leave it with my mother, because when I go and pick it up, she'll definitely smell a rat, and all mine and Marcus's plans for stealth and secrecy will be blown sky-high out of the water, so it's a bit of a conundrum. Then I think, I know exactly who will understand and not tell a soul and be utterly discreet. I can't imagine why I didn't think of this before.

I call round to see her when I know Beamish is elsewhere, because I can just imagine him putting his bumbling foot right in it.

'The thing is, Agnes, we just want to be married. We don't want any fuss, and we don't want to wait ages or get wound up planning an enormous, elaborate reception or anything like that...'

Agnes gives me a slightly exasperated look. 'Louisa. Dear. You don't need to explain that to me. Don't you think that I, of all people, know exactly what you're getting at?'

I must look nonplussed, because she laughs a bit, and then I realise.

'Oh,' I say, feeling rather dim. 'I think I've just said to you exactly what you said to me and Rachel just before we went and organised you an enormous party. Oh my goodness.'

But Agnes only smiles. 'It was wonderful, Louisa, and we will be forever grateful to you and Rachel for organising it. But if you're telling me you just want to get married quietly, I completely understand. So I'll hide your gorgeous dress and say absolutely nothing to anyone. Now, shall we have a cup of tea, and you can fill me in on what's happening at work. I'm afraid most of it goes right over Beamish's head.'

Which is not the slightest surprising.

48

Not long after, comes what turns out to be the morning from hell. I've barely unlocked the office when I take a call from someone on the A34 Winchester bypass. He tells me, and I quote, 'There's a bleedin' horsebox on its side and some horrible noises goin' on.'

My blood runs cold. As soon as he rings off, I'm back on that phone quicker than lightning. Miles is already the opposite side of the county on a rescue mission of some description, but I reach Marcus, Emma and Will, who go straight over there. It honestly sounded horrendous. Apparently one of the horses has somehow broken out and been in a collision with a lorry.

Later, Emma fills me in. Vets see some fairly horrible situations, but she's terribly upset. The horse had to be put down there and then.

'I've never seen anything like it, Lou. It was terrified, and so badly injured... And all because some idiot lost control while overtaking and ploughed into them, that's the worst bit. It happened because someone was in a hurry.'

Karina's late this morning, but I'm too preoccupied to notice,

'Sorry, Louisa,' she says when she gets here. Then seeing my face adds, 'What on earth's been going on?'

I fill her in, but she already knows. It turns out the horses were on route to Sylvie's yard, which is why Karina's so late.

'The one that survived is only a baby. He's a three-year-old,' she tells me. 'Hasn't exactly had a sparkling career on the racecourse, but if he's come through this, perhaps he's destined for greater things.'

She doesn't mention the other horse, and I don't like to ask.

'So have you seen Will?' I ask much later, cautiously, in case she hasn't.

There's a small smile there before she even answers my question.

'Yes...'

'And...'

'He came for supper. Actually he helped put Oscar to bed, and read him a story if you can believe it. I mean for goodness' sake, he's only a few months old. Far too young for stories.'

'And...' I ask brightly.

'You're so nosey,' she says. 'If you must know, Will and I talked, and that's all, for most of the night.' And she starts looking dreamy.

'Stop looking so lovestruck,' I tell her bossily. 'You were late and you've got work to catch up on.'

But *wow*. It's exciting, because I really think this is the start of something.

* * *

Marcus gets caught up with the police for ages, which is a complete waste of his time because it's far too late for the poor horses. He comes into the office at lunchtime looking exhausted.

'God, Lou. I've never had a morning like that, ever.'

I make him a cup of strong coffee, and we sit outside in the yard while he drinks it.

'You okay?' I ask sympathetically.

Marcus sighs, rather too much like Miles does, in response.

'You know, it's one thing when a horse gets sick. I can cope with that. But road accidents are almost always because there's an idiot. Which results in a horse that's so damaged you can't put it back together.'

Oh my giddy aunt. We need some light relief, or we'll all become as morose as Miles. And, right on cue, in comes Mrs Boggle. Four hours early, God bless her soul, which is entirely out of character. And she's dyed her hair bright orange. Not chestnut, or auburn, or even strawberry blonde. It's nasturtium orange and my eyes are popping out of my head.

'Mrs Boggle,' I say to her earnestly. 'I absolutely LOVE your hair...'

Meanwhile Marcus is spluttering none too quietly into his coffee. Mrs Boggle gives him a killer look.

'Don't mind him,' I say soothingly to her. 'He's had an absolutely terrible morning.'

Then I add, 'You're very early today. Is everything okay?'

'Fine, duck,' she says, still giving Marcus dirty looks. 'Only the bike's got to be serviced later. Won't have no wheels, like. Thought I better see to them loos.'

Which is immensely thoughtful of her. And off she goes to get her bucket.

I elbow Marcus in the side, hard.

'You are very rude,' I tell him bluntly.

'I know.' He grins. 'And I can be even ruder... Come here...'

But his lewd suggestions are brought to an untimely close as Karina yells out, 'Louisa? Are you there? There's a call for you...'

***

Karina's day ends at lunchtime, unless there's any reason for her to stay on. And so when Will comes in later in the afternoon, I swiftly corner him and find out exactly what's going on.

'Had a great evening last night,' he says happily. 'That Oscar is a great little nipper. I told him my favourite stories,' he says, looking all starry-eyed.

I'm not convinced that's such a good idea. I should hardly imagine that Will's favourite stories are suitable for a three-month-old baby. They're probably X-rated and full of topless nymphos, but then what on earth would I know. Maybe the obsession with the female form starts earlier than I thought.

'And how did you and Karina get on?' I ask, knowing that it's pointless beating around the bush when you're talking to Will.

'Good,' he says. 'I don't want to rush her, but she's gorgeous, don't you think?'

And he gives me a dopey smile.

***

That night, Marcus is still upset, but this time it's about something else.

'That flaming estate agent,' he says irately. 'He's farting about wasting so much of my time. He's trying to make me go and see houses that I'm not interested in. And anyway, I don't want to look at anywhere unless we go together.'

My ears prick up.

'Marcus?' I ask thoughtfully. 'Would that by any chance be Martin Slime, I mean Syme, who's supposed to be selling your cottage? Super smug, shiny suit, very sleek car?' I add, just in case it helps.

'That's him,' says Marcus bitterly. 'And what's more, he made me an offer himself. A bloody cheeky low one too.' He laughs hollowly.

'Hmmm. Martin and I go way back,' I tell Marcus meaningfully. 'And actually I happen to know that he is a bit of a sneaky bugger when it comes to house deals.'

'Now I'm interested,' says Marcus. 'Go on...'

'Well, Mr Slime has quite a substantial property portfolio. Did you know that?' I say, enjoying myself. 'I think he must have a way with the old ladies, who end up practically *giving* their homes away. To him, of course.'

Marcus is nodding slowly now. 'I get it,' he says at last. 'He doesn't let any would-be buyers anywhere near, then tells the old dears that it's obviously overpriced, then makes them a ridiculous offer.'

Golly. Even I hadn't worked out the details. Marcus's imagination is almost on a par with mine – but he must be right.

'I'll deal with that little toad tomorrow,' says Marcus.

'Oh, do give him my best,' I say innocently.

But far from amused, Marcus is furious. 'Tomorrow I'm putting the cottage on with a different agent,' he says angrily.

He's still cross after we've had supper. In fact, I've never seen him in such a mood.

'Marcus...' I run my hands up his arms and fasten them round his neck. 'Darling? Why don't we have an early night.'

But for the first time ever, he brushes me off.

'You can if you like. I'll join you later,' he says abruptly.

Suddenly it's like the wind's been knocked out of me. Did Marcus really just say that? Numb, and without another word, I take myself to bed.

I'm too upset to sleep. And I lie there in the dark for all of about five minutes before Marcus comes thundering up the stairs and hurls himself onto our bed.

'Louisa,' he says, in a very gruff voice. 'I'm so sorry. I didn't mean it. It wasn't you, it was me...' And for a split second there, he sounds exactly like Arian, which unleashes a whole other set of emotions I thought I'd seen the back of.

But then he says, 'Look, I've had one of the worst days ever. Is there any chance you could wriggle over and let me climb in too?'

I think about giving him a hard time. But he's had a truly horrible day and actually, I can't be cross with him for long. I fold back the duvet and he climbs in beside me, still fully dressed.

But it doesn't feel like the time to joke, and silently, I help him peel off the shirt and trousers, after which he falls asleep in my arms.

49

It's Saturday. No alarm clock. No horses to get up for, it being the time of year that Horace and Mavis are turned out in the field. Marcus lies peacefully sleeping. He actually has a whole weekend off. I'm thinking perhaps we ought to spend some of it talking about our wedding, because even small weddings don't happen on their own.

I creep downstairs and make us a pot of tea and hot buttered toast. When I take it back upstairs, Marcus is awake and looking more like his usual self again.

It's a rare morning that we can lie in bed without one of us having to rush off to do something. And after the tea is drunk and some of the toast eaten, he turns to me and says earnestly, 'I'm really sorry about last night, Lou. I was in a foul temper. Forgive me?'

I know he'd had just the worst day. And looking at those brown, imploring eyes and the lips I'm itching to kiss, of course I do.

'I might,' I say. 'It depends. You might need to do a little persuading, though.'

Marcus is quite happy about the persuading idea, which was quite inspired of me, I decide. After all, there's no better way to spend a lazy morning than gloriously, decadent sex.

When we do finally get round to discussing our wedding, Marcus suggests that we book a registry office.

'We can always have a church blessing later, when we have our party,' he says.

Which could be quite romantic, being secretly married for as long it takes to organise the second bit.

'I suppose...' And it's not quite how I'd imagined it, but at least we'll actually be married.

Then he says, 'I don't suppose you'd like to pay our Mr Syme a visit with me? Today? Only I've had an idea. I think you might find it entertaining.'

But before we do, Marcus calls a couple of other local estate agents and we agree to meet one of them at his cottage before we go and visit Martin. The new agent seems to think that Marcus's cottage would sell very quickly, particularly as it's already empty, and he values it far higher than Martin has.

Then, we drive into town. Marcus's face is grim as we enter the offices of Symes Country Property. Martin's sitting at his large, mahogany desk and leaps up the instant he sees me, pasting one of his smug smiles on his face. Then, when he catches sight of Marcus beside me, his face is an absolute picture.

'Hello, Martin,' I say airily. 'I believe you know my fiancé, Marcus Fitzpatrick?'

'Mr Fitzpatrick,' says Martin smoothly. 'Of course. How can I help you?'

With a face like thunder, Marcus tells him, 'I'm afraid you picked the wrong person to play your little game with, Mr Syme. I've just spent a very interesting morning with some other agents who will market my house far more cheaply than you, and interestingly, have valued it at a much higher price. One already has buyers lined up...'

Martin starts, 'Funnily enough, sir, I was just about to call you myself, ho ho.' He does that horrible smug little laugh of his.

Marcus says calmly, 'Don't bother. I am taking my business elsewhere. As of now, I no longer wish to have any further dealings with your agency.'

And just as Martin opens his mouth to protest about contracts and agreements and whatnot, Marcus adds in deadly seriousness, 'Oh, and by the way, I shall be dropping a line to the National Association of Estate Agencies – I'm sure I don't need to explain why – suggesting that they take a closer look into exactly what goes on in this office. After all, I believe you have quite a little portfolio of your own. Come on, Louisa. Let's go.'

As we leave, I wink at Martin. 'Love the suit. It's only a little bit shiny,' I say brightly, with a beaming smile in his direction.

He glares back at me, but before he can say anything, there's an almighty crash out in the street. There's a red Peugeot 205 embedded in the side of the brand-new Mercedes. Martin's day has just got a whole lot worse.

'Oh golly,' I call back to him, a look of mock surprise on my face. 'Looks like someone's just driven into an awfully expensive Merc out here. You wouldn't happen to know whose it is, would you?' And nearly get flattened as he belts out of the door boiling with rage.

'Will you really do that?' I ask Marcus a bit later, quite impressed at how he wiped the floor with smug Martin back there, who's now considerably less smug. And his car getting driven into was just brilliant. Such perfect timing.

'And how do you know about the National Association of Estate Agents? Have you done this sort of thing before?'

Marcus grins. 'Looked it up on the internet while you were in the shower! I don't think it matters whether I actually write to them or not. Our good friend Mr Syme's probably sweating nervously and scurrying around trying to cover his tracks as we speak – well, once he's had his car towed away. Thing is, he'll never know, will he! I reckon he'll be watching his back for some time to come, don't you?'

'Brilliant,' I say delightedly. 'You are so clever, Marcus. Now, can I buy you lunch to celebrate?'

And the afternoon gets better when we carry on mooching around town and stumble across a menswear shop where we find Marcus a fabulous suit just perfect for a secret wedding.

'Can I buy you a tie?' I say persuasively. 'Only I have to hide it, otherwise it'll give the game away about my dress...'

'Okay, just as long as it's not pink.'

'Hmmm, okay...' I say. *Bugger*. Pink was exactly what I had in mind, and I'd just spotted one the perfect colour. I sneakily buy it when he's not looking. On the day, he won't really mind because he'll be so happy to be marrying *me* he probably won't even notice.

That evening we go to the pub. Being Saturday night, it's packed, and we take our drinks outside and find a table in the garden. In no time we're joined by Ben, on his own because Emma's on a call, and then by Will and Karina, which is lovely and only a bit weird.

As I chat to her and Will, we end up looking at photographs from Agnes and Beamish's wedding. And I get a pang, which I instantly dispel, about Marcus and I keeping our wedding a secret, because part of me would love to be talking about it all and sharing it with our friends. But no, I tell myself. It's what Marcus and I both want, just to be married without a fuss.

Will is looking very lovey-dovey, clearly besotted with Karina. She too looks happy, even though in some ways, he's her total opposite, but then isn't that the mystery of love? And you could knock me down with a feather when an embarrassed-looking Miles comes over, characteristic frown in place, with a bony, horsy-looking looking girl he introduces as Fiona.

'Fiona works at the horse sanctuary,' he tells us, as they sit down at our table. Oh golly, she looks as serious as Miles. I can't imagine how that will work. They probably go home and play Nick Drake CDs and get all maudlin and depressed together about the poor starving horses around the world.

Then he drops a bombshell. 'Fiona and I are going on holiday,' he says, nearly managing to smile as he takes her scrawny hand in his.

Which makes us all nearly fall off our chairs.

'We're going to India to one of those welfare places where they try to educate the locals about basic horse care.'

It's not my idea of a holiday, but bony Fiona looks as thrilled as he does. What a funny old world it is.

Marcus and I walk slowly home, our arms round each other's waists.

'Who'd have thought it?' says Marcus with a grin. 'Old Miles and a girl as obsessed as he is?'

'She would have to be, wouldn't she? Marcus?' I say questioningly. 'Er, do you definitely want a secret wedding, or have you thought you might like some other kind?'

'Definitely the secret one,' he says and kisses the ear that's nearest to him. 'Why? Have you changed your mind?'

'Oh no, no,' I say hastily. 'No, our secret wedding will be perfect.' If it's what Marcus wants, then I want it too. And I'm sure it will be just perfect.

50

Oh. It's Sunday morning and I've just had a call from my mother. And to tell you the truth, I'm not entirely sure what to make of it.

'Darling,' she said, sounding a little odd. 'Now it's nothing to worry about, but Daddy's gone into hospital. They just want to give him a check-up, and then he'll be home again. Probably tonight... So don't worry, I'm sure there's nothing to worry about.'

And with that she rang off.

I go over it again in my head. Okay, so my mother phones, which she does extremely rarely, tells me my father's in hospital, and then tells me there's nothing to worry about, at least three times.

I call her back to ask what he was doing in hospital in the first place, but there's no reply and my call goes to voicemail.

'Marcus?' I call. I can hear him getting out of the shower, so I go in to the bathroom and perch on the side of the bath, watching him stand there naked as he shaves as I recount the conversation I've just had with my mother.

'Sounds to me like something *has* happened,' says Marcus, looking worried. I love that he shares my worries with me.

'Why don't you call the hospital?' he suggests.

Isn't he brilliant? So after half an hour of being transferred and cut off and ringing unmanned extensions, I eventually get through to a ward which confirms that yes, they do have a David Sparks in one of their beds.

Eventually I persuade them that I'm not an imposter and that I genuinely am his daughter, and a nurse tells me that he came in last night suffering with chest pains and feeling rather unwell.

'He's comfortable now,' she says. Comfortable. They always use that word in hospitals don't they? As if anyone could be comfortable in those horrid narrow beds with all that noise and bright lights and complete lack of privacy.

I thank her and put the phone down. I don't have a good feeling about this *at all*.

'Marcus?' I say to him. 'Look, do you mind if I nip over to the hospital and find out what's going on? Only I'm a little bit worried that there's something no one's telling me.'

Marcus comes over and hugs me deliciously close to him.

'I'll come with you if you like,' he says gently.

'Oh, I know you would,' I say, longing to have him with me. 'But you need this weekend off, and I'll be fine, you know. I'll be back this afternoon.'

* * *

I drive over there without the sense of urgency of last time, but with this anxious feeling niggling away inside me. I remind myself what the nurse said on the phone, that Dad was comfortable, but also that he'd had more chest pains and that's the bit that worries me, especially after all the changes he's been making.

I go to the ward where Dad was earlier, but he's not there. Nor is Mum. So I wait for a nurse to finish a long winded and trivial sounding phone call, before I ask where I can find David Sparks.

She looks at me and gets up to lead me away from the ward.

'He took a bit of a turn for the worse,' she says gently. 'He's actually in intensive care. Do you know where it is or would you like me to take you there?'

I shake my head dumbly, which doesn't give her an answer and start walking, then running in the direction of ICU, because that niggling feeling has just grown into a full blown feeling of fear, of the worst, and of being there too late...

This time I negotiate the swing doors with a little more care and my entrance to ICU is less dramatic. I see Mum immediately, beside a bed in which Dad is hooked up to all kinds of machines.

'Hello, Dad,' I say, trying my hardest not to show how worried I am. I kiss his cheek and then Mum's, before taking his hand in mine.

'He's being monitored and they've got him on a whole load of drugs,' says Mum in a strangely husky sounding voice.

Dad coughs and winces. He's obviously still in pain.

'I'm going to talk to one of the nurses,' I say to my parents. 'I'll be back in just a mo.'

But I can't find anyone to tell me other than what I already know. This is way scarier than last time.

We sit for ages, my parents and me. All making bright attempts at conversation, all clearly worried out of our minds. Eventually, I get up.

'I'm going home for now,' I tell them. 'But I'll come in after work tomorrow.'

'Thanks, poppet,' says Dad quietly, sounding for once quite grateful, not even trying to persuade me that I don't need to.

'Now don't forget little Benjy, Mum,' I say to my mother, in an attempt to lighten the mood. 'He'll be wanting his tea before long.'

'Oh,' says Mum startled. I think she'd completely forgotten about him.

* * *

Marcus has started cooking supper when I get home. Delicious smells of something roasting in the oven make me realise how hungry I am, and there's a bottle of wine uncorked waiting for us. As I collapse on our huge sofa, the day catches up with me.

'Do you know,' I say to him, gazing into his gorgeous, earnest eyes. 'I've been merrily bowling along all my life, not a care in the world, apart from the bullying episode in school of course – and now look. First there's my divorce, though of course I'm glad that happened because otherwise I wouldn't have you.' I stroke his stubbly cheek. 'But this, with Dad, is different. Because he's never going to be able forget that his heart could play up again at any time. None of us can forget... and it's hard to see any positive side to that. It's like for the rest of his life, there'll be a big black shadow hanging over him.'

I can't help the single tear that rolls down my cheek.

Marcus gets up and pours us both a glass of wine. Then he comes and sits next to me again, and says slowly, 'You know, that's not quite true, what you said just now. Well, it is, and yes, there will be a bit of a shadow as you put it, but I *can* see some positives. Look at how they've changed their lifestyle. They never used to do anything together, and it's brought them closer again. And you know, it'll have made all of you value each other more. Haven't you seen more of them since his first heart attack, than for ages before?'

He's right, of course, and as his words sink in, I feel a little of my tension ebb away and a little more hope creep in, as I pledge silently to never take Marcus for granted.

'Have a drink,' he says firmly, being masterful in that way that I adore, especially when he's proffering a glass of wine. 'Cheers. Now, are you ready to sample the culinary delights that I have waiting for you?'

And not for the first time I wonder what I've done to deserve this.

51

Fortunately, life decides to have one of its less eventful spells again. With Karina working more in the office, now that he's got our new computer up and running, Zac is released for more animal-related duties, though is always available in his role as Tech Support whenever we flounder. Which is often. The vets are busy as ever, especially as Beamish has all but retired. And I've had my official letter from him, confirming my new post as Practice Manager, with a far bigger pay rise than I'd anticipated.

Emma and Ben are as blissfully happy as ever. Miles is still seeing bony Fiona, much to the amazement of all of us. She's not too bad, though conversation is somewhat limited - to horses. And then there's Will and Karina, another great love affair in the making. Quite how an affable, oafish American has charmed the slightly stiff, rather posh Karina is beyond me, but that girl is seriously *in lurve*...

I'm happy to report that I hardly ever see Arian, though I occasionally hear little snippets when I catch up with Leonie and Pete. Correction, I should say when *we* catch up with Leo and Pete, because Marcus has become as much their friend as I am. Pete is doing really well. The internet business is going from strength to strength, and forget aeroplanes, he's now completely obsessed with cycling. It looks as though he even shaves his legs. It cuts down the air resistance, I'm told. Looks mighty funny to me, big hairy Pete with smooth, hairless legs protruding from his tight, moisture-wicking Lycra cycling shorts. Just hope he doesn't do his head.

Which leaves me and Marcus. And our secret wedding...

Marcus has booked our registry office ceremony for this weekend. I'm bursting with excitement, and longing to tell someone, but the only one I can talk to about it is Agnes, who has my fairy dress hidden away in her spare room. I haven't even told my parents, because with Dad only just out of hospital, I don't want cause any excitement.

On the Thursday before, when I go over after work to pick it up, she's got a bottle of champagne on ice and two glasses on her kitchen table.

'I hope you've got time?' she says. 'After all, it's not as though you've got any last minute wedding plans to see to is it?' But she's smiling. I always knew that Agnes would understand.

'This is lovely,' I say sincerely. 'And thank you Agnes, so much, for keeping my secret and not getting involved in any subterfuge behind my back.'

'Subterfuge? Oh, yes...' She gives me a look. Then she passes me a little box.

'Now Louisa, you know that old saying, something old, something new... Well, I wondered if you'd like to borrow this. I suppose it could be your something old and something borrowed all wrapped up into one.'

I open the little box, imprinted with the name of a rather posh jeweller, and inside is the most beautiful silver bracelet. Its heavy links are ornate, and there little sparkly stones inset which twinkle as they catch the light. I'm so touched at her generosity, my eyes fill with tears.

'I love it, Agnes,' I say quietly. 'It will be perfect with my dress. Thank you, so much...' And it will be, even more so because it's hers.

I sneak my dress home, and my borrowed bracelet, and hide them in the spare room which I lock. Marcus isn't home, so I go and see my lovely horses, grazing in the sun on this lovely summer evening. Horace nickers and wanders over, and Mavis just lifts her head up and carries on eating, long tufts of grass sticking comically out of the sides of her mouth. I stroke darling Horace's head, thinking in just a couple of days, I'll be *Louisa Fitzpatrick*. Married. Secretly. *Wife of Marcus Fitzpatrick*, gorgeous vet and the only man I've ever properly loved. It just took a painful divorce for me to grow up enough to realise that.

* * *

But at ten o'clock Marcus still isn't home. I'm starting to wonder where he is, because he wasn't on call and it's most unlike him not to text. I've tried calling his mobile but all I get is *Marcus Fitzpatrick, please leave a message...*

In fact I'm just thinking about going to bed without him, when the phone rings. Guessing it must be him, I leap up to answer it, ready to give him hell for not telling me where he is. But it isn't Marcus, it's Sam. The signal is terrible and he's not making any sense at all.

'Lou, something's happened... it's Marcus... break-in... he... the intruders.. Look, he's been... A & E, so you might want to get yourself down there.'

Sam's mobile cuts out altogether at that point, and I stand there wondering if I heard him right. But he definitely said A & E. I have to be there – and grabbing my bag and keys, I'm out of there like a shot.

Fortunately because it's late, the roads are quiet and so I drive far faster than is safe, thinking all the time of Marcus. And I'm there in half an hour, and even manage to find A & E in no time, as due to the number of ailing and decrepit people in my life, I've become a dab hand at navigating hospitals.

When I get to the reception, a battleaxe fixes me with a very stern look, and tells me to *just take a seat please*, until I impress on her that I'm Marcus's fiancée and that he'll most definitely want me with him. So then she calls a nurse, who takes me round to the cubicle where he's being examined.

Oh... Is that really him...

I feel the biggest rush of love as I look at him – and then shock, because there's barely an inch of him that isn't purple and blue and covered in blood. His eyes are swollen and closed, and a nurse is holding a compress over them.

'Marcus?' I whisper tremulously. 'What happened? Are you all right?'

What a stupid thing to say. He's far, far from all right, even an idiot like me can see that.

But he turns his head in my direction and croaks, 'Lou? I'm so glad you're here...' which appears to take an inordinate amount of effort on his part.

'Sshhh...' I tell him quietly and gently stroke the hand I'm holding in mine. 'Don't say anything for now. You're in hospital, you'll be fine, Marcus.'

Just then Sam sticks his head round the side of the cubicle. 'I wasn't sure you'd got my message,' he said ruefully. 'Poor bloke, seems Zac's bloody stepdad got his revenge after all. I think Marcus must have caught them breaking in. Guess they were looking for drugs. Beat the crap out of Marcus, him and his mate, before scarpering with our new computer.'

'Hush, please,' reprimands the nurse administering to Marcus. 'You're disturbing the patient.'

'Come out here, Lou, and I'll fill you in,' suggests Sam, but Marcus is holding on to my hand so tightly, I can't move.

'Um,' I say, nodding at my hand, 'bit tricky.' Tell me here, quietly.'

'Well, me and Zac were in the Dope, and as we left, this car almost ran us down. It was dark of course, but Zac stopped in his tracks and said, it's 'im, me bleedin' stepdad. Of course, when we saw where the car was headed, we followed. On foot, so we were a good ten minutes behind them. I got on my mobile and called the police, who wouldn't come out because nothing had actually happened. I told them that something was definitely about to happen, but they dug their heels in. By the time we got there, Marcus was like this. Believe it or not, that Paris kid from up at the house had covered him with a blanket and had called the police.' He nods at Marcus lying in the bed, before adding grimly, 'The office door was blowing in the wind, and the bastards were already in their car. Nearly ran us over as they left. Must have decided to leg it when Paris drove down. Just as well they didn't see it was just a kid. There are three of us who can identify him. The police will get the bastard eventually.'

Marcus is shifting uncomfortably by now, looking as though he's in quite a lot of pain.

'If you can't be quiet, I'm afraid you'll have to leave,' says the nurse, more insistently. 'Now I'm going to give you some more painkillers, Mr Fitzpatrick. You may feel a little sleepy.'

Marcus tries to grunt. Sam winks at me and says, 'I'll make sure everyone knows who needs to. I'd just sit tight if I were you.' And with that, he's gone.

Ages later they move us to a small ward. Marcus is barely conscious and I try to get comfortable in the chair next to his bed. But I'm terrified to stop watching him for even a second.

I completely lose track of time. Emma texts me to say she's collected Elmer, she'll feed my horses unless she hears from me and Karina will open the office first thing. I have an idea, now, how Agnes felt when *she* was in hospital; about how difficult it is to accept that someone else can do your job just as well as you. Well, *almost*, in my case. But I'm relieved that I can just stay here with Marcus, because right at this moment, I really don't think I could leave him.

I must have dozed off at some point, because I open my eyes to find a wash of light on Marcus. Someone's draped a blanket over me, but I'm still holding Marcus's hand. He's still sleeping, or at the very least drugged to the eyeballs, but at least he's not writhing with pain.

I think back to what Sam told me. I can quite imagine that Zac's stepfather was overjoyed to have the opportunity to settle a score with Marcus. But this time, he's pushed his luck, because there's no way Sam or Zac will let him get away with this.

As if sensing my thoughts, Marcus stirs, registers I'm still here and goes back to sleep. And suddenly I'm frightened again, because what if he's concussed or even brain-damaged? His head has been given a battering. In fact, looking at his injuries, who knows what damage has been done.

Shortly after nine, Karina sends me a text to tell me that everything's under control in the office and that she at long last understands why Beamish makes us write absolutely everything in the diary, which makes me smile a little. I text back:

Thanx so much L. x

I'm so glad she's there.

And just shortly after ten, after a doctor comes and goes again, a policeman turns up, wanting to interview Marcus, who's still unconscious.

'I can tell you what happened if you like,' I offer helpfully. 'Zac's stepfather, who already has a reputation as a stepchild beating, dog-poisoning, wife-stealing thug and who is probably a wanted criminal, broke into our office and when Marcus caught him in the act, he took great pleasure in duffing him up. And now he's in a life-threatening condition.'

I stare at the policeman, who isn't writing anything I say in his notebook. Then he clears his throat and says, 'Um Miss... er...'

'Mulholland,' I say shortly. 'And it's Mrs.'

'Mrs Mulholland. Were you actually at the premises when the above allegation took place?'

'Um, no. Of course not. I was waiting for Marcus to get home.'

The policeman raises his eyes heavenward, and says rather narkily, 'I can't take down hearsay in place of evidence. I really need to talk to Mr Fitzpatrick.'

'Well, you'll just have to wait, won't you,' I say stroppily. 'And just for the record,' I add, 'if your lot had been just a little quicker off the mark, so to speak, none of this would have happened.'

There's an impasse as we glare at each other.

'I suggest,' I say loftily in the end, just to get rid of him, 'that you'd be better off talking to Sam and Zac, who *were* there. Oh, and Paris Mankly-Talbot. They can tell you exactly what I've just told you – if you've got an extra couple of hours to spare, that is? Which no doubt you do have?'

I don't know what's got into me. Worry, I suppose. The policeman looks as though he's biting his tongue as he gives me a nod and stomps off, leaving us in peace.

'I didn't know you were so scary,' says a whisper of a voice behind me. Marcus. *Thank God*, and judging by that last remark, not too much damage done either.

I turn round, so relieved to see his eyes prising themselves open through their poor, puffed-up eyelids. I reach over and try to kiss his cheek as gently as possible, but he still winces.

'Are you hurting?' I ask sympathetically. And stupidly.

'It's better than last night,' he whispers, then winces again. 'What day is it?'

'Friday,' I find myself whispering back. And oh my God. I'd completely forgotten. There's no way we'll be getting married tomorrow.

'I'm... so... sorry... Lou,' whispers Marcus, even more quietly this time, and the next minute, his eyes have rolled up and disappeared into his head and his face has turned a horrible grey colour, as his body starts convulsing violently.

I freeze, but only for a second, because the doctors have missed something, I just know it and terrified, I grab the buzzer by his bed, pressing it for all I'm worth.

'Marcus, hold on, you'll be okay,' I cry frantically, still pressing the buzzer, but nothing happens. And suddenly the sound on the heart monitor turns to a single, high-pitched tone.

Still, no one comes, but I know that tone from all the ER TV I've watched. I know what it means, and already I'm leaping up in a blind panic, running out into the corridor screaming for help.

52

I wonder if I can ever go back to the person I used to be. I've discovered now how fragile happiness is, how quickly bliss can be shattered and how life can change, in the blink of an eye, for ever.

At first it felt like a waking nightmare. While Marcus battled heroically with the most horrific internal injuries, I stumbled through each day at a time, sitting by his bedside, then in the hospital canteen waiting for yet another operation to be over, watching as he gradually grew weaker. Unable to hope for the best, I dreaded that moment I was terrified was coming. I've wondered so many times just how much the human body can take – and discovered the answer too.

But the worst can bring out the best in people. I've found out how wonderful my friends are, each and every one of them. Emma has kept my fridge stocked with her wonderful cooking and looked after my animals when I haven't been able to; Leo and Rachel between them virtually moved in with me to begin with, to make sure I was never on my own; Karina has kept the practice running like clockwork so I haven't had to worry about that. I am eternally grateful to her. And Agnes, of course, has been an absolute tower of strength. But I'm starting to hope now, that with the worst behind me, it's time to try to move on.

So today is the day that I say goodbye to that horrible, terrible part of my life and step forward to the future. After all, isn't that the only thing to do? And I know I'm lucky that I have one.

It's a day to make an effort for – but not overly so – and I've dried my hair and left it hanging loose on my shoulders, before dressing with the greatest care, leaving me ten minutes to sit. I wanted to be alone this morning. Just to think.

But, actually, I end up with about three minutes, because there's an unexpected knock at my door. It's Emma.

'You okay, Lou?' she asks, an anxious look on her face. 'Only, I've come to get you. There isn't time to explain. Let's just say there's been a slight change of plan.'

After months of surprises, after everything that's already happened, I don't even ask what it is. I just follow her outside, to where Ben's Boxster's parked at the side of the lane.

* * *

We drive in silence.

There's far too much going on in my head and actually, I'm nervous beyond belief. That something else will go wrong, that my emotions will get the better of me. After all, absolutely nothing in life is certain. And however promisingly something starts, you can never know what will happen in the future.

At last, the drive is over and we're here.

Carefully, I climb out. We're at the tiny church near Ben's house instead of the one in the next village.

'Ready?' asks Emma quietly.

Just inside the door, there's a tiny bunch of roses tied with ribbon, with a little card with my name on it next to them. Obviously they're intended for me, so I pick them up and hold them to my nose. They smell divine. Then Emma opens the door. My stomach is lurching horribly.

And suddenly I'm not sure I can do this.

Inside, the church is packed with people, so many people, they're standing crammed in at the back. I didn't expect this. Gosh, they all look so smart... but then I suppose they would for an occasion like this. The flowers are beautiful and the warm glow inside comes from the dozens of candles everywhere I look.

Emma nudges me. 'Go on...'

I start my walk down the aisle. This isn't how I'd planned it at all. I'm overwhelmed – more than anything by the sight of my future husband, still battered and only just out of his wheelchair, but standing there in his posh suit and his pink tie, a huge smile on his scarred face as he waits for me to reach him. He's been through hell and back and his face will forever be marked from that hideous encounter with Zac's stepfather, but to me he's the most handsome man in the world. And he's looking at me as though I'm the only girl in the world for him. Well, I hope I am, because I'm marrying him.

* * *

After the ceremony is over, and months later than planned, at last I'm Louisa Fitzpatrick. And as I walk slowly out of the church arm in arm with Marcus, like the sun from behind the biggest, blackest cloud, the happiness I nearly lost comes bursting out of nowhere. A manic smile plants itself on my face and my blood zings round my body, as I want to jump with the joy of both of us being alive.

'So much for a secret wedding,' whispers Marcus in my ear, when no one else is listening. 'But I wouldn't change this for the world...'

And actually, nor would I. We wander across the road over to Ben's, slowly, because Marcus can't go much faster, but also to take in every magical second of this day. There's a huge marquee in his garden waiting just for us and if I know our friends, quite a party. But just inside the gate, I stop. I've just remembered something I have to do.

'What is it now?' asks Marcus, surprised.

'Just something, darling Marcus...' I tell him. 'It'll only take a second...'

Hitching up my fairy dress in all its ethereal glory, I kick off my shoes and fling them into the hedge. Barefoot in the cool, soft grass, just as I always dreamed of. Reaching up on tiptoes, I kiss his gorgeous face.

'Okay,' I tell him, grinning from ear to ear, wanting to dance and twirl forever. 'Now, everything is perfect...'

PS...

'You do realise that Marcus has raised the bar about proposals, don't you? I mean how can anyone beat that?' Ben asks me, after at least five glasses of champagne.

Golly. But I'm not altogether surprised that Ben is thinking about such things as proposals. I think Marcus's dice with death was a wake-up call for all of us.

'Hmmm...' I say in wondrous agreement. No one found out about the torrential rain and the thunderstorm. They all think we went on a fabulous picnic. 'It was very lovely and romantic... Awfully clever of him... Um, when are you going to ask her then?'

* * *

'Will's moving in with us,' beams Karina, before she hugs me. 'Oh, I just can't believe this is happening!' She hugs me again. Who'd have imagined we'd become friends? I must remember to thank Arian for introducing us.

Hmmm, another wedding on the cards. I can just see it... And at the Amberley Stud no less... Should be out of this world...

* * *

'Your wedding,' I say to a hyper-excited Emma. 'Are you absolutely sure you want me to be your maid of honour, after all, you don't want me to upstage you...'

* * *

'Hey, Zac, how's it hanging?' Marcus is surprised to see Zac looking so down in the mouth, today of all days.

'S'all right s'pose.'

'Something wrong?' Marcus stands there, leaning on a walking stick, which he still needs, especially when he's been on his feet for a while.

'It's all my bleedin' fault. 'Bout that fuckin' wanker that beat you up. If I wasn't 'ere, it wouldn't 'ave 'appened.'

'Do you know, Zac,' says Marcus, looking serious for a moment. 'Firstly, it certainly wasn't your fault, and secondly, that fucking wanker bastard, I am delighted to say, has been jailed for attempted murder. So all in all, there is definitely justice in that. And I am going to be fine. Now cheer up and come and have a beer.'

* * *

'Hi, Rachel. Have you met anyone who's not too intense and not too frivolous yet? Only I might know just the person,' I say to her cautiously, conscious of my husband's eyes on me, drawing me back to his side.

Husband... Hmmm, I already love saying that.

'Oh. Thanks, Lou, but actually, well, it's early days but you know, I might have...' Rachel's ears are pink. Mine prick up with interest as I start to edge back towards Marcus. 'I met him at a party. He's been through the mill, he's divorced and all that, but he's so good-looking and such a nice guy... Funnily enough, his name's Arian...'

ACKNOWLEDGMENTS

When I wrote this, I wanted to portray a little microcosm of country life. I also wanted to include the animals so many of us share our lives with, the unconditional love they give us, the heartbreak we feel when they leave us.

It's a kind of a triumph over adversity story, the kind I like to read. When life seems to fall apart around us, I like to think it's clearing the way for something better. So if that's you, I hope this book makes you smile. You may shed a tear or two, but I hope it will fill your heart with hope.

I'm so grateful to the wonderful team at Boldwood Books. To be working with you, and to see this book out in the world, are dreams come true. To my editor, Isobel, to Nia, Claire, Marcela and all of you, huge thanks for making it happen.

To my agent, Juliet Mushens, thank you and much love. I'm so lucky to have you.

To my readers, I can't thank you enough for buying my books, reviewing them, sharing them, for your messages. Without you, I wouldn't be doing this. It means the world. x

This book is dedicated to Bernard, my dearest Golden Retriever who was with me for fifteen years, and who I still miss, every day.

ABOUT THE AUTHOR

Debbie Howells' first novel, a psychological thriller, *The Bones of You*, was a Sunday Times bestseller for Macmillan. Fulfilling her dream of writing women's fiction she has found a home with Boldwood.

Sign up to Debbie Howells' mailing list for news, competitions and updates on future books.

Visit Debbie's website: https://www.debbiehowells.co.uk

Follow Debbie on social media:

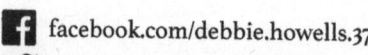

facebook.com/debbie.howells.37
twitter.com/debbie__howells
instagram.com/_debbiehowells
bookbub.com/authors/debbie-howells

ALSO BY DEBBIE HOWELLS

The Life You Left Behind

The Girl I Used To Be

The Shape of Your Heart

It All Started With You

The Impossible Search for the Perfect Man

Boldwood

Boldwood Books is an award-winning fiction publishing company seeking out the best stories from around the world.

Find out more at www.boldwoodbooks.com

Join our reader community for brilliant books, competitions and offers!

Follow us
@BoldwoodBooks
@TheBoldBookClub

Sign up to our weekly deals newsletter

https://bit.ly/BoldwoodBNewsletter

Milton Keynes UK
Ingram Content Group UK Ltd.
UKHW040941311023
431635UK00005B/147